LOVE IN BEVERLY MILLS
LOVE YOU, ALWAYS

LAUREN LACEY

Trigger Warning
This story contains explicit language, sexual content, and discusses sensitive topics such as parental loss, miscarriage, terminal illness, addiction, and suicide

Copyright © 2023
LAUREN LACEY BOOKS
LOVE IN BEVERLY MILLS
LOVE YOU, ALWAYS
All rights reserved.

No part of this publication may be reproduced, distributed, or transmitted in any form or by any means, including photocopying, recording, or other electronic or mechanical methods, without the prior written permission of the publisher, except in the case of brief quotations embodied in critical reviews and certain other non-commercial uses permitted by copyright law.

LAUREN LACEY
contact@authorlaurenlacey.com

Printed Worldwide
First Printing 2023
First Edition 2023

10 9 8 7 6 5 4 3 2 1

LOVE IN BEVERLY MILLS

LOVE YOU, ALWAYS

CHAPTER 1

NEVER MEANT TO BE- PARKER

I've been back home in Beverly Mills for half a year now, and sometimes I feel like a stranger in the city I lived in for nearly my entire life. So much has changed. Just fifteen years ago, Beverly Mills was just a small beach destination off the coast of Georgia known for a few things – hole-in-the-wall bars, small-town diners, a historic downtown, and drunken get-togethers at the pier. Fifteen years later, Beverly Mills is now known as the Beverly Hills of the South. We have tons of swank coffee shops, the multi-million dollar hospital expansion, luxe spas, eclectic boutiques, and too many new restaurants to count. It's the perfect blend of country and coastal beach living. Beverly Mills outsiders are moving to town in droves in search of better jobs, good schools, and a much slower lifestyle than the busy, bustling city of Atlanta, located about three hours west.

But despite all the changes, this is still my home. It's the town that raised me, loved me, and comforted me through my pain, and I really want to move into the next phase of my life starting today, starting now.

"I feel so blah! I'm missing something in my life, but I can't quite figure it out." I struggle to explain my feelings to Merissa, my psychologist.

"Do you feel unfulfilled?" She asks.

I think about her question for a moment before explaining further, "It feels like everyone around me is excited about something, but I feel as if I'm just going through the motions in life. Mom and Dad act like giddy teenagers when they're around each other. They're so happy and in love. I see that same passion in my younger sister, Avery. She's the fiercest up-and-coming attorney in the South. And my youngest sister? Don't even get me started. Izzy, or Izzy Loves Lilies as her 400,000 social media followers call her, is super passionate about carrying on our family legacy by taking over Dad's floral business. Everyone's passionate about something or someone, and then there's me. Just me." I slump down in my chair and throw my hands up in defeat.

"Talk to me, Parker. What do you want?" Merissa pushes me to dig deeper and admit how I really feel.

I take a deep sigh and answer, "I don't know. On paper, I'm a catch! I have a good life. I have loving parents. I have amazing sisters and an awesome best friend. And I'm super gorgeous, might I add. Hell, I'm a freaking doctor, for goodness sake, but if you take away the resume, at the end of the day, I'm just a single woman who wants love. I want to get married. I want a family. I want it all."

Merissa looks at me sympathetically. "You want everything that you deserve, Parker. You can have that, too, in your own way and in due time, but you can't continue to put unrealistic pressures and timelines on yourself. You're finally in a healthy head space. You've been single for an entire year for the first time in your obsessive, co-dependent life, and you're thriving at age twenty-nine! Give yourself some grace."

While I respect Merissa's logical point of view, today just isn't the day for me to accept or appreciate her wisdom.

"Thanks, Merissa. I know what you're saying is right, but I'm too distracted to soak it all in."

"Is this because of your parent's 30th anniversary party?" She asks.

With an exasperating sigh, I reply, "You know it. It's the talk of the town, the most anticipated event this year, and everyone's gonna be there. Seeing people madly in love with their significant others is beautiful, but it's also painful. Mom and Dad have been married since they were eighteen, and I'm nearly thirty years old, which is like forty-five by today's standards. I'll never find that type of love at this rate."

"Don't compare your journey of love to theirs. Just because your timing and circumstances differ doesn't mean your love story will be any less beautiful. As a matter of fact," Merissa looks at her watch, closes her notebook, sets her pen on her desk, and turns back around to face me. "Our time is up, so I'm going to stop speaking to you as your shrink and speak to you as your best friend instead." Her words hang in the air.

I know exactly what Merissa's going to say or who she's going to mention rather.

"Parker, you say you want love, marriage, and the whole works, right?"

I slowly answer, "Right."

"Good," Merissa smiles. "So, are you aware that Jackson's going to be at your parents' anniversary party?"

"Of course, I'm aware! My parents invited him personally, and everyone has reminded me of this fact every day for the past month."

I hate talking about Jackson. My mom, my dad, my sisters, my best friend, and even the mailman have mentioned Jackson's name to me since the town announced that their most successful townie was returning home from the big city.

Oh, and did I mention that Jackson is also my first love?

Jackson Sands and I met in 3th grade at Beverly Mills Elementary. His family moved from Atlanta to Beverly Mills for a fresh start after his mom beat cancer for the first time. Jackson and I were immediately drawn to one another, best friends. Despite the doctor telling my parents they were having a girl, my dad was adamant that I would be a boy, hence the name Parker. Growing up, my dad was determined to make me a 'chip off the old block,' so I enjoyed doing everything the 'boys' in Beverly Mills did – fishing, hunting, football, basketball, you name it, I did it – with Jackson, his dad, and mine. He was my best friend, and as we grew older, puberty hit, and our hormones grew. My best friend since 3rd grade became a super cute 8th grader with a deep voice. Then he became a 10th grader with muscles, and a few years later, he grew into a sexy, captivating, hazel-eyed stud.

But no matter how much we try to be together, fate refuses to let us be happy. As much as we love one another, our love story was just never meant to be.

"Hello! Earth to Parker!" Merissa screams. "Stop drooling over thoughts of Jackson!"

"I am not!" I lie. "I'm simply thinking that I'm tired of everyone reminding me of the first person who broke my heart too many times to count, and he's without a doubt the reason why I'm still single."

"Parker, first thing's first, let the past be the past. Jackson has turned his life around, and he's apologized to you so many times over the years. Y'all have endured so much together. Either way, you need to figure out if you want to try again with Jackson because you can't keep telling yourself that you're over him yet allow your past relationship to hinder you from moving on with anyone else – which takes me to my second point. *You* are the reason you're single now. You push everyone away, specifically David, who absolutely adored you!"

"Wow, Merissa. I thought you were an ally. This session is over! My love life is no longer a topic of discussion. It's time to open up anyway. We have children to save!" I smile, knowing that Merissa can't argue against that fact.

It's 8 a.m. on Monday morning, and it's time to open our joint practice, Beverly Mills Pediatrics and Childhood Psychology. Merissa and I always knew we wanted to be doctors. Back in college, we dreamed of opening a clinic in Atlanta, but the funny thing about life is that we can't dictate our future. Eventually, traumatic events led us back home to Beverly Mills where we've been able to transform lives and give back to our community. When Merissa's sister was finally diagnosed with bipolar and schizophrenia as an adult, she wanted to help children manage their mental and emotional health at a young age with hopes of helping them lead happier and healthier lives than her younger sister endured. And when I...well, when I experienced my own tragedy, I decided to become a pediatrician to fill a void of a painful reality that would affect me for the rest of my life.

From appointment to appointment, we go about our day putting smiles on kids' faces and alleviating parents' worries and fears.

"Another day, another feeling of satisfaction for helping kids in need. Are you ready to close up?" Merissa asks as she opens the door for me.

"Yep, I'm right behind you! Just give me a sec. I had way too much crap delivered today for the party. I don't know how I'm going to carry it all." I struggle to carry all of my packages while also kick-dragging another box with my feet.

"Well, common sense says make two trips, Parker." Merissa laughs as she carries her own bags as well.

"Common sense says these heels aren't made for walking."

We laugh in agreement, and as soon as I drag the box over the threshold of the sidewalk, I tumble over and begin to fall to the ground until...

Well, if this were a beautiful love story, a true fairy tale, I would be saved by a handsome knight in shining armor, but instead, I fall on the sidewalk and scrape my knee and the palm of my hands. Shit, that hurts! Immediately after, I hear Merissa and a surprising but familiar voice yell my name. Ignoring the first voice, I look up to the man who's trying to show immense concern while also trying to hold back a smile.

"Jackson! What are you doing here?" I ask in complete shock.

Jackson worriedly asks, "Parker, are you okay?"

"Of course, I'm okay. I fall all the time, Jackson." I shrug him off as he helps me up to my feet. I try to compose myself, dust my knees off, and wipe the wrinkles from my tight pencil skirt to look as prim, proper, and independent as possible.

"Still stubborn, I see. I'm glad you aren't hurt, so now I don't feel bad for laughing at you." He teases while gazing at me with his piercing hazel eyes.

Ugh, why does he have to be so damn handsome? I can barely think straight, but I can also see that he's undressing me with his eyes, assessing my well-defined curves and licking his lips as he stares at my legs. Yep, I still got it! I may be rusty when it comes to dating, but it's satisfying to know that Jackson still can't control himself around me.

"Ahem!" Merissa clears her throat. "Jackson, it's so good to see you again! Now, if you can stop drooling over Parker for a minute, why don't you come over here and give your best friend a hug."

Jackson refocuses his thoughts and discreetly adjusts the bulge in his pants to walk over to greet Merissa.

"Hey Ris. Did my assistant call you about the location we found for the rehab cen –" Marissa elbows Jackson like he let out a secret I wasn't supposed to know. I look at the two of them with suspicion but opt to dismiss the awkwardness. He coughs uncomfortably but continues the conversation while picking up my packages off the ground.

"I'm meeting up with Jason and the guys at Maxine's on Wednesday. I'll be here working on the hospital wing development for the next six months, so y'all will see a whole lot more of me around here."

With a joyous smile, Merissa replies, "That's awesome, and I love what you're doing to improve the hospital. You've done so much for the town already. Text me when you have some free time to go out for lunch. It's been three months! We have so much to catch up on, and I would much rather hear about your ongoings from you rather than ENews or Times Magazine. And please don't let my lightweight husband have too many beers. There better not be a repeat of what happened the last time you fools got together."

We all laugh knowing that when the Beverly Mills Boys get together at the town's favorite bar, Maxine's, things get rowdy, and the boys get kicked out.

"By the way, thank you for helping Parker carry those boxes. She thinks she's superwoman and doesn't believe in asking for help."

I shake my head and roll my eyes, then turn to face Jackson. We both have boxes in our hands, and we stare at one another, waiting for someone to speak first.

"So, where'd you park?" He asks.

"Follow me, Mr. Sands." I may never take him back, but harmless flirting never hurts, right?

When we walk to the parking garage, he's surprised to see my car, "I still can't believe you kept the car."

"I needed a car, Jackson. As angry as I was with you, I wasn't gonna turn down a brand-new ride. Besides, I love Miss Daisy. She's been loyal to me and never hurt me, unlike some people I know." I shade him with a glare.

"Touche, touche. I deserve that." Jackson agrees. "But I've been trying to prove to you that I'm not dipshit Jackson anymore. I just tried to make amends with you three months ago. I was ready to apologize and disappear from your life for good until you invited me over. Then, one thing led to another, but you haven't responded to my calls or texts since that night. How long are you gonna keep punishing me? What can I do to help us heal from the past?"

Instant anger arises within me, and tears form behind my eyes. I turn to face him without even thinking of my surroundings and start to yell.

"Really Jackson? Every time I heal, you come back into my life to cut me again. It's been seven years since you walked out of that hospital room.

It's been six years since you chose a life without me. It's been three years since you embarrassed both of us with your drunken antics on national television in front of millions of people. It's been two since I've healed from the pain you put me through. And it's been three months since we made a stupid mistake that we both agreed should have never happened. Why would I want to open up those wounds again, Jackson? I can't keep doing this with you. We only hurt one another."

When I'm done speaking, my yells have turned into a whimper. I helplessly stare at Jackson with tears streaming down my face. This is what he does to my life – turns happy, productive days into emotional cluster fucks. This is what he does to me – turn a strong, healed woman who has overcome her heartbreak into someone who's still heartbroken, but his pain radiates off of him as well. I know our failed attempts to be together aren't all his fault, but there's no point in harping on what was never meant to be.

"I'm sorry, Jackson. This is too painful to relive. We try and try and fail every time. Let's try to stay out of each other's way for the next six months you're in town."

I quickly grab the boxes from Jackson's hands, load up my car, and avoid making as much eye contact as possible. Yet, as an attempt to satisfy my painstaking desire for him and perhaps say my final goodbye, I take a step forward to give him one last kiss, but a kiss that's supposed to be short and sweet quickly turns into the kiss of life itself. It feels like our souls possessed our tongues, and we'd been waiting for this moment again for the past three months. We moan and roam each other's bodies like long-lost lovers. This feels so right, so good, but it always does when we're alone. It's the outside world that reminds us that we'll never work out. Our passion, emotions, and love have never been enough to give us the life we want together - the happy life I know we both deserve.

I reluctantly push Jackson off of me and open my eyes to come back to reality. His breaths are heavy, and mine are equally as intense.

With swollen lips and lustful eyes, I let Jackson know, "That was the last time." I get into my car, and he runs over to grab the door before I shut it.

"You were wrong, you know. The cards weren't in our favor back then, but there's no way you believe that we weren't meant to be together. I love you, always, Parker Waylen." He lets the door go and walks off,

I drive away in frustration and release a deep breath.

"Mondays suck."

The next day goes by like clockwork. I treat patients, and I have impersonal conversations with Merissa in hopes she doesn't mention Jackson's name. I make the final arrangements for my parents' anniversary party, and by the time I decide to take a break, my work day is already over.

"Hey Ris, what're your plans for tonight? Wanna go out?"

"Sorry, Parker, no turning up on a Tuesday for me. My night's gonna be filled with schmoozing stuffy old, rich donors for Beverly Mills' youngest, sexiest Mayor, my Jason bear."

"Ugh, that's even more boring than me watching re-runs of Law & Order. Have fun with that."

"Well, now that Jackson's back in town and for much longer this time, maybe you two could go out to dinner, you know, catch up on old times. Didn't you agree to try to be friends again a few months back?"

She's right. We did agree to be friends again, or cordial at least, but that was before we banged each other's brains out, which resulted in me ghosting him out of panic. She doesn't need to know that, though.

"Hmm, I'll see what my parents are up to instead. They haven't seen me in days, and Mom's been guilt-tripping me about not answering her calls while I'm at work. That woman and her video calls." I laugh and hope that I successfully changed the subject.

"I see what you just did, and I'll let you slide this time. Give Mrs. Jolene a big hug and kiss for me. I'll see you tomorrow morning!"

We close up shop and depart for the day. I was so occupied with work and the party that I forgot to turn my phone off 'do not disturb.' As soon as it disables, I receive a long text from Jackson he sent this afternoon. Crap, this'll be an interesting conversation with Mom. She loves to discuss my love life or lack thereof.

I arrive at my parents' home, a beautiful plantation-style house stretched across three acres of land. We didn't grow up in this home; in fact, we originally lived on a portion of this land in a small but cozy four-bedroom house a few steps away. We didn't come from money, and my parents aren't wealthy by any means, but they are loved and well-respected by the residents of Beverly Mills. My parents would give their last dime to my sisters and me, the church, schools, struggling businesses, and the sick – if anyone in Beverly Mills is in need, The Waylens will help. After my dad passed the family business down to Izzy and my mom retired from teaching, they expected to live happily and humbly ever after in our old beat-up home for the remainder of their lives. However, the townspeople had other plans in mind.

After Avery won her first high-profile case as an attorney, she purchased this land for my parents. Deacon's parents, Pastor Rich and Mrs. Owens, blessed the land, so anyone who steps on the grounds will be rewarded with love, wealth, and good health. We country folk believe in that type of thing. After the blessing, Izzy and I combined our money and contracted Sands Construction to build them their dream home. They deserve it. It's the most beautiful home in town for the most generous people you'd ever meet.

As soon as I open the door, I'm hit with the smell of freshly baked peach cobbler. I inhale the yummy aroma.

"Ooh, mama, that cobbler smells amazing! But who's sick?" I greet her with a big hug.

"Hey, Parker. One of my friends from choir came down with the flu, and she's slow to recover, so I'm gonna deliver one of my pies. All she needs are some peaches to soothe her soul, and she'll be back to singing in no time." She neatly packages her peach cobbler, places it in a tote bag, and walks toward the door.

"You're not leaving already, are you? I just got here. We have so much to catch up on. We haven't spoken in days." I stand between my mom and the door with puppy dog eyes.

Mom nonchalantly pushes me out of the way and says, "And whose fault is that? I swear, my daughters are slowly but surely forgetting all about me. If it weren't for your dad, I'd be a lonely old bitty." She says in an overly dramatic tone.

"Aw, don't be like that Mama! Besides, you and Daddy are too busy for us anyway. Whenever I do call, y'all are out and about cruising the town together with your friends like twenty year olds. Your social life is way more interesting than mine."

My parents married young, and they didn't wait long to start having kids. Within two years of marriage, my mom gave birth to me. The pregnancy was physically trying for her. She was diagnosed with eclampsia and suffered numerous seizures. She was considered high-risk and spent the majority of her time in the hospital. The doctors warned her that another pregnancy would be extremely dangerous to her health and the health of any unborn babies. Still, they were determined to build the family they had always dreamed of.

When I was two years old, I went to the hospital to meet my 'new' baby sister, Avery. She was so beautiful. I didn't see her mother, and I didn't know the full details about her adoption at the time, but I was in love and protective of her since the moment I laid eyes on her. She didn't look like us, so I immediately had questions. Her skin tone was golden brown, and she had a head full of beautiful curly hair. Two years later, Avery and I welcomed another Waylen sister, our baby girl, Izzy. She was also adopted, but her mother remained present in her life until she passed away when Izzy was about 9 years old. She didn't speak much English, but she left a journal dedicated to Izzy that details her heritage and family history. Our family may be unconventional, but we're a close-knit bunch that supports one another and fights for each other no matter what.

"One day, you'll be able to enjoy life unapologetically with the one you love like I do with your dad. We're living our best lives, Parker! You should too."

"That's right!" My dad chimes in as he walks into the kitchen, wraps his arms around my mom's waist, and kisses her on the cheek.

I roll my eyes at their cuteness and shift the conversation to focus on the outside construction. Izzy and my dad are transforming their backyard into a beautiful floral wonderland so they'll be able to host small, intimate-sized weddings and gatherings.

My fantasies begin to overpower my logic. "The pavilion is coming along so well. Everything looks so romantic. And the flower arrangements, dad, they're beautiful. I'd love to be married here, one day."

I quickly gasp when I realize what I just said. I haven't thought about marriage since my ex-boyfriend David. I really messed that relationship up.

My mom walks up to me and puts her hand on my shoulder. "Parker, you can have anything you want. I, for one, look forward to the day your father walks you down the aisle to give you away to Jackson. It's only right for you two to be the first to marry here."

I look at my mom in shock and confusion. "We're not getting married!"

She practically ignores me and waves me off. "Oh, shut up. A mother knows. Besides, Jackson and Frank just left here about an hour ago. Both you and Jackson have put in the work to become better versions of yourselves. He's changed, and so have you. It's time, Parker."

My mom is usually so wise, so I don't understand how she could be so wrong about this.

"I guess we'll see. Time doesn't heal all wounds."

"No, but time, therapy, forgiveness, and love do."

Mom kisses me and hurries to the door with her peach cobbler in tow. "I'm going to the hospital. Don't let your dad eat the rest of my pies. I swear that man's gonna go into a sugar coma if he keeps it up. Bye, love! I'll see y'all later."

My mom leaves me with heavy thoughts that aren't necessarily of Jackson but more so of myself. I've been through so much, and I lost so much. Yet, here I am. I know I'm ready to love again, but don't I owe it to myself to find love with someone new?

"Stop thinking so hard. You're gonna give yourself a headache, Parker," My straight to the point dad says. "Frank said the same thing to Jackson when they were here earlier today. You two are always stuck in your own heads for no reason. I was watching this talk show on tv, and they called it something," He thinks to himself. "Imposter syndrome, there's a name for everything these days. You're psyching yourself out. Your generation is a mess when it comes to love." He says without so much as a blink.

"Wow, thanks, Dad. Attaway to motivate me. I thought you hated Jackson, anyway."

"I hate anyone who hurts my baby girl, but after all these years, you're still stuck on Jackson Sands. I couldn't understand why until I got to know him better over the past few years. He lost my blessing a long time ago, but he's earning it back now. So, please proceed with caution, but have at it, Parker. Stop being so stubborn."

My dad is so oblivious to the intricacies of modern-day relationships. He and my mom think love is simply black and white. You either make things work, or you don't. But life's not that simple, not anymore, not after everything we've been through.

"Did you get his text?" He asks. "Jackson texted you today."

I look at him quizzically and remember that I completely forgot to check my texts when I arrived. I pull out my phone to see what he sent. Jackson doesn't like to text much, but this looks like a four-page letter.

I don't expect you to respond to me, but I know you're going to read my message. I know you love me. I know you're in love with me. I'm in love with you, too. We always have been, and we always will be. And one day, we'll be husband and wife. I'm willing to wait for you, but I won't wait around and let you ignore me. I'll wait for you to decide whether you want to be with me while we date one another. I think I understand why we never worked out when we tried and failed over the years. We need to take the time to get to know one another again, not through our memories together but as the individuals we've evolved into. I'm not the same man you knew years ago, and you aren't the same woman. I want to know who you are today, and I want you to know who I am. If you're willing to give us a real shot, then let's wipe our slates clean. Please allow me to take you on a first date. I want to introduce you to the best version of myself – the Jackson I want you to fall in love with. Meet me on Thursday night at 7 o'clock at The Grail, a restaurant we've never been to. It's time to make new memories together. I love you, Parker Waylen.

My dad smiles at me while I continue to read Jackson's text over and over again.

"We just want to see our children happy, and tragedies aside, you two knuckleheads make one another the happiest people on the planet. When there's love, there's hope. When there's hope, there's a future. Just explore it and see what happens."

I'm not quite sure why tears are rolling down my face. I'm happy and touched, but they're streaming down like a baby. My dad gives me a big hug. Daddy doesn't often show affection, and he rarely offers his opinion on anything that pertains to my love life, but when he does, it's sincere, and it's usually spot on.

"Thanks Dad or should I call you the Beverly Mills matchmaker?" I wipe my tears and tease.

"I'll always be your dad, and I'll always want nothing but the best for you – with or without Jackson. I'm so proud of you and all your accomplishments. Every time I think about this beautiful life I have, I think of your mom and my three beautiful, intelligent, and resilient daughters. I love you, Parker."

Yep, I'm still crying. I tighten my grip around my dad and think about how hard he's worked to give us the life we have. He's the best, and I'll accept nothing less for my future husband. This visit to my parents' house is exactly what I needed.

"Thanks, Daddy. I love you, too."

I say goodbye and head to my car, but before I drive off, I reply to Jackson's text.

I won't fight this anymore. I'm ready for a clean slate, but if it doesn't work out this time, we need to move on and stop holding ourselves back. I look forward to our first date, Mr. Sands. See you on Thursday night.

Chapter 2

The Beginning of It All - Parker

When I arrive home to my beautiful and cozy but empty beach bungalow, I throw myself on my bed and scream out loud – a sound mixed with both frustration and wonder. I can't believe I'm going to take a risk with Jackson yet again.

I thought I was over him. I thought three months ago, after our regretful hookup, would be my last slip up. I mean, I want love, but I'm not lonely, so why am I all of a sudden feeling this way – like I *need* him, like he's been the missing piece to my happily ever after.

I do agree that we need to take things slow this time around. All eyes are on us, and we need to get this right so we can determine whether we should really move forward together or apart.

No one except our friends and family know the real story of Jackson and I. No one knows about the tragedies that tore us apart and the anger that kept us away. It's crazy to believe we've known one another for so long. We'll forever be a part of each other's lives, and I'll never forget the moment we met, the day he became my best friend and the only person I would ever give my heart to.

While most of the town may call my sister Izzy *the* sweetheart of Beverly Mills, my mom, Mrs. Jolene Waylen, Jo for short, originally held that title. She has a heart of gold, and she knows everyone in Beverly Mills. She was an elementary school teacher who taught nearly every adult and teenager in this town.

She was also my 3rd grade teacher and encouraged me to speak to the 'new student' in my class. His name was Jackson Sands.

I remember Jackson's first day of school at Beverly Mills Elementary. He walked into the class with his head hanging low and watery eyes compelled by nervousness, fear, and sadness. My mom took him by the hand, lifted his chin with her finger, and found a way to make him feel comfortable on his first day of school.

"Class, we have a new student today, and his name is Jackson. What do we say when we have a new student?"

The students said in unison, "Hi Jackson, welcome to Beverly Mills!"

The fear and sadness in his eyes slowly dissipated, and a smile appeared when the students greeted him with warm hugs, enthusiasm, and kindness. Mom, Mrs. Waylen, assigned me to be Jackson's welcome buddy. For the next month, it was my responsibility to get him acclimated to the school and help him make friends. Jackson shadowed me throughout school. We ate lunch together every day and partnered together on class projects. He was so funny in a dry humor type of way, and for an eight year old, he had tons of Southern charm. Our month-long temporary buddy arrangement transitioned into a permanent situation. We became naturally inseparable.

Once Jackson became accustomed to Beverly Mills life, he made more friends. This includes the group of kids we know today as the Beverly Mills Boys. Jason, who's currently Mayor of Beverly Mills, but most importantly, Merissa's husband. Deacon, who's our hot, playboy sheriff. Gabe, the smartest tech geek in town who also happens to be Merissa's stepbrother, and Jackson, the big city millionaire real estate developer.

As we grew older, the Beverly Mills Boys joined forces with my girls - Avery, Izzy, and my best friend, Merissa. We share Merissa as a best friend.

She and Jason are the glue to our relationships, friendships, careers, and sanity.

But Jackson and I were closer than anyone else.

I remember visiting Jackson's home for the first time. He missed an entire week of school, and I was so worried that my best friend had left town without notice, not even a goodbye. I didn't know what was going on at the time, but my mom did. We arrived at his doorstep with Jackson's missed schoolwork, a card, and a freshly baked peach cobbler. I distinctly remember a handsome and youthful but somber Mr. Sands answering the door with Jackson standing in the distance. My eyes moved back and forth between the two. He looked just like my Jackson.

When we entered the home, we were immediately overtaken by the smell of fresh linens and mint. It made me feel light and refreshed – a completely opposite feeling of Mr. Sands and Jackson's mood. We stood in the foyer for about five minutes until a beautiful, frail woman with dark hair and hazel eyes, just like Jackson's, came walking around the corner. She looked young but old and tired, as if life had hit her too hard, too fast, and too unexpectantly. She may have only been five years older than Mom, but her vibrant youth had been replaced with harsh life experiences and undeserved struggles. Yet, she wore a smile wide enough to mask Mr. Sands and Jackson's pain.

"Mrs. Sands! You look as beautiful as ever." My mother compliments her and gives her a delicate hug.

"Oh please, call me Debbie. And no need for flattery. I know this isn't my finest attire, but I did pull out my most extravagant hair scarf to greet our first guests since we moved into town." Debbie teases herself and does a playful fancy twirl before nearly losing her balance and stumbling to the floor. Mr. Sands and Jackson quickly rush to help keep her footing.

"Deb, you're doing too much. Let's sit down. Save your energy." Mr. Sands says with worried eyes, but Debbie slaps his hand and laughs.

"Mrs. Waylen, please excuse Frank and his little mini-me. They keep hovering over me like I'm some delicate flower wilting away. These boys just won't leave me be. I might have to file a restraining order just so I can have some space to myself." She laughs weakly.

"Oh, please call me Jolene or Jo, whichever you prefer, and I'll be happy to replace your home with some more estrogen from time to time. We have three girls at the house, so my husband Wayne would love to hang out with you Sands men! The closest thing we have to testosterone in our household are the names of our daughters."

Both moms laugh, and the parents walk to the living room to chat. They motion for us to go play. When we're in the playroom, I try to think of something to say to end the silence.

"We miss you at school. Jason's been going overboard with his jokes. He just won't stop, and he's not funny at all. Like at all!"

Jackson finally laughs. We all know Jason isn't funny. Even today, he still tries to make jokes and fails miserably, but he's a charming politician, and he corny joked his way into the ballot box and Merissa's heart.

"Thank you for coming today. I miss you." Jackson tells me.

"I miss you, too. You're my best friend, probably more than Merissa, but don't tell her I told you that. If she finds out, she might not be my friend anymore, but that's okay because I love you, always, Jackson."

"Pinky promise?" He asks.

"Always." We wrap our pinky fingers around each other and kiss them to seal the deal.

My mom and I stayed at Jackson's house all day until she and Jackson's dad put his mom back to bed. The frowns are long gone, and by nightfall, his home feels like how it smells – light, refreshing, and filled with love.

"Thank you so much for stopping by Jolene. You have no idea how much your visit has meant to us. We needed a moment to just smile and laugh." Frank says with gratitude.

"Laughter is truly the best medicine. That and peach cobbler. Thank you for having us over at such short notice. Jackson means so much to Parker and our family. He's her best friend, and I have a really good feeling that our families will be the best of friends, too. Now, I'm gonna let Wayne know that you and Jackson are gonna join him and the girls on their monthly fishing trip in two weeks, and I'll be here to hang out with Deb. Every woman needs her girl time, ya hear?"

"I hear you, Jo. I look forward to the fun times ahead. Y'all have a good night."

We all hug and end the day on a wonderful note.

Just as my mom said, our families became the best of friends. When we were kids, Jackson and I believed our friendship and families' love for one another was so special that it even brought new life to Mrs. Debbie. Over the next few years, she changed, and so did Jackson and his dad. Her frail body miraculously became stronger, sturdier. Her skin glowed and her once hollow hazel eyes became fuller and more vibrant. The smile she plastered for visitors became more sincere and frequent. Even her hair, which was once covered by scarves, began to grow thicker and longer. Frank and Jackson became less worried and embraced life more. It was as if the brokenness we felt in the atmosphere when they opened the door years ago never existed at all. It wasn't until college that I fully understood the physical, mental, and emotional damage that cancer leaves in its wake.

The town was much smaller back then, and everyone knew one another. We went to church regularly, and we rotated between fishing, exploring historic Beverly Mills, and beaching on the weekends. Life was so simple, and over the years, the original children of Beverly Mills forged bonds that would frequently be tarnished, tattered, and tested but never broken. This is especially the case for me and Jackson Sands.

During the summer going into high school, everyone assumed we would finally 'make it official.' You know, become boyfriend and girlfriend. We were always together. We finished one another's sentences, and we may or may not have admitted at Jason's 15th birthday party that we had a crush on one another when playing truth or dare. However, Jackson needed to focus on football and schoolwork, and I needed to focus on volleyball and schoolwork. Jackson, Jason, Merissa, and I were all in the same grade and had collective plans for our futures. We promised to attend UGA together, move back home, remain best friends, and raise our kids together. That sounds pretty vague, but we were young and didn't think any deeper than that.

 By the time we began 9th grade, all the girls swooned over Jackson. I noticed his good looks well before then, but it was my job as his best friend to humble him, of course. It didn't work, though. He was the starting freshman quarterback of Beverly Mills High's Varsity football team. Local and surrounding news stations covered his gameplay every weekend. He was the star, but no matter how much of a star he was, he still made me feel like I was his everything – his galaxy.

 My mom and Mrs. Debbie would alternate picking us up after our practices. Every day, we'd do our homework together and dive deep into topics about dating, or in other words, the girls who were trying to date Jackson. If they weren't throwing themselves at him in the halls, they'd throw themselves at him in his social media inbox. I admit I was jealous of the attention he received from girls who didn't deserve to breathe the same air as him, but I tried my hardest not to show it. Yet, as time passed, our playful afterschool glances began to last longer than usual. Even more frightening, or maybe thrilling rather, was when our hugs began to feel different than what they used to. Jackson began to *feel* something, too. He'd find excuses to hold on to my waist as if he needed to scoot by me in my parent's kitchen when there was clearly enough of room to walk around. He'd get pissed off and insult any guy who looked at me for too long, and God forbid anyone gives me a compliment. We were just waiting for one of us to make that first move. I wanted to graduate from best friend to girlfriend since that summer we played truth or dare at Jason's 15th birthday party.

Not to mention, puberty was serving me well. I grew super cute, not too big but not too small, with breasts like Beyonce's and hips that didn't lie like Shakira's. My mom finally let me wear lip gloss, and I was ready to pucker up for my first kiss with Jackson. I wondered if he had noticed my physical transformation. I wondered if he smelled the perfume I sprayed on myself without my mom's permission to get his attention. I'd tie the bottom of my collar shirt into a knot to show my belly button just for him, but we remained innocent, and Jackson acted clueless. Although we flirted all throughout 9th grade, he only saw me as his best friend until the following summer at Jason's Sweet 16 Birthday party, where our love story finally evolved.

To this day, Jason's parties are revered as the most epic celebrations in Beverly Mills. He's been going all out since we were kids, and some of our most heartfelt and vulnerable memories occur at his home. Jason's parents come from old money, but he never looked down on us. He's just always been a part of the crew. Don't get me wrong, he's a showboater, but he's kind and has always only wanted to have fun, be cheesy, and support the people he loves. He's seen us all at our worst, and he treats Merissa like the precious jewel she is. His family funds the mental health wing at the hospital and named it after Merissa's sister, who struggled with mental illness and drug addiction. To Jason, we're an extension of his family, and there's nothing he wouldn't do for us, including forcing us to admit our feelings for one another.

The night of Jason's Sweet 16, Jackson and I arrive together, but we go our separate ways so I can chat with Merissa, and he can meet up with Jason and their football buddies.

"Jason really went all out with this party, didn't he? A live DJ? Caterers? And how in the world did he manage to get alcohol? Who approved this? I feel sorry for the woman who marries him. He's so extra." Merissa laughs in amazement.

"Yeah, he does the most! But that's why we love him." I respond in a disappointing tone.

"What's wrong, Parker? You don't sound like you're in a fun mood to party. Get happy!" Merissa tries to cheer me up by dancing to the music, but I can't stop thinking about Jackson.

I'm so frustrated and just begin to babble.

"It's Jackson. I've pulled out all the stops for an entire year, but he's ignored all my signals. I show him some skin. I flirt. I give lingering hugs, but nothing. Maybe I was reading him wrong all along. I really thought he was into me."

"Oh girl, he is definitely into you! Jason told me. Jason tells me everything. He said Jackson wants to ask you to the movies, but he thinks you're into David. He said David constantly flirts with you, and you flirt back, knowing it makes him angry. So, he's afraid you're going to say no." Merissa nonchalantly drops this bomb on me.

"David! I mean, he's cute and all, but I have no interest in him whatsoever. I can't believe you didn't tell me this sooner, Merissa! What the heck? You been holding out on news that could change my life forever." I yell in outrage.

"Hey, don't get mad at me! I'm simply practicing for the future – doctor patient confidentiality. Jason told me not to tell you," She shrugs. "But I do have an idea that'll get the ball rolling!"

Merissa takes out her phone and sends a text message to Jason.

You ready for some truth or dare?

Not even a minute goes by until Jason, Jackson, and their friends arrive to liven the party and announce the start of the game.

"Are y'all ready to tell the truth or dare to be devious?" He says while standing on the arm of his parents' extremely expensive furniture.

Everyone cheers, and I turn my head slightly to gauge Jackson's reaction. Our eyes meet instantaneously. Maybe he wants to know how I feel about him just as much as I want to know how he feels about me.

Merissa and Jason stand next to one another to serve as the game facilitators. These two are always scheming.

"Jackson and Parker, you're up first! Truth or dare?" Merissa asks.

All eyes are on us. There has to be over a hundred kids from school at the party. We look at one another and nod.

"Truth."

"Really, guys? You're taking the easy way out?" Jason asks.

"Give us time. We're just getting started, and I don't trust drunk Jason right now." Jackson laughs.

"Fair point. Alright, let's start off light. Jackson, do you find Parker physically attractive as in sexy enough to kiss her?"

Jason's voice echoes across the room, and everyone from Beverly Mills High patiently waits for Jackson's response.

Calm, cool, and collected, he says, "Absolutely. Parker's the most gorgeous, smartest, funniest, and selfless girl I ever met. I'd love to feel how soft her lips are."

While oohs, woos, cheers, and high-fives fill the room, my eyes go big in shock and delight. We gaze at one another as if we're the only ones in the room.

"Okay, okay, okay, calm down people! We're not done yet. Parker, do you find Jackson physically attractive as in sexy enough to kiss him?" Merissa asks.

Silence falls upon the room again.

I'm so nervous. I wish I was as smooth as Jackson, but my reply only reflects my long-awaited desire for him. I just say, "Abso-fucking-lutely."

Without thinking, without care, without fear, Jackson smiles and gently cups the back of my head and draws our faces near one another. Our lips collide, and warm electric circuits shoot through my body as he slips his tongue into my mouth. This is my first kiss ever, and I follow his lead effortlessly as if this magical moment is just one of many.

We eagerly explore one another's mouths for what seems like minutes until Jason and Merissa wrap their arms around our shoulders like proud parents. "Slow down, you two! Save the rest for my 17th birthday party." Jason laughs.

Everyone continues to cheer. We play and party like there's no tomorrow. When the festivities end, Jackson, Jason, Merissa, and I proceed to clean up the trashed areas of the house.

By the end of the night, we're all exhausted, and I'm confused. Although we had that intense moment two hours ago, we haven't had another yet. Did he not feel what I felt? I decide to woman up and ask.

"Jackson, is something wrong? Do you regret kissing me?" I grab his arm to command his attention.

"What? Of course not. Why do you ask?" He responds as if he's offended by my question.

"Because you haven't said anything to me since we kissed. I can't continue to try to read your mind, Jackson Sands. For once, tell me how you feel."

I cup his cheek with my hand to help him feel comfortable to open up to me in this moment. Of course, I'm the aggressor in this situation. I know Jackson inside and out. I have to push the issue for him to say what's really going on in his head.

Jackson sighs and finally tells me how he feels, "Everything's fine, Parker. Between school, sports, and my mom's appointments, I don't see how I could make time for a girlfriend, and you deserve someone who could give you everything. I think too much and speak too little. I don't want to bore you to death." Jackson then lowers his head to avoid eye contact. I know he can be quiet at times and even slow to speak, but I've never seen him so insecure.

Thankfully, I'm the jelly to his peanut butter, and I don't mind reassuring him of how amazing he is. "Jackson, as long as we're together as best friends or hopefully more one day, we'll always be okay. You'll never bore me. You are the most interesting, boring person I know. So do you or do you not regret kissing me?"

Jackson gives in and says, "Parker, I've wanted to kiss you forever."

His answer makes me so happy. "Hmm, how long is forever?" I smile mischievously.

"Since you've been putting lip gloss on your pouty lips. Since you've been tying your shirt to show off your soft skin to all the boys at Beverly Mills High. Since you've been wearing that perfume, that drives me crazy." Jackson stops to inhale the scent of my neck. "You smell so good, and you're so beautiful. I can hardly control myself around you." He grabs me by my hips and pulls me nearer as he leans back on the counter.

"Then don't, Jackson. Don't control yourself." I breathe heavily.

We're finally done with the chase, and we kiss again, frantically like our lives depend on it, until a loud, commanding voice interrupts the moment.

"Ahem!"

It's my dad! Even worse, he's with Jackson's parents, Debbie and Frank, Jason's parents, Marge and Jason Sr., and Merissa's mom and stepdad, Maria and Carl.

"Parker Eliza Waylen, what the hell are you doing having sex in a kitchen?" My mom screams for the entire neighborhood to hear.

I quickly come back to my senses and separate myself from Jackson. I cautiously walk across the room to speak to my mom in a low discreet tone.

"Mom, we were *not* having sex. We were just kissing. God, this is so embarrassing!"

"Embarrassing? You got that right. Wayne, your daughter's playing tonsil hockey with Jackson and on her way to making us grandparents fifteen years too early!"

Jackson tries to intervene, but it's a terrible idea. "Mrs. Waylen, to be fair, I kissed Parker first."

"Stay out of it, Jackson. As a matter of fact, you have some explaining to do. Let's go." Debbie says.

Jason's mother, Mrs. Pierce, looks around her house in anger and disgust, "Jason, have you sneaky little underaged kids been drinking alcohol? Where did you get all of this beer from?"

"Uh, I raided Dad's secret stash. Sorry." Jason lowers his head as his dad pinches his thumb and index finger between his neck. "C'mon, Son. You're gonna learn how to do manual labor today, and this is the last party you'll ever throw in our house."

We all follow our parents' orders to clean the house and go our separate ways soon afterward. What is supposed to be one of the greatest teen memories of my life is cut short and followed by weeks of punishment – no phone, no contact with my friends, and no social media. This is the longest I've ever gone without contact or communication with Jackson since 3rd grade.

Being on punishment sucks. I spend the majority of my time getting lectured by my parents about teenage pregnancy. The upside, though, is that I get to spend some quality time bonding with my younger sisters, Avery, age fourteen, and Izzy, age twelve. I hadn't realized how much my sisters looked up to me, and I definitely didn't know how fun and interesting they were. Izzy's been obsessed with all the juicy details about my first kiss, while Avery goes on and on about how Jackson is too quiet and closed off for me. I lost count of how many times I made them play Monopoly or how frustrated Avery gets because we still don't know how to play chess. And don't get me started on Izzy's favorite movie collection. I think I can recite The Princess Diaries line by line at this point. If she wasn't so obsessed with being the next social media sensation, her next calling would be to become a Disney princess. So, while I dread my time away from Merissa, Jason, and Jackson, my punishment has allowed me to build a stronger bond with my sisters.

It's the first day of my sophomore year of high school, and I'm ecstatic to see my friends, most importantly Jackson. For weeks, I've been confused about where our relationship stands or if we're even in a relationship. The night of the party was so intense, and I've thought about our kiss every day since. I wonder if he thinks about me as well. When my mom drops me off in front of the school, I excitedly greet Merissa, Jason, and Jackson with hugs and smiles. We missed one another so much.

Jackson turns to face me shyly, then looks to the ground before saying, "Parker."

I melt and reply, "Jackson."

Jason and Merissa tease us with coos and googly eyes. Jackson grabs my hand and kisses it gently.

"Shall we go to class, mi lady?"

Relieved from doubts that my feelings wouldn't be reciprocated, I respond, "We shall, my fair gentleman."

We go through the motions of first day teacher-student introductions and syllabus overviews and anxiously await lunch period to sit down and officially discuss that night. When that time comes, we're both eager to speak.

"So, about that kiss?" I look to Jackson.

"You mean kisses?" He laughs.

"Yeah, kisses," Our eyes meet, and I ramble. "I know that we've been best friends forever, and our parents have essentially given us the hint to stay away from one another, but I don't want to. I really like you, like really like you, and I don't want to beat around the bush with our feelings, so please tell me if you feel the same. If not, I completely under-."

Jackson cuts me off and gently cups the side of my face with his hand.

"May I kiss you again, Parker?"

I'm so stunned yet delighted by his request that I can only respond with a slight nod. Jackson pulls me towards him and plants a sweet, innocent kiss on my lips. It's quick but satisfying.

"Parker Eliza Waylen, will you be my girlfriend?" Jackson asks.

My first day of school hasn't entirely gone according to plan, but no complaints over here. I'm so overjoyed about Jackson that I quickly say yes and anxiously kiss him in front of the entire school body.

Jason stands at the lunch room table and announces, "Parker and Jackson are officially boyfriend and girlfriend, ladies and gentlemen!"

We hear comments like, *It's about time. We love you guys. Beverly Mills' hottest couple.* Jackson and I are pretty popular, but we generally keep to ourselves. We had no idea what people actually thought of us. They evidently also believe we were always meant to be.

After our football and volleyball practices, we meet back up to chat, hug, and hopefully kiss, but our moms arrive together to disrupt our plans.

Mrs. Debbie sits in the passenger seat and rolls down her window.

"Hop in, kids!"

We give one another a confused look and proceed to get in the car with our moms. Our fear, curiosity, and anticipation consume the atmosphere.

"Y'all are probably freaking out right now and maybe even wondering if you're on punishment again, huh?" My mom asks rhetorically. "Well, you're not. Debbie, Frank, Wayne, and I are navigating new waters just like the both of you, so we wanna sit down, have a nice dinner, and discuss some ground rules for this new relationship you, too, are developing."

When we enter Jackson's home, our fathers sit at the kitchen table, instruct us to clean up and come back to the dining room for dinner. Racked with nerves, we do as we're told, and by the time we sit down, dinner is served. I don't exactly know how to feel right now, but we just go through the motions of having a typical dinner with our parents anyhow.

When we finish eating, my dad speaks.

"It's time for us to talk about what happened the night of Jason's party."

I roll my eyes in a fit of exhaustion, and I can tell that Jackson is also annoyed. We've apologized to our parents numerous times for drinking and behaving 'inappropriately.' What more do they want from us?

My mom leads the conversation and says, "We were so shocked and overwhelmed with seeing you two," She pauses. "Displaying affectionate feelings towards one another. I mean, we knew it'd likely happen one day, but just as you two aren't prepared to manage your hormones and emotions, we aren't prepared, as parents, for our kids to start dating."

Debbie chimes in. "Now, this doesn't excuse your behavior, but we were at fault as well for reacting in haste rather than speaking with you both about your feelings and dating in general, for that matter."

My dad then cuts straight to the point, "So, Jackson, how do you feel about my daughter?"

"Dad!" I plead to my dad to stop before Jackson can answer. "This is an invasion of our privacy."

But Jackson's words come out strong and confidently, like he's been preparing all his life to answer this question.

"I really care about Parker. She's my best friend. She's assertive and passionate to the point it scares me sometimes. When I wake up, I think about her. Before I go to sleep, I think about her. She's my dream girl. I truly do apologize for my disrespectful and inappropriate behavior towards your daughter. Your family's respect means the world to me, and I would never do anything to hurt Parker."

I grab Jackson's hand and shoot him a look of admiration.

"I care about you too, Jackson."

Our parents stare at us differently than they ever have before. It's like they don't see us as their babies anymore but now as teenagers who need the chance to explore our emotions.

"Well, Son," Frank says, "If you two are gonna *date* one another, both of you need to abide by our ground rules and set some of your own. Is that clear?"

We both nod.

My mom pulls out a sheet of paper titled *The Waylen and Sands Rules to Dating while Living Under Our Roof.*

1. An adult must be present when together at the house.
2. No inappropriate touching or grabbing.
3. Be home by 12 a.m. on the weekends.
4. No talking on the phone past 12 a.m.
5. No shutting bedroom doors.
6. Academics before dating.
7. No making out in public.
8. No sex!

The rules don't seem too excessive, so we shake hands with our parents and agree to obey their rules.

"Now that we've gotten that out the way." My mom says. "Frank and Wayne, how about you two take Jackson to the living room to talk while we ladies chat with Parker?" The men leave, and my mom and Mrs. Debbie look me in the eyes.

My mom touches my shoulder and says, "You're growing up, aren't ya? A fact of life I didn't prepare myself for."

She tries to lift her head to the ceiling to prevent tears from forming behind her eyes, so Mrs. Debbie steps in to continue the 'talk'.

"I know you and my son care deeply for one another, and I'm confident that his father and I have raised him to be kind, respectful, and loving. I also know how lovely you are, Parker, so I'm thrilled that y'all are so fond of each other. However, I think Jo and I can both agree that hormones can tempt us to push boundaries, and our rules about decency and no sex can easily be forgotten when you're caught up in a moment of passion."

"Passion?" I ask.

"Yes, as in when you get to kissing and feeling up on each other. It's when you start to get horny, Parker," My mom explains. "It's inevitable, and you have to make sure you control yourself cause once you cross that line, your emotions are entangled in ways that people, let alone horny little teenagers, can't handle, and I know you, Parker. You have this *go-all-in* trait where you get a little obsessive. Imagine yourself on steroids when sex enters the equation."

"What Jo means is, don't rush things. When the time is right, it'll happen with the right person, and when you do decide to have sex, be safe. Use condoms. We aren't ready to be grandparents yet. Give us time before we have to start changing diapers again." Mrs. Debbie laughs.

I nod to Mom and Mrs. Debbie, and they both get up to hug me with my mom's embrace lasting significantly longer. Jackson and the dads return with my dad squeezing Jackson's shoulder as if their conversation was just as intense as ours.

"Well, we'll let you two talk or play or whatever teenagers do." Mr. Frank says.

Our parents leave the dining room so we can talk.

"So, how'd your talk go?"

"Terrifying. Let's just say, if I want to keep breathing, then holding hands is gonna be the only thing we can do for a while. Is that okay with you?" He smiles as he leans in closer to me.

"Absolutely not. Rules are meant to be broken, Jackson Sands."

He pulls my face to his and kisses me on the lips. "I have the most beautiful girlfriend in the world."

"So, do you want to set some ground rules of our own like our parents recommended? It'll probably be good for us, right?"

"Yeah, you're right. I know you're my first girlfriend, but I want you to be my last. Let's do this right."

We take out a sheet of paper from the cabinet drawer and come up with the following rules:

1. Stick by each other's side during tough times – as a couple and as best friends

2. Always communicate, no matter how tough the topic may be

3. No lying. Tell the truth even if it hurts

4. Support one another, no matter what

5. Choose each other, always

These rules roll off my tongue and onto the paper like liquid, but Jackson looks overwhelmed and stops me while I'm on a roll.

"Okay, Parker, these rules are really intense. Like number five is a bit excessive, don't you think? We're teens. I doubt we'll have many or any instances where I have to choose you. Like what are the actual odds that we'd be in a 'no matter what' type of situation?"

"Every situation is a no matter what scenario. These rules are important to me, Jackson."

He laughs, takes the pen away, and begins adding to the list.

1. Focus in this order – school, sports, family, and relationship

2. Be patient when communicating is hard to do

3. Respect one another's space

"I think the focus order thing can be interchangeable, but everything else is doable."

Jackson smiles and places his hand on my right cheek.

"One more thing. We have to promise not to give up on one another. I know I'm not the easiest to talk to. I'm not the easiest to support. I don't say much, but I haven't ever had to because you know my mind and heart the most. If it ever becomes too much or if I push you away or mess up somehow, please don't give up on me, Parker."

"That'll never happen. As crazy as I sound, come heartache and heartbreak, I'll never give up on us. Ever."

We press our foreheads together and exhale simultaneously with the understanding that nothing could ever stop us from loving one another.

Chapter 3

Going in Circles - Parker

My Tuesday night was a blur, and Wednesday was even worse. I can hardly focus on my patients, and Merissa's been yelling my name repeatedly to get my attention, but I can't stop having flashbacks of Jackson, except I'm having flashbacks of my life, too. It's impossible to think about myself without thinking about him.

I need to snap out of it! I need to focus on the present. I've come too far to fall back into depression over that man.

"Something's up with you, Dr. Waylen. You've been distracted in deep thought all day, and I don't like it, so get ready to tell me what's going on tonight." Merissa says as she closes up for the day.

"Tonight?" I ask confusingly.

"Yes, tonight! It's Girls Night In at your place, remember," Merissa rolls her eyes and grunts in frustration. "I can't believe you forgot. Seriously, what's gotten into you?"

I can't tell her I forgot about Girls Night In because I've been fantasizing about Jackson all week, so I lie.

"Nothing, I'm just super stressed, but I got this. Girls Night In has my undivided attention!" I plaster a fake smile and give her a thumbs up.

When I get home, I rush to clean my house so the girls don't notice I've gone into another Jackson Sands downward spiral – a sad, junk food binge accompanied by tear-jerkers like The Holiday and The Notebook. A night in with Avery, Izzy, and Merissa is the perfect distraction so I can stop obsessing over Jackson. I prepare the wine, meat, and cheese tray, and turn on the tv so we can watch re-runs of Game of Thrones.

However, while I intended to have a classy night with my girls, they clearly had other plans. They bust through my front door with shot glasses in one hand and tequila in the other. Welp, this is going to be a long night!

"Big sis! Merissa told us you've been acting weird today, so I thought it best we drink the hard stuff tonight! Please tell me you didn't hook up with Time Magazine's Douchbag of the Year." My self-righteous but means-well sister, Avery, fusses and moves past me to enter the kitchen, where she pours us a round of shots. "And don't lie, Merissa already told me Jackson 'conveniently' showed up at your work this week. That little weasel. He's so calculated." She shakes her head.

Avery slides our glasses across the kitchen island. Back-to-back, we were down one shot, then two, then three.

"Well, hello to you too, Avery. I'm gonna blame your bad attitude on work because Jackson doesn't deserve the hate you're throwing his way. And for the record, I did NOT hook up with Jackson!"

The girls stare at me in disbelief after I deny their accusations, so I give in, shamefully admit the truth, and cover my face from the embarrassment.

"Okay, so we may have made out for a few seconds, but that's it."

They all groan hysterically.

"I knew it," My youngest sister, Izzy, says ecstatically. "This is so exciting, Parker! My followers have been obsessed with you and Jackson's story ever since that disastrous interview. #whoisparkerweyland was trending for three months." Izzy's such a hopeless romantic.

"Calm down, Izzy, I can assure you, they are not back together. Yet, that is. So, Parker, what's the deal with you two, anyway? Are you gonna give him another chance or what?" Merissa quizzes me.

Everyone in Beverly Mills is invested in our relationship. I don't intend on getting back together with Jackson, but we are going on a date. I'm a walking contradiction at this point.

"No, we are not getting back together."

Avery raises her hands in defeat and downs another tequila shot.

"So, you don't plan on getting back with your first love that you seem to have a very unhealthy addiction to? You go through this every few years, Parker. Every time Jackson comes back in your life, everything is sunshine and rainbows for a short period of time, then *we* have to come in and pick up the pieces after he's shattered your heart again. It's an endless cycle of toxic love."

Avery is definitely the hard ass of the crew, and tonight, she has zero tolerance for love games. If only her ex-boyfriend Deacon, Beverly Mills' sexy sheriff, was here to brighten her spirits.

"Someone's panties are in a bunch today. Deacon must not be answering your calls again. Direct your frustration towards him, not Jackson," Izzy says. "Look, Parker, you're smart, successful, financially stable, and sexy – like all of my guy *and* girl friends think you're super freaking hot. This isn't the 1950s, where you're obligated to pine over a man, but there's also no shame in wanting to be with someone who makes you happy. Jackson makes you happy, and you make him happy, too. It may not have worked out before, but if I may be honest, neither of you would be the people you are today if you hadn't experienced the pain of your past. Just go for it, girl!"

"And there you have it!!" Merissa chimes in. "Now let's eat and binge-watch some classics."

The girls and I lounge around on the couch, drink wine, snack on cheese, and binge-watch Game of Thrones. We're two episodes in, and we're nearly at the juicy sex scene with Jon Snow.

"Take it off, Snow! You sexy Winterfell Targaryn!" Avery cat calls to the tv.

We all laugh and stare at the tv like horny housewives, then suddenly, we hear a bang on my front door.

Who in the world is knocking on my door this late at night? I walk over and look through my glass sidelight windows to see the Beverly Mills Boys standing outside my door. Jackson, Jason, Gabe, and Deacon look like the mischievous knuckleheads they've always been. I open the door but don't let them come in.

"What are y'all doing here? Jackson, why are you carrying Jason?"

Merissa runs to my door. "Seriously, Jackson? I told you to make sure he doesn't get carried away. I let him out the house for one night and this is what happens?"

Merissa helps Jason to the kitchen and pours him a glass of water. I let the rest of the guys in, and they're immediately shocked by what they see on the tv screen.

"What the hell type of porn is this?" Jackson yells and jealously glares at me.

"Cover your eyes, baby." Jason drunkenly tells Merissa as she hands him the glass of water.

"Boys, let me introduce you to the dreamy Jon Snow." I tease them and wait for their response.

"So, every week, y'all get together to objectify men? We're more than rock-hard abs and a chiseled jawline, you know?" Sheriff Deacon plops down on the couch and puts his arm around Avery. She quickly goes from Ice Queen to a deer caught in headlights, and Deacon's the headlights.

"That's exactly what y'all are. You're our little tinker toys. Isn't that right, Gabe?" Izzy gets up to flick her finger on Gabe's nose and flirtatiously smiles at him. His eyes follow her movement into the backyard, and he follows Izzy shortly thereafter.

"Is something going on between your baby sis and my baby brother?" Merissa asks with a perplexed look on her face. Merissa, Avery, and I look at Jason because we all know he's a terrible liar and can't keep secrets.

"Okay, okay, okay! They may or may not have a thing going on, but that's all I'm going to say."

The guys grunt and shake their heads at Jason.

"Sorry, man. The wife asked, so I had to tell. Happy wife, happy life." He shrugs.

We laugh and admire Jason and Merissa's relationship. They're a perfect fit.

The shock of the guys' arrival is soon replaced by tension, thanks to me trying to escape Jackson's piercing gaze. If I don't relieve some of this tension, I'm going to break out in sweats.

"Seems like Guys Night Out was fun. How much did you drink? Did you drive?"

I study Jackson's face, carefully knowing his history with alcohol and how it damaged our relationship.

Jackson's relieved to speak, "Umn no, no drinking for me tonight, and despite how it looks, Mayor Jason over here only had two beers until he started tough man crying about missing his wife. We tried to take him home, but he refused to get out of the car and sleep in an empty house. So, here we are."

Merissa informs me she and Jason will sleep in one of my spare bedrooms. I let Avery and Deacon know they can do the same. I'm sure whatever Izzy and Gabe are doing will continue in my other spare room as well.

I make an announcement for everyone to hear, "Well, boys, you've officially ruined Girls Night In, so feel free to sleep in a spare room with your wife, your booty call, or your secret plaything that we need to talk about first thing in the morning. Goodnight, everyone. Oh, and no sex! Save it for when you get home."

Everyone goes to their respective space for the night. Well, everyone but me and Jackson. He graciously insists on helping me clean my messy kitchen.

"I miss these nights. From high school and college – hanging out with the guys and then crashing your girl's night. Good times." Jackson reminisces, and we both get lost in our shared memories.

He grabs my waist to make space as he moves to load the dishwasher, a classic move he's done since we were young as an excuse to touch me, and his touch, indeed, just sent shivers down my spine and forbidden thoughts in my mind. I need to control myself and get us back on neutral ground.

"Thank you for helping me with the dishes. I figured you forgot how to do manual labor with you being a millionaire and all now." I tease him with a hip bump.

"Ha. Ha. Ha. I don't mind getting my hands dirty, Parker. You know this." Jackson smiles back at me.

Dammit. We're flirting again, but I know exactly what to say to push his buttons.

"I don't know, Jackson. How in the world will you last six months back here without your driver, fancy suits, and the beautiful women on your arm?" I wait for an annoyed reaction.

In a stern voice, he responds, "As always, the only woman I want is you, Parker. It's always been you." Jackson inches closer to me.

Determined not to give in to his declarations, I slightly push him away.

"You're not the man for me, Jackson. Our history keeps us together and apart at the same time. Don't you want to start fresh with someone else?"

"What do you think I've tried to do for the past seven years? Hell, I almost married Allie Oxford, for God's sake! I want a fresh start with you!" Jackson screams, but he realizes he just stabbed me straight through the heart with the mention of his engagement to Allie.

"I definitely remember the day you decided to commit yourself to another woman, Jackson. A woman that could give you a child, something that I could never do." I look down and rub a deep scar below my stomach – a permanent memory and invisible pain that I can never get rid of.

Jackson drops to his knees, holds his head to my stomach, and kisses my scar while moisturizing my skin with his warm tears.

"I'll never forgive myself for that night, and I pray that you believe me one day when I say I'd never leave you for that reason. I never left you, Parker. I only spared you the pain of my guilt and brokenness."

I lean against my kitchen island and rub my hands in his hair. He feels so good and strong, yet vulnerable against my body. I just wish we weren't, at this point again, comforting one another's pain – a pain and insecurity that I've moved on from. This is why we can't be together. We can never have a happily ever after.

As much as I should stop him from sweet-talking my misery, I fall back into the Jackson Sands saga and let go. Jackson begins to slowly litter my body with gentle, sweet kisses from my belly to my breast and from my collarbone to my neck. Then, finally, our lips reunite. Sweet as ever and thrilling as if it's our first time, we move frantically like addicts, ready to get our fix.

Jackson grabs my thighs and effortlessly lifts me up on my kitchen island. With our tongues tangled and fighting to breathe, I grind my hips into his. He groans, and I whimper.

We should stop, I think to myself, but the exact opposite utters out my mouth, "Jackson, I missed you. Make love to me."

No matter how many times Jackson disappears from my life, we circle back to instances like this wrapped in one another's embrace and deep inside of me all night long.

I'm conflicted between my mind and my emotions. I finally stop unclothing Jackson and speak plain and clear, "This is a bad idea. You and I both know how this ends, in tears."

He presses his forehead against mine and whispers in my ear, "It doesn't have to. There's nothing and no one holding us back now. Let's try this one more time."

He knows exactly how to turn me on. I obediently nod place my hand on top of his, and guide him down to my soaking wet panties.

He closes his eyes and moans in my ear. "Shit, Parker. Do I make you feel this way?"

"Always."

His eyes light up even more, and his fingers make their way into my body as if they belong inside me – inside every crevice. He eases one finger in slowly, and I feel my body tense as he strokes me.

I grab his shoulders, "Jackson, I need more. Please make love to me."

Without a word, he picks me up and carries me to my couch. He opens his wallet to pull out a condom but hesitates and looks at me.

"I've only been with you since the last time, but that may not be the case for you. I understand." I hold my head down and hope for a different answer than what I'm assuming.

"Only you, Parker. I only want you for the rest of my life."

I grab the back of his head and pull him towards me so our lips can meet again. Jackson's body is on top of mine, and my body is aching for him to enter me. Without further delay, the biggest and best I ever had sends lightning bolts through my body. I try to subdue my scream, but I can't, so Jackson puts his hand over my mouth and his lips to my ears.

"Shh. You have company, Parker. We don't want an audience, so scream and moan in my mouth instead."

He kisses me hard while feverishly and passionately thrusting in and out of me, and I moan in his mouth, fighting to both breathe and contain myself.

He tightens his hold on my hip with his right hand and grabs the sofa arm for support as he whispers sweet everythings in my ear and starts stroking faster and harder at a rhythmic pace.

"You feel so good. No one has ever made me feel the way you make me feel. You're perfect, and you're mine. I love you, Parker. I love you so much."

And with that, we both release, but this time it's different. We didn't just release three months of sexual frustration. We released years of anger, hurt, regret, and relief. Maybe I'm coming from a lustful place, especially after such an intense orgasm, but perhaps things could really be different. Maybe we really can make our relationship work this time around.

Once we catch our breaths, Jackson lifts his body from on top of mine and gives me a sweet and tender kiss.

"Should we shower?"

"We should." I smile.

I grab Jackson by the tip of his fingers and lead him to my master bathroom. Still behind me, he wraps me in his arms and nestles his head on my shoulder. He smells like home, like fresh linens, mint, and love. We take our time adorning one another's bodies in the shower. He's the most beautiful man I've ever seen, and, in this moment, I do believe I'm the most beautiful woman he's ever seen. I don't believe in fairy tales, but I'm willing to play into this fantasy tonight with Jackson. I'll let him continue to adore me like his queen and please me like I deserve to be pleased.

We lay in the bed together with our fingers intertwined. We have small talk and reminiscence on fun memories.

"We're officially old," I laugh. "Everyone's been asleep for an hour, but it's only 1 a.m. I remember back in the day, we used to stay up all night – drinking, playing games, and taking late-night trips to Walmart and Wendy's."

"You remember senior year, maybe a few weeks before I got drafted? You went on a serious hot Cheetos and Cookie Dough frosty binge. You woke me up at 1 a.m. every night for two weeks straight like a madwoman," Jackson laughs. "It got so bad that your dad cut you off – no more money to support your habit. You were begging everybody for chump change, and no one would spot you $10! It was hilarious, but I enjoyed those nights. We'd stay in the Wendy's parking lot for hours talking about our future until the next morning."

"I remember those nights. Y'all were so cruel to me! You could've easily just given me the money, Jackson. You, Merissa, and Jason called it an intervention."

We stay in one another's embrace until I continue with the story that reminds us of our dark past.

"And two weeks later, the accident happened. I guess that explains those weird cravings, huh?"

No words are spoken. I can feel Jackson's desire to speak, but he only grits his teeth and touches my scar.

Unable to defeat the pain of our past, we resolve to silence and find comfort in falling asleep in one another's arms.

The next morning, I wake up to the refreshing smell of fresh linens and mint. Without even opening my eyes, I know that Jackson is still asleep and spooning me, but I also smell the delicious aroma of the famous Waylen banana pancakes and brown sugar bacon. I groan in a hungry delight, and Jackson grips me tighter as he slowly wakes up to pepper my back and neck with kisses.

"Good morning." He whispers in his sexy, raspy, half-sleep voice.

"Good morning, handsome," I plaster a fake smile and revert to my hardened heart. "Jackson, we need to act like nothing happened last night. I don't want everyone to know we did it again. Our chaos affects our friends. They start asking questions, and they take sides. It's just a mess, and I don't want to bring drama or stress to anyone else's life but mine. Agreed?" I want to kiss him, but I keep a straight face as I wait for a response.

Jackson looks at me wearily as if he wants to disagree, but he sighs, throws himself on the pillow, and says, "Okay. I'm willing to be your dirty little secret for this morning and this morning only."

I happily squeal at how easy it is to get him to oblige to my demands, and unaware of my sensual body gestures, I straddle Jackson to give him a kiss of gratitude. Caught off guard yet excited, he squeezes my thighs and grinds his hips in a circular motion in response.

"If this is the thanks I get for keeping my mouth shut, I would've agreed to be your secret a long time ago." He teases as our body temperatures begin to rise.

"So, you want to have a dry hump session this early in the morning, Jackson?"

"There's nothing dry about you right now, Parker. Let me taste you. I'm starving."

He flips me over so his body is on top of mine. He's so strong, so enticing, and all mine. I know our friends are in the kitchen cooking and eating, but it's so hard to say no to Jackson, and it's even harder to say no to an early morning, confidence-boosting pick me up.

This man's mouth was made to devour me. As he works masterfully like a magician, I quickly feel myself about to burst into hot flames.

"Jackson, I can't. Slow down. I'm about to co –" I moan, unable to complete my sentence.

My body starts to convulse, and when I finish, he eases back up to kiss me on my lips.

"Still sweet as ever, like honey and whipped vanilla." He smiles so seductively.

It feels like we're lost in our own world. We press our foreheads together and give one another one last kiss before we face the music.

"Come on. Let's go deal with the mob. Where are your clothes?"

Jackson looks around and remembers we unclothed in the kitchen. We look at one another with the same thought in mind. *Dammit. We're busted.*

"Just grab one of your t-shirts and sweats out my bottom drawer."

"It's good to know you haven't boxed or burned all my things over the years." He laughs.

"Oh no, I've definitely burned some, just not all."

As soon as we get dressed, we enter the front room. Avery, Deacon, Merissa, Jason, Izzy, and Gabe stare at us with looks of suspicion.

"If you're going to make a no-sex rule when hanging out with your friends and family, then maybe you should abide by them too, Parker. I mean goodness, between last night and this morning, you two ought to be ashamed of yourselves. We didn't get any sleep." Avery says dramatically.

"That's not true. Avery snored all night long." Deacon rustles his hand in her unrealistically perfect morning hair.

She needs someone like Deacon, who could ruffle her feathers and soften her hardened exterior, and she knows he's her match. While they quietly bicker with their eyes, Izzy hands me and Jackson a plate of banana pancakes and bacon.

"Order up for Beverly Mills' favorite couple. It's so good to see you two back together." Izzy leans on the kitchen island with her hands gently cradling her chin as she waits for us to confirm.

"Sorry to disappoint, but we're not back together, and we didn't have sex last night." I look down to hide my pitiful poker face, and Jackson only nods in agreement.

Jason chimes in, "I'm the Mayor, and I can spot b.s. from a mile away."

"And as an attorney, I'll say the evidence is evident. Exhibit A, your boxers. Exhibit B, your underwear, and Exhibit C, the guilty look on your faces. Take 'em away, Sheriff!" Avery points to her faux beau.

"My pleasure! But first, we need a confession. Did you or did you not –" Izzy swings around Deacon's shoulder to say,

"Stick your P in my sister's V?"

This is everything I wanted to avoid. Thankfully, Merissa steps in to save the day.

"Hey, hey, hey, lay off! This is not truth or dare. We do not have the right to interfere in Parker and Jackson's lives. Now, leave them alone. We all know they did the deed both last night and again less than twenty minutes ago."

Everyone laughs, and we continue to eat breakfast and have casual conversation throughout the morning. It feels amazing to have the gang back together, and I wish this feeling could last. My home feels full of love, a feeling I haven't experienced in what seems like forever.

When we finish breakfast, we exchange hugs, and everyone carpools home, well, everyone except Jackson. The air is thick between us. I desperately do and don't want a repeat of last night, so I try my hardest to keep things platonic.

"So, since we've already done the deed, there's no need for our date tonight, right?" I ask him while keeping a sharp distance between us.

"Are you kidding me? I look forward to tonight, and I'll be on my best behavior. Actually, I think I should be worried about you keeping your hands off me tonight since I'm going to 'wow' you with my charm." Jackson jokes.

"Oh, is that right? Well, please do tell me what I can expect from you tonight, Mr. Sands."

"I'm pulling out all the stops for the most beautiful doctor in Beverly Mills, Georgia." Jackson begins to close the space between us. He grabs my waist and whispers, "I want to tell you everything. I want you to know me, the real me. Will you open your heart to me again so I can show you?"

His hot breath sends tingles down my spine. I'm so crippled by hot, passionate lust that my words get caught in my throat, and I can only reply with a nod. Jackson looks me in the eye, then kisses my forehead and steps back to put the distance between us again.

"Jackson, you're such a tease." I tell him in a needy voice.

"Says the woman wearing my t-shirt and sweatpants," He responds. "My ride share's here. I'm gonna head back to my dad's house, get some work done, and prep for our first date. I'll see you tonight, Parker."

Jackson catches a grape in his mouth, kisses my cheek, and says goodbye. I place my hand in that spot to savor his touch. Am I insane to think this could work again?

Chapter 4

Jackson Sands - Jackson

Parker and I have been in a relationship for two and a half years. We're seniors in high school, and it may sound crazy, but we've already planned our lives together. We both accepted athletic scholarships to attend the University of Georgia, and our parents keep telling us to focus on our education and that we're still young, but I love her. I love her so much, and I know I'm going to marry Parker Waylen someday.

She's my first best friend, my first girlfriend, my first, well, she's my first, and I know our parents gave us rules to abide by, but at least we waited until Senior Prom night to break the sacred rule of 'no sex.' We controlled ourselves for as long as we could, unlike Jason and Merissa. They've only been dating for a few months, and they jump each other's bones like jackrabbits every chance they get.

What Parker and I have is rare, and today marks the end of a chapter and the beginning of the rest of our lives together. It's our high school graduation day.

"Hey, stud. What're you daydreaming about?" Parker walks up to me in the mall food court and plants a kiss on my cheek.

"Hey, babe." I sit her down on my lap and nuzzle my face in her neck.

"Jackson! So much PDA. If I knew you were gonna be this affectionate, I would've, you know…with you a long time ago." Parker teases, then playfully pushes me away.

"I'm sorry if I didn't show you love and affection before. I guess I have to pile it on as much as I can to make up for lost time, huh? How about this? Parker Waylen, you are so amazing. You look amazing. You smell amazing. You sound amazing. You *feel* amazing." I serenade her until Jason and Merissa walk up to the table.

"Cut it out, you two horndogs!" They laugh.

"In five hours, we'll officially be high school graduates. Can you believe it? My parents are still figuring out how I made it this far." Jason says.

"Babe, I keep telling you that you're a closet nerd. You're gonna be president one day, but let's start off small. Maybe run for town mayor? You've got my vote." Merissa says enthusiastically.

"And while you're making Beverly Mills a safer place to live, Parker and I will be world-renowned doctors. Isn't that right?"

"You bet! We're gonna open a practice in Atlanta. I'm thinking plastic surgery. The rich and famous love their fillers." Parker says.

I admire my friends as they talk about life after high school. They have their futures all planned out. They know what they want to do and who they want to be, but me? I lost. The town says I'll be the first of us to make it to the NFL, which would be nice, but that's not important to me right now. I'm fully content with my life as long as I have my mom, dad, and Parker. I don't want to think too far ahead. I never could. That luxury doesn't exist for me, or else I'd have to consider everything else going on in my life. And I'm just not ready to accept a tragic truth that my parents have been shielding me from for the past few weeks.

When I get home from hanging out with my friends, I see my mom's strained face and my dad walking beside her as if he's ready to catch her if she falls – a familiar thing he used to do when she was sick with cancer, for the second time, a few years back. They brush off the interaction to greet me with warm smiles.

"Jackson! You're home. Are you ready for your big day, sweetheart?" My mom asks.

"Absolutely." I greet her with a strong hug and a kiss with the hope of transferring my strength to her weak, tired limbs.

"We're so proud of you, Son. You're my proudest achievement, the best thing that ever happened to us." My dad gives me a bear hug and pats me on the back.

My mom says my dad and I are one and the same. We're men of few words but passionate about the ones we love, and he's the best father I could ever ask for and, per my mom's words, the best husband a country girl could ever dream of. I hope to live up to that one day. I hope to be that man for Parker.

"Oh, my boys. I don't know how or why God chose to bless me with two of the most amazing men in the world. Frank and Jackson, y'all are everything that I've ever prayed for. You've taken care of me when I should've been taking care of you. You've seen and been through so much, Jackson. Your strength has given me strength. Thank you for making me so proud."

My mom stands up to hug me, but she loses her balance and nearly falls to the floor until Dad and I help her sit back in her chair. This has been my normal ever since I was a kid.

"I'm fine!" She yanks her arms from our grip, and this time, when she speaks, it's out of embarrassment and frustration. She's usually so calm and unafraid, but for a moment, she lets her guard down, and I see nothing but fear and uncertainty. I can't play the fool anymore. I have to say something.

"Is it back?" My parents ignore me, so I repeat myself even louder, "Is the cancer back, mom?" My voice cracks, and my eyes widen. I played this conversation out in my mind a million times. Still, I didn't prepare myself for the heap of emotions that are overtaking me right now. I've shrunk down to the scared little boy who's seen his mom battle cancer time and time again, only for it to come back every time with vengeance.

"Today is your high school graduation, Jackson. It's about you and you only. There's no need to focus on anything else." She tries to reassure me, but it isn't working, so my dad chimes in to back her up.

"After your ceremony, you're gonna go celebrate with your friends and have fun. You deserve it. Any other conversation can be saved for tomorrow, okay, Son?" My dad pulls me in for another hug.

His tear drops on my shoulder. They don't need to answer my question. Enough has been said, and my fears have been confirmed. A few hours later, I put my feelings aside, put on my game face, do as instructed, and try to be a normal teenager.

"It's go time, baby!" Parker runs up to me and wraps her arms around my neck. Naturally, I swing her around into a full circle and kiss her soft, comforting lips. Though I'm worried about my mom's health, I don't want to alarm Parker, Jason, or Merissa.

I don't want to put my problems on them. So, for now, I'll keep everything to myself. I can't really focus on graduating when the most important person in my life is suffering. My dad and I are my mom's biggest supporters, and the thought of her being in need makes me want to drop everything and be there for her like she's always tried to be there for me, even when she couldn't.

"Jackson, hun, are you okay?" Parker asks.

"Yeah, babe. I'm sorry. My head is spinning in circles." I try to reassure her that I'm fine, but it's hard to hide anything from Parker. She knows me inside and out.

"Jackson, I know when something's wrong. You've been out of it since you got here. What's going on?" Parker grabs my hand and squeezes it tight. I want to tell her, but it's not the right time. Not now.

"I'll tell you later, okay? Don't worry. Let's get ready to walk and celebrate. I wanna share this moment with you."

I give her an endearing kiss on the forehead, and we walk to our chairs on the football field. I'm sitting next to the love of my life, who's full of energy while staring at my mom, the woman I love the most, who's in the bleachers, draining all her energy just to cheer me on. What a bittersweet day.

Most graduating seniors head down to the pier for our graduation celebration. I'm not in the mood to party tonight, but my parents wouldn't let me sulk at home. So here I am, sitting alone outside at a party full of people having the time of their lives. I just want to be by myself, sit on top of my car, and drink a beer. I don't want to ruin Parker and my friends' night with my depressing personal problems.

"Jackson," Shit, Parker found me. "Jackson, how long have you been out here? I've been looking for you."

Parker observes what she sees - me drinking a beer with three other empty beer cans surrounding me.

"Jackson, you're wasted. What's going on? It's time to have that talk, now!"

She slides next to me on the hood of my car and grabs my hand. We both stare at the sky in still peace for nearly five minutes. She waits for me to speak, but instead of words, only tears form, and I finally let go and break down my hard, expressionless exterior. Parker holds me in her arms and comforts me while I cry.

I finally muster up the words to say, "Mom's sick again."

Parker holds me tighter and kisses my temple, "Oh, Jackson, I'm so sorry. When did you find out?"

"I don't have many details yet, but I saw it plain and clear today. She's been losing weight, and sometimes she's too weak to stand. I finally asked what was happening, and I was met with a dismissive silence worth a thousand words. Parker, I don't know what to do. I need to be there for her. I need to be there to help my dad help her." I start to panic.

"Shh, shh, shh Jackson, calm down and breathe," Parker places her hand on my back, "One thought at a time. Let's slow down and think everything through. Yes, your mom will need all the love and support we can give her, but it'll stress her out even more if her one and only son puts his life on hold for her. Let's find out what's going on before jumping to conclusions, okay?"

Parker kisses me and sits in my lap so I can hold her as close to my heart as possible.

"I love you, Parker. You always know how to make me feel better." I squeeze her with dear life so I can feel her body heat closer to mine.

"I could make you feel even better if you weren't so drunk, Jackson. I know you've been hit with bad news today, but I don't want to see you get wasted like this again. It scares me. You've been drinking so much lately. Don't turn to alcohol when you feel like you're falling, let *me* be your safety net, not this. I'm the one that will always love you, especially when you're down."

I kiss the top of her head, and we fall asleep on my car. This is the perfect escape, even if only for a few hours.

Talk about the hangover of my life! My head is pounding, and I feel nauseous as hell. I would say I'm never drinking again, but I said that last time. I could hardly remember anything from last night. However, my senses are still consumed with the smell and taste of Parker, so I probably need to apologize to her for getting drunk again.

But right on cue to interrupt my thoughts, my mom prances in my room with vibrant energy and enthusiasm – a different pep in her step than I've seen her have in the last few weeks.

"Rise and shine, Jackson!"

"Ugh, mom! Please close those curtains. I have a killer headache." I groan and bury my head into my pillow.

"Oh really? Well, I wonder why! You reek of alcohol, Jackson. Now, you may have graduated high school, but you're only eighteen, and you're still living in my house, so you still have to abide by our rules. I'd roll over in my grave if you throw your life away over alcohol. It's addictive, and I'll be damned if I lose you to it like I lost my bastard dad."

The last thing I ever want to do is cause my mother pain or, even worse, disappoint her. I never met my grandfather, but I've heard endless stories about him. He was a drunk, a mean, cold, deadbeat drunk. He did things to my mom and grandma – caused them physical pain that I could never imagine doing to anyone. I always say that I'll do everything within my power to never be like him, yet here I am, drinking whenever I can just to get through the day, just like he did.

I need to stop being weak. I need to be stronger. I need to be more like my mom and less like my grandfather. All my life, I've tried to prove myself worthy of the people who love me, yet I continue to be a burden to everyone around me. Back in elementary and middle school, at my mom's sickest moments, I tried to imitate my dad so I could be the strength she needed to beat cancer, but she just got sicker and sicker. I tried to stay out of their way as much as possible so they could focus on her health. I tried not to cry when I was in pain. I tried not to speak when I needed to ask a question. I tried not to be too happy. I tried not to laugh too loud, especially when I saw my mother in so much pain. I always tried my hardest to make things easier on them, but I've always felt like it was never enough. I was waiting to mess up, and lately, I've been screwing up and making nothing but bad decisions.

I feel the same way when it comes to my relationship with Parker. She's too good for me, and I can't get rid of that inkling feeling that I'll hurt her. It angers Parker every time I drink, and it angers me to anger her. I'm waiting for the day she up and leaves me. She deserves everything, but how can I give her everything when I have nothing to offer.

When I snap out of my state of self-loathing, I realize Mom is bent over with a painful grimace on her face. Shit, my selfish, self-pitying ass can't do anything right!

I rush over to my mom's side to check on her, "Mom, are you okay?" I ask while holding her hand.

"Don't worry about me, Jackson. I see you over there, lost in your thoughts. You're putting yourself down again. Don't do that, Jackson. Talk, laugh, or cry out your feelings, but please don't hold them in. You deserve to be happy, to be loved, and praised. I know I missed out on so much when you were younger. You had to be strong and brave at such a young age, and I'm sorry for that. I'm sorry I couldn't give you a fun, carefree childhood. I'm sorry you're always on edge, but please try to remember, these negative thoughts you have don't reflect who you are."

My mom encourages me, and then we put our foreheads together and say in unison, "Because despite everything, we are still wonderfully, beautifully, and fearfully made." A mom-and-son sort of secret handshake that started ever since I could remember. My mom's voice soothes me and brings me back to a place of peace and reassurance of who I am, but it's easy for the darkness to creep back in, especially considering that my mom, my anchor, won't always be around to center me, sooner rather than later.

My dad walks into the room with my mom's bag in hand. I look at them in confusion and ask, "Where are y'all going?"

"To the hospital for some routine tests." My dad responds without making eye contact.

"Frank?" My mom stops him in his tracks and squeezes his arm.

My dad relaxes his muscles, softens his tone, and says, "I'm taking your mom to the oncologist," The three of us sit on my bed. My mom nods to my dad, and he continues to speak.

"About a month ago, your mom went to the doctor because she'd been feeling off for a while, a similar feeling she had before. The doctors ran some tests to see if her cancer returned." My dad lowers his head and takes a deep breath before continuing, "This time, they found tumors in her breast."

A tear falls down my mother's cheek, yet she's the one who comforts me.

"It's gonna be fine. We caught it early, and the doctors are gonna treat this aggressively. I'll have surgery in a week to remove the mass, then chemo. Then, in a few months, I'll be rooting you on at your first college football game. Before you know it, I'll be cheering you on at your graduation. A few more years down the line, I'll get to watch you marry the love of your life. Then soon after, I'll hold my first grandbaby."

"Hey, now. We should talk about this timeline of yours. Let Jackson stay a kid for a little longer before we think about grandbabies." My dad laughs.

"Jackson, don't worry about your old mom. You've worried about me all of your life – always waiting for bad news. We want you to have as much fun, *sober* fun, before you head to college, and maybe you should also speak to a professional. You know, like before? You're making a big transition from high school to college. Everything you do is gonna be scrutinized by coaches and the media. And my health," My mom pauses. "My health can be unpredictable, and you need to be able to talk through how you feel, or else you may find unhealthy ways to manage your anxiety and depression, like drinking, for instance." My mom says as she caresses my back.

"Your mother's right, Jackson. We won't always be around to protect your secrets. You can't continue to go untreated. You need to get some help before you spiral out of control. It may not happen tomorrow or next week or a month down the road, but it'll happen eventually, and you could destroy yourself or those closest to you. Your condition is serious, and you have nothing to be ashamed of, Son. If you really want to be there for your mom, then the best way to do that is to get yourself some help, too."

My parents are pleading with me. They're confronting an issue that I've been avoiding. Ever since I could remember, I only wanted one thing, which was for my mom to be cured – no more cancer. But since I couldn't make that happen, I controlled the narrative for every other aspect of my life – my emotions, my education, football, my words, how I'm perceived by others, and my relationships. But lately, the more I try to neatly package my life together, the more everything seems to come undone.

I take a deep sigh and look to my parents, "Okay, I'll schedule an appointment to speak with Dr. Kaiser next week, but you also have to be open with me, too, about treatments, about your pain, about everything."

We all agree. This is a turning point for our family. My parents feel comfortable enough to finally level with me about my mother's health. They also expressed their feelings about my mental health, a topic I've avoided for years. There's an unspoken respect between us, as if they now trust me to handle the severity of our circumstances.

"Do you mind if I tag along? I – I'll stay out of the way. I'll be as quiet as possible. I just –"

My mom interrupts my stammering words, "Jackson, I think that's a great idea, and don't feel like you need to stay out of the way. You've never been a burden. Without you and your dad, I don't think I'd still be alive. Y'all are my anchors, and I'm thankful you're here now for me, yet again."

I hug my parents, and we leave to go to the hospital to begin another long journey to recovery.

It's the day of my mom's mastectomy. She's the strongest woman alive, and she and Mrs. Waylen are making jokes about finally being able to throw away her bras. Parker is back at our house, cleaning, prepping the rooms, and reorganizing my mother's essentials so everything can be as easily accessible to her as possible. She hates relying on us at home, so it'll be a nice surprise for her to come home and still feel like the superwoman she is.

I only have a few more weeks left until Parker and I have to leave for summer training, so I need to focus my time and energy on Mom's recovery. She needs my undivided attention, and I'm afraid of what'll happen when I leave. I told my coaches about everything that's happening, and as understanding as they seemed, I worry about making a bad impression by missing practices and not being as focused as everyone else on the team. If I lose my scholarship, then I'd be letting my parents down, my friends, and the town. Everyone expects me to excel, but I don't know how much more I can bear before I fail and become the disappointment I've always believed myself to be.

A few days later, we arrive home and escort my mom to her room to rest. Parker outdid herself. The house looks brand new, not a dirty dish or speck of dust in sight. When my mom opens her eyes from her nap, she's happily surprised to see that her bed and nightstand have been rearranged and loaded with all of her must-have items – tv remote, medications, phone and charger, snacks, water, and tissues are all at her disposal.

"I'll take it from here, boys." She jokes, and she shoos us away.

I feel a lot better about leaving now. I never got around to calling Dr. Kaiser, but I don't think it's necessary again. My mom's surgery went well, and for the first time in a long time, I'm confident that everything's going to be alright, and I think I can manage my mental health by myself, for now.

So much has changed in just two years. My mom underwent a single mastectomy but had to get her second breast removed months later. The cancer hasn't spread, and her health has gotten much better. She's even attended almost every home game this season. I know I shouldn't get my hopes up, but I'm just happy to be able to speak to her every day.

Parker and I are doing great. She decided to forego playing volleyball next season to focus on her pre-med studies, and she's also inspired me to study business. When it was time for us to decide on a major, she, Merissa, and Jason already had their futures figured out, but I finally admitted that I had no idea what I wanted to do with my life. Ever since I was five, my existence centered around caring for my mom and putting myself second. I never thought about my passion or future separate from my mom or Parker. I don't just want to be an NFL player. I want to do some good, so I'm going to turn my desire to help others into a non-profit that supports families impacted by cancer.

"I can't believe I'm dating Beverly Mills' hometown hero and college football's national treasure! Can you believe you made First Team All-American as a college Sophomore? You're truly one-of-a-kind Jackson Sands." Parker sits on my lap and gives me a passionate kiss.

"I'm definitely not one-of-a-kind. I actually consider myself to be your standard regular guy. What'd you call it? I'm basic."

"And you're basically crazy, Jackson. You really do underestimate yourself. When you're not killin' it in class, you're killin' it on the field. You call your parents at least once a day, and you find it in your busy schedule to make time for us even when you don't have it. Your grades are still good, and your non-profit will help so many families. You're far from basic. You're pretty damn spectacular. I would've buckled under pressure if I were you, but nevertheless, I'm so proud of you, Jackson." Parker wraps her arms around my neck and smiles.

"Thank you, Parker. I really appreciate you."

"Oh no, I am *not* done boosting your ego, big boy," She smiles. "You're on sports news every weekend, and nearly every girl on campus wishes she could have you, but they can't because you're all mine."

"Always, Parker Waylen." I hug her with all my strength, afraid to let her go.

"What're your plans for tonight?"

"I'm going to the Gamma party with a few of my teammates. Do you wanna come?"

"Absolutely not! And if Jason isn't one of your teammates going, then you don't need to go either. A lot of those guys you've been hanging with are leaches, and they don't have your best interests in mind. Y'all just get super drunk and belligerent. I don't like it, Jackson. It isn't who you are."

Parker tries to get off my bed, but I grab her wrist and plead, "I'll only have one drink, that's it! I promise. We're celebrating. You said it yourself, I'm a hotshot."

"Don't use my words against me, Jackson Sands!" She rolls her eyes.

I kiss her neck to try to ease the tension, "I'm sorry, but seriously, I promise I won't get drunk."

"Well, who's bringing you back to the dorms?" She asks.

I smile mischievously and run my fingers through her hair. "You're gonna pick me up, and I'm sleeping at your apartment."

"You mean *our* apartment? Just move in already. You and Jason practically live there."

Parker and Merissa moved into their first apartment last semester, which means we have more alone time to ourselves. She wants me to move in with her, but I'm too embarrassed to tell her that my family is flat broke. My dad's construction business has taken a hard hit since the housing market crashed. He's had to hire two more people to fill my mom's role of managing the admin and operations for the company, and before that, he dumped all of our savings into her cancer treatments. If it weren't for football, I wouldn't even be able to attend school. I know Parker wouldn't judge me. Hell, she may even try to set up a fund to raise money, but I don't want to be a charity case, and my father wouldn't want to be pitied, either. I just need to focus on making it to the NFL so I can eventually take the financial burden off my parents. They deserve a chance to be stress-free for once in their lives.

"I mean your apartment, Parker. I told you, I like living on campus. It's all a part of the college experience." I grab her by the waist and position myself on top of her.

At times, I feel like I'm close to a mental breakdown; the pursuit of perfection is overwhelming, and I know I could lose it all in the blink of an eye – football, school, Parker, my mom. I need a distraction, and Parker has always been the only person that makes me feel like I can really have it all, even if only for a moment.

"Kiss me." I whisper softly in her ear.

"No." She giggles.

"I'm serious. I need to feel your lips on mine. I'm in my head again. I need you, Parker."

I try to be as vulnerable as I can without revealing that I'm in constant fear, constant stress, constant worry, and constantly insecure.

She cups my face with her soft palms, pulls me nearer, and gives me a sweet, tender kiss that puts my mind at ease. As she pulls away, my eyes are still closed, my tense jaw loosens, and my ice-cold expression softens into a smile.

"Don't worry, Jackson. I'll always be here to calm your fears. I'm right here. Just be with me in this moment."

Her assurance and how she easily expresses her love and care for me sends me into a spiral of sensual heat, and I feel her need for me, too. Though I may not be able to express my inner struggles, I can do my best to show her my appreciation by worshipping her for the goddess she is.

"I want you, Jackson." She lets out breathy moans as I trail kisses down her stomach to her inner thighs.

"Keep going?" I ask.

"Please."

If I could, I'd stay here glued to Parker's body, kissing her skin all day and night. Her smell is distinct, like drizzles of honey and whipped vanilla. I could live off her scent alone. I methodically position my tongue between her thighs until I feel her legs flinch and her hips buckle. She pants and pushes my head deeper inside her. It satisfies me to know that she's satisfied.

Seconds later, she almost violently comes, but her face is as gently beautiful as ever. Afterward, I reposition myself next to her so our eyes meet.

"You make me see stars, Jackson." She says to me as she tries to catch her breath.

"Good, because you're my everything. My galaxy." I respond with a rough kiss that turns into Parker rolling on top of me.

"I know you're exhausted from work and classes. We can finish this later. I just wanted to thank you."

"Thank me for what? Don't be silly. Let me show my appreciation to you."

Parker straddles my lap and begins to grind her hips against mine and teases, "Are you sure you don't want me, Mr. Sands?"

"I always want you, Parker. Always."

"Then don't ever deny me again."

Parker pulls out my hard erection, and I see her eyes go wide. I can't help but laugh.

"Why are you looking like that? You've seen me naked a million times at this point. You've felt me a million times too."

"Shut up! It just looks bigger every time." She rubs it against her opening before slowly sliding it inside of her.

It's hard to maintain my composure. She's my first and only, and I am hers. My body bends to her will, but when we're like this, she unleashes a beast that I can't control. Thrust after thrust, we move in unison until I can't contain myself anymore. I try to lift her off me to catch my release, but her inner walls squeeze and clinch me tight.

"No, Jackson, don't pull out, please. Let's start a family." Parker begs.

We've been together for four years, but we've never crossed that line. Unprotected sex, yes, but I never actually came inside of her. We always agreed that we want to graduate, get married, and start a family. This decision could change our lives forever. I hesitate, but my body's in autopilot, and I can't help but come inside the love of my life.

We lie next to one another, feeling closer to each other than ever before. I'm sure we share the same thoughts – whether this could be the beginning of the next phase of our lives. How could it work? How would it work? Nonetheless, I can't help but smile and wrap my arms around Parker at the thought of having a child with her.

But our joyful silence is interrupted when I receive a text from my dad. *It's your mom. Can you come home?"*

Chapter 5

First Date Jitters - Parker

I've anticipated this night all week, and I even closed my office early for an afternoon of pampering. My hair looks flawless, my eyebrows are waxed, and I even got a super cute new gel polish on my fingers and toes. I'm pulling out all the stops to both impress and let down Jackson tonight. I know we just had sex, really great sex, but I'm not sure if I want more. Neither time nor favor has been on our side over the years, so I don't see how we could be together this time around, but I'd be lying if I said I'm not interested in what he has to say. I already know who Jackson is. I know him better than anyone, so what else could I learn about him? What else is there for him to learn about me?

An hour passes, and I'm still questioning whether I should go on the date or flake on Jackson. Why am I so nervous about this fake first date, anyway? I'm actually freaking out. My palms are sweaty, and my head is spinning. Maybe I should cancel. I have work to catch up on anyway, and I need to focus on my parents' anniversary party. This entire date thing is clearly a distraction that I just don't need.

I plop down on my couch in despair until I hear my doorbell ring.

"Who is it?"

"Your conscious!" A sarcastic, sharp voice responds.

Why is Avery here? She's the last person I expect to see. I love my sister, but she's structured and predictable. She wouldn't just pop up for no reason.

I open the door in concern, "What's going on, Aves? What's the emergency?"

"You're the emergency, Parker!"

She brushes past me, throws her expensive handbag on my couch, and turns to me with her arms folded.

"Why did I just find out from Merissa that you're going on a date with Jackass. I mean Jackson Ass-sands. Or Jackson – whatever his name is."

"Don't be like that, Avery. You love Jackson."

"I don't love him for you!" She rolls her eyes and sits down on the couch.

I slump down next to her to calm her nerves. "While I understand your concerns, Avery, it's my life. I'm not going on the date anyway."

"What? Why not?" Her eyes widen in shock.

"I'm confused. Do you or do you not want me to be with Jackson?"

"I want you to figure that out for yourself. Figure out what I already suspect. I don't mean to be cold, but you deserve everything good, and the worst moments in your life involve Jackson somehow."

I'm the older sister, yet Avery has always been stronger, more emotionally balanced, and resolute in her decisions. She may be adopted, but she's my blood. She's my family, and she always talks sense into me.

"I wish I could be like you, Avery. You're so steadfast. If I had half of your willpower, I'd probably be married by now instead of obsessing over the same man for a decade. I'm pathetic."

"You're not pathetic, Parker. You're hopeful. Dick-matized and hopeful," She jokes to lighten the mood. "Seriously, though. You aren't weak. I've seen you love hard and fearlessly since we were kids. That's a strength that people wish they had. Your love for our family made me want to seek out my birth parents. When I didn't get the outcome I expected, your love helped me realize that y'all are the only family I'd ever need. Hell, your passion and forgiving nature even rubbed off on me because I can't seem to get rid of Deacon. What I'm trying to say is that you are light and you've always shined it in my life, our family & friends, and especially Jackson's. I just want you to be with someone who brightens your life as well."

I appreciate Avery's sincerity. I never knew she felt that way about me, but I still wish she knew the Jackson I know. He's the exact opposite of selfish. His depression and anxiety attacks always crippled him, and he never found a way to cope with the death of his mom. He's selfless to a fault. He aims to please everyone around him despite his happiness and well-being. He depletes himself for others' sake, and when he's at his lowest, he holds in his pain until he breaks.

Dammit, here I go again, sympathizing with Jackson instead of myself! After I recovered from my accident, I worked extremely hard to get to know myself again, separate from Jackson, because, for so many years, I voluntarily became whoever I needed to be to make his life more comfortable and to make him feel better. He needed it. He needed it more than me. I always made sure to cheer for him at all his games. I always made sure he completed his assignments. I always made sure he felt confident about himself. I always made sure he didn't drink too much. I just always made sure he was taken care of. No questions asked, and no time for myself to think about anyone else but Jackson Sands' well-being. I thought my traumatic experience and years of therapy helped break my obsessive and co-dependent tendencies. Yet, I've been in knots since Jackson's arrival and sunken back into a dark place I vowed never to return to.

"Hey, stop thinking so hard. Let me help you get dressed." Avery pulls me off the couch and goes to my closet.

"Hmm," She places her hand on her chin and looks me up and down. "You need something tight and short to show him what he's been missing.

Not too short, though. You don't want him to think he's getting lucky tonight. Let's leave his mind to wander."

Avery pulls out a red satin dress that drapes at the bosom. This must've been one of those. *I bet I'll look sexy in this, but I will never wear it* purchases.

"Whoa! I can't wear this! It's practically an under slip." I try to put it in the closet, but Avery snatches it back.

"Oh no, Parker. You are definitely wearing this. One thing I know about dating is how to tease and make men sweat; the only thing *you* know is how to give in and give it up to Jackson. This dress will drive him crazy, but the real question is, can you control yourself and keep it on by the end of the night?"

I snatch the dress from her hands and eye it up and down. This is totally not my style, but everything about this night is unconventional.

"I'll be on my best behavior, Avery." I respond and smile innocently.

She rolls her eyes and hands me a pair of clear, chunky-heeled stilettos.

"Okay, the group chat will go live at 7 p.m., so keep your phone on vibrate. Merissa, Izzy, and I are your accountability partners. This date will test whether you're really over your addiction to Jackson. No kissing, no fawning, and no sex!"

I feel like I'm getting a lecture from Mom and Dad all over again, and we all know what happened to those dating rules they gave us back in high school.

"Okay, okay. I hear you, Aves."

Avery gives me a thorough look and smiles like a proud mama.

"Well, my work here is done. I'll let you finish the rest. Remember, phone on vibrate! It's going down in the group chat tonight during your 'first date.'"

I nod, and she leaves for the night. I finish getting ready quickly. I haven't put this much effort into getting dressed since our one year anniversary. We were only Juniors in high school, so we didn't have much money or freedom, but Jackson had all the creativity in the world. He took me to the pier and set up the most romantic dinner on the beach. He showered our cheap little beach tent with rose petals, swooned me with a love song, and we ate a delicious shrimp, mussel, and scallop linguine. Then, at the end of our date, Jason and Merissa showed up to illegally blast fireworks in honor of our special day. It was perfect.

Jackson's words were often stifled by his insecurities and fear, so he always tried to go above and beyond to showcase his love for me. He had a football game our sophomore year of college on the day of our four year anniversary, and to be honest, I actually forgot about it that year, but Jackson didn't. After the game, eleven of his teammates hand-delivered a love note that recounted a memory for each year from the past eleven years we'd known one another. Then, four of his teammates hand-delivered my favorite snack, hot Cheetos, and a poem highlighting his favorite things about being in a relationship with me. It sounds corny, but it was special. It was personal, and it was from Jackson's heart.

I still have time left before I have to leave, so I decide to rummage through my box of *Jackson's Things* to find the notes and poems.

"Aha!" I read the notes, and my heart begins to melt.

Another year down and a lifetime to go

My love for you continues to grow

You are my safe place, my light, and my peace

You and I are meant to be

He's such a romantic and a goofball at the same time.

6th grade memory:

Do you remember when we went to Destin for our September fishing trip? Our parents forgot to check the weather. There was a hurricane alert. We packed up our tents and bundled up in the RV we rented. It was so cold, and we were short on blankets. We cuddled together that night for the first time. It was also my first woody. Thank you for always being my first everything.

Oh my gosh, good times! I haven't looked through this box in years, not since David confronted me about still being in love with Jackson.

Is this our senior prom picture? I can't believe I wore that hideous tickle me pink dress. That night was unforgettable. Everyone talks about how their first time was terrible, and they regret it, but not me. We had our prom at a hotel, which is a terrible idea, by the way. Why would any high school think it's okay to host a prom at a hotel so horny teenagers can check in afterward to do adult activities. And that's exactly what we did. We lost our virginity that night, but unlike the horror stories I heard, Jackson was soft, gentle, and mindful of how comfortable I was the entire time. I could tell he was nervous as well. It was the best thirty seconds of my life.

But as much as the beautiful memories melt my heart, the painful memories quickly ice it frozen again. That same night, Jackson met up with friends to go to a senior prom night bash. He got wasted, of course. It was prom night, so I gave him a pass and told him to go have fun, but in typical Jackson form, he went overboard. Not to mention, he had been acting off and emotionally distant again. I found out later that it was because Debbie's cancer came back. Still, I wish he felt comfortable enough to talk to me back then rather than drown his sorrows in alcohol. Shot after shot. Beer after beer. The more he drank that night, the more out of control he behaved.

I begged him to come back to the room with me for another thirty second love making session, but he was loud and mean. I remember grabbing his arm and telling him he was acting like someone else, someone I didn't know.

He yanked his arm away from me like I was a stranger to him and screamed, "Like my grandfather, huh!" Then, he nonchalantly continued to drink with friends. I was so confused and didn't recognize the man I loved.

He never spoke about his grandfather. All I knew was that he chose alcohol over his family, and the mere thought of him triggered Jackson.

After his blowup, I went back to the room and waited for him to come back, which was hours later. He apologized for how he treated me, and we slept in one another's arms for the rest of the night. I was content knowing that I was lying in the arms of the love of my life, but in hindsight, I wish I had known the early signs of alcoholism so I might have been able to get him the help he needed to prevent the tragedies that occurred years later.

Chapter 6

The Crack Before the Break - Jackson

I can't get my dad's last text out of my head. *It's your mom. Can you come home?* Immediately after I read his message, I called my dad's phone, but he didn't answer. I don't plan on going back home until after finals in three weeks, but I'd drop everything in a heartbeat if something happened to my mom.

"Jackson, what's going on?" Parker asks.

I've been so frantic, pacing back and forth and calling my dad over and over again, that I forgot Parker was still in my room.

"Jackson!" She yells.

I finally stop pacing and sit beside Parker on my bed, "Something is wrong with my mom. My dad's not answering, and I don't know what to do. Should I pack a bag and leave for the weekend? Should I wait for him to call back? I need him to answer and tell me what's going on!"

Parker rubs her hand on my back and rests her head on my shoulder. She doesn't say anything. She never needs to. Her silence alone comforts me as tears roll down my face.

I haven't cried in nearly two years. I feel both heavy and relieved, and after what feels like hours, my dad finally calls me back, and I make sure to answer on the first ring.

"Dad?"

"I'm sorry to freak you out, Son. I know you're busy with exams."

"It's okay. Tell me what's going on with mom."

Ever since I confronted my parents about withholding my mom's health issues from me two years ago, we agreed to keep an open line of communication within our family. No more secrets to spare my feelings.

"Well –" My dad pauses for a few seconds. "Your mom is sick. We've been in and out of doctor appointments all week. We would've called you sooner, but everything's been a bit overwhelming. Tougher than before." My dad stops speaking. I can hear him release a soft, exhausted breath through the phone.

"How bad is it?" I ask.

"The cancer's spreading, but we're going to undergo treatment. The doctors say there's a strong chance that it'll work. We'll need to be aggressive, but Mom doesn't have the strength she used to, so we need to be very cautious."

My dad continues to speak, but I've already zoned out, and Parker takes the phone out of my hand to talk to him.

"Hi, Mr. Sands. It's Parker," She tells him with a soft and gentle concern that calms the both of us. "I'm here with Jackson. We have you on speakerphone. I hope you don't mind."

"Of course not, Parker," my dad speaks somberly. "Ma has a tough road ahead of her, and we'll need to be strong to help her get through it, stronger than ever this time around. I just wanted to let Jackson know what was going on. I hate doing this over the phone, but I didn't want to keep you in the dark, Jackson. I'm sorry, Son. I sent an emotional, erratic text earlier. Please don't feel like you need to come home. We look forward to seeing you in a few weeks."

My dad hangs up the phone, and before I can say anything, Parker speaks.

"I know your dad said not to panic or do anything rash, but if you feel like you need to go home, we can pack a bag and leave right now. I know you. You're going to be a wreck unless you see your mom with your own eyes."

I want to respect my dad's wishes and carry on with my life as usual, but Parker's right. These are unusual circumstances, and I won't be able to function, let alone continue with school without seeing her.

"Would you really go with me? I mean, I don't want you to cancel any plans."

"Of course, Jackson. Merissa and Jason are also driving down. They've been driving back and forth nearly every weekend to help with her sister's transition from rehab. I know you and Jason haven't been as close as you used to be, but I think it'll do you some good to have people around who really care about you right now."

I consider what Parker says, and it doesn't sound like a bad idea. Jason has always been a brother to me, but our everyday interactions have changed. He doesn't hang with many of our teammates. When he isn't with Merissa, he spends most of his time studying and traveling with the debate team, but he's always been there for me when I needed him, so maybe this is the perfect time to reconnect.

"Let's do it," I reply. "Let 'em know we're tagging along."

A few hours later, Parker, Jason, Merissa, and I load our bags in Jason's truck and hit the road back home to Beverly Mills for the weekend. At first, the drive is awkward. I'm sure that Jason and Merissa have discussed the decline of our friendship just as much as Parker and I, but I'm ready to hash everything out to end our rough patch.

"So, to prevent this drive from being three hours of pure hell, let's address the elephant in the room." Jason says.

Parker and Merissa agree, "Yes, let's talk. Please!"

I want to bury the hatchet with Jason. I miss having a guy that I can talk to. I've become good friends with a couple of teammates, but we mostly party and drink together. With Jason, I can talk about my mom, my relationship with Parker, and even my emotions. He's my best friend, and now is the time to apologize and repair our friendship.

"I'll start off by apologizing. I don't know when the rift began or why, but I miss you, man." I confess.

Jason clutches his steering wheel tight. "Jackson, if you think I'm letting you off the hook that easy, you must think I'm a damn fool," Jason responds with a straight face. "I'm sure you don't remember when or why *I* began distancing myself from *you* because you've been shitfaced all year."

"C'mon Jason, you're overexaggerating."

"I'm serious, dude. After every game, win or lose, you go out and party with Hank and the other offensive linemen. I don't. It just doesn't appeal to me," Jason speaks bluntly with a weary expression. "I grew up listening to you tell me stories, dark stories about the abuse your mom endured from your drunk grandpa - a man you never met, yet you've compared yourself to your entire life."

No one says a word. I look back at Parker to try to read the expression on her face, but she looks down and twiddles her fingers.

"I don't compare myself to him, Jason. I just don't want to hurt the people I love like he did."

"Oh, so your solution to not being like him is to drink too much and too often, just like he did?" He snaps back at me.

I subconsciously ball my fists in frustration, but I manage to control my anger and maintain my composure.

"I don't drink that much. I don't have a problem. My drinking doesn't affect my schoolwork. It doesn't interfere with football or get in the way of my relationship."

Jason looks at Parker in the rearview mirror and asks, "Parker, has Jackson's drinking ever been an issue for you?"

I turn around to look at Parker again. This time, she bites her bottom lip and looks at me with hesitant eyes like she wants to speak but doesn't for fear of hurting me with the honest truth.

I turn back around to Jason to end this conversation.

"That's enough, Jason. You're entitled to believe what you want about me, but I don't judge you and your rich friends – those future lawyers and politicians that you hang out with."

"You mean my debate buddies? I'd much rather hang with them than a bunch of dudes who have hangovers every night. I'm all for having fun, but I know when to draw the line."

Parker interrupts, "Maybe Merissa should sit up front."

"No, let the guys duke it out. Communication is healthy." Merissa says.

"I wouldn't call this communication, Merissa."

Jason's frustration gets the best of him. He just lets loose on me.

"Well, this is the most talking we've done in months. Honestly man, I'd like to get back to a place where I can just talk to you, but you're always tense. You're either stressed about football, stressed about Parker leaving you, stressed about not being good enough, stressed that people won't like you, or stressed about what people think of you. You're a ball of stress, and you think the bottom of that bottle helps relieve it, but it alienates you from us, your real friends and family."

"Well, tell me how you really feel, Jason." I sit back in silence. Jason not only humiliated me, but he humbled me as well. He revealed every struggle, every thought, and every insecurity I've ever dealt with in my entire life. He exposed the feelings I push down and lock away every day. He sees me fully, just like a brother and a best friend should.

"I don't have a blood brother, Jackson, but I do have you, and that's more than I could ever ask for. I just don't want you to push us away because you fear we'll leave you. Hanging with Hank, Josh, and our other teammates may be fun, but will they be there for you when you're down? Do you feel comfortable opening up to them? Why aren't they with you right now? I'll always be here for you, bro. Always."

"I appreciate that, Jason, and I'm sorry for how I've been acting lately. Sometimes it's just easier to be around people who don't care so I don't have to deal with what's really going on. I always feel like I have something to prove. I'm expected to be the best player. I have to maintain my grades. I constantly worry about my mom. I got a constant fear that everything and everyone I love will leave. I'm sorry for being so stupid. I've been a complete douche. My bad, Jason," I take a sigh of relief. "Can we move on, or do you want me to grovel some more?"

Jason reaches his hand over to pat me on the back. "Ris, do you think Jackson needs to beg a little bit longer?" Jason looks back at the girls.

"Hmm, I don't know, babe. Jackson does *seem* apologetic. Maybe you should ease up off him. We forgive you, Jackson." She smiles at me.

"Good, now lay off my man, Jason! He's been through enough for the day, okay?" I wink at Parker as she steps in to defend me.

"You get a pass for this weekend and this weekend only, Jackson. In all seriousness, though, we're here for you. We love Mrs. Debbie. She's been like a second mom to me. I've practically lived at your house longer than mine."

Merissa grabs my shoulders from the back seat, "Yeah, Jackson. Deb's the best. We'll help you get through this. Remember when we were stuck in a snowstorm in North Carolina for our 7th grade class trip? Our parents all freaked out and traveled there to rescue us, and your mom managed to find a snow plow truck from God knows where to take us home. She does things that defy common sense and reality. Doctors were so concerned when she got sick the next day. Yet, she recovered a full week later and returned to taking care of the people she loves the most – you and Mr. Frank."

"Yeah, Jackson. She's strong. If anyone can get through this, it's her. She's already done it time and time again." Parker chimes in.

I lay my head back on the headrest and think about how hard my mom's fought to stay alive and won every time.

"Thanks, y'all. You have no idea how much your support means to me."

Without realizing it, a tear falls from my face. I try to look out the window to avoid my friends' reactions, but nothing gets past them.

"Jackson Sands, are you crying?" Jason yells.

"I am not." I coldly respond.

"That's okay. Get it all out." He laughs.

"Yeah, yeah. That's enough about me. Merissa, how's your sister doing? I'm glad to hear she's back home."

Merissa's sister, Iyanna, is about five years older than us. Merissa's parents were married young, and unfortunately, her dad was killed in action during a military mission while they were pregnant with Merissa. Her mom was strict and wanted her children to work as hard as she did, but Iyanna never healed from the pain of their dad's death, and it didn't help that Merissa's mom never spoke about him either. She didn't have time to grieve while raising two daughters and working two, sometimes three jobs to make ends meet. Merissa's mom had to choose between survival and supporting her daughters through the loss of their father. It caused a strain in their relationship, and by the time Iyanna reached 6th grade, she was labeled as 'difficult.' She'd skip class, disrespect the teachers, and have disruptive emotional outbursts. When she began high school, she started hanging with the wrong crowd, then drugs followed shortly after – it started out with weed but quickly escalated to pills, then cocaine, and now...whatever she can get her hands on. Their family, like mine, has been through so much if not more. Yet, they continue to hope she'll recover, and I hope they're right this time.

Merissa sighs and explains her family situation, "Honestly, I think she's going to stay sober this time. For years, my mom cried and prayed endlessly for her to overcome her addiction. Iyanna's stolen money from my parents. She's physically fought us during her drug binges, and last time, she nicked my mom with a knife and threatened to kill herself. Thankfully, Dad was there to subdue her. She's done it all at this point, but how many times can you hit rock bottom before you rise to the top?"

Parker rubs Merissa's shoulder and gives her a comforting hug.

"I believe in her, Ris. She's been sober for six months, and Carl has taken the reigns to help mend your family."

"That's true," Ris responds. "I really wish we would've met with a therapist sooner. I don't blame my mom entirely. She did what she had to do and raised us how she thought we should've been raised. Still, I always think about the person Iyanna could've been if she received her diagnosis much sooner than recently. We could've gotten her the help she needed. What if she never even turned to drugs to cope with how she was feeling in the first place?"

"You know now, and that's what matters. My mama always says there's no explanation for why we endure pain, but there is a reward when we get through it, and that's peace. Peace is coming."

There's a content silence in the car as everyone revels in their own thoughts, and sensing the need to ease the tension and sadness, Jason turns up the music. We sing our favorite songs, make fun of one another, and reminisce on fun times from elementary on in. Before we know it, we're getting off of I-16 South and onto the Beverly Mills exit. We're home.

When we arrive in town, Jason drops me and Parker off at her house so I can be in a happy, light, energetic headspace before I face reality.

Walking into the Waylen's home, I'm hit with the smell of banana pancakes. Breakfast for dinner – a Waylen weekend family tradition I love to be a part of. Izzy's now a teenager obsessed with flowers and fairy tales. She's also shy and a lot more reserved than Parker and Avery. Speaking of

Avery, she walks into the kitchen, grabs a pancake, and eats it out of her hand. She stares at me and doesn't say a word, which sends frightening chills down my spine.

"Hi, Jackson. You've come to return my sister to us, I see." She gives me a cold, condescending smile.

"Hi, Avery. You look happy as usual." I snap back in my monotone voice.

"Well, everyone's not loved and adored like you. Some of us have real-life problems that we have to deal with."

If only she knew, my problems are as real and complicated as hers.

Parker intercedes, "Don't mind her, Jackson. Avery's just stressed out about meeting her birth mother. Everything's going to be fine. She's going to love you just as much as we do." The two close-knit sisters give one another a hug.

"Thanks, sis. I'm just nervous. While every kid waits to turn eighteen to graduate and go to college. I've just been waiting for the moment to find out who I am and where I come from."

Mrs. Waylen walks into the kitchen and is disturbed by the tense conversation. "Is Parker playing mediator again?"

Mrs. Waylen gives Parker a tender hug from behind and nestles her chin in her shoulder before she turns her attention to me.

"Jackson, what a lovely surprise. We never get to see you now that you're a future NFL star. I thought the tv screen was the closest I'd ever get to seeing you again. It's been so long!" Mrs. Waylen exaggeratedly says to me.

"Mom! Stop being so dramatic. You know Jackson has a lot on his plate between football, classes, media attention, and family – please cut him some slack."

I take a few steps towards Mrs. Waylen to hug her and kiss her on the cheek. "Good evening, Mrs. Waylen. I missed you, too." I laugh.

"Jackson, how many times do I have to tell you to call me Jo. You are the most well-mannered, formal person I know. I'd like to think you see me as a second mom after all this time."

While her comment is sweet and well-intentioned, I could only think about the words *second mom* because who will I really have if and when my first mom passes away? I come back to my senses to force a laugh, but Mrs. Jolene is intuitive and recognizes the discomfort in my voice.

She moves closer to me, hugs me tight, and whispers discreetly, "Everything's gonna be okay." She rubs my back and lets me go with the understanding that she won't mention what my mother's going through, but she's always there for me if needed.

Izzy runs up and grabs me by the hand to show me her flower display, "Jackson, you're back! Check out my lilies! Aren't they beautiful? Maybe I'll decorate you and Parker's wedding someday. Y'all are so perfect."

I look up at Parker and signal for help. Izzy means well, but she thinks too highly of me. Like many others in Beverly Mills, she has fantastical ideas about how perfect I am. It's too much pressure to live up to everyone's expectations.

Parker walks over to Izzy's display to express her enthusiasm, and I slowly ease away to avoid any more interactions with the Waylen sisters, but unfortunately, Avery comes back to me to finish our conversation.

"Are you excited about me moving in with Parker and Merissa in the fall?"

"Am I excited about you probably kicking me out of the apartment just for being there? No."

"Whatever I do is in Parker's best interests, Jackson. She quit volleyball to spend more time with you, for goodness sake. Her life revolves around you."

"That's not true. She quit volleyball to focus on her studies and get hands-on experience in a doctor's office."

Avery scoffs, "If you really believe that, you're even more clueless than I thought. Do you know the one thing that you and Parker have in common?"

"You're gonna tell me anyway, so proceed."

"You compromise your feelings for everyone else, even at your own expense. I have an eye for observing others, Jackson, and from what I see, you two have a weird co-dependent relationship. You have this whole damsel in distress vibe going on, and Parker has a hero complex. When are y'all going to have a normal boyfriend and girlfriend relationship? No drama. No stress. Just go out on dates and have fun together. What are you gonna do when Parker's the one who needs you? How're you gonna reign in those thoughts to be the hero she needs for once? You have issues, Jackson, but Parker's too blind to see it because she has her own problems – she's addicted to you. I'm just waiting for one of you to realize your relationship is unhealthy."

Avery genuinely scares me. She's a no b.s. straight shooter, and I can't tell if she hates me, feels sorry for me, or wants the best for me. Either way, she knows something about me that not even Parker knows. I actually *do* have issues. I *am* suffering, and I fear my extreme anxiety and depression could break me at any moment.

I obsess over my fears of not being good enough. They consume me so much that my stress levels soar through the roof, causing headaches and bouts of depression until I just ultimately shut down.

My first anxiety attack occurred in 2nd grade before we moved to Beverly Mills. My teacher dismissed class, but I was paralyzed, and the only thing moving was my shaky hands. As crazy as it sounds, I was breathing so hard that I could barely breathe at all. The school nurse called my parents, and we all assumed it was a one-off incident, but after a consecutive number of episodes and a noticeably sharp decline in my social skills, they referred me to Dr. Kaiser, a child psychiatrist based in a small town that we never heard of, Beverly Mills.

I promised my parents that I'd start seeing Dr. Kaiser again a few years ago, but I never followed through. I've been so busy that I didn't make my mental health a priority, but now, I don't think I have a choice but to resume my treatments because, once again, life has paralyzed me, and I can't move forward without getting help.

While my friends prepared to return to Beverly Mills for a weekend, I packed heavy with the expectation of taking a leave of absence from school. My academic bereavement request was expedited and approved, permitting me to complete my Spring exams under supervision at the Beverly Mills Public Library. This isn't how I intended to end my sophomore year of college, but family comes first, and come hell or high water, I'm going to be there for my mom until the absolute end.

A couple of weeks pass by quickly. I have a daily routine – wake up, make breakfast, take mom to her doctor appointments, go to therapy, organize her meds, help dad with small construction projects, make dinner, clean the house, and go to sleep to do it all over again the next day. Mom isn't getting better, but she isn't getting worse, so I call that a win. As exhausting and time-consuming as our new normal has become, I'm determined to enjoy every minute I have with her. Parker and I text and talk throughout the day, which anchors me back to a peaceful state of mind amidst all of the chaos, but it's going to be extremely difficult to split my time when she comes home for summer break this weekend.

Over the last few weeks, Dr. Kaiser's helped me organize my thoughts, feelings, and priorities. He challenged me to open myself up to the people who love me the most, which means I need to tell Parker about my depression and anxiety. Dr. Kaiser says letting go of my need to control things, eliminating the idea of perfection, embracing life as it happens, and confronting my fears are the ongoing actions I need to take to best manage my mental health. I'm ready to begin this journey of healing and evolution, and I really hope Parker doesn't mind the good, the bad, and the ugly that may come with it.

"Your friends come home from break today, don't they?" Dr. Kaiser asks as we end our session for the day.

"Yeah, this is the longest we've been apart since elementary school."

"Well, give yourself permission to live a little, Jackson. Remember, you're entitled to be happy, and you deserve to have some fun. Have you thought about telling Parker about our sessions? I know how much she means to you, and from our conversations, it seems like your relationship is fueled by intense emotion and dramatic events, but communication, honesty, and vulnerability should always be front and center."

"I've thought about it but don't know whether I'm ready to disclose something so deep and personal to Parker. I know we've been working on my communication skills and breaking through my fears, but I'm unsure now is the time to dump all of my issues on her."

"Ah, Jackson, you're retreating again. Are you unsure about letting people in, or are you fearful about letting people in? And be mindful of the negative language you use when referring to yourself. You mentioned *dumping my issues* rather than language, such as expressing myself or discussing my mental health condition. An issue is a problem. You aren't a problem, Jackson. We've been working together on and off since you were a young boy. Now, you're an ever-evolving young man who's strong and getting mentally and emotionally healthier each day. If anyone in your life views you as a problem, then they don't deserve to be in your life at all, Jackson. However, I have a good feeling that your friends will support you and be proud of you for being open and honest with them. You'll appreciate their support, especially if you feel yourself drifting back into that dark headspace, but they can't help you if they have no idea what you're going through."

Dr. Kaiser is right. I feel like I've grown so much in just a few weeks, but I clearly have a long way to go until I'm comfortable and confident enough to openly discuss my thoughts and feelings.

"Thank you, Dr. Kaiser. I'll keep working on myself, and I look forward to our next session. I'm sure there will be a lot to discuss on Monday."

"Have a great weekend, Jackson. I'll see you next week."

The weekend is here, and summer break has officially begun for my friends. My dad took a rare Saturday off so he could spend time with Mom, which clears my schedule so I could spend time with Parker, Merissa, and Jason. However, as much as I want to see my friends, I'm physically, emotionally, and mentally drained.

Parker, Jason, and Merissa want to hang out at Maxine's Bar & Grill tonight, but I don't have the energy to go. Action Jackson would suck it up, put on a smile, and have a few drinks to get through the night, but those days are over. I don't want to be someone I'm not anymore. I don't want to get to that point again where I feel overwhelmed, like my head's going to explode at any minute. I'll text them and offer a different plan of action instead. You can do this, Jackson – no compromises. Put yourself first. Do what's best for you.

Beverly Mills Crew Group Chat

Jackson: Hey, I know the plan tonight was to meet up at Maxine's but I've had a hell of a week so I think I'm gonna stay in.

Jason: Lame, old man!

Merissa: No worries, Jackson. We completely understand. You should rest. We'll stop by tomorrow.

Parker: Jason and Ris, it looks like you two are on your own for the night. I'm gonna go hang out with my man!

Jason: Wow, you dropped us quicker than sizzling bacon on the 4th of July.

Merissa: What does that even mean Jason?

Jackson: Lol. It means that Parker knows I'm better company.

Merissa: Nonsense! She's just horny.

Parker: On that note, goodnight, everyone! I'll see you soon, Jackson. 😊

An hour later, Parker shows up at my house wearing ugly, snuggly pajamas and holding a pan pizza. She offloads her hands and preps for our stay-at-home date night as soon as she can.

I grab her arm to give her the embrace I've longed for since I left campus weeks ago. Parker turns to me and wraps her arms around my neck. Her body melts perfectly into mine. She stands on her tippy toes, and we passionately kiss one another. It's taking everything in me not to take her on this couch right here, right now.

"I missed you, Jackson Sands."

"Oh really, how much?"

Parker nibbles on my ear and says, "I can show you better than I can tell you."

She starts to playfully untie my sweatpants, but I'm hungry and impatient, and I need more now. I lift Parker up, and she wraps her legs around my waist.

We continue to kiss while I carry her upstairs to my room. I lay her on my bed, and we explore one another's mouths. Her lips are so soft and taste like honey and vanilla, but I still need more. My hands move wildly down to her firm breasts, and my mouth follows shortly after flicking them back and forth with my tongue.

"Oh, Jackson!" She moans.

She slides her shorts off to allow easier access, and I part her legs and slide my finger in slowly, then rub my thumb on her clit in the circular motion that drives her wild. I watch her as her body jerks in and out of ecstasy. She looks so beautiful like this – hot, sweaty, and out of control. When Parker comes back to her senses, she strips off the remainder of her clothing and pulls me on top of her.

"You're a wild man, Jackson. This is a new side of you, and I love it," She gives me a deep kiss and says, "It's been so long. Don't hold back. I want you hard and deep."

I'm so turned on right now, and sex talk isn't my specialty, so I avoid it because I don't want to make a fool of myself, but hell, I'm working on letting go anyway, so here goes nothing, "I want to fuck you senseless." I whisper in her ear.

Parker's eyes go wide in shock and curiosity. I've never spoken to her like this before. Call it inexperience, preference, or maybe nerves, but I've always been a slow and gentle lover with a few position switches here and there but I'm feeling bold, confident, and unrestricted, and a lot less insecure than my usual self.

"Do you trust me, Parker? Let me have my way with you."

Parker's already in a haze of sexual bliss. She smiles lazily and says, "Have your way with me, Jackson."

Without hesitation, I flip Parker on her stomach and pepper kisses down her spine. I grab her perfectly round cheeks with my hands and give her a firm smack.

"Ow!" Parker yells in both pleasure and pain. "Do it again, please."

After a few more playful smacks, I enter inside of her. I feel free and animalistic, and I can barely restrain myself as my body slams into hers like a violent storm in the peak of September.

"Yes, Jackson! Harder." She screams.

I don't know what's gotten into me, but I instantly pull her hair to steady my stance.

"Parker, I'm about to –" This time, before *I* can finish my sentence, I let go harder than I ever have in my entire life. We collapse on my bed beside one another, and Parker leans in closely to nuzzle her head into my chest.

Exhausted, breathing heavily, and glistening with sweat, she says, "Jackson, that was so…different."

I tilt my head down and look into her eyes. I'm embarrassingly curious and feel myself retreating back to classic Jackson. I'm usually so cautious about everything I do and say, so I hope my attempt to *not hold back* hasn't backfired on me.

"A good different or bad different?"

"It was good, *really* good. The best." Parker lifts up her head to meet my lips with a deep kiss. "We should slow down, though, unless you're ready for round two?" She says with a raised brow.

"I'm a young college athlete with high stamina, but even I'm not afraid to admit that I need to take a break afterward. Let's go downstairs and see what lame movies we'll fall asleep to."

"Jackson, need I remind you that I have great taste in movies! You're the one that always chooses the duds."

We head downstairs to eat pizza and watch a scary movie, but midway into a gory scene, Parker turns her attention towards me.

"Jackson, is everything okay?"

"Yeah. Why do you ask?"

She initially hesitates but eventually continues to speak, "Well, you haven't mentioned your mom or how she's doing. You're surprisingly more relaxed than usual. And that sex," Parker shakes her head in awe, "It was mind-blowing. You don't seem like yourself, and I want to make sure there isn't anything you're not telling me, or maybe you're hiding something from me?"

I have every intention of telling Parker about my mom and my therapy sessions, but tonight, I want to be stress-free. No heavy conversations. No tears. No worries.

"I don't really want to talk about it, Parker. So much of our relationship over the years has been dominated by my heaviness. I promise we'll talk in detail tomorrow morning, but I want a night where we can be a happy, normal couple that enjoy a movie together. Can we please do that?"

"Okay, Jackson. I understand. Just know that you can always talk to me. You know that, right?" She rubs her hand on my face, and I kiss her forehead in return.

"I know. You know it's hard for me to communicate my feelings and thoughts sometimes, but I'm going to do better. I'm going to do better for you. I'm going to be better for everyone."

"I like the sound of that, but don't put too much pressure on yourself. I'll always be here when you're ready."

Parker falls asleep in my arms, and all I wish I could do is freeze time and enjoy this moment of peace.

The next day we meet up with Jason, Merissa, Gabe, Deacon, Avery, and Izzy at our favorite food spot, The Breakfast Nook. We're long overdue for a friend group reunion. Izzy and Gabe are the youngest in the group, 10th graders at Beverly Mills High, but they're also Parker and Merissa's younger siblings, so they get the privilege of hanging out with college students. Deacon and Avery just graduated high school. Avery will attend UGA in the fall with us, but Deacon's going to attend Kennesaw State University.

"So, how does it feel to be high school graduates?" Parker asks Deacon and Avery.

"It feels like a big weight's been lifted off my shoulders," Avery says.

"I don't know. I'm gonna miss high school. I mean, we grew up with so many of our classmates, and now we're all going our separate ways," Deacon responds. "I may live near Atlanta for the next few years, but I think I'm definitely gonna come back home and lay down some roots."

"Lay down roots, as in get married and make babies?" Izzy asks.

"Deacon, you're already thinking about your future wife and kids, huh? Anyone in particular?" Merissa directs her attention to Avery.

"Oh no. Don't look at me. I do *not* want kids." Avery shakes her head.

"Don't worry, Avery. I don't plan on giving you any…yet." Deacon laughs.

Avery rolls her eyes. She clearly wasn't expecting Deacon to snap back. They kinda dated briefly throughout high school, but those two are always hot and cold. It takes a lot to break down Avery's defenses, but as much as they argue, I still say they're gonna end up together ten or fifteen years down the road.

"Well, you won't have much time or interest in dating for at least the first semester, anyway. Give yourselves time to acclimate to your class schedules, make new friends, and join a few clubs. You know, find your own way," Merissa says. "Our first week of school was so nerve-wracking. Thankfully, Parker and I had each other. We partied almost every night at the start of freshman year."

"What kind of parties? Frat parties with drugs and alcohol? Are the parties really as wild and crazy as they are on TV?" Izzy asks.

"Even worse!" Merissa laughs.

"We were lucky to be connected to Jackson and Jason as freshmen. They befriended a lot of upper-classmen, athletes, and party houses when they left early for football training. I wasn't one of the 'cool' athletes, but by the time Ris and I started school, we were already invited to nearly every social event of the semester."

"Take my advice, and don't do what we did! We barely woke up on time for classes." Merissa says.

"So, what're everyone's plans for the summer?" Jason asks everyone.

Before anyone could answer, the waitress approaches the table to take our order.

"Oh my word, the Beverly Mills High superstars are all back together! It's so good to see you kids. I miss serving y'all."

"We miss you too, Miss Marcie." I give her a winning smile.

"Mr. Jackson, don't you dare flash me those beautiful pearly whites. Parker, if I were twenty years younger, I'd snatch that handsome young man of yours right up."

"Miss Marcie, I don't know if you're being serious or joking." She laughs.

"She's serious." Jason says.

"I feel like a piece of meat."

"Delicious meat, apparently." Parker laughs.

"So, what are you kids eatin' this morning?"

Everyone, except Izzy, orders a hearty meal, The Nook's famous pancakes with scrambled eggs and bacon. When our food arrives, many don't seem to notice, but Avery takes a considerable interest in Izzy's lack of appetite. I know I shouldn't pry, but I can't help but observe.

Avery lowers her voice to speak to Izzy.

"Please, Izzy. Eat something. You can't keep starving yourself."

"Leave me alone, Avery. I'm just not hungry right now."

"You never are, Izzy."

I saw Izzy a few weeks ago, but I didn't notice any physical changes because she wore a baggy t-shirt and sweatpants, but now I see a difference. She's still adorable, but she's also extremely thin, much thinner than I've seen her before. I don't want to overthink it, so I'll let it go, for now. There's no need to put her on the spot, and if there's one thing I learned from Parker, it's best not to comment on a woman's weight or age.

After we finish eating, Parker reveals big news to everyone. "So, Merissa and I are interning at the hospital this summer."

"That's awesome! Congratulations. I'm sure I'll see you all there," Gabe says. "So, y'all are dead set on being doctors?"

"Definitely for me. At first, I thought I wanted to be a plastic surgeon, but honestly, after everything my sister's gone through over the years, I've really shifted my focus to mental health. I think I can really make a difference." Ris says.

Parker places her hand over Merissa's and squeezes it tight.

"Becoming a doctor would be a dream come true. I'm not sure what I want to specialize in yet. I'm still waiting for my aha moment!" Parker explains.

"What about you, Jason and Jackson? What are your plans for the summer?" Deacon asks.

"Absolutely nothing!" Jason laughs. "Just kidding. We have to report back to campus next month for football training, but in the meantime, I'm gonna work as a media assistant in the Mayor's office."

"I think you're going to do great in politics, Jason. Defy the norms and prove that an honest, kind-hearted person is fit to run for office."

I see Jason blush for the first time since I've known him. Merissa and Jason are so supportive of one another, just like Parker and I. I hope things remain the same between us as I continue to focus less on our relationship and more on my mother and myself.

"Jackson? What about you?" Deacon asks.

"For the next month, I'll mostly focus on my mom. That's really my only concern at the moment. I wanna be there for her as much as I can. I want to help as much as possible before I leave. I even told them that I could push my training date back by a week and that coach would understand, but my dad's adamant about me returning to school. They want me to act like things are back to normal, but they aren't. Mom takes a million medications a day. They help with the pain, but I think the pills are just band-aids." I unload my feelings to my friends without even thinking about what they may think of me.

Parker rubs my back and lays her head on my shoulder.

"We're your family too, Jackson. Whatever you need, let us know. My mom and dad will be Mrs. Debbie and Frank's personal assistants 24/7. She has an entire village at her disposal." Izzy says.

"But how are *you* doing, Jackson? You need to make sure you're taking care of yourself while taking care of others." Merissa asks.

I was going to tell Parker about my therapy sessions with Dr. Kaiser in private, but since I'm around a group of people that I trust, perhaps this is the best time to open up and be honest about everything that I've been dealing with.

"Actually, I do have something to share with everyone."

All eyes are on me. I never like to be the center of attention, primarily because of my anxiety – I'm fearful of saying the wrong things and embarrassing myself, but I have to find the confidence to be comfortable with who I am, flaws and all.

"I've been battling –"

As soon as I'm about to open up to my group of friends, I'm interrupted by a group of Beverly Mills locals.

"Is that UGA's quarterback, Jackson Sands? Can we please get your autograph? My son plays football for Beverly Mills Middle School. He really looks up to you." One of the men says.

Now distracted by town locals, everyone begins to have side conversations. Then, after a few minutes, we pay the bill and leave the restaurant. I'm a little frustrated but more disappointed that I didn't get to share my feelings with the group. It would've been a major turning point for me, a real proud moment, but like so many other situations in my life, things never quite go the way I plan.

"Jackson, are we still on for the movies tonight?"

Crap, I completely forgot about our date night. For the past few months, my dad's been contracting small side projects, and he works nearly every weekend now so he can pay for my mom's treatments and hospital bills. My mom would practically shove me out the door if she knew I had plans tonight with Parker, but there's no way I could leave her alone at such short notice.

"I'm so sorry, babe. It must've slipped my mind, but I can't tonight. Dad's in Valdosta this weekend working on the new stadium, so I'm staying at home with Mom. Rain check?"

Parker pouts and playfully moans, "You sure you don't want company? I can bring some Chinese takeout and your mom's favorite rom-com?"

"As tempting as it sounds, I think I'm gonna pass. Mom had a rough morning, so I'm gonna try to force her to take it easy and rest."

"Good luck with that. Mrs. Debbie marches to the beat of her own drum. There's no way she's going to sit her butt down."

"You're right about that."

"Well, hopefully, you can get some rest too, Jackson. You look so tired. Are you sure everything's okay?"

"I'm fine, especially since you're here now. I've missed you so much." I grab Parker by the waist and give her a gentle kiss, and we go our separate ways.

Parker was right. I am exhausted. If you asked me over a month ago what my summer plans were, I'd say spend time with my girlfriend and best friends. Instead, every day, I feel like I'm jumping from one tedious task to the next, and I have to stay on high alert since my mother's health could easily take a turn for the worst at any moment.

When I get home, I open the door to the smell of my mom's muffins. This woman just won't let up.

"Ma, what are you doing? You were just under the weather this morning. You should be resting."

"Oh, Jackson," She dismisses me. "I felt a burst of energy this morning and the urge to make your favorite – blueberry muffins. You used to ask me to make muffins for dinner all the time." She scurries around the kitchen like the energizer bunny.

"They do smell delicious, but the last time you cooked them, I got really sick!"

"Because you and your dad decided to have an eat-off to see who could eat the most muffins in three minutes. Don't you dare blame my cooking. Blame you and your dad's competitive spirits." She laughs.

Watching my mom cook makes me think about the years in between her bouts of sickness. She's always been so full of energy and made sure dad and I were taken care of. She was always out and about doing somethin' – whether taking me to practice, grocery shopping, managing the construction business, or volunteering at my school, my mom was involved in everything when she was in good health.

"Why are you staring at me like that?"

"I was just thinking about you. I don't know how you do it."

"Do what? Cook muffins?" She asks obliviously.

"No, just do everything. You work, cook, clean, volunteer, and raise me and Dad," I laugh. "Our lives are like a tightly run ship, and you're the captain. How do you find time to relax, let alone sleep?"

"Well, that's the trick of being a parent, Jackson. I sleep in the moments in between and the hours unseen."

"What the heck does that even mean?"

"It means when you finish football practice and go to your room to shower, take your time and don't rush to move on to the next thing. Milk the time you have to yourself and enjoy it. When you're overwhelmed with studying for exams, take a break. Even if you have twenty minutes to spare, take a power nap. We're the captains of our own lives, which means it's important to take care of ourselves before we try to do anything for anyone else."

I think about what my mom says, and I make mental notes on things I can do to help alleviate my stress and anxiety.

I give my mom a kiss of gratitude and continue our conversation.

"You always know how to make every moment a teachable lesson. So, tell me, where do you find your moments of peace?"

"Is this get to know your mom day?"

"No, it's just me spending time with you is all."

"Well, I actually do have a few guilty pleasures that I like to partake in from time to time."

"Hmm, dare I ask what those are? What really goes on when Dad and I aren't home?"

"Oh hush! A woman's gotta have a life outside of her husband and kids, you know."

"As you should."

"Okay. So, ever since we got this new cable box with all these channels set up, I've discovered so many new tv shows. I can even record them! And let me tell you, I *really* liked those housewives! Ooh, Jackson, they are so spicy – a real hoot," My mom goes on and on about her favorite reality tv shows as if she's been waiting to discuss them for ages. "Oh my gosh, and you gotta watch this singing show! They turn their chairs around if you sound real good. And Blake Shelton's a judge! Don't tell your dad, but I just love that man. He's so adorable. I bet he knows how to throw a party."

"So, you're a reality tv junkie now? All I ever heard growing up was '*Tv is the devil's play, Jackson. Who needs tv when you have homework to focus on?*' blah, blah, blah." I imitate my mother's voice and mannerisms.

"Don't make me sound so pious. Besides, there hasn't been much else I could do over the years but stare at a stupid tv screen. I been mostly confined to the house after all the treatments and 'groundbreaking' trials that were supposed to cure me,"

Suddenly, my mother's playful tone turns somber, and I notice tears swell behind her eyes.

"I been fightin' for over fifteen years Jackson, and I don't know how much longer I can keep it up. I just wish I could fast-forward to the good scenes, but I feel like I'm getting much closer to the credits this time around. My kidneys are shot, my liver's holding on for dear life, and I feel weaker and more tired than before. I just –"

My mom can't bring herself to finish speaking. Her words are replaced by sobs and unregulated breathing. She keels over with her hands tightly gripping the oven handle, and I walk over to hold her fragile body in my arms. As much as I want to cry with her, cry because of her, cry over her, I preserve my emotions and be the strength that she needs in her rare time of vulnerability. In all my life, my mom has never mentioned her pain or physical weakness. She always remained positive, enthusiastic and full of hope, which enabled my dad and I to always be confident in our future as a family and comfortable knowing that she'll make it through. Now, for the first time, I don't see that hopeful light in her eyes. I don't see my incomparable, unbreakable, three-time cancer-surviving mother. I see an exhausted and defeated woman with so much more love to give – if only she had more time.

"I just need more time." She whispers.

I put my mom to sleep in her bed, lie beside her, and whisper, "Because, despite everything, we are still wonderfully, beautifully, and fearfully made."

When she's finally in a deep slumber, I release a stream of uncontrollable tears I've been holding back that symbolize the love I have for her, the loss I'm anticipating and the pain I have no idea how I'm ever going to recover from. This is the last time I'll allow myself to crack before my entire world breaks.

Chapter 7
Every Moment Counts - Parker

Jackson and I have weathered through many storms before, but this may be the toughest. I want to support him while he supports his mom, but it's hard because he barely has time for me.

I've been home for summer break for a month, yet I've only seen him a handful of times. I'm just glad I managed to keep myself somewhat busy interning at the hospital. However, tomorrow's our last day together before he returns to school for summer football training, so I'm planning a romantic evening at the beach. He needs a few hours to de-stress and relax. I want to be that for him – his safe haven, his peace during this time of chaos.

However, today is all about Mrs. Debbie, and Mom has planned a surprise girl's day luncheon at the town banquet hall. Mrs. Debbie is as equally loved by the people of Beverly Mills as my mom. She and Frank Sands have done so much to revive the town's infrastructure. Sands Construction launched the Beverly Mills Beautification Project. They rebuilt homes for the town residents after we were struck by hurricanes Irene and Matthew. They renovated Beverly Mills Elementary and one day, they hope to build the much-needed expansion for the hospital – a place Mrs. Debbie spent nearly half her time over the last ten plus years. Given her latest diagnosis and the uncertainty of the future, Mom and the other Beverly Mills moms want to celebrate their best friend.

Merissa, Avery, Izzy, and I put the final touches on the banquet tables before Mrs. Debbie and my mom arrive at the hall. Though it's a girl's luncheon, Mr. Sands and Jackson are hanging back in the kitchen to assist with the heavy lifting and provide physical assistance to Mrs. Debbie if needed.

When they enter the building and walk through the doors, we all yell at the top of our lungs, "Surprise!"

Debbie buckles her knees in shock at the room full of women who have come together to celebrate her.

"What in God's name is going on here?"

"It's a girl's day luncheon for you, Deb. We want to let you know how much we love and appreciate everything you've done for us. We love you, sis." My mom gives Mrs. Debbie a heartfelt hug.

I haven't seen much of her since I've been back home. Most of her time is consumed by doctor's appointments and sleep. She resembles the woman I met in 3rd grade – fierce but fragile, beautiful but hollowed and frail, yet determined to keep going. And while she's usually a master at maintaining her resolve during times of sadness, today is different. She looks more vulnerable than I've ever seen, and she's wearing her fear on her sleeve, heightening her emotional response. I think she knows she won't win this time, and she breaks down in tears of bittersweet happiness as she embraces dozens of her friends.

Though she's excited and joyful, my heart still breaks for her. It breaks even more when I look through the banquet kitchen window and see the tears in Jackson and Mr. Sands' eyes as they gaze at the woman they love and adore like no other. She is their light. She's what makes their hearts beat steady. Jackson and Frank are just alike – tense, quiet, and filled with worry but Mrs. Debbie is the peace that puts their minds at ease. They feel their peace slipping away fast, and I feel their sorrow from across the room.

"Wow, you've really outdone yourself today, Jo. The spa, nail salon, this extravagant new hair, the clothes. I feel like I won the lottery or somethin'. This is all so beautiful. Did you get Wayne to arrange the flowers, too?" Debbie asks in gratitude and amazement.

"Oh, it's nothing, Deb. This day is all about you! And Wayne actually had a lot of help from Izzy. That girl's so talented and whimsical. She's gonna take over the family business one day and transform it into something we could never imagine."

The luncheon goes off without a hitch. We eat, laugh, sit back, and listen to the women reminisce about their weekday meetups and Monday mimosa dates. At the end of the luncheon, Mrs. Debbie takes the mic to make an off-the-cuff speech.

"I'd be remiss to be the guest of honor and not make a speech, so here I go. Jolene, Marge, Eleanor, and Maria, you all have been the best friends a girl like me could ever ask for. Y'all are my family, and we definitely act like it with all the fights we had over the years, especially between Jo and I." The group of women laugh. We all know how forceful and bossy my mom can be. "Jo, you were the first person to greet me when we moved to Beverly Mills. I was sick back then, and I'm sick now, but I'm so grateful that you've never gotten sick of me. I'm grateful to all of you. My family was small growing up, and I never had sisters until I moved here. You group of women have helped me be a stronger woman, a more loving wife, a better mom, a loyal friend, and a hopeful Cancer survivor over and over again."

Mrs. Debbie holds the mic in one hand and rests her arm on the table for support. The exhaustion begins to show on her face.

"I've been blessed, so so blessed to know you all, but most importantly I've been blessed with the most supportive husband and most selfless son."

Mrs. Debbie looks back at Jackson and Frank and mouths *I love you*. They do so as well in return. Tears flow down nearly everyone's faces as she continues to say what feels like her parting words to her group of friends.

"I hope I've been able to pour into y'all's lives like you've poured into mine. Finally, I think I'm gonna shut up now because I'm tired, and I'm not afraid to say that I don't have much time left to live on this earth, so I'd like to spend as much time as I can laughing with y'all, spending time with my son, and having sex my with my husband."

The ladies erupt in laughter, and my mom high-fives Mrs. Debbie and says, "Get it, girl!"

Despite the high emotions and somber moments, the celebratory luncheon is a success. We honored a strong, tenacious, positive, and powerful woman in Debbie Sands. I didn't get to text or talk to Jackson much during the gathering, so I attempt to check in to see how he's doing, especially after his mom's speech. His responses are dry, and his conversation is short. He's shut me out entirely at this point. I wish I knew what to do to show him that I'm here as an outlet for him to release his pain.

As we clean up the hall, I approach him cautiously and place my hand on his forearm, "Hey Jackson, how're you feeling?"

"Hey, Parker. I'm okay. Y'all did an amazing job with the decorations. Mom hasn't been this happy in weeks. It was nice to sit back and watch her smile again. I also enjoyed admiring you from afar."

Jackson swipes his thumbs across my jaw, wraps his arms around me, and presses his lips to my forehead. It feels so good to feel his touch again.

"I'm sorry if I've been distant lately. I promise I don't mean to push you away. I just can't seem to find the time to –"

I interrupt his self-deprecating speech, "It's okay, Jackson. You being here and reassuring me that we're still okay is good enough for me. I love you. I'll always love you."

He exhales a sigh of relief and gives me a sweet, tender kiss.

"My dad and I will finish up here. Go home and relax. I'll call you when I'm home."

"Are you sure? I don't mind helping, especially if that means spending more time with you." I try not to sound too desperate, but I desperately want to feel that powerful connection we've always shared.

"We got it, babe." Jackson says in a steel tone.

"Well, okay then. Don't forget to call me when you're done. I love you."

"Love you, too." He smiles and gets back to work.

That night, he forgot to call.

The next day, I wake up feeling uninspired and worried. While I should be excited about my special date with Jackson, I fear he'll cancel or just forget about it altogether. I want to call and text him first thing in the morning, but I also want to give him his space. So, I wait, wait, and wait some more to see if he'll ever call. He doesn't.

It's 10 a.m., and I've grown anxious, so I decide to video call, and he surprisingly answers on the first ring.

"Parker, I was just thinking about you." Jackson puts on a big smile, but his voice is groggy, his hair is messy, and he looks exhausted.

"Are you just waking up?"

"Kinda, sorta. Mom had a rough night last night. She's been sick all morning. I think Dad's gonna take her to the hospital today to make sure she hasn't taken a turn for the worst already." Jackson runs his fingers through his hair and tries to fight through his sleep.

"Well, you should get some more rest. Are we still on for later?" I ask hoping for a yes.

"Actually, I was wondering if I could come over? I know it's last minute, but I'd love to spend more time with you. I'll be busy with training for the next month, and then I have to jump right back into the regular season. I want to spend as much time as I can with you today."

My face lights up, and I don't even try to hide my excitement. "I'd love that, Jackson. Hurry up and get your ass over here now."

He gives me a half-hearted smile and hangs up the phone.

Two hours later, we're at a midday movie matinee watching a scary movie. I glance over to look at his face, and for a moment, I see a glimpse of happiness. I see a care-free twenty year old. I see the peace we bring to each other's lives. He subconsciously displays small gestures of affection, like lightly rubbing his fingers against my arm when he squeezes me closer to him to comfort me from the horror scenes. I feel like we're us again until his phone vibrates, and the worry creeps back in. Life just loves to hand him lemons.

"It's my Dad. I need to step out to take this." Jackson excuses himself and comes back a few minutes later with an apologetic look.

"What's wrong?"

"I'm sorry, Parker. My dad needs to take care of an emergency at one of the construction sites, so he needs me to take Mom to her appointment."

"I can go with you. I'd really like to help."

"That's okay. My dad's gonna meet us there later. I hate to cut our date short, but my mom needs me."

"Please, Jackson. I want to be there for you and your mom."

He thinks it over and texts his mom to ensure it's okay. Not even a minute later, Mrs. Debbie texts him back, and Jackson finally gives in.

"Mom says she's excited to see you, but Parker, if you feel uncomfortable or feel yourself getting emotional, please let me know. Dad and I always try to stay positive for Mom's sake, but I'd understand if your emotions get the best of you. She won't look like the woman you saw yesterday."

I nod my head and begin to mentally prepare myself to see Mrs. Debbie. We make a few stops before arriving at Jackson's house, and I feel nervous. I've visited the Sands' home a million times before, but this doesn't feel like home. This feels dark, daunting, and different than what I expected.

Jackson kneels down next to Mrs. Debbie's bed and rubs the side of her face.

"Hey, mama. How're you feeling?" He asks in a soft voice.

She places her hand on his and tries to suppress her cough, "I'm doing much better, Son. I could probably run a marathon right about now." She jokes.

"Well, let's save that for another day. Parker's in the hallway. Is it okay if she comes in?"

"Yes, of course," Mrs. Debbie tries to sit up on her elbows, then weakly raises her hand to usher me into her room. "Come sit, Parker." She pats her hand on the bed, signaling me to sit beside her.

"Hi, Mrs. Sands." I feel so awkward and uncomfortable, just like Jackson said. I don't know if I should hug or kiss her on the cheek, so I resolve to a pathetic wave and cautiously sit down on the bed.

"I'm so glad you're here. Thank you for coming."

"You're thanking me? I didn't do anything, Mrs. Sands."

"You can stop with the formalities now, Parker. Loosen up. I'm far too tired and weak to not speak plain." She says sternly.

"Well, okay then, Debbie!" I laugh. My shoulders relax, and I sit beside Debbie as if it's just a normal day.

"Attagirl!" Debbie smiles wide. "Jackson, I hope you've been treating my daughter-in-law well." She turns to him with a stern look on her face.

"Ma, where'd that come from?" Jackson laughs sheepishly.

"Because we all know how you shut people out. Isn't that right, Parker?"

"That's right, Debbie and Jackson's shut me all the way out. This is literally my first time seeing him since we've been home." I say in the most dramatic way.

"Wow! Are y'all really ganging up on me right now?" He laughs and shakes his head.

"Oh, I completely forgot. My mom made our lunch for the day." Before Debbie can respond, I run to the living room to grab my tote bag and set the table. Debbie slowly drags her feet while Jackson holds her arm to guide her to the kitchen.

"By the way, I'm not moving slow because I'm weak. I'm moving slow because I don't want to eat your mom's cooking." She complains.

Jackson laughs, and I gasp in shock.

"Debbie! You love my mom's cooking, especially her peach cobbler!"

"I assure you, Jo did not bake me a peach cobbler. I don't smell no peaches. I smell vegetables and unseasoned meat." Debbie plops down in her chair.

"Oh, you can smell that, huh?" Jackson eyes her suspiciously.

I peep into the tote bag, and Debbie is exactly right. My mom neatly prepared four labeled Tupperware bowls packed with lean, healthy food.

"Let's see what the chef prepared today," I take a long whiff of each bowl teasingly and put the food on our plates. "Mmm, turkey meatballs with a butternut squash dipping sauce. It smells so delicious!"

"What the hell is butternut squash dipping sauce? Your mama's gonna run me to my grave if she keeps cooking me these foreign foods. What else do we have?"

"Hmm, we also have a sweet potato chili and, last but not least, a strawberry mango salad."

"Yay." Debbie responds in an unenthusiastic tone.

"I'm impressed Mrs. Jo cooked all this food, Parker. Please tell her thank you for us."

"All jokes aside, Parker. Please do tell your mom thank you. I'll begrudgingly scarf down as much food as my body allows. Jackson and Frank's culinary abilities are limited, so my taste buds are desperate to try anything besides fish and dry chicken breast."

"I thought you loved my cooking!"

"Oh no, Jackson," Debbie places her hand on his cheek. "I love *you*, but I hate your cooking, Son."

We all laugh and continue to eat our lunch. Debbie, unable to eat much, only takes a few bites of her food, but her face is filled with satisfaction and joy. Despite the circumstances, spending time with Jackson and Debbie feels so good. They have such a playful and loving mother-son relationship.

"Okay. I'm gonna go get cleaned up." Debbie scoots her chair back and winces as she stands up to walk to her room.

"I'll help you, ma."

Jackson tries to grab her arm, but she pulls it away. "No, you will not, Jackson. I can dress myself. And believe it or not, I can also wipe my own behind." Debbie waves him off, then turns to us before slamming the door, "You two aren't high schoolers anymore, so you have my full permission to get a little frisky while I get ready for my appointment."

"Go get dressed, please!" He yells and buries his face in his hand.

I can hardly contain my laughter.

"What are you gonna do with that woman? She's a hoot!"

"A hoot? Her low-country twang is rubbing off on you already." Jackson pulls me in close, then playfully hugs me and nibbles on my ear.

"Jackson," I whisper. "Your mom's in the other room." I barely try to push him away.

"Did you not hear her when she said we could get frisky. You don't want to disobey my mom now, do you?" He asks with a raised brow.

After a few tickles and hot breaths to my ear, I give in to Jackson's antics. I lean back on the kitchen counter, and he hovers over me like a tall, gentle giant. He kisses my ear and drags his breath across my jawline to my lips. I've missed his tender touch so much. I tug at his shirt to pull him closer to my body, and he nudges my legs open and moves his leg in between mine. Desperate for friction, I lay my forehead and left hand on his shoulder and grind against his thigh. I move my right hand down his shorts to gently squeeze him, and Jackson gasps softly and mutters cuss words, which makes me even more eager to please him. I grind against him at a steady pace and move my hand up and down in a swift and relentless motion. Jackson pulls my hair back to claim my mouth once more. We both softly moan as we come against one another's bodies.

With his forehead against mine, Jackson laughs, "Did we really just dry hump in my parents' kitchen?"

"We definitely just had a horny teenager moment. Your mom's gonna kill us. Look at my face. I'm flushed!"

I run to the sink to clean myself up, but Debbie's country tone radiates through the walls and startles us both.

"Okay, put your clothes back on! I'm comin' out."

Debbie marches out of her room with her purse on her shoulder but quickly stops in her tracks. She stares at us with squinted eyes.

"You two look guilty. Reminds me of Frank and I when we were your age. Your dad couldn't keep his hands off of me. He still can't!"

"That's gross, ma. Why would you put those thoughts in my head?" Jackson expresses a playful look of disgust, but I smile as I think about how angry and disappointed our parents were just years prior when they caught us kissing in Jason's kitchen.

Debbie motions us to hurry and leave, "Alright, let's go. I don't wanna be late."

An hour later, we sit in the oncologist's office, waiting to receive Debbie's latest prognosis. Mr. Sands arrived late but still in time to sit next to Debbie to hold her hand. Jackson paces back and forth in an anxious heap, and I do my best to calm him by gently grabbing his wrist to get his attention.

"Hey you, everything's gonna be alright." I bury my head in his chest and wrap my arms around his waist, hoping to transfer my stillness to him.

Jackson sighs deeply and whispers in my ear, "Thank you."

Dr. Myers, Debbie's longtime physician, enters the office with a patient folder filled with scans. Jackson's parents stand to greet her with a hug. Her facial expression reads serious, and I'm unsure whether that's good or bad.

"Frank and Debbie, thank you for coming in today. I'm so glad that you took your coughing and fever seriously." Dr. Meyers says as she sits in her chair and lays a collage of scans across her desk.

We stand behind Debbie and Frank, anxiously anticipating the doctor's explanation of the x-rays laid out in front of us.

"These are your scans from about six months ago," Dr. Myers points out. "These are your scans from three months ago, one month ago, and these are your scans from five days ago."

From scan to scan, we notice numerous circles – like small to medium-sized balls. I have no idea what I'm looking at, but the Sands family is well aware.

"We also reviewed your blood results from your last visit, and I can confirm that your breast cancer has metastasized to your liver and lungs."

This is my first time accompanying the Sands to one of Debbie's appointments, and I suddenly feel like I don't belong in the room. I wrap my arms around Jackson's right arm, and Debbie squeezes Frank's hand tight. We brace ourselves for the remainder of Dr. Myers' bad news.

"Debbie, you've been my patient for nearly eight years now, and I'd like to think we've even developed a friendship, so I want to be as honest with you as possible. It's fairly common for breast cancer to spread to the liver. Generally, the life expectancy afterward is about two to three years. However, when it spreads to the liver *and* lungs, the odds are much more slim."

"Just say it. It's okay. Tell me how long I have." Debbie nods to Frank, then turns around slightly to touch Jackson's hands, which are now gripping the chair so tight he could break it in half at any moment. She turns back around to give the doctor the go-ahead to continue with the painstaking news.

"Six months to a year – the latter being very rare." Dr. Myers hesitates. "You were the first patient I worked with when I moved to Beverly Mills. I'm so sorry that we can't do more." Dr. Myers tries to get a hold of her emotions. Debbie smiles and begins to speak so she can regain her professional demeanor.

"You've done so much already. You all have," Debbie looks around the room. "Doc, how can we make the time I have left as smooth and painless as possible for me and my family?"

"Of course, we'll forego radiation and surgeries. At this point, they'll serve no use. We can begin hormonal therapies and immunotherapy, we'll add three more medications to your existing daily regimen to relieve your pain, and we'll provide you with the information for palliative care support for you and your family. Now, we can also do chemo. However, you know how that goes – you'll experience exhaustion, weakness, and sickness on top of how the cancer already makes you feel. It won't allow you to have the peace and comfort you want during this time."

"I agree, Dr. Myers. No chemo this time. Now, let's discuss further details, together, as a family."

Frank takes out his phone and dials a few numbers. The appointment turns into a conference call. The best of Beverly Mills gather together in support of the Sands. All the parents - Jason, Merissa, Deacon, and mine are on the phone. For the next hour, we sit together as a big Beverly Mills family and discuss what to expect and how to work together to make the last months of Debbie's life filled with love, comfort, and peace.

What's only been a few hours feels like days. We're all emotionally exhausted. Although we hide our feelings, we still look defeated. With everything that's happened today, the date night with Jackson completely slipped my mind. It's menial to even think about, given the news we received.

Debbie rides back home with Frank and Jackson and I ride back to his house together. The silence in the car is deafening. I place my hand on top of Jackson's, and he turns to me with a weak smile.

"You should rest tonight. You and Jason have to get on the road tomorrow to return to school. Do you want to spend time with your family instead?"

"I'll text you and let you know. Mom is probably spent, so she'll sleep for the rest of the night, but we'll play it by ear."

I reach over to kiss his cheek and head to my car, but before I get in, Jackson grabs my arms and pulls my body to his. He holds me so close, so tight I can barely breathe.

"Thank you, Parker. Thank you for being with us today. I love you."

I wrap my arms around his waist to savor his sweet embrace. After the moment ends, he kisses my forehead with both his lips and tears. I drive back home with tear-filled eyes and a feeling of dread in the pit of my stomach that I can't seem to let go.

That night, I don't hear back from Jackson, and I won't until a week later. I try to give him his distance, but I can admit that I don't quite understand that concept. For seven days, I call in the morning to wish him well, call in the afternoon to check on him, and call in the evening to tell him goodnight. The only response I receive is, "I'm okay. I'm just really tired. I'll give you a call when I'm free."

Over the next few weeks, I keep myself busy with work at the hospital, split time between home and Jackson's house to help care for Debbie, and send unanswered texts and voicemails to Jackson's phone. He's obviously okay because I overhear Debbie's conversations with him. So, for now, I'll let everyone continue to think our relationship is perfect, but we're back to where things were months ago when he kept things to himself and pushed the people who love him away.

Today's the day I go back to my second home. Classes start again in a few days, and Merissa and I want to make sure we familiarize Avery with the school campus. Jason and Jackson didn't have practice, so they were supposed to come down to help us, but I only see Jason. Sometime later, I read a text from Jackson that says, "Sorry I couldn't make it. I just need time to think."

Jason scoffs and rolls his eyes, "What he means is he needs time to drink."

I look at him with wide eyes filled with disappointment.

"Jason, did he really go back to drinking? He's been dry the whole time he's been home."

"He's definitely back to drinking. I think it's even worse than before. He missed a few practices. He told Coach he was sick, but when I checked on him, he was passed out on the floor. It was bad, Parker."

This is what I feared, and all I can do is brace myself for the long road ahead. I know we can get through anything, but that pit at the bottom of my stomach forms again, and all I can sense is heartbreak, grief, despair, and pain. I need to muster up the strength to help Jackson overcome this storm.

Chapter 8
First Date Part 1 - Parker

This feels like the build up to a movie, and I'm all set for my first date with Jackson Sands. I have my hot girl dress on and my sexy heels that flaunt my irresistible legs. I'm ready to make him long for me like a deer that panteth for the water. I'm definitely going to hell for saying that.

When I arrive at the restaurant, I notice a sleek red Aston Martin that sticks out like a sore thumb in a parking lot of mini-vans and pick-up trucks. It must be Jackson's. It's showtime.

I take a deep breath and give myself a quick pep talk. "You got this, Parker. You're successful, beautiful, strong, and confident. Okay, let's do this."

I approach the hostess, who greets me before I can introduce myself.

"Dr. Waylen?" She asks.

"How do you know my name?"

"Mr. Sands told me to keep an eye out for a breathlessly beautiful dark-haired woman with big brown eyes."

I tuck a lock of hair behind my ear and lower my head to hide my blushed cheeks.

"He also showed me a picture so I could identify you," She chuckles. "Follow me, Dr. Waylen, and please leave your keys with valet." The hostess directs.

I oblige and follow the hostess. As I approach the table, Jackson looks up from his phone and he walks up to greet me with a chaste, soft kiss on the cheek then pulls my chair from under the table for me to sit down.

"You look stunning, Parker."

"Thank you, Jackson. You look rather handsome yourself."

"Your server will be right with you. Enjoy your meal." The hostess leaves us alone to partake in a classic staring contest. The first one to give in and break the ice loses.

"Why are you staring at me like you didn't just see me this morning?" Damn, I lost.

"I like to admire art." He laughs and takes a sip of his water.

I roll my eyes, "You're so corny, Jackson. If you want to woo me, you have to work a whole lot harder than that."

"I don't want to *woo* you, Parker. I want to win you over."

"You want to win me? Like a pig at a fair?"

"No, win you over as in earn the privilege to be in your life again." Jackson's so witty. That's new. He always had an irresistible Southern charm, but as bad as it sounds, he wasn't always the quick to think on his feet type. He must've learned a few tricks over the years while he was building his fuck boy reputation.

"That's cute, Jackson."

"I'm actually really nervous about tonight. I wiped my palms three times so far. I was afraid you wouldn't even show up, to be honest." He admits.

"I almost bailed like five times. I'm still shocked I'm sitting here right now."

"Wow, dagger to the heart. No pressure on my end or anything."

After a few flirtatious glances back and forth, our nerves settle, and our date starts to feel like old friends reconnecting. We find a comforting space within each other's presence.

"Thank you for meeting me for dinner. You've no idea how much this means to me. For years, I wondered if I'd ever have the chance to be this close to you again on friendly terms. I didn't even think I deserved that much, so now I'll do everything in my power to stay in your good graces." Jackson places his open palm in the middle of the table, and I lay mine on his.

"Thank you for inviting me. I look forward to getting to know you better, and I'd really like for you to get to know me better."

He nods in agreement.

"Let's start now," he says, "Ask me anything. Whatever you want to know."

Jackson just gave me the open door to ask him *anything*. Should I go hard or soft? Should I keep things light or dig right in? Let's go hard!

"Do you plan on staying for six months only, or would you consider moving back to Beverly Mills for good?" I ask, curious as to whether it would even be logistically possible for us to have a future together.

Jackson thinks carefully before answering, "Atlanta's my home. It's where my son and I live, and I don't want to uproot him from his familiar surroundings. My relationship with him is important. It grounds me,"

I do understand Jackson's point of view, but if we were to continue to rebuild a friendship, let alone enter into a relationship, then my needs have to be fulfilled as well. My world doesn't revolve around him anymore, and I won't be the one to compromise this time around.

"However," He continues. "I would make whatever needed adjustments to ensure we have a healthy, happy future together."

I smile and feel comfortable enough to continue my inquisition.

"So, what type of father are you? What's your son like? I've seen the pics your dad posted of him on social media. He's adorable."

Stay strong, Parker. You've come a long way. You can talk about this. You can talk about your first love's child that he had with another woman.

I give Jackson a faint smile, but he looks at me with thoughtful, sincere eyes. He squeezes my hand and rubs his thumb across mine as strength to get through his answer to the question I regret asking.

"I'd say I'm playful. I'm also a softie, so maybe I spoil him too much. I can't help it. He's such a great kid. His humor is very dry, and he says what's on his mind, like my mom. Jax is smart, and he's really starting to communicate a lot more, too. He's recently become obsessed with wrestling, so if you happen to see me return to town one day with a black eye, it's all his fault." He laughs.

"A black eye? Wow, I have to meet this little dude. It sounds like he knows how to put you in your place. So, how's your relationship with Allie? Do you get along? Do you ever occasionally get romantic with one another?"

I need him to answer this question because I know how persistent Allie is. She tried for years to get Jackson's attention. Would I have to deal with a crazy ex? There's no way she'd be okay with not being *the* Mrs. Sands, and she's the closest anyone has ever been to the title.

"You're not holding back, huh? I haven't been romantic with her since the engagement, and the intimacy was forced, so to speak. It took us a while to get along after ending the engagement, but now, we co-parent well enough. Jax lives with me during the weekday, and she usually gets him on the weekends."

"Wow, that's not much time to spend with her child. The weekends only? What's up with that? What type of mother would agree to those terms?"

"I'm in no position to judge. Allie's a decent mom, but my son has a form of autism, Asperger's Syndrome, to be exact. You gotta have patience, energy, and time for any kid, but just a bit more for one with special needs. I was a crap father starting out. I was traveling for football and partying, but she was there for the 2 a.m. ER visits. She missed work to take care of him. She's the one who noticed he needed extra attention. I missed out on the first few years of his life due to my struggles, but Allie's at a point in her life where her company's expanding, and she's extremely busy. My life's more stable. I can close deals from my bed, so it's just easier for me to be the one to take care of Jax on a daily basis. She gave me primary custody a year ago, and now I'm the luckiest dad in the world. I get to come home to the coolest kid ever."

The pure joy on Jackson's face when he talks about his son melts my heart. Enthralled with the fantasy of adding to Jackson's family unit, I slip up and ask another triggering question.

"Do you want more children?"

He looks into my eyes and answers earnestly, "Yes, I'd love to have more children with my future wife."

Just as my words slipped from my mouth, so does a tear from my eye – a happy, unexpected tear. Jackson wipes it from my face and cups my cheeks with his strong hand.

Shortly after, our waitress comes to take our order.

"Oh my god, you're Jackson Sands!" She looks no more than twenty-one, and her fangirl demeanor solidifies that. "I'm a huge fan of your ex. I graduate from fashion school in just a few weeks. My senior project is inspired by her Ode to the 90s collection. She's a fashion genius."

Our waitress is oblivious to Jackson's irritable facial expression as she proceeds to mention his crazy ex over and over again.

"Ahem." He adjusts his voice and points his head toward me until her eyes slowly move from Jackson to me. Eureka! She finally gets it.

"I am so sorry! I didn't even realize you were here on a date. Please forgive me, ma'am. Sometimes, I get carried away and stick my foot in my mouth. I'll just be quiet now and take your order."

"It's okay. I, too, was once a fan of Jackson Sands," I try to make the young girl feel better about her excusable blip. "I'll have the shrimp, mussel, and scallop linguine, and he'll have the same, but with extra shrimp."

Jackson raises his eyebrow and smiles at me in surprise.

"What? Did I get it wrong?" I ask.

He softly laughs, "On the contrary, you got everything correct. Color me impressed."

The waitress interrupts our intimate stare, "Would you two like to pair a wine with your pasta for the evening?"

"None for me. I'll have a sweet tea." Jackson says.

Surprised by his response, I add, "Well, color me impressed, too."

I follow suit and order the same. When the waitress leaves, we continue playing our game of questions.

"Okay, let's take a break from me and focus on you." He suggests.

"Oh no," I shake my head. "I didn't offer myself up as an open book like you, Jackson. You can't just ask me anything and expect an answer."

With a slight smirk on his face and a hint of mischief behind his eyes, Jackson replies, "I promise. Light questions only."

I nod for him to continue, and that damn Jackson just goes right in!

With a glare, he asks, "How long have you been single?"

"That is NOT a light question, Jackson."

"You already agreed to answer, so shoot." He laughs.

"Hmm," I ponder, to prolong the suspense. "I've been single for a year."

"So, you haven't dated anyone since David. Did you love him?"

I knew he was going to ask. Jackson's going to hate this answer, but I have nothing to be ashamed of, and I certainly don't live for his approval anymore. I do and screw who I want.

"Yes, I loved him. I was in love with him."

Jackson clinches his jaw tight.

"I see." He sits back in his chair and eyes me from head to toe.

With an exasperated reply, I indignantly reply, "Stop judging me. You're trying to make me feel bad, but I don't."

He holds his hands up in defense and says, "Hey, I have nothing against the man anymore. He's a cool guy, but he and I are complete opposites. I knew that wasn't gonna last."

"It didn't last because of you and your meddling, Jackson. You wouldn't leave me alone!"

He laughs, "You could've blocked me, Parker."

"I shouldn't have to block you. You should've just respected my wishes and left me be."

"So you could make a mistake and be with a guy you'd never love as much as me?"

"I tried to move on, which you're still struggling to do."

"At least I admit my feelings instead of stringing along someone who's been obsessed with you since high school."

"Oh please, Jackson, you've been jealous of David since high school. Did you expect me to not date anyone after we broke up? Be a nun for the rest of my life?"

"I would've preferred *that* over you dating David. He waited years for me to be out of the picture, then took advantage of you during a rough time in your life."

"He did not take advantage of me. He was there for me when you were too drunk or stoned out of your mind. We became friends and then started dating later on. I don't owe you an explanation, regardless. Why would you even bring him up? You got yourself all riled up, and now we're arguing again, and if I recall, you were one step away from marrying Allie, of all people! She's the most desperate woman in the Coastal Empire."

He stares at me with an unreadable expression and says, "So, I guess we're even, huh?"

I let out an uncontrollable laugh. For a moment, I forget that I'm on a date with Jackson. What began as playful banter turns into words of disdain and resentment.

"Not even close! David and I had real love for one another. He helped me, and I'll always appreciate how good he was to me, but you can't say the same about Allie. That entire engagement was a mess from the start, and from what I've seen and heard, you two brought out the worst in each other."

I regret my words as quickly as they come out of my mouth. I can see the hurt on Jackson's face, but as much as I care about his feelings, my feelings are equally valid.

He's still sitting back in his chair with his arms folded in deep thought as he carefully chooses his next words.

"I apologize. I let my jealousy get the best of me. I'm glad he was there for you when you needed it the most, and I'm sorry I wasn't."

His apology is thoughtful and filled with genuine emotion. I see tears prick the back of his eyes, but before I can appreciate this moment of sincerity, Jackson changes the subject.

"So, I have a question. It may seem random, but it's driven me crazy for years." He discloses.

"Oh really?" I playfully tease. "I'm nervous now. What thought-provoking question has been keeping you up at night?"

"You promise to tell me the truth?" He asks with sincerity.

I thoughtlessly reply, "Is this the question?"

"I'm serious, Parker. You have to tell me the truth." He insists.

With a big sigh, I respond, "Yes, Jackson. I swear to tell the truth, the whole truth, nothing but the truth, so help me God."

"Okay, I'll hold you to it then," Jackson hesitates for a moment before proceeding. "Why'd you quit volleyball back in college?"

He catches me off guard with this stupid question he already knows the answer to.

I agitatingly respond, "*This* is the question that's been wracking your brain? All that whiskey must've damaged your memory because my explanation has always been plain and clear."

There's a slight hint of irritation in my voice, and I can tell that my mention of his drinking habit stings him a bit also. He shifts uncomfortably in his chair yet still holds his gaze, attentively waiting for my answer. I sigh and abide by my promise to tell the truth.

"For so long, I told myself that I quit to focus on school, but honestly, I just wanted to spend more time with you." I embarrassingly admit.

Jackson's strong, broad, and proud shoulders slump at my admission. I see the guilt written all over his face as I continue to explain the poor decisions I made when I was a young and head over heels in love college student.

"Nearly every decision I made until a few years ago was centered around you and our relationship. It was unhealthy. I was so obsessed with the idea of us and our future that I was willing to put my life on hold just to make sure *we* were solid. Between my classes, practices, games and everything you had going on, I really believed something had to give. I was a twenty year old small-town college girl who wanted to support her superhot football superstar boyfriend that the entire nation adored. A part of me felt like I'd lose you to the fame, girls, and drinking. The bigger you became, the smaller I felt I was in your life, so I decided to quit so I could be seen by you again."

Jackson reaches over the table, places his hand on top of mine, and rubs his course thumb over my fingers with a look of concern and says, "I would've never asked you to quit on my behalf. I know I made mistakes and took you for granted, but did I really make you feel like you weren't important to me?"

I shake my head to half-heartedly reassure him, "No, Jackson. Well, not until later on. In high school, freshman, and sophomore year of college, my insecurities were mostly all in my head, but junior and senior year of college was the worst. You shut me out completely and I compromised my feelings to be your supportive, forgiving, and agreeable girlfriend. To tell you the painful truth, I probably would've settled with being your barefoot and pregnant wife with no dreams or aspirations of my own if I continued going down the emotionally dependent road I was on."

He lets out a soft laugh. "So, maybe our journey through the fire over the past years was a good thing?"

I laugh in return. "I wouldn't say all that. But our years away from one another did allow me to evolve into the person I was supposed to be."

Jackson nods slowly in agreement. I wish I knew what he was thinking. I thought I knew him completely, but the Jackson Sands I'm on a date with tonight is someone different, and I haven't quite figured him out yet.

"What are you thinking?" I curiously ask.

"I'm thinking about how strong you are, how strong you've always been. I know I had my fair share of screw-ups, but every time I've succeeded in life or overcome obstacles, it's because you were there to encourage me. I hate that you gave up something you love because you thought you'd lose me. I guess we both felt the same way. I psycho-analyzed everything I did because of my insecurities. I felt like I wasn't good enough for you. For all the love you'd given me my entire life, I gave you nothing in return and constantly feared losing you. Your love for me kept me alive, and because of you, I'm the man I am today."

I hope my cheeks aren't as flushed as I think they are.

"Are you putting on that millionaire charm that the blogs and influencers all rave about, Jackson Sands?" I bat my eyes and play with my earrings.

He responds with a boyish grin, "Absolutely not. Don't believe everything you read. Although, I'm flattered that you keep tabs on me."

"Don't be. It's hard not to read or hear about your comeback story. You went from college superstar to a short-lived NFL champ to a playboy trainwreck, and now you're a redeemed businessman. In ten years, there's gonna be a movie about you. Just make sure whoever plays me is drop-dead gorgeous."

"No one is as gorgeous as you, Parker." Jackson says with a straight face. His words pierce through me, and my heart begins to pound.

It may be maturity or perhaps just age, but Jackson's confidence and calm bluntness is a side of him that I've never seen before. He's reserved yet forward and way more open than I've ever known him to be. When we were young, he struggled with expressing his thoughts. Whether good or bad, I'd have to coax him to speak, but this Jackson exudes confidence, awareness, and authority. Our heavy conversation tonight still feels light, and his touch is soothing rather than tense. He makes me nervous, afraid, giddy, apprehensive and turned on all at once. For once, I'm not the supporter or comforter. He's dominant. He's taking control and isn't afraid to go after what he wants me.

Before I can break the sexual tension, our waitress returns with our food.

"Here are your entrées, Mr. Sands and Dr. Waylen." She says as she delicately places our plates in front of us.

"Oh, you know my name now? I almost feel as special as Jackson."

"I had no idea who you were by face, but our manager told me to personally give Dr. Waylen the VIP treatment. Had I known who you were, I would've raved about you rather than Mr. Sands over here."

"Should I be offended?" Jackson laughs.

"Hush, Jackson. I'm enjoying the spotlight for once. Please keep going, Miss."

"The work you and Dr. Pierce have done for the city this year is amazing. I can't wait for next year's Block Party and the Beach Bum Fest! Your events are epic, and you donate all proceeds to causes that benefit Beverly Mills' children in need. You're an angel, Dr. Waylen."

"Why, thank you," I read her badge to address her properly. "Danielle. I really appreciate your kindness. Dr. Pierce and I are just fortunate and thankful to give back to our wonderful community."

"Well, you have my deepest gratitude. Enjoy your meal, and please let me know if you need anything else." Danielle walks away to tend to her other tables.

My food smells delicious, and I'm ready to dig in, but Jackson's unreadable smile freaks me out again.

"Why are you staring at me with that goofy look?"

"I'm on a date with a celebrity. I'm just fanning out a little bit, is all." He jokes.

I roll my eyes. "Oh, you're a fan, huh? How does it feel to be the nobody for once?"

"Quite nice," He admits. "You deserve all the praise. As much as you've grown into your own, you're still the loving, selfless Parker you've always been. The work you and Merissa have done here inspired me to choose the hospital as my new passion project. I wanted to be a part of the great work being done. After running away for so many years to escape the painful memory of my mom's death, I knew something or someone good would bring me back to Beverly Mills, and it was you. The good in my life has always been you."

For the first time tonight, I sense a hint of nervousness in Jackson's eyes. He's pouring his heart out to me and nearly holding his breath as he awaits my response. I debate whether I should reciprocate my feelings or torture him a bit longer. Perhaps I'll make him sweat.

I cut into my perfectly cooked scallop, and before I could mind my words, I close my eyes and moan as it melts into my mouth. "Umn, Jackson, this is so delicious. You have to taste it."

Jackson's eyes go wide, and his thoughts go elsewhere, "Indeed I do." He raises his eyebrow and smiles flirtatiously.

Finally aware of my gestures, I blush embarrassingly, "Oh, I'm sorry. Great food does something to me. It's one of my top three most enjoyable pleasures in life."

"And what're these top three most enjoyable pleasures you speak of?"

I take a sip of my sweet tea to gather the courage to dive into a topic that could easily dictate the mood for the rest of the night, "Great food, great company, and great sex. No particular order." I smile and take another sip of sweet tea.

Again, Jackson nods with an unreadable yet comforting smile. We continue to enjoy light-hearted conversation and flirtatious banter until we're stuffed and satisfied.

"The food was so good. We have to come back another time." I exclaim.

"Already planning our second date, huh?" He excitingly asks.

"I guess I am. I really enjoyed dinner. Thank you, Jackson."

He nods. "Thank you for finally giving me a chance, but the night isn't over yet, Parker."

"It isn't over? What more could we possibly do? It's getting late."

"It's barely 9 o'clock. Don't you have a social life?"

"Social life as in lounging around my house with the girls and binge-watching late 2000's tv shows?"

"Tragic," Jackson shakes his head. He catches Danielle's attention and gestures for the check. When she brings the check to the table, Jackson doesn't even look at it. He neatly tucks four $100 bills in the sleeve and returns it to her. Her eyes go wide in shock.

"Keep the change, Miss Danielle."

"Thank you so much, Mr. Sands and Dr. Waylen. Y'all have made my night. It's been a pleasure to wait on you."

She barely contains her excitement, and Jackson's unfazed response is so natural, as if being generous is just a part of who he is.

"Have a lovely evening. We look forward to seeing your designs in stores. Keep up the great work." Jackson stands up, extends his hand to mine, and helps me out of my chair.

He looks at me in pure desire then asks, "Are you ready to have some more fun?"

Curious, nervous, intrigued and possibly even scared, I ask, "What do you have planned next?"

Yet, he only replies, "You'll see."

"I don't want to be out too late. You know I hate driving at night. I get really bad PTSD." I inform him as we exit through the restaurant doors and head toward our car, but within seconds, I halt to a complete stop. "Wait, where's my car?"

I begin to panic.

"Don't worry. Jason and Merissa took your car home. I'm driving." He looks at me with a devilish smile.

"What? Is that why I was instructed to leave my keys with valet? Jackson Sands, you sneaky little –" Before I could rip him to shreds, he steps closer to me, his chest to my breast.

He lifts my chin to meet his eyes and whispers in my ear, "Sneaky, yes, but we both know there's nothing little about me, Parker."

His breath is hot and intoxicating in my ear. He moves one hand to the nape of my back, maneuvers the other from my chin to my mouth, and then brushes his thumb across my bottom lip.

"I've been fighting the urge to kiss you all night long. Your lips are so perfect. Can I have a taste?" He asks.

Dammit! Say no, Parker. Please, say no. No, no, no, and no!

Yet, the exact opposite slips out. "You never have to ask, Jackson."

He runs his fingers through my hair and commandingly pulls my mouth into his. He plunges his tongue into my mouth, and his hands move lower down my body. I feel a pool of wetness form in between my legs. I have to force myself to regain control by placing my hands on his chest to put distance between us so my need for him doesn't put me in an all too familiar precarious position.

I open my eyes and pace my breathing, "We have somewhere else to be, don't we?" I remind him.

"Right. That's right. Let's get going." He says as he tries to regain his composure as well.

Once we're settled in the car and on the road, I check my phone. I completely forgot about the date night group chat and have nearly 100 unread texts.

"Holy crap!" I accidentally say out loud.

He worried asks, "Is everything okay?"

"Yeah, I told the girls I'd check in during our date, but I guess I was having such a nice time with you that I forgot."

He smiles confidently, "Well, I guess I can mark off great food and great company as two of your enjoyable pleasures for the night. I wonder if I can mark off anything else for you."

"Jackson Sands, you are trouble. That is not happening. As a matter of fact, I'm checking in with the girls now. They'll hold me accountable and make sure I don't fall for your irresistible charm." I pull the hem of my short dress down and read my messages from Merissa, Avery, and Izzy.

Help Keep Parker's Legs Closed Group Chat

Avery: Send a picture of your final look to us now, you sexy bitch!

Izzy: You're gonna turn heads tonight, Parker!

Avery: You mean she's gonna make a few heads bulge.

Merissa: Ew Avery! You're so nasty! Get your mind out the gutter for once. Parker is NOT going to have sex tonight. Isn't that right, Parker?

Avery: Parker isn't responding. They probably skipped dinner and went straight to the bedroom.

Izzy: No, no, no. I have faith in you, Parker. Stay strong and have a lovely date!

Jackson turns his focus from the road to me, "What are they talking about?"

"Oh, nothing. They think we skipped dinner and went straight to sex."

"Wow. They think so little of us."

"I mean, I think they're justified, Jackson. You are my first love and the best I ever had." I unashamedly admit.

He smiles and continues to drive while I read more messages.

Help Keep Parker's Legs Closed Group Chat

Avery: Ok, I'm getting worried. It's been over an hour and you haven't responded.

Izzy: Maybe because she's having a wonderful date and not thinking about us. They're falling in love all over again.

Avery: Or not.

Merissa: Everything's going well. Jason and I just peeked into the restaurant and snapped a picture. See.

"What the heck?" I yell.

"What happened now?" Jackson nearly slams on his brakes.

"Sorry. These girls are crazy. They're acting like this is the most excitement they've had in years. I guess Merissa took a picture of us when they went to pick up my car."

"Let me see."

I show him the picture, and he smirks, "We do look good together."

"Well, be that as it may, it's intrusive and kinda creepy."

I keep reading a few messages in which Merissa reveals Jackson's surprise.

Help Keep Parker's Legs Closed Group Chat

Izzy: You got the girls sitting nice and pretty tonight, Parker! I love it.

Avery: Shoutout to her personal stylist, Miss Avery. Izzy's right. Your Waylen whoopee cushions are looking extra plump tonight.

Merissa: You did that girl! Parker looks drop-dead gorgeous.

Izzy: Jackson is looking quite scrumptious as well.

Avery: I'll admit. Jackson the Jackass does look sexy AF tonight.

Izzy: I'm dying to know what's going on.

Merissa: Spoiler alert ladies! They're spending the night at the beach.

I stop reading my messages and look at Jackson in a screaming fit of fury, "We're spending the night at the beach?!"

'Operation Keep My Legs Closed' just became a lot more difficult.

Chapter 9
When His World Shattered - Parker

How do you put glass back together? If one piece is out of place, if one thing goes wrong, the glass shatters all over again. Jackson is fragile as glass and I can't fix him. I can't make him smile anymore. I can't make him feel better. I can't make things go back to how they used to be when we were happy and secure in our love.

We're inching toward the end of fall semester of our junior year of college. I quit volleyball, and I could probably take on more classes, but I arranged my schedule strategically so Jackson and I could spend more time together. My plan backfired.

He practices five days a week with games on Saturday, and when he isn't at practice, he's busy in 'study hall' with his teammates, yet his grades have dropped tremendously so I've been doing some of his assignments to help maintain his GPA. He needs as much help and support as possible right now and since I have extra time on my hands, why not help him out? He stops by the apartment on Wednesday nights to watch a movie but he can barely keep his eyes open and he and Jason come over on Friday nights for their pre-game dinner.

Saturday nights are frustrating to say the least. Jackson is a superstar now, a projected top five NFL pick so everyone wants his time, and this semester, he's chosen partying and the limelight over me. Jackson goes home on Sundays to spend time with Debbie. I used to visit with him, but he stopped asking me to go and I eventually got the hint to stop volunteering to accompany him. I know this version of Jackson is temporary. This is all a phase and he's trying his best to cope with the impending reality that his mom could die at any moment so, despite how he treats me, he needs me to be by his side now more than ever before.

"It's homecoming! Are you ready to party?" Merissa asks as we lay out on the drill field wearing our significant others' practice jerseys.

I need to have some fun and stop worrying about Jackson. "This week will be epic! I actually think I may let loose and get wasted."

"Wasted? Girl, we're getting shitfaced! Jason's frat is sparing no expense for tomorrow night's neon party. Do you have anything to wear? I hope it's tight, bright, and hugs your curves just right! You need to blow Jackson's mind and show him what he's been missing out on because you're a sexy mofo!" Merissa slaps my butt playfully.

"I don't need to show off my goods to anyone else. Jackson already knows what he has. He's just been occupied with other things, that's all." I respond unconfidently.

A deep velvety voice cuts through the noise of hundreds of students out on the lawn to butt in on our conversation.

"If anyone ever takes you for granted clothed or unclothed, they're an idiot."

Merissa and I are still laying down but we see a tall, tanned, and handsome, muscular-framed man towering over us. As soon as we stop lusting over his statuesque body, we sit up to get a closer look. He looks so familiar and eventually it clicks with Merissa.

"David? Are you David Gallinari from Beverly Mills?" She asks, still in awe of his beauty.

The corners of his mouth curve upwards and his teeth are even more perfect than his face, "Indeed I am. It's nice to meet you. What's your name?"

"I'm Merissa and this is –" Merissa starts to introduce me but David interrupts.

"Parker. You're Parker Waylen."

With an impressed yet confused look on my face I ask, "How do you know my name? Have we met before?"

"A few times, in passing. I went to Beverly Mills High. I was a senior when you were a sophomore."

"Well, I must have left quite the impression if you remember me."

"How could anyone forget you? You're the most beautiful girl that's ever lived in Beverly Mills." He says unwaveringly and shakes my hand.

David and I stare at one another like it's just us and nothing else matters. I'm so intrigued. I don't remember much about this person but he's clearly into me, and it feels kinda nice to feel desired, but I suddenly realize our handshake turned into two hands intertwining. I pull back as fast as I can and apologize.

"I'm sorry. I didn't mean for my hands to linger like that. I don't know what got into me."

"No need to apologize. I got lost in time as well." His smile is shy and sweet.

He looks as nervous as I feel. I haven't felt this hot and flustered in so long, but since Jackson isn't the person that's making me feel this way, everything that's happening right now is wrong.

Right on cue, Jason and Jackson approach us and I see the anger in Jackson's eyes.

"Jason. Jackson. Hey, you two!" Merissa greets Jason with a hug and an exaggerated kiss.

I hug Jackson and as he leans in for a kiss, out of awkward instinct, I turn my face so his lips meet my cheek instead. Why would I do that? I've never done that before, but then again, Jackson has barely shown me any public displays of affection all semester so I won't let him assert his dominance now just because this new guy is around.

Jackson backs away and looks at me and David. "So, what did we just interrupt? You seem to be quite cozy with my girlfriend of five years. I'm Jackson Sands. Who the hell are you?" Jackson puts his hands in his pockets and waits for David to answer.

"That's David Gallinari, Jackson. Another fellow Beverly Mills townie. You're hardly recognizable without those braces and that bad haircut you used to wear. You look like a stud now, man." Jason jokes.

David laughs and thanks Jason for the backhanded compliment, but Jackson's expression is still stone cold. I remember Merissa mentioning something years ago about a guy named David who used to have a thing for me. Could this be the David she was talking about? Holy crap! It is!

"David! Now, I remember you! We had two AP classes together. Oh my gosh, you do look different! I mean, you look great." I can't believe I just told David he looks great. Jackson looks at me in shock so to soften the blow, I grab Jackson's hand and lean into him to make it clear that we're together.

"Thanks. I just started grad school this semester for my doctorates in physical therapy."

"Congratulations. That's really awesome. It's always exciting to connect with fellow Beverly Millions or Beverly Millinites or whatever we're called." Merissa says.

"I don't think we're called any of those, babe."

We all laugh and the heavy tension ceases, but we still feel the anger radiating off Jackson.

"Well, it was really great catching up with y'all. Maybe we can hang out sometime. I'll see ya 'round." David eyes me one more time then hurries away to escape Jackson's glare.

As soon as David's out of earshot, Jackson turns to me and yells, "What the hell was that, Parker? You flirted with another dude in front of me. And not just any dude, David Gallinari! He's liked you since high school. I can't believe you just disrespected me like that. Is that what you do now when I'm not around?"

Unable to get a word in, I shake my head to deny his accusations then try to place my hand on Jackson's chest but he moves it away.

"Jackson, calm down! And don't you dare talk to Parker like that after everything she's had to put up with!" Merissa yells.

"Babe, let's stay out of this." Jason pleads.

Merissa reluctantly agrees and she and Jason let us know they'll meet up with us later.

"Jackson, listen to me. I wasn't flirting. I was just flustered and caught off guard. We're in the middle of campus arguing in front of classmates, professors, and your football groupies. Let's talk about this somewhere else, please?"

He pulls away and looks at me indifferently. "No, I'm good. I have class. I'll hit you up later."

He turns away from me but stops when he sees the group of girls listening in on our conversation and speaks directly to Allie Oxford, the most desperate, conniving girl on campus. She's similar to one of those mean girl villains from a movie. I'd always used to say people like that don't actually exist, until I met her. She comes from money, and she isn't afraid to say it. She's also wanted Jackson since freshman orientation.

"Hi ladies. You look beautiful today." Jackson spitefully flirts with them.

"Why, thank you, Jackson. Is there trouble in paradise? Is your little country bumpkin causing you a problem?" Allie indirectly insults me and flirtatiously puts her dirty little pen in her mouth.

"Nope, no trouble at all. I hope to see you at the homecoming festivities this weekend." He looks at Allie for two seconds too long.

Tears of anger, hurt, and embarrassment fill my eyes. I push Jackson from behind. He barely moves, but it's a reaction that shocks the both of us, "Screw you, Jackson. You're a fucking jerk." I wipe my eyes and proceed to go to my next class.

I'll be damned if I get berated in front of everyone because I forgot to worship the ground that Jackson Sands walks on for once.

It's been hours since our public spectacle in front of the student body and Jackson's been texting my phone like crazy. First, he sent heartfelt apologies. Then, he started begging for forgiveness. But now, these are definitely drunk texts.

Jackson: You mean the world to me Parker. I apologize for being a jealous jerk. You do so much for me and I take your love for granted. Please forgive me.

Jackson: I love you so much. I was an asshole for my behavior and I promise to never disrespect you or talk down to you again.

Jackson: Please talk to me. Answer your phone please. I miss your voice.

Jackson: You're the brightest star in my life. You're my galaxy. I need you. Please don't leave me.

Jackson: What are you doing Parker? Answer your phone! Why are you ignoring me?

Jackson: We get in one little fight and this is how you react? Unbelievable.

Jackson: Come over, tonight. Let me make it up to you. The image of you smiling in that dude's face is pissing me off all over again. I want to see you.

Jackson: I don't think I can drive tonight. Sleeping over at Hanks, but I wish I was with you instead.

I can't deal with a drunk Jackson tonight. I much rather stay at home and slum it with Avery and Merissa, but Merissa is with Jason at a party and Avery is out with her freshman friends. So, I just go to sleep. Hopefully by tomorrow, Jackson has found his common sense and steps to me correctly.

The next day, Jackson stops by my apartment after his practice unannounced and with his overnight bag in his hand.

"Did I say you could sleep over, Jackson?" I ask with a sharp attitude.

He scoops me up and twirls me around with hopes of buttering me up.

"No, but I was hoping that you miss me as much as I miss you. I'm sorry, Parker. I was a dick, a big dick, the biggest dick you ever had." He playfully pouts and gives me puppy dog eyes.

"You've barely spoken to me outside of drunk texts. What've you been doing since yesterday, Jackson? Hanging out with Allie Oxenfry?"

He laughs but I'm dead serious. I saw pictures of them together at a party all over my social media feed. She was hovering over him like a weirdo. Her new name should be Helga and Jackson's acting as oblivious as Hey Arnold right now.

"Hell no! I immediately regretted speaking to her in the yard. She's been following me everywhere ever since. She's like a stalker or something." He cringes.

"Serves you right then, Jackson. You really hurt me, and I'm sorry I overlooked you or showed what seemed to be too much interest in David, but I promise you, it was innocent. I just forgot for a moment how it felt to have someone look at me like I was special. He looked at me the way you used to. I don't want David. I just want to know that I'm still the girl you're in love with. I want to feel that."

Jackson's face is ridden with guilt.

"I'm sorry Parker. You deserve so much better. You're my everything." He takes his hand and caresses my face and kisses my lips, then my ears, and then my neck. His sensual touch forces me to let out a breathy moan.

Jackson lifts me up effortlessly and I wrap my legs around his waist. Our tongues are in a wrestling frenzy and he carries me to the kitchen to gently place me on the counter.

"Let's go to my room, Jackson."

"No, I want you right here. Just like this." He whispers in my ear.

It's like a switch just turned on and my need for him just grew ten times more. I pull him into a hard, desperate kiss and undo his pants as fast as I can. Jackson pulls my dress from over my head and I now sit before him in my bra and panties. He unclasps my bra then takes a hand full of my breast to his mouth. He moves his hand up my thigh and rips my panties like a wild beast then circles my clit with his thumb as I tilt my head back and enjoy the rush of ecstasy creeping up inside of me.

"I can't take it anymore, Jackson! I can't control it." I cry.

"Not yet, Parker. Wait for me." He commands.

I impatiently pull him closer. He plunges inside of me and we both gasp at how good we feel. Jackson thrusts over and over until my thighs begin to tremble and he tells me, "Now. Come with me."

I release the loudest, most intense orgasmic cry of my life. I can barely control my breathing and my legs feel like putty. Once Jackson levels himself, he worships my body with kisses then gently lifts me off the kitchen counter and gathers my clothes.

"What we just did goes against all the house rules." I laugh.

"We'll let this be our little secret," He winks. "C'mon, let's shower. We gotta get going."

"You have an early game tomorrow. Where are we going?"

"It's homecoming, Parker! We're going to Jason's neon party and I know you've been too pissed off at me to go shopping so I bought you something to wear." Jackson unzips his gym bag nervously. He's never purchased clothes for me before. This is hilarious.

"Jackson Sands, I can't believe you bought me an outfit. Are you sure you got the right size," I look through the different outfit choices he selected. "Jackson, these are so cute! I hope you return what I don't wear though. I don't like the idea of you spending all this money on me. We're broke college students until you make it to the NFL."

"For once Parker, stop tending to my needs and get dressed. Let me treat you for once. I haven't done that in a long time. I wanna show you off to the entire school tonight."

I let out a sigh and give in. "Okay, okay. I think I'm gonna wear the sports bra and high-waist leggings. I'm feeling the 80's vibe. What do you think?" I hold the up the outfit and wait for his approval.

"I don't know how I'm gonna control myself all night watching you in that sexy, tight glow in the dark outfit. I'm getting excited just thinking about it." Jackson picks me up and slings me over his shoulder.

"What are you doing?" I laugh and pathetically protest. "I'm gonna make love to you in the shower. We're gonna get dressed then go have some fun." He smacks me on the butt and we do just as he says.

Before we walk into the party, Jackson tells me that he isn't drinking tonight. He wants to remain sober so he can focus on the game tomorrow.

"You know my weaknesses, Parker. I really don't want to drink tonight, but I give in easily especially when everyone expects me to be down for a good time. Will you keep me in check?"

There's a hint of vulnerability in his request. I squeeze his hand and reach up for a kiss.

"I gotchu, babe."

For the first time in months, we have fun together – just the two of us. We talk, dance, kiss, and joke around all night long, and we ignore sneers from Allie the Stalker who foolishly thought she stood a chance with my Jackson. It feels so good to know I'm the apple of his eye again.

The next morning we're awakened by loud banging on the door. We're the only ones in my apartment so I assume either Merissa or Avery left their keys. The banging persists so I hop out the bed and throw on one of Jackson's shirts, and he sleepily walks over to the kitchen wearing only his boxers.

"I'm comin'! I'm comin'! Why do y'all keep –" I open the door expecting to see my sister or best friend but instead it's Mr. and Mrs. Sands!

"Surprise!" Debbie yells, but not for long when she glances over to see her half naked son in my kitchen. Then, she looks me up and down and I realize I'm just as unclothed as Jackson.

"Mom? Dad? What are y'all doing here?" Jackson tries to cover his privates with a gallon of milk and hurry back to my room.

I quickly grab the throw blanket from my couch and wrap it around my waist.

"Well, we were trying to bring you in on the surprise of showing up to Jackson's game, but I think Frank and I are the ones who are surprised, instead. Isn't that right Frank?" Debbie laughs.

"This is so uncomfortable," Frank says. "Son, do you have on clothes, yet? Do you always walk around naked like this?"

Frank and Debbie look around at my messy apartment which is sprinkled with clues of last night's post-party sexscapades.

"Uh, yes, sir. I have on clothes." Jackson comes out the room now fully dressed in a t-shirt, sweatpants, and even socks.

"Hey, Dad. Hey, Mom." He gives his dad a hug then squeezes his mom tight and kisses her cheek.

"Hey, Son. It's so good to see you. Now, under normal circumstances, I would give you two a good cussin' for all of your fornicating, but I'm getting kinda happy 'bout the idea of Parker giving me a grandbaby before I die." Debbie says.

"Don't talk about those things, Deb." Frank says.

"Talk about what, death or grandbabies?"

"Both!" Frank and Jackson say in unison.

We laugh light heartedly and sit down to catch up. Maybe it's her makeup or perhaps the pure joy of seeing her son but Debbie looks really good. She's still thin and frail, but her face looks fuller since I last saw her a few months back. However, looks can be deceiving because when I look at Frank, his expression and demeanor is the exact opposite. Frank looks exhausted and as Debbie speaks, he keeps looking at her as if he's just waiting to catch her or waiting for her energy to be spent from putting on this *everything is okay* facade.

I tidy up my small living room space for the Sands and I head over to the kitchen to clean the counters that we had sex on all night long. Then, I open my fridge to cook breakfast for my surprise guests.

"Are y'all hungry?"

"Oh, I can definitely eat." Mr. Sands replies.

"So, why are y'all here? It's not safe for you to be at a game surrounded by nearly a hundred thousand crazy football fans. It isn't sanitary either. Your immune system could be compromised by anything. What were y'all thinking?"

"Who are the parents here? Now, I'll be damned if I miss out on my son's homecoming game! Watching you on a tv screen doesn't even compare to being in those stands. It's an adrenaline rush, I tell you." Debbie says.

Jackson sits down next to his mom and lightly lays his head on her shoulder while she plays in his hair. He looks like a little kid again, finding comfort in the arms of the woman he loves the most. After a while, Jackson comes in the kitchen to assist me with laying the spread of banana pancakes, bacon, scrambled eggs, and fresh fruit.

"Oh, my goodness! You've outdone yourself as usual, Parker. Always going above and beyond. Frank and I would've been happy with a bowl of oatmeal, but I'm not complaining. This food is delicious! You get your cooking skills honestly, that's for sure." Debbie compliments.

"It helps that I have someone to cook for. Jackson is the most starving man alive. He inhales food. He's gonna eat me out of a house and home soon."

"He gets that honestly, too. Frank's stomach is a bottomless pit."

"We just appreciate good cookin' is all and the best way to show our appreciation is to eat up everything we can." Jackson responds.

"That's right, Son." Franks agrees and they both fist bump from across the table.

"We miss your Sunday visits, Parker. Where you been?" Debbie inquires.

I look at Jackson who looks back down and continues to eat his food. Debbie and Frank notice.

"Oh, I see. Jackson's been pushing you away *again*, huh," She shakes her head and looks to Jackson. "You know, Dr. Kaiser wanted us to check in with you. He said you called him in a frenzy this week, something about losing Parker. He said you may have had an episode."

Jackson stops eating and gives his parents a knowing look.

"Who's Dr. Kaiser? An episode?" I ask.

"Oh goodness, Jackson! You haven't told her?" Debbie sounds off disappointingly.

"It's not a big deal, ma," Jackson says nonchalantly. "Parker, I've been seeing a therapist here and there, on and off for a few years."

"A few years! Jackson, how could you not tell me this? What's going on?"

"This is why I didn't tell you. I don't want you to worry. It's really nothing."

"Jackson battles crippling anxiety and occasional depression. He has ever since he was a little boy. It started when I first got sick. Dr. Kaiser's been working with him to manage his anxiety and stress levels. It's why we moved to Beverly Mills in the first place."

Debbie places her hand over Jackson's but he adjusts his hand slightly to take her hand into his.

"I'm sorry I didn't tell you, Parker. I thought I could shield you from that part of myself. I didn't want to be a dark cloud hanging over your head."

"Well, maybe if you'd be more open with her, she could replace that dark cloud with some light." Debbie chides.

"That's what your mom's done for me, Son. You and I are one and the same in many ways. We think we can handle everything on our own, but when you have someone who loves and cares for you, you gotta learn to let them in. Mama's my sunshine."

Franks smiles at Debbie and she lets go of Jackson's hand to caress Frank's face.

I'm so angry at Jackson, and this secret has ruined my mood entirely. Sensing my displeasure, Debbie looks to me and says, "Don't let my son's foolishness destroy what was meant to be. He's a complicated boy at times, but he means well. He dwells too long on his shortcomings and he often forgets that despite everything he's wonderfully, beautifully, and fearfully made. If you can, please be there to remind him."

I nod yes to Debbie's request. Jackson leans over to me and whispers, "Sorry, I wasn't completely honest with you."

"For our entire lives, Jackson?" I stare emotionless.

He lowers his head in guilt and shame. Feeling sorry for the complexed and conflicted man I love, I grab his hand and kiss his shoulder blade. "Your mom did say you Sands men are difficult. She wasn't lyin' about that."

We continue to eat our breakfast and enjoy each other's company. Afterwards, Frank and Debbie get ready to leave to check-in their hotel and rest before the game. Before she goes, Debbie pulls me to the side for a few words in private.

"How are *you* doing, Parker?"

"I'm doing great Debbie. I really am." I smile wide to try to convince her.

"Hmm, if you say so. A mother knows her son and a woman knows the dissatisfaction that comes from unreciprocated devotion. I know how devoted you are to Jackson's happiness but remember to put yours first. Jackson is a work in progress. I know it. You know it. We all know it. Things are gonna get ugly, real fast and real soon. I mean very soon, Parker, and if things don't work out between you two, I completely understand. Jackson's happiness and well-being is not your responsibility but please promise you'll check on him from time to time. I don't know how and I don't know when, but I do know you'll be his saving grace that pulls him from rock bottom."

"Yes, ma'am. I promise I'll be there for him in any way I can."

Debbie pulls me in for a big hug and his parents leave. I turn to Jackson and look at him sternly. He plasters a sheepish uh-oh smile on his face and rubs his hand on the back of his neck.

"You have some explaining to do, Jackson Sands."

For the rest of the morning, we sit together on my couch and discuss his lifelong struggle with anxiety and bouts of situational depression triggered by his mom's cancer. He tells me about the pressures of trying to be perfect and his constant fear of losing it all – football, school, me, and his mom, on a daily basis. Jackson's been hiding his anxiety attacks and mental breakdowns from me for years. He hid his pain from everyone for nearly his entire life thinking it's in everyone's best interest, yet it's only to his detriment. All of this time, I thought I knew Jackson Sands inside and out, but I never really knew him until now. Now that he sees I love him still for who he is, flaws and all, he can finally be himself fully, unapologetically, fearlessly and without shame. He never has to be alone again.

The last month has been a whirlwind. Jackson opened up to all our friends about everything and they were just as shocked as I was, but together we made a vow to support him no matter what. Our official unofficial title is the Beverly Mills Accountability Crew. As Jackson's best friends, we're going to make sure he attends his virtual and in-person therapy appointments with Dr. Kaiser. We're definitely going to make sure we support him over the next few days and for however long after because we're home for Christmas Break and things aren't looking so good right about now.

We've been preparing for this moment, but you can never be fully prepared to lose a parent. Jackson asked me to stay with him every step of the way and that's exactly what I'm doing. We've only been home for a week and it feels like hundreds of people have come and gone to say their final goodbyes. Jackson and Frank have barely slept. Mom, Merissa, the Beverly Mills Moms, and I've rotated between cooking, cleaning, and helping Frank and Jackson manage their final affairs.

Jackson and I have barely had a moment alone in days, so we decide to sit on the porch for a breath of fresh air.

"I think today's the day." Jackson sits in a rocking chair, eyes full of sorrow with his head titled back on the hard plank of his house.

"How do you feel?"

He lets out a soft, exhausted chuckle. "I don't really know how to answer that question, Parker. It's a weird kind of question."

"But you still *feel* something? How do you feel?" I ask again.

He thinks for a moment before speaking. "I feel like I'm holding my breath, and when I let go, my mom will let go, then everything's gonna go dark."

I take Jackson's hand and we sit in silence for a few minutes. He doesn't cry but I hear his pain in his deep, loud breaths. I feel his pain in his limp hands, and I see his pain through his tired dragging eyes.

As soon as we begin to synchronize our breathing at a calm, steady pace, Mrs. Hernandez, Merissa's mom, peaks from around the front doorway, "Parker, can you come in here for a moment?"

I hurry up and follow Mrs. Hernandez to Debbie's bedroom. "She wants to speak to me?" I point to my chest for clarification.

Mrs. Hernandez nods her head and lightly knocks on the door. My mom is in the room giving her best friend one last hug goodbye. Before she walks past me, she squeezes my arm to give me strength to endure the conversation to follow. I walk in the room and sit next to Debbie, whose laying in the bed taking slow, course breaths and fighting to keep her heavy eyelids open.

She looks at me with a weak smile and says, "My sweet Parker."

"Hi, Debbie. You're quite popular round here, aren't ya?"

"I don't know what it is about me, but I can't seem to get people to leave me alone. It's like I'm having a going away party or something." She laughs.

Debbie still manages to be her sweet, humorous self even in her last days of life. I can't help but feel a pang of sadness take over me as I look into her eyes.

"Don't look so sad, Parker. Today's a good day. I've survived cancer for over fifteen years. It tried to take me out so many times, but it only won once, just this once."

"You're the ultimate champion, Debbie. The best I've ever seen do it." I respond and wipe my tears.

"You know it. Now, let's talk about your future." She tries to sit up on her pillow, but she doesn't have the strength.

"My future?" I ask. "Isn't this supposed to be one of those conversations where you make me promise to take care of Jackson, love him endlessly?"

Debbie waves me off. "Oh, Parker. I'd like to think you'd know me to be quite the worldly woman by now. I only want to remind you how special you are. You love hard and you're so passionate about others. I just hope you remember to love yourself the hardest and make sure your dreams and goals are your first passion. Everything and everyone else will follow accordingly including our Jackson."

I smile appreciatively. "Yes ma'am."

"*Now,* we can talk about Jackson," She says. I grab ahold of her hand and listen intently fighting to hold back tears.

"Oh, Jackson. He reminds me so much of Frank when he was young. Quiet, mysterious, and conflicted. It took me years to get him to open up to me. I reckon it's taking you the same with Jackson, but when Frank finally opened up, he never looked back. He's been nothing but the most attentive husband and caring father. I don't know what the future holds for you and Jackson, but I do hope it's filled with forgiveness, redemption, happiness, and love; however it happens and in whatever order, I just pray for it to be so. I'm not going to ask you to love him endlessly, but I am going to ask you to love him in spite of. He's gonna keep mistakes for a while and he may even push you away for good, but I hope you can see him for the man he'll become someday and love him anyhow. You became a part of this family the moment we met, and I'll forever love you, Parker."

"I love you, too, Debbie. You've been a second mom to me. I really hope we can experience decades of happiness like you've shared with Frank. I think we're getting there."

"Oh Parker. Your happiness will be even better and I know you'll never stop loving each other even through the most difficult times."

I lean over to hug Debbie and she whispers in my ear, "Goodbye, daughter. I think I'll spend the rest of my time left with my two boys. I know it'll take some time but thank you in advance for the beautiful life I know you and Jackson will eventually share together."

I hug her tight and say, "Sleep well, Mrs. Debbie."

Before I open the door, I wipe my tears so as not to show how much of a wreck I am to the crowd of people outside and I signal to Jackson and Frank to tend to Debbie.

"She'd like to spend time alone with you all. Just you two. Y'all head in and mama and I will let everyone know to head home for the day."

Frank and Jackson enter the room and close the door. My mom and I inform visitors that they'd like to have some privacy over the next few days. When they're all gone and the house is clean, my mom, dad and I say our goodbyes to Frank and Jackson and we head home for the night. By 9 p.m., I'm in my bed sending a prayerful text to Jackson to try to lift his spirits. He doesn't respond but that's expected.

At 3:15 a.m., my phone rings and it's Jackson. Barely awake and coherent, I answer.

"Jackson, is everything okay?"

Jackson doesn't respond. I only hear heavy breathing and endless sniffling on the other end.

"Jackson, are you okay?" I ask louder and in increasing panic.

"No." He says. That's all he says and that's all I need to know.

"I'm coming over." I hurry out the bed and throw on the nearest piece of clothing I could find.

My dad rushes out of his room in fear. I must've woken him with all of my scrambling around.

"Parker, what's going on?"

"Jackson needs me." I quickly answer then leave the house to console the love of my life.

When I arrive to Jackson's house, the medical team is already on the scene. Frank stands outside and watches as they place Debbie's bagged, lifeless body in the ambulance. He's usually stoic and unexpressive, but tonight he's completely broken and unable to maintain his composure. Buckled at the knees and bent over, Pastor Owens offers Frank his shoulder to cry on, but he cries out Debbie's name instead. I look around for Jackson, but he's nowhere to be found so I enter the house and after searching a few rooms, I find him in his mom's room. He's sitting in the corner with his knees close to his chest, rocking back and forth. His eyes are swollen and tears flow profusely down his face. He looks up at me and I run to him.

"She's gone, Parker. She's gone. My mom's gone. I don't know what to do." He cries.

I wrap my arms around Jackson and hold onto him with dear life.

"It's okay, Jackson." I try to console him.

"She's gone. My mom's gone. She's gone. What am I gonna do?" It's all he can manage to say.

For the next four hours, I sit on the floor with Jackson and hold him in my arms as he cries himself to sleep. I'll never forget the night Jackson Sands' world shattered and it'd be years until the pieces of his life could be put back together again.

Chapter 10
First Date Part 2 - Parker

Jackson's done it again. He made a unilateral decision about what he *thinks* is best by planning an overnight date. Does he think he's going to get laid? If so, he can guess again. My legs are staying closed tonight. I can't believe him. Everything was going so well. He wooed me with a nice dinner. We had great conversation. Then, he oversteps as usual! I have to hear from Merissa that he devised a plan to get me in his bed.

"Parker, did you hear me?" Jackson raises his voice.

"Huh? What'd you say?"

Jackson looks back and forth between me and the road ahead. "I said it was supposed to be a surprise. I asked Jason and Merissa to grab a few things from your place so we could spend more time together on our date. I apologize for overstepping or making decisions without speaking with you first. I was just so excited that you finally said yes that I went all out and started planning. I'm sorry, Parker."

I take a deep breath and roll my eyes, "I forgive you, but that's strike one, Jackson. Three strikes and no more dates, no kisses, no nothing."

He lets out a sigh of relief and flashes a cute smile.

"Deal. I'll be on my best behavior from here on out."

We pull up to the northside of Beverly Mills beach which piques my curiosity. The northside of the beach is reserved for the wealthy, affluent residents. They often throw posh parties, but tonight it's completely empty, yet there's a sign that says *This beach is closed for a special event.*

"Jackson, I don't think we're supposed to be here. There's some type of special event going on."

"*We* are the special event, Parker."

Jackson grabs my hand and leads me to the shore where I see an elaborate set up of candles that form the shape of a heart. In the middle of the heart is a beautifully decorated table with a satin covered photo album and two plates of peach cobbler.

"I'd like to tell you a story of how I found love in a little town called Beverly Mills." Jackson waits for my approval.

"Go on." I respond, thoroughly impressed with Jackson's effort. This moment reminds me of our first anniversary date on the beach, a more upscale version, of course.

We walk to the table and Jackson cuts a slice of peach cobbler with his fork and feeds it to me. It's so delicious that I let out an involuntary moan.

"Did my mom make this?"

Jackson nods and pulls out my chair for me to sit. He then opens the photo album and reads the opening message.

When I was a little boy, I moved to a town filled with people I never saw before, but when I met a girl named Parker, she changed my life forever. My love for her grew when she and her mom showed up to my house with a beautiful smile and a fresh baked peach cobbler. We made a promise to one another to love each other, always and it's a promise that remains to be unbroken. This album is a physical representation of what loving someone wholeheartedly looks like.

"May I have the pleasure of accompanying you for dessert this evening, Parker Waylen?"

I caress his cheek and respond, "The pleasure's all mine, Jackson Sands."

We enjoy one another's company and look through the photo album that chronicles our lives together from elementary school to college and moments in between. Our lives together, even despite the pain, have been our own unique love story. Jackson and I continue laughing and reminiscing over fun times, heartfelt experiences, and intimate moments we shared. When we finish, he takes my hand and walks me over to a beautiful white king-sized canopy beach bed drenched in lilies and roses with neatly folded sleepers on top.

"This is beautiful." I look to him in pure awe of his attention to detail and willingness to go the extra mile for me.

"Can we fall asleep in one another's arms and wake up on the beach together like we used to?" He asks.

I feel like I'm in a trance. I'm a yes girl at this point. Whatever Jackson wants from me, he can get it. My poker face disappeared the moment my feet touched the sand. As much as I try to be hard and steadfast like Avery, I just can't. I'm like putty in Jackson's hands. I wear my heart on my sleeve and I really want to believe that Jackson has changed. I *need* to believe that he's changed. I pushed away a possible shot at love before, at real happiness with David, with hopes that Jackson would one day evolve into the man Debbie once told me he'd be, and I hope I don't regret this.

"I'd love to fall asleep under the stars and wake up next to you as the sun rises, Jackson. It'd be the most beautiful sight ever."

He turns to me and brushes his finger over my lip and says, "Yes, it is the most beautiful sight ever."

We change into our clothes and lay underneath the covers. I'm so nervous that I get goosebumps. Jackson notices my uneasiness and pulls me closer to his body.

"Are you cold?" He asks as he rubs my goosebumps away.

"No, I'm just afraid." I answer honestly.

"You and me both." He admits.

"What are you afraid of, Jackson? What have you got to lose?"

"Everything. You're my everything. You've always been my everything. Our memories together and occasional run-ins over the years are what's motivated me. It's what's kept me sane, but I need more, Parker. I don't want to screw this up. Not this time. Not ever again," Jackson puts his hand in my hair and turns to look me in the eyes as we lie next to one another. "I promise to never push you away again. I'm not the same Jackson you knew before. I want to show you all of me. I want to give you my all, Parker."

"I want that too, Jackson, but it's a big risk. I could've been happy with someone else. I could've been married, but I'm not because I wasted years hoping and praying for you to be the man I knew you could be. I'm starting to think I'm as crazy as everyone thinks I am. How can you be so sure you won't break my heart again? You broke me down so many times Jackson. What if you decide to go get drunk one day –" Before I can continue to express my fears, Jackson cuts me off.

"I don't drink anymore. I haven't had a drop of alcohol in three years."

Jackson's admission nearly takes my breath away. I'm not really sure what to say next.

"You're quiet, Parker. What are you thinking?"

Carefully choosing my words, I answer, "I'm just surprise is all. I never thought you'd quit drinking. You were –"

"Addicted," He says. "So, I don't know if you recall, but a few years ago, I did this really awesome interview where I proclaimed my love for you on national tv."

"Oh yes, I remember that, Jackson! What a lovely interview that was. My name went viral #whoisparkerwaylen and your meltdown was the #1 used meme that year. Don't tell her I told you this, but Avery still uses it when she's having a bad day."

"Wow. One of these days, I'm gonna win your sister over."

Jackson smiles, but his expression reverts back to the seriousness of the moment.

"After that interview, I went on a serious drinking binge. Allie was understandably pissed off at me. She told me to stay away from her and threatened to get an order of protection to keep me away from my son. I felt like I lost you for good. My dad and I were on the outs about my drinking and my crazy lifestyle. I missed my mom so much it hurt, and I just felt my world was crashing down. I was hopeless and the only thing I thought I could do to get through the day was drink. I wanted to kill myself."

A tear falls down Jackson's face, and I wipe it away with my hand then lay on his chest as he continues to tell his story.

"After my binge, I took some pain pills and anti-depressants. I failed as a son. I failed as a father. I failed my mom. I failed you. I failed at life and I was ready to end it all, but as soon as I felt myself slipping away, I read your text. You said you'd always love me. You told me to get help. Then, it was like my mom spoke through you and said –"

Together we both say, "Because despite everything, we are still wonderfully, beautifully, and fearfully made."

"What happened next?"

Jackson continues, "I called Jason. I couldn't say much. I was drunk, high out of my mind, hysterical, and having one of the worst anxiety attacks of my life. I don't even know how much time passed, but sometime later, Jason, Merissa, my dad, and your dad showed up."

"My dad? Why didn't anyone tell me about this? I would've come to support you."

"I told them not to, Parker. You've supported me enough. You sacrificed enough and I wanted you to be happy. I knew you'd drop everything, all the good things going for you to carry my burdens."

I can't believe Merissa managed to keep this from me. I can't believe my dad hid this from me. I can't believe I almost lost Jackson for good. He's been through so much and I should've been there for him.

"Hey, come back to me." He says and lifts my chin so we look one another in the eyes.

"I'm sorry, Jackson. I'm so sorry you had to go through that, alone. I wish I could've been there."

"I'm so thankful I went through it, Parker, and I was never alone. I had your words to push me and I had Jason, Ris, and our dads to see me through. I stayed in the hospital for a day or so after getting my stomach pumped then I went to in-patient rehab for six months."

"Six months? How'd you manage to keep that a secret from the media?"

"Money. Lots of money," He laughs. "After rehab, I started going to therapy again. I attended AA meetings every day for 180 days straight. Twice a day on stressful days and there were many of those. After about a year, it became easier. I didn't feel the daily need to drink anymore. I honestly didn't know what life was like without alcohol until I got sober. It's like I'd been feeding this demon since high school. A drink here, a drink there. Giving it just enough to get stronger, just enough for my bad habit to survive. Then came college, and it grew as my fame grew. It grew as my pain grew. I fed it so much day by day, month after month, year over year until my need to drink became stronger than me. It damn near ruined me, Parker. I'm so thankful to be alive. I'm thankful to be next to you right now. This moment means everything to me, and I finally feel like I can be the man you deserve."

I lift my head off Jackson's chest, adjust myself to level with his face, and pull him in for a kiss.

In a soft voice I say, "You've always been that man, Jackson Sands. Always. I'm so proud of you."

"You have no idea how happy it makes me to hear you say that. It took me a long time to get here, Parker. I've hurt people. I've hurt you. I stayed away for so long for that very reason. I never thought I'd ever have a chance to be with you again, but I know I couldn't truly be happy if I didn't try one last time. Do you think –" Jackson hesitates. "Do you think you could see yourself falling in love with me again?"

Rather than say yes, I decide to show Jackson instead. I lean into him and kiss him again.

"Is that a yes?"

"It's a no, Jackson. I can't see myself falling in love with you because I've never fallen out of love with you."

As soon as I confess my feelings, we see beautiful fireworks in the night sky. We both smile and press our foreheads together then lie next to one another under the moonlight of Beverly Mills beach exchanging kisses here and there and talking for hours until the sun rises.

I no longer see the young and troubled boy who broke my heart. I see the matured man that Debbie told me needed time to make mistakes, time to heal, time to find his own way, and time to earn redemption.

He finally found his peace and I may have finally found the piece I felt was missing to my happy ending.

Chapter 11

When Her World Shattered - Parker

It's been five months since Debbie passed away from cancer. Her death changed everything, specifically the trajectory of Jackson's life.

In January, just a few short weeks after the funeral, Jackson led his team to the college national football championship and won. What should've been a momentous occasion for him was heartbreakingly somber. He gave an impassioned speech dedicated to Debbie at his post-game interview and that was the last time he spoke of her ever again.

Since then, he's been alarmingly calm and disturbingly cool at seemingly all times, which has created a distance between us that I've been trying my hardest to close. A part of me suspects that he's pacifying his pain with alcohol, and he hides it too well for me to catch him.

"Hey, big sis," Avery plops down on the couch next to me. "You're all packed up and ready to go?"

"Yep, I even packed all of your things too since you've been m.i.a. all semester." I side eye Avery. She embarked on a journey of self-discovery this year. She joined a few cultural appreciation clubs and she has her own friend group separate from us, but most importantly, she's been on a journey to discovering who she is as a black woman adopted into a white family. It's been wonderful to watch her come into her own.

"I've been crazy busy this year, but I can't wait for summer break. I need a break from everything especially silly college boys. I miss the slow pace of Beverly Mills. Do you and Jackson have any special plans for the summer or does he have plans with his football 'bros'?"

I laugh at her dumb jock impression, but honestly, that's all Jackson really makes time for these days. It's like he's avoiding what's real so he doesn't have to confront the pain of losing his mom.

"I don't know. Jackson's so wishy washy. One minute he wants to spend time together and the next he's avoiding my calls and texts. I'm being sensitive and understanding to everything he's been through since Debbie's passing, but it's getting harder and harder to put up with. He tells me just enough to get me to stop nagging him. I remind him about his therapy appointments with Dr. Kaiser, but there's no telling if he's actually being transparent in his sessions. He says he hasn't had a drink in months, but I don't believe him. Something's just off."

Avery lays her head on my shoulder and speaks her truth, "If you think he's drinking, then odds are he is, Parker. Jackson is the type of person to hide how he feels, hide what he thinks, and hide what he does. You know when he's being honest with you and it sounds like he isn't. You gotta decide whether you're going to save him or if you're going to let him make his own mistakes. I told you a long time ago that y'all's love is toxic. When are you gonna realize it?"

"We're not toxic. We're soulmates, Avery."

"Same thing." She shrugs.

"You're so pessimistic, Aves. C'mon, let's hit the road."

We're back in Beverly Mills for the summer and for the first time in forever, I don't have my life planned out. I want to wing it – spend quality time with Jackson, sun bathe on the beach, relax around a few bonfires, and just enjoy being in love in Beverly Mills.

When Avery and I pull up to our parents' driveway, Jackson is already there waiting for me. I run up to him to give him a big hug but I stop an inch away from his lips. He smells. No, he reeks!

"Jackson, what the hell? You smell like beer and lots of it. Were you drinking? Did you drive?"

Jackson shakes his head and dismisses my feelings. "Parker, don't be ridiculous. I'm fine. I only had a few beers before I came over. I met up with a few teammates before I got on the road then met up with the Gabe, Jason, and Deacon when I got in town. It's no big deal."

He smiles and tries to bring me closer into his embrace, but I pull away.

"No, you told me you weren't drinking anymore. You lied to me!"

"Stop overreacting. I didn't lie. Beer is barley, not alcohol." He laughs and opens his car door to grab a beer from his back seat.

"Semantics, Jackson!" I move slightly towards his rear car door to slam it shut and stop him from grabbing his drink, but he's much stronger than me.

"What are you doing?" He laughs.

"I swear to God, Jackson, if you grab that damn beer from your car, I'll kick your door in so damn hard. Don't you dare!"

Avery butts in and tries to end the conflict before it gets any worse.

"Hey Jackson, maybe you should go inside."

"No, I'm good. I think I'm gonna head home. I don't have time for her shit." He glares at me.

"For my shit, Jackson?" I quickly snatch his keys out of his hands and Jackson lunges forward to try to grab them back, but he's too drunk and loses his balances.

"Give it back, Parker. Why do you have to do this? You're starting an argument for no reason!"

Avery still stands between us. "Hey, both of you back up, now! Mom! Dad!" She calls out to our parents.

"I'm calling Dr. Kaiser." I tell Jackson.

"What? Why would you do that? What good is that gonna do? You think being a tattle tale's gonna give you brownie points? It's just making things worse between us."

I call Jackson's therapist and walk further away from him and Avery so I can try to get Jackson the help he needs.

"Dr. Kaiser's office. This is Jasmine. How may I help you?" His secretary answers.

"Hi Jas, it's Parker Waylen. How're you doing?"

"Parker! It's been so long. How are you? How's Jackson? I hope he's doing well."

"What do you mean? Jackson just had an appointment this week."

"Umn, no. He said he found a new therapist that was closer to his school. That was about two going on three months ago." She informs me.

"What? Are you kidding me? I've been asking him about his sessions every week and he acts like everything's been going great." I look at Jackson from across my yard and he stares back with a stupid look on his guilty face.

"Jackson!" I scream. "You frickin' liar!"

My mom and dad finally come rushing out the house.

"What is going on here?" My mom asks.

Avery explains, "These two love birds are arguing. Jackson's drunk and apparently, he's been lying to Parker about going to therapy."

My dad takes his hands off his waist and pats Jackson's back, "C'mon, Son. Let's call your dad."

Jackson rubs his hands over his face and bows his head in shame. He follows my dad into the house and I look over at my mom. She looks disappointed in me, but I don't know why. I'm only trying to help Jackson. He needs help and I seem to be the only person trying to save him.

"You're not a superhero, Parker. Now, get in the house girls." My mom sternly commands.

Less than thirty minutes later, Frank shows up. I hadn't seen him since the funeral five months back. He looks unkept with a 5 o'clock shadow and scraggly hair. I can tell he's still in mourning just like Jackson.

My mom keeps us separated from one another so I can't hear what my dad, Jackson, and Frank are talking about. When they finish, Jackson briefly glances at me before walking out my front door.

My parents tell me they're going to drop Jackson's car off to his house. I ask to go with them but they tell me to stay home and wait for them to get back so we can *talk*. This is not the way I thought my summer would begin.

An hour later, my parents enter the house and call me into the dining room.

"Come sit, Parker." My mom tells me.

We all sit down at the table and my dad begins to speak angrily. "What you did today was foolish. Jackson is a loose cannon. He drove to my house drunk! What if you would've gotten in the car with him? Something terrible could've happened, Parker. I don't even want to think about it! Both of you behaved recklessly!"

"Fussin' like little schoolkids out in the open, Parker. What's going on?" My mom asks.

I slump down in my chair. I'm twenty-one years old now, yet I feel like a little kid who can't intelligently articulate myself.

"It's Jackson! He's doing everything to ruin our relationship. He lied to me about going to his doctor appointments. He lied to me about his drinking. He barely spends time with me anymore. I don't even know if he still loves me."

My unintelligent feelings roll out my mouth as fast as diarrhea. I've been dying to vent to someone. I don't even care who right now, but I'm sure I'll regret spilling my guts to my parents later on. They probably think I'm silly, immature, and naïve, but my relationship with Jackson has become exhausting, and I'm trying my hardest to be the glue we need to stay together.

My dad looks disappointed and irritated, but my mom looks at me sympathetically and says, "Parker, I don't mean to upset you or sound harsh but Jackson is not your responsibility. As sad as it is, he had a mom. She's no longer here, and you shouldn't try to take her place. You're gonna run yourself ragged, otherwise," She scoots her chair closer to me and places her hand on top of mine. "Parker, you're approaching your last year of college. By the grace of God, you've done okay with your studies, but barely. Your dad and I think you and Jackson should probably take some time apart to focus on yourselves and think about your futures."

I pull my hand away from hers in a disapproving manner. "You want us to break up?"

"Yes!" My dad interjects. "Jackson has issues that he needs to work out, Parker. Now, I've watched you run after this kid for years. You chased after him and catered to his every need. My daughter should be focusing on med school. You've lost your focus a long time ago. I don't even know who you are anymore. Every word that comes out of your mouth is about Jackson. What about you, Parker? You can't live for this boy!"

"Your dad's right. Avery told us that you didn't score well on your last MCAT exam. Your grades dropped significantly this year, and you're behind on med school applications."

I have to defend myself against these baseless attacks that have nothing to do with me and Jackson. "I feel like y'all are ganging up on me. I'm not the one who needs help. I don't need an intervention, Jackson does. Can't you see that?"

My dad slams his hands on the table and unleashes his fury and screams, "I don't give a damn about anyone else but my daughter whose throwing her life away over a damaged boy whose two drinks away from rehab!"

Stunned by my dad's reaction, my mom tries to rectify the situation.

"Parker, what your dad's trying to say is –"

"He meant exactly what he said, mama."

Offended by the conversation with my parents, I get up from the table and go to my room to call the person I know would be on my side, but Jackson doesn't answer. I'm so taken aback by my parents' anger, that I completely forgot our blow up was the cause of it all. I'll just wait to speak to him in the morning.

A phone call never came the next day or the next. It takes days for Jackson to answer my calls, and when he does, his response is underwhelming.

"Jackson, are you punishing me?"

"What? You sound ridiculous. How can I punish you?" He laughs through the phone. He's tired, agitated, and distant as usual.

"I don't know, maybe because you haven't called me. You haven't answered my calls. You didn't even bother sending me a text. I know you heard my voicemails. You're obviously ignoring me."

"I've just been working with my dad over the last few days. It's been good for the both of us. Our relationship's been a bit strained since mom died so it's nice to reconnect with him. I'm sorry for not texting or calling. The other day was just a lot. I wasn't myself and you weren't yourself."

"I agree. We were both beside ourselves. I never want us to get to that point again. I'm sorry for overstepping and calling Dr. Kaiser's office. I'll start setting better boundaries between us."

"Boundaries are good, but honestly, I think we need to do more than set boundaries. I think we need a little bit of space from each other, Parker."

"What do you mean by space, Jackson?" I start to panic on the inside but manage to maintain my cool.

"Listen, I'm at a job site right now with my dad, but let's talk more tonight at the Bonfire."

"Of course. I'll see you tonight. I love you."

"I'll talk to you later." Jackson responds.

What the hell, he didn't even tell me he loved me!

Later that night, me, Merissa, Jason, and Jackson head to the beach. This is our first time at the 21+ Beverly Mills Alumni Bonfire. We've heard so many stories about this annual event and now that we've received an invite, it feels like we've officially grown from Beverly Mills adolescents to Beverly Mills adults.

Jackson barely spoke to me in the car and I'm assuming he told Jason about everything that happened earlier this week just like I told Merissa every minute detail also. Unsurprisingly though, Jackson gets ready to put on a show once we walk to the beach. He throws his arm around me and gives me a big fake smile and a kiss on the cheek. I guess it's time for me to play his loving, doting girlfriend who just a few hours ago was hit with the cliché scape phrase 'we need space.'

"You want me to be fake happy, Jackson?" I look at him with disdain.

"Parker, not tonight. Let's just have a good time. Just be chill. All of Beverly Mills is here and ready to greet us." He says irritatingly.

"They're here to see you, Jackson. College's national football champion and soon-to-be first round draft pick, but sure, go ahead and put on your famous fake persona. I'll just hang around by my lonesome. It's whatever, Action Jackson."

As we approach a big crowd of former classmates and upperclassmen, I watch Jackson's 'on-screen' personality at work. He's handsome, charming, talkative, and even funny at times. He's everything that he's not behind closed doors. He's fake. Fake, fake, fake! I feel my anger and frustration getting the best of me. His arm's no longer around my shoulder. I don't even think he notices me right now. Grown ass women are throwing themselves all over him. Men are trying to get his attention to ask him questions about football. This is not my Jackson. I drift away from the crowd and find Jason and Merissa cozying up to one another at one of the fire pits.

"Hey, love birds. As cute as you two are right now, I can't help but be jealous."

"What? Jealous of us? We act like an old, boring couple. There's nothing to be jealous of." Merissa smiles back at Jason and nestles her head in his chest, and he kisses the top of her head in return.

"Oh my goodness, look at that right there! Y'all are adorable."

They both laugh and look at me with pained expressions. "Have you and Jackson spoken yet?" Ris asks.

I look back at Jackson to see him with his left arm around a thirsty fangirl while holding and a beer in his right hand.

"No, he's busy being Action Jackson right now so no time for me." I give them a fake smile and change the subject. "How's your sister doing?"

Ris' sister was doing so well after rehab. She started taking her meds, going to NA, and even began rebuilding her relationship with Ris and their mom. For almost two years she was on the right track until she started dating a guy she met in one of her meetings. It was too soon, way too soon.

"Uh, not great." Jason tightens his embrace to comfort Ris as she speaks.

"She called me last week and Jason and I almost fell for her con. She said she wanted to get clean again. We even researched facilities while we were on the phone, but by the end of the conversation when we were ready to take action, she flaked. She said a few dollars would suffice for now. I just want her to be okay. Mom says she isn't ready to be helped, but I don't understand how she can just give up on her own daughter like that."

"You and your mom's been through a lot too, babe. The lying, stealing, violent outbursts. Remember the nights your mom would drop you off to my house when we were kids so she could drive all night looking for her on street corners? She's been doing the same thing for years. Your mom's tired." Jason says.

"Iyanna's sick, Jace. Sick people need help the most." She cries.

I look at the two of them and I can't help but admire how they communicate and support one another. This is what Jackson and I used to do, but I don't even know the man I'm staring at anymore. A few seconds later, a different man appears in front of me and blocks my line of sight to Jackson.

"Excuse you, you're in my way." I look up and notice a flattering, familiar face. It's David.

"I know." He smiles at me with a twinkle in his eye. "May I sit?"

I look at Jason and Merissa. They shrug approvingly, but he specifically waits for me to respond.

"Sure, why not."

David sits next to me, close enough for me to feel his body heat but far away enough for us to maintain an appropriate distance from one another.

"Is this your first alumni bonfire?" He asks.

"Yeah, there are so many people here. It's kinda overwhelming." I try to keep my attention on David, but I can't help but worry about Jackson and the onslaught of women gathering around him.

"I'll be happy to distract you. I'm sure it can't be easy dating the famous Jackson Sands."

David tries to shift my focus from Jackson to him and I guess I could at least play into it a bit more, to protect my sanity at least.

Merissa and Jason join in on the conversation. "Try being his best friend. It's a whole job!"

We all laugh and David and I have small talk and get to know one another.

"Did you bring a date tonight?" I don't know why I just asked him that. It's none of my business.

"Yeah, which lucky Beverly Mills babe did you happen to bring?" Merissa chimes in.

David laughs and looks down embarrassingly. "Well, she's actually from our school, but after tonight, I don't think I'll be dating her anymore. She's been occupied for the past hour." He points his head towards Jackson's direction.

I squint my eyes to get a better look at the faces surrounding him and to my horror I notice the last person I want to see.

"Allie! You're dating Allie?"

Merissa nearly spits out her drink, and Jason has a wow expression on his face. David looks like a deer caught in headlights.

"Am I missing something here? I feel like I'm the only one who doesn't get the joke."

"Allie is obsessed with Jackson. She'll do anything and *anyone* just to get close to him."

For the first time tonight, I laugh harder than I have in weeks.

"How is this funny, Parker?" David asks.

"I don't even know. I don't know if I'm impressed at how much of a strategic stalker she is or if I'm shocked that you, a smart, handsome guy like yourself fell for her tricks."

While I continue to find humor in the situation, Jason and Merissa stop laughing and David looks at me with curiosity. What did I say? I think for a moment and realize that I may have just flirted with David Gallinari!

I try to clarify my statement, "I mean, you're obviously not an ugly guy. You're decent looking, definitely not better looking than my Jackson."

Oh crap. I just keep digging a deeper grave. David must think I'm an idiot, but he just laughs at me.

"You're all good, Parker Waylen. You're funny. Very interesting and funny."

He and I look at one another in blushing form, but Jason and Merissa look toward Jackson's direction. I notice their eyes moving and I turn around to see Jackson and Allie walking toward us. He has an unfazed confident expression on his face but he's looking directly at me and I can tell that he's pissed.

Jackson gives him a firm handshake and says, "David, it seems like you're always around Parker when I'm conveniently not around."

Dismissing Jackson's snide comment, David's turns on his staggering wit and charm.

"Beverly Mills is a small town so it's hard not to cross paths with the mesmerizing Parker Waylen." Jackson's presence doesn't seem to faze David. He flirtatiously smiles at me and Jackson moves towards me to mark his territory.

"Babe, aren't you gonna introduce me to your friends?" Allie asks while craving the attention that no one bothers to give her.

"Y'all, this is Allie, a friend from school."

She rolls her eyes and makes it apparent that she isn't happy. "Well, we were having a blast over there talking to all the small town locals about UGA life, football, and what not. Isn't that right Jackson?" She winks at him.

"Okay, this is all types of disrespectful." Merissa gets up, walks over to me, and grabs my hand. "Do you wanna get outta here?" She asks me.

I look up at Jackson to gauge what he's thinking. "Do you still wanna talk?"

"Yeah, let's do that." He says, still stoic, without regard or care.

"I'm gonna head out, too. I think it's time for me to take Allie back to her hometown where she belongs. Right, babe?" He nicknames her sarcastically, but the girl is such a nit wit. She doesn't even realize she's the butt of the joke.

David and Allie leave and Jason and Merissa wait up for us in the car. We sit down so we can address his infamous line 'we need space.'

"So, you're still entertaining David, huh?" He scoffs.

"I'm not entertaining anyone, Jackson. David's really nice and he's been nothing but respectful to me tonight. Yet, you let Allie fawn all over you. She touches your arm and shoulder, and she boldly flirts with you in front of my face, yet I'm entertaining David? Puh-lease! You're such a hypocrite. You want space from me anyway, remember?" I scoot further away from him, but Jackson moves in closer.

"I don't know what I want Parker, but I know what we're doing isn't working. Everything about us is just too intense for me to handle right now. You hover over me to the point I can't breathe. I don't even know what it's like to miss you."

"Well, I miss you every day, Jackson! I even miss you when you're with me because you're so distant. It's like you're trying to push me away. Is that what you want Jackson? Do you want to break up?"

"This is what I'm talking about! Everything with you is all or nothing. I just want us to slow down. Our entire relationship has been you making 'sacrifices' for me and that's not a relationship. It makes me feel bad because I'm not asking you to do that. I want you to be my girlfriend, not a martyr, not my nanny, and damn sure not my mom, Parker!"

His anger sharpens the cut of his words which sting me to my core. I always thought I was exactly what Jackson needed, *who* he needed to help keep his life on track. From the time we were kids to now, I've always cheered him up, distracted him from the pain of his mom's bouts with cancer, encouraged him, motivated him, and pleased him. I was always there for him. That's what best friends do. That's what people who love each other do. That's what soulmates do. Is my love too intense? Or is he just being ungrateful for everything I've done to keep us together?

"Jackson, I've never tried to guilt trip you over anything I've done for you. I love you and when people are in love they take care of one another!"

"You don't get it. I need space to breathe. I need space to figure out the next chapter of my life. I'm going to the NFL and you're going to med school next year. Maybe we should start adjusting to not spending as much time together is all I'm saying and the time we do spend together should be focused on fun like every other couple our age."

I still disagree. I don't do lighthearted fun, but I nod to appease his demands, anyway.

"I can dial back the intensity, Jackson, but you have to make some changes, too." I look down at the beer in his hand.

"How many times do we have to have this conversation?" He rolls his eyes and stands up to walk away.

"Until you do the right thing and get some help. Look," I grab his arm to stop him from walking away. "How is your behavior any different than your granddad? You drink so much and so often Jackson. It changes you. It makes you mean, dishonest, and dismissive, and you tend to take all your frustration out on our relationship."

I don't know if he's really listening to me, but he assures me yet again that he'll slow down.

"I'll try to do better, but I won't make any promises. I wish you could feel how hard it is to be me sometimes. My team depends on me. I have to stay on top of my schoolwork. I have to do intrusive, uncomfortable interviews. The town sees me as their hero. My life is constantly under a microscope. There's so much pressure and I feel like I'm gonna explode at any minute. Then there's you. You're always telling me what I should do, what I need to do, and that I'm not doing enough. If my mom was here, things would be so different, but she's not and I'm doing the best I can, Parker. I really am so if I want to have a drink to calm my nerves from the intensity of performing and pleasing everyone then that's what I'm gonna do, okay?"

We don't exactly come to a resolution, but it's the closest happy medium we'll reach and as long as we're still together, I'll settle for that. Jackson throws his arm around my shoulder and we leave the beach the same way we arrived, both displaying fake smiles portraying two young adults who appear to happily in love in Beverly Mills.

For the past month, Jackson and I have been working on implementing ways to have more 'fun' and I have to admit, we should've done this years ago. We agreed to spend as much time together as possible before he leaves for football training. No sad or heavy conversations, just unbridled fun and lots of sex! We even took a romantic couple's trip together.

This has been the perfect weekend getaway in New Orleans. We've enjoyed delicious beignets, second line parades, soothing jazz music, thrilling alligator tours, and flavorful Nawlin' style gumbo. I mean, we've taken plenty of trips before, but this one feels like such a breath of fresh air.

He's giving me the attention that I've been desperately craving for the last six months, and per his request, I've stopped monitoring his drinking for now and on our last night in New Orleans, we lay in one another's tipsy arms and enjoy pillow talk.

"I'm glad you decided to go back to work at the hospital for the remainder of your summer. I was worried you initially decided not to on account of wanting to spend time with me."

He moves my hair out my face to look me in my eyes.

"Well, initially, that was my plan." I laugh. "But I'm glad I'm working again too. I miss watching the doctors do their thing. I imagine myself doing the same, but lately I've been wondering if I'm really cut out for it, you know med school and becoming a doctor. I didn't really apply myself like I should've last year. I didn't even score as high as I needed to on my MCAT." I admit to Jackson.

"Parker, are you serious? Why didn't you tell me you've been struggling? I would've helped you or at least made sure you focused on your studies."

Challenging Jackson, I pounce on top of him and playfully pin him down by his wrists. "Do you really think you could've *made* me shift my focus from you to myself?"

"I've been told I could be very convincing, Miss Waylen," Jackson takes control and flips me over so I lay underneath him. "Nope." Jackson says and rolls over beside me.

"No what, Jackson?"

"No, I'm not doing anything with you until you get it through your hyper-intense brain that you need to stop worrying about me and focus on scoring higher on your exam. Do you want to be barefoot and pregnant popping out little Sands babies every year or do you want to be a well-respected doctor who saves people's lives every day?"

"Why can't I be both? Why can't I be your loving wife and mother to your kids *and* a well-respected doctor?"

"One life changing moment at a time, Parker. Focus on your number one priority which isn't me or marriage or babies. It's you, your career, your future, and your happiness. I'm gonna ignore you if you try to spend any extra time with me."

For the first time in a very long time, the tables are turned. He's worried about me the way I'm always worried about him.

"Okay, Jackson! I hear you. More studying, less obsessing over you. Now, can we have mind-blowing sex?"

"You're so sexy when you listen to me." Jackson whispers in my ears and trails kisses along my jaw.

"And you're so sexy when you tell me what to do." I ease my hand down into his gym shorts and begin to caress him. "Tell me what to do, Jackson."

He lays me on my side and pulls me closer to him so my backside rubs against his front. I grind against him until I feel his breaths get heavier as he slides his hand into my panties and his fingers inside of me.

"I wanna hear how good I make you feel, Parker. Moan for me."

I moan loudly and breathe heavily. Still spooning me, he removes his fingers then enters me so wildly I can vividly hear my skin clash against his.

"Do you hear how sexy that sounds?"

"Yes, Jackson!"

He puts his wet fingers in my mouth and I suck them dry.

"You love how sweet you taste, don't you, Parker?"

All I can do is moan and whimper as he dominates my body.

"You can have it all, Parker. Marriage, babies, career. We'll have it all together."

"I love you, Jackson Sands."

And with that said, we fall asleep in each other's arms content with how far we've come and ready to embrace the next phase of our lives, together.

We're halfway through our first semester of senior year and we spend way less time together, yet I think we're stronger and happier than ever before. My sole focus is passing the MCAT and getting into my top medical school of choice, Emory School of Medicine. Life couldn't be better.

And today's a bitter sweet day because it's homecoming. This time last year was a turning point in our relationship. Jackson disclosed his struggles with mental health but most importantly it was one of the last beautiful memories we made with Jackson's mom. She's was filled with so much joy to see her son play for the last time.

"Are you excited about your game, baby? It's our last homecoming ever!" I stand on my tippy toes to give Jackson a big kiss.

"Don't mention this to anyone, but I'm so nervous, I could damn near shit myself. College went by so fast. I don't think I could've survived without you, Parker. I love you."

"I love you, too. Now, c'mon you have a game to win and I have a certain someone to cheer for in the stands."

One thing Jackson Sands can do is throw that damn ball. Reporters, scouts, agents, and coaches have all been trying to get Jackson's attention all year. His precision is near perfect. He can run and throw under pressure. He's the future of the NFL and he's all mine. Merissa and I sit next to Frank and cheer as loud as we can for our beaus. I sometimes forget that Jason is even on the team. He doesn't care that he's been warming the bench for four years. He's a decent player, but he's passionate about politics. His family has the connections to put him in front of the right people, and his charisma is all he needs to put him in a position of power.

I can't believe the four of us managed to stick together through these chaotic years, and today is a day to remember. As the game clock nears the end, Jackson takes a step back for his last throw of the quarter, but as soon as the ball leaves his hands, a player from the opposing team lowers his helmet and slams into Jackson's shoulder. We can hear how hard he hits the ground. The crowd goes crazy in anger and concern on both sides of the field. The refs blow their whistles and commotion breaks out between the opposing teams. Jackson is still on the ground barely able to move. He tries to move his left arm over to grab his right shoulder but he winces in pain. Minutes pass and me and every fan in the stadium wait in angst as we watch college's #1 quarterback and the love of my life get medically assisted off the field by his trainers and team doctor. Frank rushes out the stands and head towards the locker room to check on his son.

"Parker, you need to go to Jackson, now." Merissa says. I nod and follow Frank accordingly.

Frank and Jackson are in the training room with the team's sports medicine staff. I wait for them for forty-five minutes after the game ends.

Reporters, students, and fans all wait around for news about Jackson's injury. I hear whispers and rumblings about whether it's a career ending injury and whether his future in the NFL is over. What pricks! Just a few hours ago, he was the best in college football and now all of a sudden, he's done for? The nerve of them!

"Can y'all all just go away! You're talking about Jackson as if he's not a person. This is his life, his health! If you don't actually give a damn about his well-being then get the hell away and stop using him for your own gain!"

I snap at the media and strangers who have no idea who my man is in real life and I don't regret it. Jackson's going to want privacy and he doesn't deserve to get hounded by these vultures after he just got pounded on the field.

A few minutes later, he comes out with his arm in a sling. He puts on a brave face for reporters and fans but I see right through his façade. He pulls me close with his good arm and gives me a kiss then in a low, discreet voice he says to Frank and I, "Y'all, please get me out of here. Please."

Without hesitation, we rush through the crowd, head to our cars, and drive to my apartment. We carry Jackson's equipment and bag inside and I place pillows on my couch to try to make it as comfortable as possible for him.

"What did the doctor and trainers say?" I ask the Sands men.

"He has to get x-rays on Monday, but they suspect he has a torn rotator cuff and dislocated shoulder."

Jackson throws one of his socks across the room out of frustration.

"In other words, my arm will never be the same. My career is over before it even began."

"Don't say that, Jackson. Don't assume anything just yet. This could very well be a minor injury. You'll be back on the field in no time playing in the SEC championship and getting your second national trophy. That should be what you're thinking about." I sit next to Jackson and massage his neck to help calm his nerves.

"Parker's right. Don't get down on yourself, Son. That dirty play isn't gonna trip you up. You're a Sands. Sands men can overcome anything, right?"

"Yeah, you're right, Dad." Frank and Jackson give one another a parting hug and I spend the rest of the evening taking care of him.

The next few days blow by fast. We expected the best, but we received the worst news. The hit caused a large tear in Jackson's rotator cuff. Jackson's out for the rest of the season.

The following week, he undergoes surgery and everyone who loves Jackson is here to support him through this difficult time especially Dr. Kaiser.

We've been shielding Jackson from tv and social media for days. He's the topic of every conversation and there's speculation about his future all across the airwaves. They say Jackson's draft chances have dropped from top 3 to 2nd round at best, but he doesn't need to know that.

"How long am I out, doc?" Jackson asks the surgeon.

"You had a large tear, Mr. Sands. You need to take care of yourself. No heavy lifting, wear your sling, and no alcohol. If you follow your post-op instructions, you could possibly be back on the field in six months."

"Six months? The draft is in four. How am I supposed to remove the recruiters' doubts if I can't throw the ball?" Jackson freaks out and grimaces in pain.

"Calm down, Son. Let's take it one day at a time. You're young and strong. It may not even take that long to heal." Frank places his hand on Jackson's good shoulder offering the hope he needs.

"In the meantime, Jason's moved your belongings into the apartment. Merissa's moved out and so has Avery. You're officially under my care."

"Us living together? This is either gonna go really well or really bad, Parker."

"Well, I'll use this experience as practice for the future. You're my first patient. C'mon, let's go home!"

Frank and I get settled in at my apartment. "I'm gonna leave you two alone to do whatever it is that you do. Take it easy, son. No television. No phone. Just rest and focus on the next day, alright?"

"Yes, sir and I'm sure Parker will enforce those rules, by any means necessary."

"You know it!" I chime in.

Jackson and I decide to lay low and refrain from going back to Beverly Mills for Christmas Break. We've had plenty visitors – coaches, trainers, Frank, my parents, Merissa, Jason, Avery, and Deacon. Company keeps Jackson distracted from the pain of his injury and sickening stress over his impending future.

After a long day of cuddling and relaxation, I still can't get Jackson to stop worrying.

"What if I never play again? Like, what if I recover but my arm isn't the same? It's happened to so many quarterbacks before. What makes me different than them?"

"What makes you the same as them? You're a Sands man, remember? You overcome obstacles over and over again. What if you do play again and prove all the nay sayers wrong?"

"So, there *are* nay sayers? Turn on the tv, please. I need to know what they're saying. My future's on the line. Please, Parker?" Knowing my most vulnerable parts, Jackson nibbles my ear and kisses my neck. "Five minutes, that's all I want." He begs.

I open the drawer to pull out the remote control and hand it to Jackson. Just as he suspected, his name is in every sports headline. *Will Jackson Sands recover in time to play next year? Is Jackson Sands still a top 5 pick? Is Jackson Sands strong enough to last in the NFL?* Every channel is questioning his ability to recover and maintain the same level of high-performance game play.

"Turn it off, Jackson. I see the anger in your eyes. Screw them. No one's as dedicated as you. I know you'll do what needs to be done to get back on that field. They get paid to be negative, but nobody knows you better than yourself. You're gonna recover and be twice as better than you were before."

"I hope you're right. Thank you for being here for me." Jackson kisses me on the forehead, and for the rest of the night, he looks over his rehab schedule and I study for my morning MCAT exam.

Let's just say these past few weeks have been on the up and up for me. Not only did I ace my MCAT but I met all of my application deadlines for my top medical schools of choice. I'm just three months away from earning my Bachelor of Science in Biology and with the help of Jackson and our difficult talk about giving one another emotional space, I was able to regain my focus and prioritize my studies. I don't often have moments to shine. I'm usually the girl rooting for the guy, but it feels really good to root for myself. I can get used to this.

What's also been easy to get used to is living with Jackson. I know he moved in so I could help him through his recovery, but we have a nice rhythm going. We go to classes, he goes to physical therapy, I come home to cook dinner, he comes home to eat, we do our schoolwork, shower, prep for the next day, and sleep peacefully next to one another. Our lives have become so drama-free, much less stressful than years before.

As we lay on the couch with Jackson's slinged arm propped up on pillows and my legs across his lap, I try my hardest to focus on my next practical exam but Jackson keeps throwing popcorn at me.

"What are you thinking about over there?"

"I'm trying to study. Maybe you should do the same. You have a test tomorrow in Professor King's Non-Profit Funding class, and you need to pass this course. It would look so bad if you fail this class right before you intend to launch your non-profit."

"Calm down, I got this in the bag. King's been helping me with the Be Strong, Hold On Project for weeks now. Everything's all set to launch in June. He even volunteered to participate in community outreach over the summer." Jackson nonchalantly informs me while flipping through channels.

"What the heck, Jackson! Why didn't you tell me about your launch? This is huge. I feel so out of the loop."

"Ah, don't be. Things are being set in motion so quickly. Just last week, Jason secured another donation. I'm telling you Be Strong, Hold On is going to help so many families. I'm talking about Make a Wish on steroids type of influence."

Jackson's been working so hard on his non-profit since the idea came to him our sophomore year. He's been waiting to launch after he gets drafted so it can gain the visibility it needs to make the biggest impact as possible. He doesn't mention his mom much anymore, but this organization is a symbol of how much she will always mean to him.

"So anyway, like I said. Don't worry about my class. I have a doctor's appointment tomorrow anyway, so I'm excused."

"Why do you have an appointment? It isn't time to check in again." Jackson has a few more weeks left until the doctor clears him to start training and participating in on-field practices again. He's recovered quicker than the average athlete, but I fear he may have overworked himself with his rehab and constant in-home exercises he's been doing to get back on the field.

"It's nothing serious. I just need another Oxy script. I still feel pain in my shoulder. Sometimes it's so painful, I can barely lift my arm. I just need some meds to dim down the pain." He shrugs.

"Be careful. Some doctors prescribe pain pills like candy. How many refills have you had already?"

Jackson shrugs again, "I dunno. Just a few."

"Jackson, at this point, you should only take them as needed. Actually, you shouldn't be taking them at all anymore. A regular aspirin or ibuprofen can help with your pain. It's much safer."

"You're not a doctor yet, Parker. If the doc recommends a light pain reliever, then I'll take that. If he doesn't, then I won't. He's gotten me this far so why would I not trust his judgment all of a sudden? In a few more weeks, I won't be in any pain, but until then I need my script and I need it bad." Jackson then raises his eyebrows in mischief, "Unless you have another medicine in mind that I can take."

"Oh, I got your medicine alright, Mr. Sands."

We flirt, laugh, and make love for the rest of the night and do the same for many weeks to follow up to Draft Day.

Jackson's been on edge for days, his doctor and trainer cleared him to begin on-field activities, but I'm still trying to determine whether it's because his shoulder is back at 100% or if it's a strategic move to improve his chances of getting drafted in the first round again. Either way, something doesn't feel right because I know for a fact that Jackson just picked up another Oxy script two days ago.

"Are you sure you don't want me to come with you? I've always wanted to make that *oh my God, I can't believe you got drafted* look in front of tv cameras."

"Knowing how dramatic you are, you'd probably go viral. But no, I think you should stay with your sisters. Izzy needs you."

"Are you sure? This is one of the biggest nights of your life. I feel so bad for not being there for you."

"You've been there for me every step of the way. You'll be with me tonight, too. Cheer for me through the screen. I'll be listening out for your loud mouth, and when I get back, I'll buy you as many hot Cheetos and cookie dough Frosties you want."

"You better, Jackson. I'm having cravings as we speak."

I lay my head on his chest and take in his homey scent of fresh linen and mint. We embrace one another and say our goodbyes then Jackson drives a little over an hour up the road to Atlanta for the NFL Draft.

My sisters arrive a short time later and it's the first time all three of us have been together in months. Avery and I planned this evening as a celebration of Izzy who just returned home from a treatment facility for individuals who struggle with eating disorders. I had no idea she was battling anorexia and apparently, she's been battling it for years. I've been so wrapped up in my life that I neglected my duties as a big sister.

Compared to Avery's rejection by her birth mother and a recent situation she refuses to discuss that's prompted her to transfer schools and Izzy's self-esteem issues, my problems and past troubles seem so minuscule. Yet, I'm so thankful that I'm finally in a healthy headspace to give them the love and support they need now.

After we eat dinner and watch a movie, we turn to ESPN to watch the draft.

"Does Jackson know if he's going in the first round or not?" Izzy asks.

"Not really. His coaches tried to get as much positive press as possible over the past few weeks. He's been giving interviews, and they've been filming his training sessions, but there hasn't been much response on the other end. I can tell he's stressed out, and if I'm completely honest with y'all, I don't think Jackson's shoulder is even half as healed as he's telling everyone."

I confide in my sisters about Jackson's desperation to get into the league. As much as I want him to fulfill his dream, I also don't want him to compromise his health which is exactly what I think is happening.

"Parker, if that's true, he could damage his arm permanently. Are you going to confront him?" Avery asks.

"Eventually, yes, but I don't know how much good it'll do at this point. If, I mean when he gets drafted and signs his contract then it's all gas and no brakes from here. He's not going to stop playing until he physically can't play anymore, and if I do confront him, then I'd be reverting back to dramatic, intense Parker who tries to control and micromanage Jackson's life. It's like I'm damned if I do and I'm damned if I don't." I huff and lay back on the couch in defeat.

"So basically, you're going to be a yes girl just like everyone else around him. How is that a relationship? You may think you're happy, but you're just allowing Jackson to have his way, and this issue is clearly bothering you. If you can't talk about this with him then your relationship's not as healthy as you think. I'm just saying, you might be hurting him more than you're helping him, Parker. Don't sweep this under the rug."

Avery's right. We've been getting along so well ever since Jackson told me to stop hounding him, but that may only be because I turned into a lap dog. All I've ever asked Jackson to do was to be better i.e. stop drinking, limit his partying, spend time with me, and communicate more. I guess we'll have to see how that goes now that life is returning back to normal. No more injury, no more sling, and no more lounging around the apartment anymore. Our perfect little bubble is about burst and I really hope we can survive the real word.

The draft's started and I'm getting restless. My nerves are so bad right now that I can barely keep my food down. The first, third, fifth, seventh, ninth, and eleventh pick have been called. None of them are Jackson. I'm trying to text him something funny, sweet, or encouraging after every pick to help keep him calm, but I'm running out of things to say. Finally, we hear the commentators mention Jackson's name. They're discussing the next team, The Miami Thunder, and their search for a young, dynamic quarterback. This might be Jackson's moment and he just texted, *I think this is it, babe.*

The announcer speaks, "For the fifteenth draft pick, the Miami Thunder select Jackson Sands."

My sisters and I hug one another and jump for joy! I can't control my tears and neither can Frank as he embraces his son. The pride on his face beams through the tv screen. This is the happiest night of my life. I know this is a huge accomplishment for Jackson, but I feel like it's an accomplishment for all of us – Jackson, Frank, Debbie, us, and all of Beverly Mills. I'm so proud of him and I can't wait for him to get home so we can celebrate.

About thirty minutes later, Jackson calls.

"Parker, we did it!" He screams.

"You did it, Jackson! I'm so happy for you. I haven't been able to stop smiling!"

"You and me both. It's crazy over here. I've given like five interviews already. I just wanted to call and tell you I love you."

"I love you, too."

"Alright, I gotta get back. It's gonna be a long night so my dad and I are gonna check into a hotel in the city. I'll text you when we're through. I can't wait to come home to you."

He still makes me blush. I love when he says home. I'll leave Jackson be for the night so he can tend to his post-draft obligations. My sisters and I spend the rest of the evening eating junk food, making fun of one another, and imagining my future with Jackson. Our lives have fallen perfectly into place. Passed the MCAT – check. Got accepted into Emory's Medical Program – check. First round draft pick – check. Graduation – almost! Our last hurrah is in three weeks and I am so amazed at how far we've come.

I've had knots in my stomach for days now. I feel weak and nauseas, and I can't shake this feeling that something bad is gonna happen and it's all because of Jackson. It's been three days since Jackson got drafted, and I've barely heard back from him. He told me he had next day meetings scheduled with the Thunder's coach and his new teammates. My response? Okay, cool, I understand. What I don't understand are the posts that I see online where he's popping bottles at a Miami nightclub. Random strangers are tagging me in posts of Jackson with all types of women all over him. The comments are insane.

This isn't Jackson's girlfriend.

Doesn't he date his high school sweetheart?

Major upgrade from his small town country girl.

So much for young love. He's in the big leagues now.

This man is so hot. I'd hate to be his girlfriend #sandstheman #actionjackson

I've blown a gasket since this fiasco began. My texts went from *Jackson, are you okay?* to *Jackson, you lying piece of shit!* really quick, and Merissa just texted me an SOS alert.

Merissa: Have you spoken to Jackson yet?

Parker: Nope. I've been going crazy waiting for him to call or text.

Merissa: You can make that happen tonight, here in Athens.

Parker: Merissa...explain.

She texts me a picture of Jackson at a party with his teammates.

Parker: Send me your location. I'm on my way.

I got your small town country girl! Without thinking, I hop in the car wearing Jackson's sweatshirt, my daisy dukes and Uggs to find Jackson Sands, who's seemingly America's new heartthrob, but I'm gonna rip him a new one! I'm fuming right now. He's been back in town for God knows how long and still hasn't bothered to call me and from what I can tell from everyone's social, it looks like he's been drinking, a lot, and I bet he's been taking those damn Oxys too.

I pull up to the party house and there has to be at least a couple hundred people here. I'm sure word got out that Jackson's back in town so everyone and their mama wants to hang out with UGA's quarterback turned NFL pro. I texted Merissa when I arrived so she's already waiting for me by the front door.

"It's about time. You gotta get your boy outta here. Jason and I just happened to be at the coffee house nearby and everyone was talking about a huge rager in honor of Jackson tonight. Lo behold, here we are! Jason's been trying to get him to cut back a little at least, but we've been here for forty-five minutes and I've seen Jackson down about six shots. He's right over there."

Merissa points me in Jackson's direction and I push pass the crowd of people to make my way to him. Jason pulls him down from the couch and meets me halfway. As soon as Jackson sees me, his eyes go wide and he flashes a silly smile on his face.

"Hey everyone! Parker's here. My girl is in the building!" He wraps his arms around me and spins me around.

"Put me down, Jackson," I wiggle out of his grasp. "What the hell is wrong with you? You've been m.i.a. for days. You ignored all my calls and texts. I've been sick to my stomach worrying about you. But then I see you all over social galivanting in Miami of all places! Is this how things are gonna be now? If so, I'm not having it, Jackson. I will leave and never see you, again!"

Many eyes are on us now so Jackson takes my hand and leads me outside. He breathes in the night's air and looks at me again.

"The world is ours, Parker," He grabs the sides of my face with his hand and kisses my forehead then lowers his head to kiss my lips.

"Jackson, slow down for a minute," I push his arm away to regain control of the situation, it flinches and he winces in pain at my touch. "Jackson, let's go home. We can celebrate together and properly without all these strangers. I can take care of your arm, too." I whisper discreetly, but he pulls away.

"C'mon, babe. It'll just be a little while longer. This is a big deal. We're a big deal, Parker."

"No, Jackson," As much as I don't want to make a scene, seeing Jackson behave recklessly worries me and his cavalier attitude towards me is really starting to piss me off. "Where's your phone? Why haven't you responded to any of my texts or calls? Why do I have to be tagged and ridiculed on social media by strangers on pictures of you partying with other women?"

Jackson looks confused as if he caught a bout of temporary amnesia, but he quickly regains his memory. "Oh crap, I'm sorry, Parker. I broke my phone on draft night. I ordered another one and it should arrive in the mail tomorrow. I haven't had any down time to update you."

"But you had enough down time to go to a club? You had enough down time to go from Atlanta to Miami!"

"My new teammates dragged me there. It was like a team bonding experience. I couldn't turn them down. I didn't want to make a bad first impression. I didn't pay attention to any of those women. I promise. I imagine you were losing your mind at home. I'm really sorry, babe. I didn't mean to be so stupid." Jackson inches closer to me and almost makes me forget about his screw up until he nearly stumbles over his feet.

I come back to my senses and see him for what he is in the moment, drunk and full of shit. I won't let him off easy, not this time.

"Jackson, come home with me now or don't come home tonight at all. Your choice."

We stand toe to toe and I wait for him to respond. He rubs his red, tired eyes and releases a sigh of frustration.

"Okay. Let's go home."

Jackson opens the driver's side door for me then walks around to the passenger side, but he lets go of the handle. "I forgot my team bag in Hank's room. I'll be right back. I'm gonna go and grab it. Three minutes, Parker. Just give me three minutes."

Jackson runs back in the house to get his belongings, but one minute quickly turns into three then five then ten then fifteen. The party is getting rowdier with people coming and going and I just want to get home so I don't have to be on the road with a bunch of drunk idiots.

I roll down my window and ask a few students to please tell Jackson to hurry up. They look at each other, laugh off my request, and enter the house party. I wait a few more minutes, but it's getting late and I need to study for my final exams. I can't be Jackson's babysitter for much longer so I text Merissa and Jason to let them know I tried as well, but to no avail.

The craziest, wildest parties are always thrown at the end of the semester and Jackson may have reached his goal of going to the pros, but we still need to pass our exams and walk across that stage in two weeks.

I'm trying my best to drive slowly and watch out for student pedestrians, but it's freaking dark out here and I still feel nauseous with worry. I can't take this feeling anymore. I'm a few miles away from my apartment, and the streets finally look clear so I pull over on the side of the road next to a tree and puke my brains out. As soon as I lift my head, I bend back over to puke some more. I can't make it stop and I'm gagging in pain. This night couldn't get any worse.

Still tired, weak, and on the verge on vomiting again, I slowly walk back to my car, but before I could make it to my door, a car full of loud students wailing out their windows and blasting music zips around the sharp curb. The driver's going so fast and barely gripping the wheel, and the car on the opposite side of the road flashes its bright lights blinding the loud and wild man driving the car. For a millisecond, he makes eye contact with me which sends him into further panic and he loses control of his steering wheel. He drives off the road and my only reaction, the only thing I have time to do is to open my car door to protect myself, but that isn't enough.

Boom! Is all I hear, all I see, all I feel. My energy instantly leaves my body. I feel powerless and consumed with pain. I see red. I see blood when I look down. I can't move. My feet are about an inch above the ground. I'm smashed between two cars and I'm in so much pain that it hurts to even think, but I must be in shock because I speak right away.

"This can't be the end."

My manic breathing is slowing down. It's getting slower, slower, and slower. I felt like something bad was gonna happen tonight, but I never fathomed it'd be this. How'd I get here? How is it I've lived my entire life for Jackson, only to die because of him. I'm surrounded by people yelling for help, yet I'm all alone.

"Miss, stay awake please! The ambulance is on its way."

"Don't let me die like this, please, not like this. Call Jackson. Call my mom. Please, don't let me die." I release a weak, desperate cry.

And just like that, it all goes to black.

I open my eyes slowly to combat the bright, blinding light directly above my face.

"Wayne, look she's waking up. She's waking up!" I hear a shaky yet familiar voice to my left.

"Parker?" Another frightened yet familiar voice calls out my name.

I lay in a low inclined position wrought with confusion about where I am or what's happening to me. My casted arm is in so much pain but that's nothing compared to my leg, or my thigh, or my knee – I can't even tell what's damaged. My entire leg is slightly raised and overwhelmed with metal rods and contraptions so I freak out and try to wiggle my hips to adjust myself to sit a little higher.

"Ahh!" I scream super shocked by the pain I now feel on the right side of my stomach, maybe my abdomen. "What's going on? What's happened to me?" I look to my left where I see my mom and dad, who have a well of tears flowing down their faces.

My heart's beating fast and I just want answers. I look to my right to see Jackson, Merissa, Jason, Avery, and Izzy. The doctor comes in and asks for everyone to leave the room, but I insist they stay.

"Miss Waylen. You've been unconscious for four days. Do you remember anything about the accident?"

I can't remember everything verbatim, but I still try to recollect the events from the other night. "I went to a party to take Jackson home," I look up at his teary-eyed face but he lowers his head in disgrace. "But I left alone. I wasn't feeling well. So, I –" Pain takes over my body again to the point I can't finish my sentence.

"It's okay. Take your time, Parker. You just endured immense trauma to your body. Don't over exert yourself in any way." The doctor says.

"No, it's okay. I can continue. I remember pulling over to the side of the road to throw up. I've been so stressed, tired, and nauseous lately. I've been worrying myself sick or I must've caught some type of bug." My mom and Izzy's faces are spent with grief and sadness while Avery and my dad's faces are filled with sadness and anger. Merissa turns to Jason and he comforts her in his arms. Jackson cries softly. I see that he wants to come closer to me, but he stops himself.

I continue to tell them what happened, "A driver came round' the corner, lost control and his car crashed into me. That's all I can remember. All I know is I thought I was gonna die." Thinking about my accident expends all of my energy. I close my eyes, take a deep breath, and ask the doctor to tell me what happened next.

"Well, the great news is that you're alive, Parker. Based on the injuries you sustained and the amount of blood you lost, the odds of your survival were slim to none. Your left leg only sustained minor bruising from the crash and your right shoulder was dislocated due to the immediate impact of it slamming against your car. We did, however, have to conduct two surgeries to repair your torn acl, broken shin, and broken femur shaft or what may know as the thigh bone. Based on the severity of your fracture, we would expect, with the proper care and physical therapy, a year to fully heal and recover."

"A year?" I react subconsciously to the doctor's bad news and jerk my body forward. "Ah, dammit!" I scream again and start to panic. I try to locate where my pain is coming, but it's everywhere. "What's happening?"

"Please, try to lay back, Parker. Your body is fragile at the moment and you have to try to do as little as possible and that especially means no sitting up right now." The doctor hesitates but continues to speak, "I'm not sure if I feel comfortable to proceed. It's also against hospital policy to have this many people in the room at once. I think I should tell you the next details in private."

"We're not leaving Parker's side." Avery says sternly.

"It's okay. I'll be fine, y'all. Can my parents stay at least?"

"I think that's a good idea." The doctor answers.

"Jackson?" I look to him to see if he's going to come closer to me or stay nestled in the corner of the room.

"Parker's awake now, Jackson. You can leave." My dad says coldly.

"Dad, please. I can fight my own battles. Jackson can stay, for now."

Merissa, Jason, and my sisters wait outside the door. Jackson slowly moves to my right side, sits in a chair, and squeezes my hand to help brace me for what comes next.

"The most extensive damage you endured was to your abdomen. Your uterus to be exact. When the car crashed, a metal bar from the grill of the car pierced directly through you. The amount of blood loss was extreme and even more so was the damage to your baby's gestational sac. We tried," The doctor clears her throat. "We tried everything, but we couldn't save your baby."

I feel Jackson's tears on the top of my hand. I'm in shock. I shake my head in disbelief.

"What're you talking about? I wasn't pregnant. What do you mean, my baby?" I ask the doctor.

"You were at least 12 weeks pregnant, Parker."

I'm immediately overwhelmed with tears. "No. No, no, no, no. That's crazy. I wasn't. I wasn't pregnant. I would've known. No, you're lying. There's no way I was pregnant. There's no way I lost my baby."

My eyes are blurry and my face feels hot. I look to my mom and her face lets me know the doctor's telling the truth.

"Umn, umn." I shake my head and wipe my eyes. "No, no, no. Show me my baby, then. Give me my baby, now! Where is she, huh? Where's my baby? If I had a baby, give her to me, now. Where is my baby?" My angered tone is drowned out by tears and heavy breathing. All I can do is sob, pant, and sniffle. I can't believe this is happening.

"I'm sorry, Parker. Your baby's gone." The doctor reiterates.

"No, you're lying! Somebody, please tell me. Where's my baby? Please, please, please, please. Tell me where's my baby? This can't be happening. Mom? Dad?"

My gasps are so loud and my nose is stuffy from crying. My world is crashing down on me. I just lost my child. It's someone I never knew existed until now yet I feel like my everything has been taken away from me. I look down to my right to see Jackson uttering sorry over and over again.

"Jackson, where's our baby? What happened to my baby? Don't tell me I lost my baby. Please, just let me see it." My mother runs two steps over to be closer to me and kisses my forehead. I take turns sniffling and crying hysterically.

"We're here. We're here, baby girl. Let it out. Let it all out, Parker." My mom brings my head to her chest.

"I'm so sorry for your loss, Miss Waylen," The doctor interrupts. "If you want me to come back in a moment to discuss the outcome of your abdominal surgery, I can. This is a lot to handle, and I would like to give you time to process."

"What more is there to say? What else is there, mama? I don't want to hear anything else. Everything I ever wanted is gone."

My mom tries to comfort me, but it doesn't work. "I know, Parker, but we'll be here. We're here for the next part."

She nods to the doctor to continue.

"As I mentioned, there was a lot of blood loss. We tried to control the bleeding, but the vessels that provide normal blood circulation to your uterus were too severely damaged. You went into hemorrhagic shock so we needed to perform a blood transfusion and –" She sighs. "In very rare cases such as this, in order to save your life, we had no choice but to perform an emergency hysterectomy."

A combined cry and laugh of disbelief escape my mouth, "A hysterectomy?" My eyes move back and forth from my parents to Jackson and once again I'm overcome with sorrow.

"That means I can't have another baby. I just lost a baby and I'll never have a baby again? This can't be real. Why is this happening to me? Please, tell me mama, why? Dad, what'd I do wrong? Why would God do this to me? I don't know what I did wrong, but I'm so sorry. I'm so so sorry. Please, I've tried to be good all my life. But what'd I do so bad to deserve this? I just want my baby back. I want my life back. I wanna be whole again. Everything's been taken from me. Everything."

My mom holds me the best she can without hurting my bruised and broken body. My tears have blocked my vision, but I feel Jackson's rough hand brush against mine. I look at him one last time and I unleash my pain, anger, and hurt in a fit of somber cries.

"You ruined me, Jackson! I loved you. I protected you. I supported you. I bled for you. I'm bleeding because of you. I've given you my everything and you've taken everything from me in return. You broke me. You killed our baby! How could you do this to us?" I'm exhausted. I'm tired. I'm weak. I can't say anything else.

"You should leave now, Jackson." My dad says.

Jackson looks at me, then at my parents, and back at me again. "Parker, I love you."

"Now!" My dad's voice is so loud, it rings through the halls of the hospital.

Jason comes into the room to pull a pitiful Jackson away and out of my life. I don't know how I'm going to recover from this or if I ever will, but I'll never allow myself to be so consumed with love that I abandon my better judgment and common sense. I'll never put anyone before myself again. Starting now, I have to think about what's best for me. I have to rethink my entire life specifically one that doesn't include graduation next week, med school in the fall, and getting married and having children with Jackson Sands, the man who shattered my world and broke me into a million pieces.

Chapter 12

The Anniversary Party - Parker

I can't believe it's been a month since Jackson and I started dating again. It still feels unreal. We aren't exclusive, but it seems we only have eyes for one another. We also haven't had any arguments or meltdowns. I haven't called him a piece of shit and we haven't ghosted one another…yet. So maybe maturity does come with age.

"What're you daydreaming about over there?" Jackson eyes me from across the room.

He just got out the shower and he looks so hot and steamy.

"You wanna know what I'm thinking now or five minutes ago?"

"I think I know what you're thinking now," He sprawls across my bed wearing nothing but a towel. "What were you in deep thought about?"

"I was just thinking about us. The past few weeks have been so good and so unchallenging. I guess I'm wondering whether things are just too good to be true, ya know?"

"No, I don't," Jackson answers. "We're finally at a point where we can stop waiting for the worst to happen. It's time to live Parker, and tonight is the perfect night."

"The perfect night for what exactly, Jackson?"

"For us to go public with our relationship."

"We pretty much already are. We've been out on like ten dates, what's more public than that?"

"I don't want to be afraid or hesitant to kiss you when we're out in public. I want everyone to know that we're back together, especially David."

"David? Here you go, again. David are I are the past. I just need time to think about what you're asking. I want to be with you but thirty good days is just too soon and it doesn't erase 8 years of bad history between us."

Jackson rolls his eyes and hops off my bed, "I'm getting dressed."

"What? Where are you going? Are you seriously gonna act like a little kid?"

"I'm gonna go pick up my suit. I have to make sure I look my best so your ex doesn't try to sweep you off your feet tonight."

I laugh so hard that I can barely contain myself, "Oh, this is funny! The millionaire heartthrob Jackson Sands is intimidated by a little competition."

Jackson quickly regains his confidence, tilts my chin upward, and gives me a short yet sweet kiss on the lips. "No one can compete with me."

My eyes are still closed, and my mouth begs for more.

"You're such a tease, Jackson."

"I'll see you tonight."

That same morning, I meet up with the girls for our monthly mani, pedi & champagne appointment.

"Hey, hey, hey, my beautiful Beverly Millinites!" Merissa greets everyone in the salon. The town loves their Mayoress.

"Merissa, I would've never pegged you to be the political type. Remember when you had that rebellious streak back in high school?" Avery says.

"Who didn't rebel in high school?"

"I didn't." Izzy raises her hand.

"Aw, that's true. You were too obsessed with Disney movies and naming flowers after me and Jackson."

"Don't remind me of that! I was so lame back then. And thin. So, so, thin." Izzy leans back in her chair in embarrassment.

"Don't be so hard on yourself, Iz. I was having an identity crisis at sixteen. Parker was chasing Jackson's tail around town like a puppy, and Merissa picked the lock to the principal's office door, twice!"

"Hold on, what? Merissa!" Izzy gasps.

"Listen, we all had our fair share of issues back then but look at us now, though. We're killin' this game of life. But I think out of everyone so far, Parker's changed the most." Merissa says.

"I agree. We've watched you rise from the ashes, girl. I'm still amazed at how strong you are." Avery compliments.

"Oh please. Y'all are just saying that. My strength's no more than yours, especially yours, Avery. It helps that we have each other, too."

We take a moment to appreciate one another and Merissa proposes a toast. "To the Waylen sisters and the Mayoress Pierce. May we continue to fulfill our dreams, make beautiful memories, and live happily in love."

Avery, Izzy, and I guzzle down our champagne but Merissa places her flute back in her cup holder. "Ris, don't be a party pooper. Drink up!"

"No drinking for me. I think I'm going to hold off on alcohol for a little while, at least for a couple more months." Merissa smiles and places her hand on her stomach.

We get the hint, and we're filled with excitement and joy over Merissa's news.

"Oh my god, you're pregnant!" I hop out my chair midway through my pedi to run over to Merissa and give her a hug. "This is so exciting! Congrats, Ris. When'd you find out? What'd Jason say? How far along are you?"

"Just gimme a sec!" She tries to gather her thoughts.

"Thirteen weeks! After so many miscarriages, we lost faith, but at least we're finally past the first trimester. Still, please don't say anything to anyone. We want to wait until I'm either that damn obvious or until late second trimester – whichever comes first."

"You're asking us to keep the most exciting news we've heard all year a secret?" Izzy asks.

"We'll try, but the moment I see Jason, I'm giving him a high five." Avery laughs.

"Have you thought of baby names, yet?" Izzy asks Merissa.

"Of course, I have! If it's boy, we'll name him Jason Harmon Pierce III. If it's a girl, we'll name her Ashlyn Iyanna Pierce." Our hearts break at the mention of her sister's name.

"Those are beautiful names, Ris. Boy or girl, I'm gonna spoil Baby Pierce. If Jason thought he couldn't get time with his wife now, just he wait. He's gonna have to call the police to keep me away from you and that baby."

I give Merissa one more hug and think about the beautiful bundle of joy that'll enter our lives soon.

While my sisters are busy on chatting with Izzy's followers on live, Merissa looks to me and whispers, "I really appreciate how happy you are for me. You've always been like a sister to me, but I hope my news doesn't bring up any painful memories."

"Thanks, Merissa. I'm fine. Nothing can overshadow the joy I feel right now, and you and Jason deserve this. You're my best friends, and I know that baby's gonna be sassy, strong, and fabulous like *her* mama and Aunt Parker."

I'm telling Merissa the truth. I used to feel so much sadness at the mention of pregnancies and babies. I used to break down at the mere thought. It hurt, and I'm sure if I were to continue to dwell on the things I can't have, I'd be in tears right now, but I'm not in that place anymore. I'm better. I no longer feel broken because I know I'm not.

"What are y'all wearing tonight to the party?" Avery interrupts our heartfelt moment.

"Well, the theme is A Glamorous Spring in Beverly Mills, whatever that means," Merissa sneers at me since I chose it. "So, Jason's going to wear a fitted emerald green tux with black accents to match my tight mermaid dress. I want to show off my figure as much as I can before this baby starts bumpin'. What about you, Avery?"

"I'm wearing a red tulle dress with a sexy high split and a plunging neckline!"

Avery's going to look gorgeous. If I had a body like hers and a face like that then I would wear the exact same thing.

"You go girl! What is Deacon gonna wear?" Merissa asks Avery.

"How should I know? We aren't 'on' right now, but hopefully he wears red, too." Avery looks worried.

"Oh goodness, here we go again!" Izzy huffs and rolls her eyes.

Merissa and I feel the exact same way. Avery and Deacon have the most complicated relationship.

"I told y'all, Deacon's my best friend with occasional benefits. He can do whatever he wants and I can do whatever I want." Avery explains.

"I just don't get how that works. If Jackson even dared talking to another woman, I'd kill both of them. I'm getting angry just thinking about it."

"Whoa, Parker. I thought that crazy side of you didn't exist anymore." Avery laughs.

"Oh, she's alive and well, just tucked away in a cage ready to pounce in case Jackson screws up again."

"I'm so glad I don't have to worry about that. I enjoy being single and I don't want to ruin the relationship I have with Deacon by being in an actual relationship with him. He and dad are the only men I could ever count on in my life. I don't want to lose that. But I do know, he better not bring a plus one tonight especially this new girl named Alyssa that keeps popping up out of nowhere. I really don't like her."

We all know Avery and Deacon are a perfect match. He may have a reputation as the slutty sheriff, but he'd do anything for Avery. A few years ago, when she met her birth father for the first time, guess who was right by her side? Not me, not mom, not dad, not Izzy, but Deacon. They love each other, and I can't wait until they finally admit it.

"Izzy, what are you gonna wear tonight? Or what type of flower print are you gonna wear?" I ask.

"It's a surprise. A few of my followers actually designed some dresses for me to wear. I'm gonna reveal my choice on Live, tonight!"

"Why would you chance something like that? You don't even know these people." Avery says.

"But I do. I love my little lilies and they love me. I've captured my entire life online since high school. They've seen me struggle with my weight. They know your stories. They met my birth family. They do know me, and it makes me feel good to know that I've help so many of them who experience similar journeys as me. Plus, I'll be helping a young, budding designer build their business. Hundreds of thousands of people will get to see their design."

"I guess that makes sense. I love what you're doing for people, but please be careful. There are lots of crazies out here and you're opening yourself up to danger by being so open with everyone." Avery warns.

"Thanks for your concern, big sis, but if anyone were to ever bother me, I have a whole village ready and willing to fight for me."

"Do one of those villagers happen to be my brother? What the heck is going on with you and Gabe? You two are so secretive. The thought of y'all boning is driving me nuts!" Merissa squeals.

"Boning? Now hold on, we haven't had sex, yet." Izzy's face looks frightened. She basically cringed at the word sex.

"Izzy, are you still a virgin?" I ask.

She pauses. We all pause and wait for Izzy to answer.

"That's none of your business!" Izzy avoids eye contact.

"What the hell, Izzy? You've had boyfriends. You really haven't you done the deed? You're a twenty-five year old virgin. That's *very* rare." Avery rubs her hands together and begins to concoct a scheme in her head.

"Oh no, Avery. I see those wheels spinning. Don't even think about trying to plan Operation Get Izzy Laid! When it happens, it happens. I'm not waiting for my prince charming or saving myself for marriage or anything like that. I just haven't had a desire to, do *it*."

"Say it." Avery tells Izzy. "Say the word sex, you dirty little virgin you."

"Ugh, sex! I haven't had a desire to have sex." Izzy raises her voice and covers his face in embarrassment.

"I think it's cute, Izzy. There's no time limit on when to have sex."

"Thanks, Parker. The frustrating thing about myself is that I'm super confident when it comes to decorating, arranging flowers, and talking to thousands of people online, but I suck at dating and men don't really desire me especially when they find out I'm a Waylen. It's hard being the younger sister to you two. I've always been seen as 'innocent' which translates to boring and naïve, if you ask me. No guy *actually* wants that. They want the assertive, gorgeous southern belle type like you Parker or the confident, sexy supermodel type like you Avery or the ideal wife type like you Merissa."

Avery interrupts Izzy and grabs her hand. "Or the stunning, charming, and kind type like you Izzy."

Izzy's cheeks go red. "Thanks, Avery."

"Well, I happen to know that your kindness has surely done something to my little brother. I haven't seen him smile in a very long time until you showed up in his life. My parents are so happy to see Gabe smile again and it's all because of you. Don't underestimate how amazing you are, Izzy"

Izzy may not actively struggle with anorexia anymore, but she definitely still struggles with self-esteem issues. She's so beautiful. I wish she could see what we all see. Someday she will, and I look forward to supporting her through that journey.

"Thanks. Gabe is special to me. I hope he can feel the same about me one day. I really want to find love, but honestly, I haven't really had many examples for what a healthy relationship looks like."

How could Izzy think that? She's surrounded by love in Beverly Mills. "What the heck, Izzy. We *are* attending mom and dad's 30th anniversary celebration tonight! What's more healthier than that?"

"They're old. I'm talking about young, happy couples that are in love and thriving. Merissa and Jason, y'all are a good example, but at the same time, y'all are kinda kinky and have lots of sex in public. No offense to you Avery, but I think your whole arrangement with Deacon sounds fun, but I think its gonna lead to heartbreak. Parker, you and Jackson just got back together and let's not talk about the stress y'all put us through for years. I'm glad that y'all are giving it another go but being in an emotionally charged relationship isn't appealing to me."

"Wow, you just ripped us to shreds, Izzy. Once you decide to take a risk, you'll see that relationships aren't like the fairy tales in your Disney stories. But I do agree with you about Parker," Avery says. "Everyone loves a good second chance love story, but Jackson was the original gas lighter. He's growing on me now, but back in school, he was sketch as hell. I was fed up Junior year when Parker planned a romantic night for their anniversary and in classic Jackson form, he bailed at the last minute. Parker was pissed off and sent him raging texts about his lack of effort and his response? *Parker, it's not that serious. We'll have plenty more anniversaries to celebrate.* Ugh, I can't!"

"To be fair, he was going through a lot that year and Parker isn't innocent!" Merissa says. "Parker has mastered the art of the savior complex.

She'd guilt trip Jackson every chance she got. She'd volunteer to do things then hold it over his head."

"Ah, yes! You remember her go to line? 'After everything I've done for you!' " Avery laughs.

I'm just sitting here watching my sisters and best friend make jokes about my love and dedication to Jackson. "How dare y'all. First of all, I'm right here. Secondly, I only wanted to remind Jackson of how much effort I put into the relationship."

Izzy chimes in, "Oh, we know how much effort, Parker. You reminded everyone, everyday! But okay, okay, enough teasing. Your turn. What are you and Jackson wearing to the party?"

"It's a surprise. Just know as the mistress of ceremony, I'm going to look dazzling and Jackson will be my trophy husband."

Izzy's eyes go wide as if I said a forbidden word. "Husband? Whoa, slow down, sis. Have y'all even discussed marriage yet?"

"No, not really. I mean, he mentioned marriage a few times, but nothing major. We haven't actively discussed it. Should I be worried?"

"It's only been a month since you've rekindled your relationship, but I do think it's important to make sure y'all are on the same page. I've never heard him and Jason talk about anything other than football when I'm around so I can't help you there, but given that sham engagement he had years back, maybe his thoughts on marriage have changed – for the worst."

Much of the remainder of our morning consists of drinking more champagne and freaking Izzy out with our wild sex stories. By the time we finish bonding, I'm starving and ready to go home to spend time with Jackson.

As soon as I pull up to my house, I see Jackson waiting patiently for me.

"I think it might be time for me to get a key."

"Hold your horses, cowboy. You have to earn that right. Besides, I kinda like seeing you out here in the heat waiting for me to rescue you."

I'm barely next to him, but Jackson's already prepared to envelop me in his strong, warm embrace.

"Get over here, already. I've missed you." He says as leans back on his car and wraps me in his arms. We take a deep inhale of one another's sweet calming aromas that we've longed to smell again after being away from one another for so many years.

"Honey and vanilla."

"Mint and fresh linens."

"Home." We say in unison and stare deep into one another's eyes and smile.

After we grab the groceries out the car, Jackson turns to me and asks, "You ready to eat?"

"Eat what, Jackson? Are you gonna cook?"

Jackson's never cooked for me before. The most I've seen him make was oatmeal and scrambled eggs, occasionally.

"Why yes, I am. You're going to sit back and relax on the couch, while I serve brunch."

"I like the sound of that, Mr. Sands."

I stretch my body across the couch and watch Jackson show off in the kitchen. He pulls out the eggs, bread, vanilla, bacon and milk. I'm getting so turned on just watching him in my kitchen wearing a tank, jeans, and my 'Kiss the Chef' apron with a wash towel over his shoulder.

"So, where'd you learn how to cook?"

"In rehab," Jackson answers as he masterfully cooks French toast and scrambled eggs. "The in-patient center used to offer all types of stress relieving classes and fun things for us to do in-between treatments and group sessions. I realized I needed to take advantage of the cooking class when I was hungry one night and the only thing I knew how to make was a pb&j. I started taking classes, learned a few recipes, and explored new ways to add a twist of fun to my dishes. When I got out of rehab, my classes came in handy when Jax would spend the night with me because, to my surprise, he loves watching the food channel. We cook all types of meals – homemade lasagna, spaghetti, mac and cheese, pizza you name it and Jax and I will bake it."

"It seems like rehab served you well."

"It was the best thing that ever happened to me after my public meltdown. Don't get me wrong, there are times when I still struggle. I called my sponsor that day we were in the parking garage after you kissed me and ran away. I just needed to reset my mind. Everything's unpredictable with us and our past is painful. I knew I'd feel anxious and stressed, but I'm not the prideful or embarrassed knucklehead I used to be so I'm not afraid to seek help or take a step back to refocus."

I smile at Jackson's maturity, but I'm also apprehensive because I don't want to be his kryptonite. I don't want to be the reason he relapses. "Do you think it's healthy for us to be together? I don't want us, this relationship, to be the catalyst that spirals you back into drinking."

"Our relationship is the exact opposite, Parker. Our relationship is home. It's what's motivated me to stop drinking. It's what connects me to the good memories of my mom. It's what's kept me sane all my life. I should've OD'd, but it was our bond that didn't allow me to break."

I walk to Jackson who's now prepping the table with syrup drizzled french toast, cheesy scrambled eggs, turkey bacon, fresh strawberries, cantaloupe, and bright orange mocktails poured in champagne flutes. I clasp my arms around his neck, and he places his strong hands on the nape of my back then kisses my forehead. Before he can walk away to finish his presentation, I beg for more.

"Don't stop. I love your touch."

Jackson's hot breath on my skin gives me goosebumps as he slides his lips from my forehead down to the bridge of my nose. He lifts my chin, and gives me a sweet peck on the lips.

"Let's eat." He smiles.

Still in the mood to wine and dine me, Jackson pulls out my chair and hands me one of his signature drinks. "This is a non-alcoholic concoction that I like to call The Jack-in-the-Box. Do you like it?"

I take a sip of the drink and I can't believe how delicious it is! It's rich, smoky, and sweet.

"Oh my goodness, Jackson. This taste so refreshing."

"I aim to please ma'am." Jackson walks to the other side of the table to sit down to eat his food.

Like every day for the past month, we sit comfortably at the table and enjoy each other's company exchanging sexually flirtatious glances and making sensual noises with every delicious bite.

"Thank you, Jackson. I don't know what's more delicious – the food or you." I raise my eyebrow and try to give my best seductive facial expression.

"Don't get me started, Parker. We've got a few hours until the party starts. There's a lot more we can do with this food other than eating it. If you want us to be late to the party, just say so."

"Ooh, don't tempt me with a sticky time." Ready to accept my challenge, Jackson gets up from the table and walks behind me. I feel his body heat overpowering mine. He leans over my shoulder and swirls his index finger in the saucer of warm syrup. He drops drizzles down my neck, chest, and in between the crease of my breasts. I turn to look him in the eyes and level my mouth to meet his sweetly drenched finger. He watches me suck every bit of syrup off his finger and when he thinks I'm finished, I maneuver my tongue to nudge a second finger in my mouth.

"You taste so good," He tells me as he sucks my neck clean and swipes his tongue across the top of my breasts. "How much time do we have?" He takes his fingers out my mouth and looks at me with hunger and desperation.

"Three hours." I breath heavily and I consider taking control of Jackson, right here and now, but he beats me to the punch. Before I can say anything else, he lifts me up and lays me on the table. He pulls my shorts down and I quickly pull my shirt over my head and lay bare naked under his deep, crippling gaze.

"You're a work of art, Parker." Jackson pours warm syrup and whipped cream all over me. He licks every crevice of my body excruciatingly slow. I moan and giggle at his every touch, and he feeds me strawberries while he feasts on me.

"You taste so sweet." He sits strategically between my legs then gives me a mischievous look as he grabs one of the strawberries off the table.

I raise my brows in curiosity. "And what are you gonna do with that, Jackson?"

He smiles and says, "Finish my desert."

Jackson takes the cold strawberry and dips it inside me.

"Jackson," I yell. With his mouth suctioning and nibbling my pearl and the cold strawberry tickling my insides, I'm nearly pushed to the edge, and I feel myself damn near pulling Jackson's hair out of his head. My orgasm rushes through me so fast that it knocks the wind out of me. He lifts his head and wears a proud smile on his face then reveals the juicy strawberry and takes a bite.

This man is so sexy. "Give me more."

He pulls me by my thighs then wraps my legs around his neck and moves in and out of me. His thickness fills every bit of space and my gasps reflect the impact of his outrageous girth.

"Tell me you love me, Jackson." I lay on the table with my breasts bouncing up and down looking Jackson in his eyes as he tries to control himself from abruptly releasing.

"I love you, Parker. I love you so much," He leans his body over the table and pulls me up by the back of my neck and professes his love to me via whispers in my ear.

"I've only ever loved you. I want to marry you. I want a family with you, Parker."

"Don't stop. Keep talking to me. Tell me I'm yours."

"You're mine, always. Forever and always, Parker."

He can't contain himself any longer and neither can I. We climax into an exhausting wave of sexual bliss. Jackson lays his rock hard body on top of mine to regain his breath then picks me up from the table and lays me down on the bed.

"I'll run your bath water. You should soak and relax before the party." Jackson kisses me on the cheek and takes a shower.

Our sex is passionate every time and lately he's been whispering sweet everything's in my ear in the heat of the moment. Marriage and kids have never really been a hot topic for us, even in college, we never really put a time stamp on things or talked about what a family together would look like. Now, my earlier conversation with the girls is starting to bother me.

"Jackson?" I walk to the bathroom and watch him clean his masterpiece of a body through the shower glass.

"What's up?"

"Let's talk about marriage."

He laughs at me and dismisses my suggestion and continues to lather his body, but I don't budge.

"Oh, you're serious?"

"Yes, I am." I brush my teeth and wait for him to respond.

"What about marriage?"

"Well, when do you want to get married? It's been years, Jackson. Why haven't you ever settled down? I have questions and I need answers."

"It's hard to take you serious when you have toothpaste suds in your mouth." He exits the shower and wraps a towel around his body.

"I'm serious, Jackson! Per my social media and blog research, you've dated a lot of women, like really good looking, successful women – aside from a few questionable influencers and 'fitness models' of course, but you never married."

I rinse my mouth out and Jackson turns to me to wipe some toothpaste residue from my face.

"I could never do things like this with them."

"Like what?"

"Be real. Be comfortable. Be in love. There were some flings or situationships that lasted longer than others but they were mostly fueled by sex, alcohol, or convenience. Parker, I do want to get married. We're twenty-nine now and I want it all. I'm finally ready to have it all, but the only person I could ever see myself sharing my world with is you. I always knew I'd end up with you. I'd marry you tomorrow if I could, but I know you need time so I'm just patiently waiting until you're ready."

"Oh whatever, Jackson."

"Now, you're the one who needs to take me serious. I'm not kidding. I want to marry you. I want to have children with you, no matter how they're created. They'll be ours, together," He reassures me and lightly slaps my butt. "Now get in the tub. We have a grand entrance to make tonight."

We get dressed in separate rooms to surprise one another with our outfit choices.

"I'm ready when you are." He yells from the other side of the house.

"I'm coming out."

I slowly open the door to my room and nervously lift my head to meet Jackson's eyes. I unveil my leg through my high split, champagne mermaid cut dress. Jackson's mouth is open, but he's speechless.

"You look beyond sexy. I – I've never seen you look so…suggestive."

I laugh nervously at his lack of vocabulary to describe how speechless I'm making him.

"What am I suggesting right now, Jackson?" He looks as equally sexy in his two-piece slim fit champagne suit and gold tie.

He raises his eyebrow and pulls me closer so I can feel the thick bulge in his tight pants.

"I hope it's what I think it is." He kisses my neck.

"It's not. Now, let's go celebrate my parents' love."

"And ours too? As in exchanging kisses throughout the night in front of all of Beverly Mills? Taking adorable photos together for the world to finally get the official answer to #whoisparkerwaylen?"

"Oh, gosh!" Jackson's been nagging me about announcing our relationship all week. "Why is this so important to you, Jackson? Why do you want to bring everyone else into this peaceful bubble that we're living in?"

"Because it's not reality. If we're really going to be together then we shouldn't be a secret. I do interviews nearly every week where I'm asked about my love life. I don't live a life of lies and secrecy anymore. If I do, then I might as well slip back into my old habits. I want to be myself at all times, and that also means being devoted to you and open about who the love of my life is. It's important to me."

"Okay," I cup his face with my right hand and affectionately kiss his lips. "If it's important to you, then it's important to me. But," I pause. "Once the world knows we're *kinda* together, things will change. People won't see me as Dr. Waylen anymore. I'll be called Parker, the woman who dates Jackson Sands again. That's not me. That's not who I am and as soon as I'm portrayed as that, I expect you to step up and defend me."

"I promise you, Parker. You'll be known as Dr. Waylen, the strong, supportive, and loving woman who I owe all of my success to. You're my star, my galaxy, my everything and everyone will know."

We leave the house and head to the venue. The old vintage building is definitely giving me old Beverly Mills glam vibes and this interior décor reads Great Gatsby meets Old Hollywood. The old Parker would've micromanaged every aspect of party planning, but the adult Parker stepped back and allowed the experts to do their job and they did not disappoint! Lush gold linens drape the walls and the candle-lit tables are garnished with pearls and ostrich feather floral arrangements.

I have a few minutes to spare before the party begins so I practice my end of night speech, but as I'm in deep thought, I feel an arm wrap around my waist and I turn to see Jackson adoringly eyeing me. His touch calms my nerves and pacifies my insecurities.

"Don't give me that fake smile. I see the worry lines on your face. What's going on?"

"I'm getting a stage freight. Love doesn't love me very much, Jackson. People won't say anything directly to my face, but I know what they say about me. I've had two disastrous relationships with two of Beverly Mills' most eligible bachelors. Everyone thinks I'm a trainwreck. Who am I to speak about love?"

"You're selling yourself short, Parker. You're the epitome of love through your family, friendships, your career, what you do for the people here in Beverly Mills, and what you've done for me. You're filled with love and you give it freely even when others don't deserve it. Throw those cards away and just say what you have to say. You're gonna do great."

Jackson's pep talk is all I need to hear. Once the ballroom doors open and guests pour in, all of my fears go away. All of the who's who of Beverly

Mills are in attendance. The music is loud, drinks are flowing, everyone is having a great time, and we're just waiting for the guests of honor to arrive.

We're in full super couple mode. Everyone and their mama are prying into our relationship, asking intrusive questions, and making off the wall comments.

High school math teacher: It's so nice to see you two back together. I would've never thought a + b would equal c with you two.

Jackson's former high school teammate: Y'all are back together? Parker's cute and all, but that swimsuit model you dated years back was smokin' hot.

Pageant coach: Love always finds its way back home. Jackson just needed time to sew his wild oats, that's all. You know how men are.

Church choir director: I like David better.

I pull Jackson to the side and whisper discreetly underneath my breath, "Jackson, I can't take this. Since when did people become so invested in our lives? I feel like we're characters in a soap opera."

"That's an accurate comparison if you think about it."

Jackson thinks this is funny, but I'm offended and now I feel even more insecure than I did before. Thankfully, at the top of the hour, my parents enter through the tall, steel doors. My mom looks radiant. She and my dad walk into the room hand in hand. Mom's wearing a white custom fit and flare dress with a sweetheart neckline and straps that hang off her shoulders and dad replaced his flower apron and overalls for an all-white tuxedo with black lapels.

"Dang, mama. You are sexy!" Avery whistles through the crowd.

"Who knew our parents were so hot!" Izzy laughs.

"I did. Haven't you seen their social media? Completely inappropriate." Even after thirty years of marriage, my parents manage to make love look easy, happy, and painless.

My parents make their way through the crowd hugging and chatting with their friends and residents of Beverly Mills. When they make it to the stage, mom grabs the mic and makes an impromptu speech.

"I'm not one for emotional speeches and dramatic moments. I'll leave that to my daughters and their handsome dates. Aren't they cute, y'all?"

My mom points to Avery, Izzy, and I who are accompanied by the three handsome men that always seem to creep their way back into our lives – Jackson, Deacon, and Gabe.

"Wayne and I want to thank everyone for coming tonight. We've been so blessed to be surrounded by the love of this town. You're all a part of our love story, and I hope you can feel the love in this room tonight because it's a beautiful sight to see. To my husband of thirty years, back in the day, if you would've told me that we'd get married at eighteen and have our first child at twenty, I would've laughed my butt off and called you crazy, but I have the most fulfilling life thanks to you. We fell in love when we were twelve, and I've fallen in love with you over and over again every day since. Thank you for putting up with my craziness over the years. I know it hasn't been easy, but we're here and I'll keep loving you and fighting for us for the next thirty years of our lives together. I love you, Wayne Waylen."

My dad doesn't bother to grab the mic, he grabs my mom's hand instead and pulls her closer to him then stares into her eyes like Jackson often stares into mine. The Beverly Mills crowd cheers 'kiss her' and so my dad does.

Their happiness brings me so much joy and I can't wait for Jackson and I to celebrate our love story someday as well.

The party's going so well. We eat, dance and have the time of our lives with people we love. I even notice David from across the room and after a few glances and attempts to get my attention, I make my way over to greet him.

David is hands down the second most sought after bachelor from Beverly Mills. Jackson is first, of course, but David is tall, handsome, and he has the most gorgeous smile I've ever seen. We haven't spoken in a year, but I have referred a few patients to his physical therapy centers when needed. Like Jackson, David's built quite the impressive career for himself. He owns one of the most successful chain of pain management and physical therapy rehab facilities in the Southeast.

"David, I'm so glad you could make it." I give him a friendly, appropriate hug well-aware of Jackson's eyes piercing in our direction, but I can't help but linger; he smells so good.

"Parker, you look beautiful as always, and I see you've spared no expense for this party. It's lovely."

I can tell by David's gaze that he's reminiscing about our times together, and in this moment, I am too. He poured every bit of love into our relationship and I always only ever gave him just enough.

"Are your parents here?"

"Uh, yes," David points me in the direction of his parents who are showing off a woman's ring finger to friends. Her back is turned so I can't see her face, but that ring is massive. "They're right over there with my fiancé."

Whew, gut punch. The mention of the word fiancé takes my breath away. I was supposed to be that girl for him. I know I hurt him towards the end of our relationship, but he looks happy tonight and he's finally engaged so why am I not happy for him? I hope my facial expression doesn't reflect how miserable I suddenly feel.

"Fiancé? Wow, congratulations. That's...such great news. How – how long have you been together? I mean – where'd you meet?" My words are flowing out my mouth like gibberish.

David laughs and plays coy. "We met at a convention a week or so after our breakup. We've only been dating for a few months, but nowadays a few months feels like a few years."

"You got that right. There's no such thing as the two year rule anymore, might as well skip the getting to know you phase and jump right into marriage, huh? You're practically marrying a stranger!" Oh crap, he might take that as an insult.

"Well, we were together for two years and that didn't quite end well for us so why not try something different." Yep, he took it as an insult.

"David, I didn't mean it like that."

"No, it's okay. I'm happy and it looks like you've finally gotten what you always wanted as well." David and I look over my shoulder to see Jackson wearily smiling back at me. I signal him to come over to us and he perks up and moves as fast as he can as if he's been anxiously awaiting the invitation. David's parents and fiancé motion their way to us as well and when I turn my attention back to them, I'm immediately stunned by what I see. It's David's fiancé, and she looks just like me!

I'm so taken aback, that I grab the chair next to me for support and forget to hide the shocked look on my face. I need to recover quickly.

"Wow, you're so beautiful!" I compliment my doppelganger.

When Jackson finally reaches me, his reaction is even worse, "Whoa, I thought you were Parker!" I elbow him in his side.

"Jackson, this is David's fiancé. I don't think I got your name."

"Pia, my name is Pia. You're Jackson Sands and Parker Waylen. I've heard so much about you two!" David's fiancé steps toward me like she's going to give me an excruciatingly annoying hug. Instead, Jackson extends his hand and blocks her from invading my personal space.

"It's nice to meet you, Pia. I see David has a type." I step on Jackson's toe and we both try to contain our laughter.

"I hear congrats are in order to the love birds. David's a great man. One of the best men I know. I'm so happy for you both." I flash David a sincere smile and he does seem to be genuinely fond of his Parker blow up doll.

"Thank you, Parker. Jackson, I'd love to pick your brain about some ideas I have for a pain management facility here in Beverly Mills. I've been thinking about contracting Sands Construction for the build."

"Hold on, since when did you two become so friendly? You hated each other, especially after the business deal fiasco."

"Whoa, stop living in the past, Parker." Jackson jokingly puts his arm around David's shoulder.

"Jackson's right. After a very hefty 'no strings attached' donation to my first facility, we were able to squash things and move on. It kinda helps that you weren't in the middle anymore, too." David shrugs.

"Wow, so I was the problem, huh?" I laugh.

"Definitely." Jackson responds.

Jackson and David step aside to have a private conversation and I'm left to have girl talk with Miss Pia who's smiling way too hard in my face right now.

"Okay, it's just me and you now. Can you stop trying so hard? It's really freaking me out."

Pia looks at me like she's confused, but after a moment, she finally relaxes her face.

"Thank God! I can't put on this childish act anymore."

"Act?"

"Yes, the happy go lucky fiancé. David and I are engaged, but he's been on edge for weeks, and when I finally got fed up with his angst behavior, I made him tell me what the hell was wrong and he showed me the invite that said *Hi David, I hope you're well and I miss you like crazy. I wanted to personally invite you to my parents' 30th anniversary party.* He's been trying to coach me on things to say and do all night long. Do you know how long it took for me to be his number one? I've been in your shadow for too long, Parker. Hell, you think I don't recognize our uncanny resemblance to one another? But I'm okay with that as long as I know he's mine. Why couldn't you just leave him alone? He was finally at peace. Why'd you have to ruin my happy ending?"

"I'm sorry, Pia. I had no idea. If it makes you feel better, David and I haven't had sex in a year."

"I know, Parker, but that doesn't mean he was over you. He was heartbroken after the break-up. Yet, you continued to have occasional hookups here and there with him knowing he was in love with you. I had to sit through so many stories about you. I had to sit and listen to him cry and get frustrated about being your second choice to Jackson, but here I am, his second choice to you. Let's end this right now. Don't write him. Don't hug him. Don't speak to him. Just don't. From what I've heard, you and Jackson are two selfish people who belong together. Leave it at that and please stay away from my fiancé." Pia unapologetically bumps my shoulder as she walks past me then grabs David's hand to lead him to the dance floor.

Jackson walks back up to me curious to get the scoop on my chat with Pia. "So, how was your conversation with Parker 2.0?"

"You know, I really like her," I wrap my arms around Jackson's neck. "She's feisty and she told me to stay away from her man. Pia definitely put me in my place. Don't bother David ever again – noted."

"That's actually kinda funy. Hey, will you dance with me?"

"I've been waiting for you to ask, Mr. Sands."

We shimmy our way to the dance floor with our friends and family. From the tootsie roll to the bump, we do our thing and for the first time tonight, we kiss. We kiss passionately in front of the people we love, cameras, and I'm sure social media feeds. Right now, I feel confident in our future and I don't harbor any of the hurt from the past. I'm ready for the world to know that I'm his and he is mine again.

It's time to give my end of night speech. We're all exhausted so I'm going to make this as short and sweet as possible.

"Since it's already the end of the night and it's past most of your bedtimes, I'd like to tell you a story – a Waylen love story that our parents used to tell my sisters and I when we were kids. There was once this country boy named Wayne. He didn't have many friends and he'd spend most of his time selling flowers with his parents at the local market. But one day, he met this loud and obnoxious, but ridiculously beautiful girl named Jolene. She ran into him and made him drop his basket of flowers. Instead of getting angry, Wayne was speechless when he looked into her beautiful bright eyes. Jolene also thought he was kinda cute, so she decided to help him pick up his flowers. 'I've seen you around,' She told him. He said, 'I know. I've seen you six times in three months and today I purposely stood in your way so we could finally say hello.' Jolene was intrigued at the shy boy's forwardness. He grabbed a few flowers from his basket and twisted them together to create a beautiful floral bracelet. He slid it on her wrist and said, 'One day I'll give you more.' Jolene ditched her group of friends and decided to sell flowers for the remainder of the day with Wayne and his parents and she did so every weekend for the next four years. For Jolene's high school graduation gift, Wayne placed a ring on her finger made out of flowers that resembled the bracelet he made for her the day they met. And again, he said, 'One day I'll give you more.' She said, 'You've given me more than I could ever ask.' Wayne said 'And I'll keep giving you more so you'll never have to ask.' And here we are tonight, gathered together to witness three decades of giving more affection, more laughs, more time, more patience, more kindness, and more love. Love is here in this room so cheers to Wayne and Jolene Waylen! And cheers to love in Beverly Mills!"

    As the guests in the room cheer and embrace their friends and significant others, I look to Jackson in the crowd and he mouths *I love you*. I blow him a kiss, but then glance over to the left where I notice the only visibly unhappy person in the room, David. He stares at me expressionless but I feel his pain. A part of him is broken just like I once was. I feel terrible that David's treating his new love like how I treated him.

    I was in denial back then and I didn't consider how my lingering feelings for Jackson would affect anyone else. I was selfish and now I see myself in David. I once lived in a fantasy world where I idealized a life with Jackson and it damn near killed me.

David's seen the worst of me and was a part of my journey to uncovering the best of me, and I'll forever be thankful to him, but I broke him down like Jackson once did me, and if he can let go of his fantasy of *us*, then he, too, can experience real happiness with someone who loves him back because everyone deserves to celebrate a 30th anniversary someday.

Chapter 13

Walking Away - Parker

"That's it. You're doing great. Keep going. A few more steps." My physical therapist encourages me to take a few more steps without my cane. I feel a little pain, but I've been through worse.

"I'm doing it, David! Oh my god. I'm doing it!" It's been a year since I walked on my own without the help of a wheelchair, brace, or my cane.

"I told you, you're strong. You're ready for this, Parker. A few more weeks and you're gonna be running again in no time."

"I don't know about all of that, but I wouldn't mind doing a light jog here or there."

"You will, in due time. Is Merissa picking you up today?" David knows the answer is yes. He's been asking me the same variation of this question for weeks now. How are you getting home today? Do you have a ride? Who's picking you up?

"Yes, Merissa's picking me up today, but she won't be able to next week. She has to study for exams."

David's face lights up, "Oh really? I'll be happy to take you home. Maybe we could grab something to eat, also?"

"Yeah, maybe we can."

It's David's first year as a PT in Emory's Physical Therapy department. He's been working with me for about six months and we've come such a long way. Twelve months ago, doctors were skeptical about whether my leg would ever function normally again. After four surgeries, a metal rod and twenty screws, I'm walking again – slowly and with a cane but that's better than nothing.

"Is that a for real yes?"

"Why do you sound so surprised? A girl's gotta eat."

"With everything you've been through, I just wasn't sure you'd want to hang out with anyone quite yet."

"David, you've become such a good friend to me. I'd love to hang out outside of these four torturous walls! Besides, I've been cooped up in my apartment for months doing nothing but online classes. I need something different."

David smiles at me and helps guide me to the door where Merissa waits for me. He hands Merissa my belongings and they exchange a friendly hug.

"Hey David! How's our superwoman doing today?"

"Wonderful. She took about twenty steps on her own. No cane. No support. Just Parker and her unyielding strength."

"I'll get this for you."

"You don't have to hold my bag or open the door for me, David. I can do that on my own."

"I know, but it'd be rude not to. Sometimes I think you forget that I am a Southern gentleman."

"You're too good to me to forget."

He and I hold one another's gaze for a moment too long for Merissa's comfort.

"That's enough, you too. David, tell Parker goodbye. Parker, tell David goodbye."

We say our goodbyes and leave the hospital, and I pull out my phone to immediately text David.

Parker: Sorry, you know how protective Merissa is.

David: Everyone needs a friend like her.

Parker: And everyone needs a friend like you. I appreciate you, David.

David and I text every day. It's usually funny memes and small chit chat here and there, but lately I've noticed he's been more attentive to me. He calls to check in. He massages the knots in my legs, and he even cheers me up when I start to think about Jackson. Merissa breaks my trance to lecture me about my love life and remind me about my vow.

"You're not ready, Parker. I like David a lot. He and Jason get along great, but you're still in recovery from your accident and from your relationship with Jackson."

"Why do we have to talk about him, Merissa?" I groan and place my hands over my ears.

"Because I know, Parker. I know he's been texting and I know you've been answering his calls."

Merissa's right. We officially broke up last May the day before college graduation. Days after my dad ran him out of the hospital room, I received a piss poor pitiful text from Jackson.

I'm sorry about everything. I promise I'll never forgive myself for what's happened to you and our baby. You were always my galaxy guiding me through the darkness, and now that I've lost you, I don't know what to do. I don't deserve you. I probably never have and I probably never will so I'll try to stay away from you for as long as I can, if I can. Goodbye, Parker.

While my best friends were walking across the stage to receive their diploma, I was recovering from my second bone fracture operation. I looked forward to that day for so many years. I dreamed about the moment I could say, I did it, but it never happened – not for me.

A few weeks after graduation, the school allowed me to take an alternative exam remotely from the hospital. I passed all my courses and a few weeks later received my degree by mail. My mom called me to celebrate, but it was an underwhelming moment of an accomplishment that I worked so hard to achieve.

I was bed-ridden in a hospital for over a month. Nothing felt real to me anymore. I cried every day for so many reasons. In the morning, I'd wake up in a depressing fit because my life was a nightmare and sometimes, I much rather stay asleep than face my reality. I'd cry when I look down at my stomach and see the nasty, brutal scar that reminds me of my accident, but I cried the most when I think about the loss I experienced. I still cry. Not only did I lose my baby, but I lost any chance of carrying another. I'll never have the chance to get back what I lost. Every day for months, I'd pray for a rainbow but I received storms instead. It's a torturous feeling – having someone taken away from you so suddenly, so abruptly, so cruelly. I feel an emptiness inside of me and I feel incomplete knowing that an essential part of my womanhood has been stripped away from me without my consent. They say it was to save my life, but what exactly do I have to live for now?

I'm damaged goods. I'm broken and I know it, and I don't need Merissa to continue to remind me of how I got to this point.

"Merissa, I'm not getting back with Jackson. We've just been talking about wedding stuff. Our best friends are getting married in two weeks and it's our responsibility to plan the wildest joint bachelor slash bachelorette party ever. Whose idea was this anyway?"

"Oh, you know it was Jason's idea. The thought of male strippers grinding on me nearly gave him a heart attack. You should've seen the look on his face when I was showing him videos of what *really* happens at bachelorette parties."

"Merissa! Both of you are terrible. You're not even supposed to see one another the night before the wedding."

"Traditions are for fools. I want to celebrate my last night of singlehood with the love of my life. We should celebrate together like we've done every other momentous occasion in our lives."

"I'm so happy for the both of you. I love you and Jason so much."

"We love you, too which is why you need to stay clear of Jackson. Parker, he's not right. Not yet. And you know it."

Jackson just finished his rookie NFL season as the starting quarterback for the Miami Thunder. The Thunder weren't even considered playoff contenders until this season. Jackson led his team to the AFC East Championship and only lost by a field goal. He's the hottest name in sports and recently voted GQ Magazine's Sexiest Man Alive. If he isn't busy on the field or making millions from endorsements, then he's partying every night and by the looks of his social, he has a new woman every day of the week.

I want to believe that I was more than just a girl he once knew. I want to believe that I'm still the one he thinks about at night and wants to wake up next to in the morning, but I lost faith in my hopes and dreams a long time ago.

"I'm not going to entertain Jackson's crap, Merissa. My only focus is recovery."

But I actually *have* entertained his crap. At first, Jackson's messages started off as distant, cautious chats.

Jackson: I'm sorry to bother you. I know it's been a long time, but I wanted to connect with you about planning Merissa and Jason's final hoorah. I understand if you don't want to speak to me. I'm sorry again for bothering you.

I thought I could handle this style of communication. There aren't any feelings involved via texts and we only needed to discuss party plans, but over the next week, our messages became less impersonal and more familiar.

Jackson: Do you think we should rent a party house or book hotel rooms?

Parker: Ooh, good question. Shouldn't they be separated the night before? I can see them trying to sneak in the bed together for a late night quickie.

Jackson: You're right, but we'll likely be able to have more fun at the house than a hotel.

Parker: How much fun can we have in one night? We'll have to sleep at some point. We have to wake up super early for the wedding.

Jackson: Ok, compromise?

Parker: Maybe. What do you have in mind?

Jackson: Rent a beach house. Girls stay downstairs. Guys stay upstairs.

Parker: Lights out at 1 a.m. no exceptions.

Jackson: Deal.

Parker: Nice doing business with you, Mr. Sands.

Jackson: I miss this.

Jackson: I crossed the line. I'm sorry. It's hard not to with you.

Parker: I know what you mean. Sometimes, I wonder what your life is like now. Mine is definitely not how I thought it'd be, but I see you're happy.

Jackson: Don't believe what you see.

Parker: Okay. I won't.

Jackson: Are you happy?

Parker: Well, I'm practically learning how to walk again. Taking online classes aren't ideal for me right now so I'm struggling to keep up with med school. My best friend and sisters practically babysit me because they think I'm too emotionally fragile to be on my own. And I look at my handsome ex-boyfriend's profile every weekend to see which new girl he's banging. So, idk Jackson. Do you think I'm happy?

Jackson: I'm sorry. I shouldn't have asked you that.

Parker: Unless it's about the wedding, we really shouldn't be speaking. It's not healthy for me.

Jackson: I'm sorry. I just miss you, Parker. I want to see you so bad. I look at our pictures every day. I'm miserable without you. Please, don't believe what you see online. It's all fake. You're the only who knows the real me.

Parker: Bye, Jackson. I really need to focus on my schoolwork.

Our conversations continued. I tried my hardest to push Jackson away, but he's relentless. I'd be a fool to think that what we're doing is okay, but everyone knows I'm a damn fool when it comes to Jackson Sands.

"Parker! Are you listening to me? This thing with David. Your calls with Jackson. What are you trying to do?" Merissa asks.

Ugh, I'm trying to think about the illicit affair I'm having with Jackson behind my friends and family's back!

"Huh? Nothing, Merissa. David's just really nice, and I don't think I would've made this much progress without him. He's been so supportive and encouraging. He goes the extra mile for me, that's all. And Jackson? Well, like I said, that's nothing. It's been a year and I wouldn't dare give him the time of day."

"Well, just be careful. David really likes you, but you still need to focus on yourself. I'm so proud of how far you've come, but you're only halfway there, Parker."

Inspired by her sister's lifelong struggle with mental illness and drug addiction, Merissa decided she doesn't want to be a medical doctor at all. After graduation, she enrolled in Emory's Graduate Psychology Program. She wants to be a child psychologist, and I know she's going to be an excellent doctor.

"I'll be careful, Merissa. I promise. I won't let Jackson break my heart again."

Later that night, Jackson randomly video calls me. My hair is tied up in a messy bun and I'm sitting in bed wearing my reading glasses and one of his old t-shirts. I look like crap, but I don't have time to change or put make-up on so I put my finger over my camera so he can't see me. Jackson hasn't video called me since the night he was drafted.

"Hello?"

"Parker? I didn't think you were gonna answer."

"Well, it is late and you probably shouldn't be calling me, but I figured it was an emergency or something." I feel a cramp in my hand and for a moment, I completely forget how I look and remove my finger from in front of the camera lens.

"Wow, you look beautiful. You look so real. I bet it'd feel like home to lay next to you right now."

I start to feel a warm discomfort down my spine. I know the way I feel is wrong, but I haven't felt this sensation in a year. For every second Jackson stares at me with that look of hunger, my lust for him grows. I bury my face in the palm of my hands to hide my embarrassment and shame of being turned on by the man who makes a daily mockery of the love we once shared.

"I look a mess, Jackson."

"You look like my dream girl. I wish I could I touch you right now."

We're treading into deep waters. I know I should hang up, but I don't.

"Touch me how, Jackson?"

"The way you like. I just want to feel your soft skin again, Parker. I'm getting turned on thinking about my hands exploring your body."

My breathing slows and I feel myself getting hot and bothered for the first time in months.

"We have to stop, Jackson. This isn't right. You're not right."

"Let's just give us what we want, what we need – just this once."

I think about what Jackson's asking me to do. I know I'm going to regret this, but my common sense takes a back seat. Jackson props himself up on his bed in a comfortable position and I reach over to my night stand to grab my vibrator.

"Turn it on, Parker. I want you to close your eyes and imagine me there instead."

I place my vibrator directly on top of my most sensitive place and I gasp so loud that I even startle myself. The thought of Jackson's mouth on me sends my body into a frenzy. I see Jackson stroking himself and I hear his jerking hand movement loud and clear.

"I wish you were on top of me right now." He moans.

"I miss you so much, Jackson."

My imagination has taken off and I'm near the edge as I think about being intimate with Jackson again.

"I don't care about those other women, and I don't want you to be with anyone else, Parker." He tells me.

"I won't, Jackson. I only want you. You're still the only one."

My climax catches me so off guard that I drop the phone. I hear Jackson grunt loud and moan my name. When I pick up my phone, he's moved from his bed and into his fancy bathroom to clean himself up. Then, a door opens and I hear noise.

"It's so loud in your house. Are you having a party?"

He doesn't respond, but he closes his bathroom door instead. I hear multiple women in the background calling Jackson's name and shouting 'babe.' I just masturbated on the phone with my ex-boyfriend while he has women at his house that he'll likely have sex with later on tonight. My brief moment of bliss is gone and I'm back to being embarrassed, ashamed, disrespected, angry, and a damn fool. He *is* still the man he was twelve months ago. He's just not right. Not yet.

"Jackson, you just used me for a quick nut. Don't ever call me again."

I end the call and cry in my pillow. Love used to sustain me, but now it only hurts. Every thought of him, good or bad, comes with emotional baggage, and my sisters and best friend aren't here to help carry it for me. Sometimes I rather die alone than to cry alone so at least I won't have to wake up the next day and deal with life all over again.

I should've recorded my journey to recovery to remind myself how strong I am because I just gave my newfound strength and dignity away to the same who obliterated it in the first place. Now, I'm back at square one, again. I'm back to being Parker. The girl who lived for Jackson Sands. The girl who supported Jackson Sands. The girl who gave her all to Jackson Sands. The girl who was ruined by Jackson Sands. But most pathetically, the girl who is still in love with Jackson Sands.

I reach out to Merissa to get her grief counselor's information and I make an appointment for next week. I know I'm depressed, and I know I need help. I won't be like Jackson and make false promises to myself. I'm going to be whole again and I don't want to continue to be Jackson's fool.

Later in the week, David and I head to the hospital cafeteria to grab something to eat.

"When you asked me if we could hang out after our session, I was thinking a restaurant or coffee shop not the hospital."

David laughs but I can tell that he's nervous and second guessing his location choice for our non-date date.

"I'm sorry, I just didn't want you to feel uncomfortable. It's only been a year since you experienced three tragedies at once – the car accident, a break-up, and your loss. I don't want to force any type of intimacy on you, including being in a restaurant where we'd be in such close proximity to one another carrying on with tense conversations."

David's so thoughtful. Our friendship is special and I can be myself around him. It's pure like the way me and Jackson's bond used to be. I'm not oblivious and naïve. I know David is interested in being more than friends, but I need us to be just the way we are until I can figure out how to stop wanting Jackson and start wanting a happier life for myself.

"You're always thinking about my well-being, even when I'm not considering my own. I wish I cared about myself more. Like – I don't hate myself. I don't exactly hate my life. I just feel nothing, and that's scary. It used to make me feel good to care about others more than myself, but now I feel neglected and left behind."

Still sitting down next to one another in the cafeteria, David looks at me empathetically, wraps his arm around my shoulder and pulls me closer to his chest, "You may feel like that, but you aren't. Feelings are unreliable, but who you are is fixed. Parker, you're good. You're honest. And you love. So many people choose not to love yet you do."

"And look where that's gotten me? A year of loss is the cost."

"I can't argue with that, but I can say with loss comes strength and with strength comes perseverance, and with perseverance comes your comeback story. What's your comeback story gonna be?"

I think long and hard about my future, something I stopped doing months ago. My life has always been predicated on what others would do. My career of choice was tied to Merissa's aspirations. The way I saw myself as a woman was based off my desire to be Jackson's wife. And my idea of having it all meant both love and children. I don't have any of those things and to think about them would mean I'm stuck in the past, and given where I am in life right now, it's impossible to make a future out of my past.

"Honestly, my comeback story doesn't exist."

"Yet," David says. "Let's start small. What's something you'd like to do that would make you proud of yourself? Tell me an accomplishment you can actually work towards within the next few days or weeks."

"Walking." I laugh.

"Too vague. Try again." David challenges me.

"Walking without my cane."

"Now, we're getting somewhere. What about walking without your cane? Be even more specific."

"I don't know. I might be pushing myself too hard, but what about walking down the aisle in Merissa's wedding without my cane? Do you think I can do it?"

"I know you can." David kisses my knuckles and I realize that I'm still leaning into his embrace. "I'll help you reach your goal, every single one, but I'm not gonna go soft on you so I better not see you slackin'."

"Deal."

David extends his hand to shake mine, but I decline. "Promises are more powerful than deals."

I give him my pinky finger and we promise to work together to help me help myself rediscover who I am.

"Parker, it's so nice to meet you. Merissa's told me quite a bit about you and your lively adventures growing up."

Dr. Martin is the grief counselor Merissa referred me to. She's an older woman and a bit quirky, too. I haven't seen many counselors wear beach sandals. Correction, I haven't seen any counselors wear beach sandals. This is Atlanta. We don't even have a beach.

"I like your shoes."

"Why, thank you. There a conversation starter." Dr. Martin says.

I like her. Her attitude is refreshing. It drowns out my darkness.

"Sit."

I find the nearest chair to her desk and do as told.

"So, tell me why you're here. Who have you lost? Yourself, a loved one, hope?"

"All the above." I answer hesitantly and she takes my hand and places hers on top of mine. Her gentle touch alleviates my tension and nervousness.

"When did your grief begin and where is it today, Parker?"

"I loved someone who wasn't ready to receive it. He was my first love. He was my everything."

"That's heavy. You existed because of him?" Dr. Martin leans on her desk and rests her face in her palms like she's just a longtime friend listening to me vent.

"What do you mean?"

"You said this young man was your everything so you gave him all of your love and now it feels like you don't have any love to give to yourself. You're grieving the loss of love for yourself. Okay, keep going. You're so relatable."

This woman is so weird, but I keep going because I think she gets it. "I was trying to get him to stop his reckless behavior and one night after an attempt to save him from himself, I got in a car wreck that left me with a severely broken leg, a dead child, and a hysterectomy."

She squints her eyes and squeezes my hand tight, "The strength you have to retell your trauma is commendable."

"I don't retell it often, but I do think about it every day." I confess to Dr. Martin.

"That's understandable. Over time, trauma can transform into a testimony and if you want, only if you want to, you can choose to turn that testimony into purpose."

"But how? What is there for me to learn? What can I share with others besides don't chase after a man?"

She chuckles, leans back in her chair, and shrugs her shoulders.

"I can't answer that for you, Parker," Dr. Martin looks down at my leg. "Your leg looks great. It's just a scar now – a beautiful scar. How bad was it?"

"It was pretty bad. I broke two bones. I have a metal rod in my leg. I had 4 corrective surgeries. I wore a brace for a few months, but now I just use my cane for support. Honestly, I can't believe I'm even able to walk again."

"You're healing. What a beautiful testimony," She smiles. "Parker, may I ask a personal question?"

"I think it depends on the question, doc."

"That's fair. Do you still cry over your losses?"

"Yes."

She nods her head and says, "You know, I lost a son twenty years ago. He was 7 years old. He was the sweetest little boy. I still cry. I cry when I think about his laugh, the pranks he'd play on me, his adorableness, and I even cry when I think about the wonderful life he would've had if he were still alive. Those tears aren't tears of grief anymore. They're tears of gratitude and they comfort me if I ever feel my mind play those 'what could I have done differently' tricks on me. Tears aren't always sad. Tears aren't always bad. When you get down on yourself, think about how far you've come and where you could've been then use your tears as a muzzle for your troubling thoughts."

"Thanks. I'll try that, but what should I do when I think about my baby? I wish I had the chance to make memories. It's like being given a gift only to have it taken away before I could open it. I miss something that I never really had, and I long for something that I'll never be able to have again."

I rub the scar on my stomach, a constant reminder that I'll never be able to conceive.

"Motherhood is beautiful, and thankfully, there's more than one way to become one. You can either wait for a miracle or come up with a new plan for yourself like adoption or surrogacy. Motherhood is still in the picture for you, but are you willing to paint a new canvas for your future?"

"I haven't even thought about that. I guess I've been so stuck on the disappointment of not being able to get pregnant and the thought of feeling like half of a woman. I always feel like something's missing inside of me. I don't know if it's the baby or if it's my body. Either way, I feel incomplete."

"That's a common feeling many women experience after a miscarriage and even a hysterectomy, but believe it or not, you can control how you feel about yourself. You're no less than the next woman, and our ability to give birth doesn't define who we are. You dictate what you want your future to look like. It may not happen according to your plan, but you can strive for it, and in due time, with the right person, or even by yourself, you'll get everything you deserve. In the meantime, cry. Release your pain, let out your anger, and try to smile afterwards at the fact that you're still here. Your body is healing, your heart is mending, your mind is getting stronger each day, but most importantly, you're finally getting help."

I really enjoyed speaking with Dr. Martin. I thought I was going to walk into her office and not say a word, but she made me want to open up. She made me feel like there's hope, and tonight I'm going to cry my heart out and smile afterwards because I think tomorrow is going to be a much better day.

It's the day before Merissa and Jason's wedding and the night of their Jack and Jill bash aka joint bachelor and bachelorette party. This is such a stupid idea, but oh well, it makes sense that these two would want a joint party. They're practically joined at the hip. Speaking of hip, mine is killing me! I've been re-learning how to properly balance my weight when I walk and let's just say, now I understand the struggle toddlers have when they start taking their first steps.

I'm so glad I have David's support. He's literally been there for me every step of the way, and I hope he accepts this last minute invitation because there's no one else I would rather have by my side tomorrow.

Parker: Hey you.

David: Hey v.

Parker: Very funny. Are you in Atlanta or Beverly Mills right now?

David: I'm in good ole' Beverly Mills hanging with my parents. What's up?

Parker: I was wondering if you'd like to be my plus one to the wedding tomorrow. I know it's super last minute so I completely understand if you can't make it. This day is just so important and I couldn't do it without you. Also, I enjoy spending time with you.

David: You had me at be my plus one.

Parker: 😊 My dress is red. Yes, I know, red 🙄

David: I may have a clown suit that I can pull from my closet to match.

Parker: Merissa's gonna kill you.

David: Alright, alright. I guess I'll wear my Sunday's best.

Parker: Thanks, David. And apologies in advance if I text you when I'm tipsy tonight.

David: I look forward to reading drunk Parker's texts.

Parker: I might get a little spicy.

David: I love jalapenos.

Parker: Lol. Bye David.

"FYI, ladies. David's my date to the wedding, tomorrow." I announce to Merissa, Avery, and Izzy.

We're hanging out at the beach house Jackson rented to pregame until the party bus gets here. I've been so busy the last two weeks with my physical therapy and counseling sessions that I haven't entertained Jackson's advances one bit, and there's been many, and most seemed to be drunk texts, of course.

"Parker, you look so hot. Please tell me what type of chaos you have planned for the evening?" Merissa asks.

"You'll see when we get there. In the meantime, Avery will explain the rules for tonight?"

Avery stands in front of us and waves a big rubber dildo puppet in the air.

"Avery!" Izzy lets out a horrified gasp.

"I'm the fun police for the night, and if I notice anyone crying or moping then you're gonna get punished."

Merissa's grad school friends break out in laughter and cheer but Izzy is indignantly confused.

"What the hell, Avery. How exactly are you gonna punish us?"

Avery slides the dildo puppet on my cane and says, "I'm gonna slap you in the face with my dick."

"This is gonna be a wild night!" Merissa says.

"I think I need a shot!" Izzy pours tequila shots for all of us and I make a toast.

"Cheers to Merissa. May you enjoy having sex in public with the same man for the rest of your life."

"We do not have sex in public. That's a rumor!" Merissa yells.

"It's not. I saw you, Merissa. You literally hooked up outside dad's flower shop. I think you and Jason have a problem and admitting it is the first step."

"Our future mayor and mayoress like to get a little freaky, and that's okay."

Avery defends Merissa because she and Deacon are just as freaky, or sexually open, I guess is the right term.

I don't think I'm going to be able to handle all this sex talk tonight. I haven't had sex in a year, and after that phone sex debacle with Jackson, I need to stay far away from him because as terrible as he makes me feel, I still fear I might be tempted to break my dry spell. I need to keep David on standby. He grounds me.

We're on shot number #4 and my phone keeps going off, but I don't know where it is. Merissa finds it and decides to embarrass me in front of everyone.

"The boys are here! Let's head out," Merissa scrolls through my other unread messages as well. "Parker, if you screw Jackson tonight then I'm kicking you out the wedding!"

"What? Why would you say that, Ris?" Izzy asks.

"Let's see. From Jackson, sorry about the other night. You made me feel so good. You're still the only woman for me. From Jackson, I can't wait to see you tonight. From Jackson, I don't think I'll be able to control myself when I see you." Merissa reads Jackson's texts aloud and I see the anger on everyone's faces.

"Clearly, I didn't respond, y'all. I'm sticking to my word. I will not do anything with Jackson Sands. My lips are closed and so are my legs."

Avery grabs my cane and points the dildo puppet towards me, "Good, because if either one of you go near each other, you're both getting a dick to your face."

Avery's wasted and she's probably going to get arrested tonight, but I'm here for it. Merissa's the first one to get married out our friend group and we're ready to party hard and regret it all later.

"It's about time. I missed you, baby." Jason pulls Merissa on his lap and wraps his arms around her waist.

"It's only been a few hours, Jace." She blushes.

"Y'all are doing the most right now." Izzy rolls her eyes.

Everyone's laughing and having a fun time together, but I notice Jackson's busy texting on his phone. The Jackson I knew could barely string together a paragraph, but he's texting like a mad man right now and he looks extremely irritated maybe even distressed.

I almost walk over to him but Izzy and Avery both say, "Don't you dare."

A few minutes later, he transforms into Action Jackson and brings over a bottle of champagne.

"Are y'all ready to get this party started?" He sprays everyone with the champagne then we drink up.

The liquor and champagne warm my insides and Jackson's gaze is making me flustered.

"Stop staring at me like that?" I hang back on the bus so Merissa and my sisters don't see me speaking to Jackson.

"Why not? You look cute when you're drunk." He whispers in my ear.

His hot breath makes the hairs on my arm stand and my body shiver and his deep voice forces me to moan.

"I need to catch up with the girls." I use my cane to help step down off the bus, but Jackson grabs my hips to give me all the support I need. One hand holds my body still while the other slides up to the back of my neck. I haven't forgiven Jackson for what he's done to me or how he's treated me in the past year, but my body feels differently as I close my eyes and lean into his touch.

I slightly turn my body to face his with hope that I have the strength to tell him goodbye and walk away, "I can't be seen with you." I tell Jackson although we move closer to one another.

"Just one kiss," He says. "I just want one kiss and I won't bother you for the rest of the night."

"I can't do this, Jackson."

His phone rings and the caller ID says 'The Devil.' Jackson looks at his phone and denies the call. That same look of irritation and weariness from earlier shows on his face. What has Jackson gotten himself into? What's going on in his life?

While he's distracted with his personal matter, I limp away to stand in the line to enter the swanky club with my best friends and try my best to avoid Jackson Sands at all cost.

The club is hot, crowded, and filled with men and women ready to mark their prey for the night, but Jackson rented out the entire VIP section so we can celebrate Jason and Merissa in private.

"Bro, I see you spared no expense. Is this how you do it in the NFL?" Jason's two shots away from a blackout and Merissa is already annoyed.

"Jason Harmon Pierce, get your ass off that chair! You're behaving like you have no home training." Merissa yanks Jason's arm and continues to rip him a new one.

"Ris, we're only getting married once! Lighten up. C'mon, dance with me." Jason drags Merissa to the dance floor and does a personal strip tease for her. It doesn't take her long to get in the groove and laugh at his antics.

While the two lovebirds are busy grinding on one another, Izzy, Avery, Deacon, Gabe, and I take shot after shot after shot while Jackson's a few steps away arguing back and forth on the phone with someone.

"Okay, I'm done for the night! No more drinking for me. I'm at that sloppy point where I might bust my ass or something. I already have one busted leg, I can't afford to break another!"

"Did Parker just tell a joke? Yeah girl, you must be drunk!" Izzy takes the drink from my hand and instructs me to follow her finger with my eyes.

"I'm fine! I needed this. I needed tonight. I wish I didn't have a freakin' peg leg. I wanna dance!"

"Who needs a dance floor? Let's dance right here." Avery's so drunk that she attempts throw me my cane but hits Jackson in the head instead.

"Whoops, sorry Jackson!" Avery's unapologetic tone adds to Jackson's irritation and he snaps.

"Avery, what's your problem? I've tried to avoid you, yet you're still acting like I've done something wrong. Can't you get that stick out your ass for one night?"

"It was an accident, Jackson! Lighten up."

"You're always judging people. I've never done anything to you, yet you keep poking!"

Jackson's angry about something and taking all of his frustration out on Avery for no valid reason, and Deacon is not happy.

"Jackson, back down, brother. Right now!" Deacon steps to Jackson.

"It's okay Deacon. I can handle myself. He's just being typical Jackson who never takes ownership for his actions."

"Yeah, okay, Avery. What'd I do now?"

"You do everything wrong, Jackson. Look at what you've done to Parker. You broke her and you left her to pick up the pieces while you make millions and screw every whore you meet. You're a selfish, cold-hearted narcissist who doesn't deserve to be in the same room as my sister. If she didn't need that cane to stand, I'd take it from her and slap you in the face with that big dick, you dick head."

"Avery, that's enough!" I try to tame her rage, but she's too far gone and I'm not physically strong enough to take control of the situation.

"No, Parker. He doesn't deserve silence. He deserves to know who he really is. Jackson, you're pathetic. If Debbie were alive, she'd be ashamed of how you treated Parker. She'd be heartbroken to know you killed your baby."

Jackson unleashes a barrage of emotions towards Avery. "You think I don't know that! You think I don't think about what I did every day? Every fucking day! I never deserved Parker and I've tried everything to stay away. So, good job trying to *tell me* who I am. I already know I'm a loser. I'm a coward and I hate myself."

Avery regains her composure and adjusts her tone to de-escalate the altercation. She's angry at Jackson, but like all of us, we care for him more than we dislike his actions, and we all hate that he truly does hate himself.

"Jackson, I really didn't mean to hit you. Let's have some fun and tackle this topic another day. Truce?"

"Truce. I'm sorry for snapping at you. I've been thinking about this night for weeks, all of us hanging out again. It's the first time we've been together in a long time, and I feel wrong for even being here. I don't deserve to be a part of this family."

Jackson's painful admission reminds us that we're not enemies. We're all best friends. We're all family. I decide to speak on behalf of the group.

"Yet, you're still family, Jackson. We all are. Our relationships may have changed but families don't stop loving one another."

We all look to Jason and Merissa to get their attention, but they're too busy feeling up one another on the dance floor. This night is for them, and I think we all lost sight of that for a moment.

"I couldn't have said it better myself, Parker," Deacon chimes in before kissing Avery on the cheek and directing her to the dance floor. "C'mon, let's dance that tequila out your system."

Izzy and Gabe make their way to the dance floor as well which leaves me and Jackson by ourselves with so much to say but nothing to say at all.

"For the record, I don't think you're a loser."

"As much as I value what you think of me, your opinion is biased," Jackson smiles at me and hesitantly moves closer to the booth. "May I sit?"

"It's a free country." I regretfully give him the go ahead to invade my space.

"How are you?" He looks down at my leg and he's consumed with guilt.

"I'm doing better. The doctor says I'll be walking again on my own in no time."

Jackson runs his hand through my hair and tucks a lock behind my ear. "I'm sorry for abandoning you. I should've been there for you."

"I don't think my dad would've allowed that, and to be honest, I don't think I would've wanted that either. For months, I regretted ever loving you," I speak honestly and it feels good not to care about how Jackson feels about what I have to say. "But I guess that's neither here or there, right? You're happy now and I'm getting better and that's all that matters."

"I wish I could say something other than sorry."

"Let's not talk about it. I'm trying really hard to get past what I thought my life was going to be like. We only have to be around each other for one more day, then we can get back to our real lives."

"We can create new lives together, as friends, if you want."

"I don't want that, Jackson. I want to experience life without you."

"That's fair. I won't push, but I won't give up either."

"What are you two talking about?" Izzy comes back over and asks.

"Oh, nothing. We were just chatting about how I'll never get back together with him again."

"Whew, burn!" Gabe teases.

"Very funny. I was only making small talk. That's all." Jackson clarifies.

"It's probably best if you make small talk with someone other than Parker, given your history and not so recent trauma." My ever so mature baby sis advises Jackson.

"You're right. I'm sorry again, Parker."

"It's alright. Maybe we should get going, though." I point over to Jason and Merissa who are practically dry humping in front of everyone.

"Oh crap, there about to have sex in public again!" Izzy yells.

"Let's get them out of here before they get arrested for indecent exposure." Jackson helps me stand and we head back to the party bus.

For months, I wondered what I'd say to Jackson when I'd finally see him for the first time in a year. I had a whole speech prepared, and I was ready to curse him, but I immediately wilted the second he touched my neck. When we get back to the beach house, we're all exhausted and emotionally wired. We lounge around on the couches and start to reminisce about the memories we enjoyed together from childhood to now.

"I can't believe y'all are getting married. We're still so young. I don't think I'll ever get married." Deacon says as he lays his head in Averys lap while she massages his scalp.

"Sure, you won't." Merissa laughs and rolls her eyes.

My view on marriage has changed in the past year as well. Jason and Merissa are still so young. I know we live in a small town in the deep South where it's normal to marry your childhood sweetheart and pop out babies by 19, but it still feels unreal.

"I have to agree with Deacon. Don't you think twenty-three is too young to get married? And you've only been with each other. You never had a chance to what do they call it, sew your wild oats."

"A year ago, you wouldn't have said that." Merissa's eyes move to Jackson.

"Low blow, Merissa." Jason checks my drunk best friend.

"Sorry, Parker. But to answer your question, I don't think we're too young. We've all grown up together. We've laughed together. We've cried together. We're all pretty much married to each other in a sense. Jason and I are just making it official, that's all." Merissa shrugs and sloshes her words.

"That's putting it lightly, babe. You made my life so much more than what I ever thought it could be. Being a part of your life makes me want to give you all of mine."

Jason and Merissa give each other a heartfelt kiss and it just makes me think about the love Jackson and I used to share. Merissa must notice the gloomy expression on my face because she suggests for us to play a classic game that we're all too familiar with.

"Parker, truth or dare?" She asks.

Mischievous expressions circle the room.

"Ris, we are not playing this game! It's late and we have to wake up early."

"Boo! Don't be a party pooper, Parker." Gabe throws a pillow at me.

"Gabe, how dare you not take my side? You're always the good conscience."

"Not tonight. The night is still young and you need to have some fun."

"My baby bro gave the final word, Parker. So, truth or dare?"

"Truth."

"When was your last orgasm?" Merissa sits up then leans over to look me in the eyes.

"I am not answering that question. Merissa, you're piss drunk."

"If you don't answer, then you have to take a shot."

"Ooh, raising the stakes! You are cutthroat tonight, Ris. I love it!" Avery says.

"Ugh, okay," I look at Jackson to gauge his expression and he's staring back at me waiting to hear my answer as well. "My last orgasm was about two weeks ago."

"Two weeks ago?" Merissa squeals in excitement. "So that's what you and David do when we aren't around."

Jackson's mood instantly sours and he gets up to walk to his room, "I'm going to bed."

"Sit your ass down, Jackson. Stop being a brat. You don't get that right." Merissa's voice echoes through the room and Jackson sits down like an obedient little boy.

"To answer *your* question, Merissa. No, that is not what David and I do because we are just friends. And there are many other ways to enjoy intimacy without being with someone else." I try to hint at masturbation, but everyone's looking at me like they're dumb.

"Ugh, I'm not gonna say it so stop trying to make me."

"You're an adult woman who likes to jack her snatch. It's cool, we all do it." Avery's carefree bluntness makes us erupt in laughter, but Jackson wants to know more details.

He wants to know if the last time I came was to the thought of him. "Was it phone sex? Was that the last time you had an orgasm?"

We disregard anyone else in the room and stare at one another. I nod my head yes and he smiles.

Merissa puts two and two together and she outs us. "I knew those text messages weren't innocent! Dammit, Parker and Jackson! You are NOT allowed to be together! You gotta stop!"

We sigh and turn to our friends who are visibly pissed off at us.

"Okay, okay. They get it, Ris. Jackson, you're up next. Truth or dare?" Jason asks.

"Uh, dare." Jackson doesn't sound too confident in his choice because he knows Jason lacks a considerable amount of common sense and social awareness especially when he's drunk.

"Now, we're starting to have some fun." Jason rubs his hands together and prepares to stir the pot. "I dare you to ask Parker for permission to kiss her."

"What the hell, Jason!" Avery yells.

"Did you listen to anything I *just* said? Yeah, no, that's not happening, Jace." Merissa says.

"Parker can't handle that." Izzy says in concern.

"First of all, I'm right here and I can handle anything. I'm not weak y'all, but Jason, screw you for that stupid dare! Jackson, ask me for permission."

"Are you sure?" I know Jackson still wants me, and we both know any type of physical touch is dangerous, but I'm also not the delicate flower everyone seems to think I am. I want to prove them wrong.

"Kiss me, Jackson! Let's get it over with." He caves in to my demand and pulls my face towards his. What should be a quick peck on the lips turns into a deep, long tussle of tongues. I forgot how warm and comforting it felt to be wanted, to be desired, and to be touched by Jackson.

I hear everyone sneering in the background specifically Avery saying, "We can't let her go down this road again."

My common sense heeds her words and I push Jackson away. His body wants me as much as mine wants his, but we know it's wrong to act any further than this.

"See, I told you I could handle it." I look at my sister and give them my proudest *told you so* smile.

"You can't fool us Parker, but whatever you say. Alright, it's your turn. Truth or dare?" Avery directs her attention to Izzy.

"Truth."

"If you had three wishes, what would they be? Anything you want!"

"Ooh, hard question. My first wish would be to see my birth mom again. My second would be to see myself how others see me. It sounds silly, but I don't always feel like the person y'all say I am." Izzy nervously tucks her hair behind her ear. "And my last wish," She looks at me and Jackson. "My last wish would be for Mrs. Debbie to still be alive then maybe we would all be different. Mr. Frank would be happy. Jackson wouldn't drink so much. Parker wouldn't have gotten in that accident. We would all still be together like the family we used to be."

I wipe a tear from my eye and Izzy apologizes.

"I'm sorry to ruin the vibe. I'm a silly drunk nineteen year old and I'm getting all emotional!"

I'm startled when I feel Jackson's hand touch mine. He doesn't say anything or even look at me. He only needs to touch my hand to make the painful memories that I couldn't seem to forget for an entire year subside for the moment – with just his touch.

"Well, I think we should get some rest. Long day tomorrow, remember? C'mon, Ave. Let's go to bed." Deacon lifts Avery and cradles her in his arms and they head to sleep.

Gabe and Izzy go to their rooms to rest and so does the future bride and groom.

"Then, there were two." Jackson walks to the kitchen to pour himself a drink and I follow.

"Are you ready to see our best friends tie the knot tomorrow?" I attempt to make small talk so I can stop thinking about our kiss.

"I'm looking forward to the wedding, but I'm not looking forward to seeing every person that ever lived in Beverly Mills." Jackson shakes his head and takes a swig of his glass of whiskey.

"Oh, so you don't want to talk about football, being rich, or your love life? Everyone's gonna be all over you." For a moment, I forget about our past and playfully place my hands on Jackson's arm and chest like I used to and while I'm oblivious to my familiar comfortability, Jackson isn't. He rubs his hand on my cheek and slides it down to my neck then to the nape of my back. Jackson pulls me closer to his body and I finally make the first move and finish what we started minutes ago. Shifting my weight to my good leg, I wrap my arms around his neck and hungrily kiss Jackson.

Aware of my limited mobility, he picks me up effortlessly and carries me to the bedroom and when our kiss finally ends, I'm conscious of what will most likely happen next.

Jackson lays me down gently on the bed and kisses my forehead, "Goodnight, Parker."

What the hell! This isn't what's supposed to happen. He's supposed to be all over me. As Jackson walks away, I grab his arm and ask him to stay.

"Just for the night, please, Jackson."

He looks at me and it looks like he's debating whether to stay or leave – make the smart choice or the worst. He chooses the latter and strips down to his boxers and gets under the comforter. I take off my clothing and lie next to him in my bra and panties.

What am I doing? Why am I doing this? There's no way I could be so horny that I'd throw away my pride and growth to invite Jackson into my bed, yet here I am so horny, so wet, and so ready for something to be inside of me other than my trauma.

"Are you okay?" Jackson asks as he tries to keep his distance to make me feel more comfortable.

"I am. You can get closer to me if you want, Jackson."

"That's not a good idea, Parker. I shouldn't even be here. I don't want to hurt you again. All I do is hurt you." Jackson slowly rubs his hand over my scarred leg.

I breathe heavily and say nothing as he moves his head under the blanket. His tears moisturize my skin as he presses his lips to my leg and kisses my scars from top to bottom. I instinctively react to the sensitivity of his intoxicating touch and pull his hair which causes Jackson to hunger for me even more. He continues to move upward to my thigh, another wound that has recently healed then to my stomach, the most traumatic wound of all, one that's still open, one that still hurts, a wound that will probably never heal. He settles there and we both release a year's worth of cries. We finally grieve all that we've lost together – our future, our love, our family.

I wipe away his tears and ask Jackson to hold me.

"You're still perfect to me, Parker. You're not damaged. You're perfect."

I turn to face Jackson and press my body against his. "Maybe, we can try this again. Maybe, we can be what we need for each other this time around." I whisper to him.

"I can't, Parker. Just give me more time to sort some things out. I love you so much, but there's something I need to tell you."

"Will it ruin this moment? Will what you have to say hurt me, Jackson?" My eyes are pleading to him not to tell me the truth and I know he doesn't want to disappoint me again.

"What do you want me to say, Parker?"

"Say nothing, Jackson. It's been a year since I've felt you. You're my first and still my only. I just want to feel loved by you again." Tears flow profusely down my face and Jackson catches my words with his mouth.

I undress and he enters inside me. This feels better than the first time, better than the last time, and it will be more memorable than anything I've ever experienced.

I gasp so loud that Jackson has to put his hand over my mouth.

"Does it hurt?" He asks. He's attentive, careful and moving painfully slow.

"I'm okay. You can give me more." I give him my approval and claw my fingernails into his back.

"Parker, I love you. I'm so sorry for everything." I can taste his salty tears and I know he tastes mine as well.

We're crying and hurting and making love all at once. I've been trying to fall out of love with Jackson for over a year yet all I can think about right now is how much I love him.

He whispers in my ear, "I'll love you, always."

My body erupts and Jackson releases a cry so loud that I now have to place my hand over his mouth. We lie next to one another on the bed like we used to and fall asleep in each other's arms.

I deserve to feel like this, even if it's for one night.

"What the hell?" It's the morning of the wedding and Merissa's standing in her robe staring at me and Jackson's naked, entangled bodies.

Jackson's so startled that he jumps out the bed and wraps himself in the sheet. "Merissa, we were just – I was just –"

"Get out, Jackson! Go help Jason." She rolls her eyes and looks at me in disappointment.

Jackson fumbles his words and rushes out the room half-naked.

"I knew you couldn't handle being around him. What were you thinking, Parker? Now your head's going to be all screwed up on my wedding day."

"Merissa, I promise. Your day is going to go off without a hitch. No drama and no freak outs, but please don't tell Avery and Izzy about this."

"Oh, trust me. I won't. I will not be breaking up any fights or calling an ambulance on my wedding day. I just hope you know what you're doing messing around with Jackson, again."

"It was just one time, Merissa. It was no big deal. Now go, I have a wedding to get ready for."

But it wasn't just one time. We opened the door to explore a possible future together again. This is our second chance.

After everyone showers and gets dressed, we hop in the limo and head to the Pierce's estate for the wedding and reception. I'm in awe of the beautiful décor. I have no idea how they managed to make a red and black color scheme look so rich and decadent.

"This is beautiful! Everything must have costed a fortune." I tell Merissa as we finish prepping her look.

"Perks of marrying into a disgustingly rich family, I guess."

"That definitely helps." A quiet voice chimes in from the doorway.

"Iyanna?" Merissa is both surprised and elated to see her sister. "You came. I can't believe you made it." Merissa tries to hold back her tears but fails.

"Did you talk to mom?" She asks.

"Yes, I rode with her. Sorry we're late. I don't have many clothes so I didn't know what to wear."

Iyanna relapsed years ago and she's frequently seen hanging around town with other known drug users. She's a functioning drug addict and I think we've all accepted it. Merissa and her mom sent her to rehab and mental health facilities over six times, and she'd get better after a while but only for a few months.

"Oh, you didn't need to worry about that." Merissa rushes over to the corner and unzips a garment bag. She takes out the bridesmaid dress that she ordered months ago for Iyanna. "I prayed for this moment. I had this made for you just in case you showed."

The small red dress is a perfect fit for Iyanna's frail, malnourished body, and it's custom tailored with mesh long sleeves to cover her old and fresh track marks. Merissa wipes her sister's tears and we help her get dressed and put on make-up so she can help celebrate Merissa on her special day.

David texts me to let me know that he's here. I meet him in the kitchen and he gives me a hug and kiss me on the cheek. I'm excited to see him, but I feel extremely guilty about sleeping with Jackson last night. I know I shouldn't, but I just do.

"I didn't receive any crazy texts so should I assume you had fun last night?"

"Fun is an understatement. We were sloshed!"

"I haven't heard that word since college."

"It was college level bad."

David smiles and rubs his hand on my cheek. His hands feel just as good as Jackson's or maybe I'm still sexually charged from the amazing sex I had last night. Either way, I'm so lost in my thoughts and turned on by his touch that I *accidentally* let out a sensual moan and his eyes light up in arousal.

"Are you ready to walk today?"

"Yes, are you gonna cheer me on?" I ask flirtatiously.

"Always." David kisses my knuckles and I give him my cane to place near the alter, and as soon as he leaves, Jackson appears.

"Oh god, Jackson! You scared me!" I laugh and hold on to his strong arms for support.

"So, did you confess to your boyfriend about hooking up with me?" Jackson doesn't even bother to hide his irritation.

"Um, no because he isn't my boyfriend. He's just my wedding date, Jackson."

"How convenient." He rolls his eyes and sloppily leans over the counter. I'm pretty sure he's been drinking. I'm pretty sure he's drunk.

I rub his back out of concern, but he moves away to avoid my touch.

"Jackson," I move closer to him. "What's going on? I thought we were in a better place, especially after last night."

"I told you, I can't be with you. I'm no good for you, Parker. I'm sorry for hurting you, again."

"What does that mean?"

He walks away leaving me pissed off and confused as hell. He used to say I was dramatic, but that was next level. I don't have time for Jackson to throw me off my game. I need to get ready to walk into the next phase of my life, literally.

The wedding party lines up and I'm up first. Over a hundred people turn in their chairs and look at me. My parents, friends and people of Beverly Mills have watched me go from a wheelchair to a leg brace to a cast to a cane, and now I'm finally walking again on my own. I see the tears in my parents' eyes. I see David with a proud smile on his face, and I look forward to see Jackson with tears of sadness and wonder. He sees my strength. Everyone does and with every step I take, I limp a little less. With every smile I see, I walk a beat faster. I feel powerful. I feel like I'm one step closer to the Parker Waylen I'm supposed to be.

When I get to my mark near the officiant, everyone cheers and Jackson gives me a faint smirk before looking away aimlessly again. The rest of the wedding party walks down the aisle – including the starlet of the day. Merissa looks like a fairy princess that has it all. Everything she ever said she wanted is happening and I'm genuinely happy for her, even more surprising, is that for the first time in a very long time, I feel hopeful.

The wedding was beautiful and classy like Merissa, but the reception is all about Jason! This is not your typical wedding DJ and they're serving burgers and fries.

"I had to compromise and this is the deal we came up with. My perfect wedding in exchange for Jason's college frat style reception. I'm officially married to a man child." Merissa laughs.

"May your days be long and your patience be even longer!" I raise my glass.

Jackson's still acting distant towards me, but I've been too distracted with the wedding to care. Besides, David's arm is around my waist and he's the only person on my mind at the moment.

"David, we need to talk about Parker's catwalk she did down the aisle today." Merissa cheers me on.

"She didn't walk. She damn near ran." He looks me in my eyes and pulls me closer to him.

"Y'all are so extra. It took me forever to get down there."

"Girl, please. You're a track star!"

Jackson and Jason walk up to us with big drunk smiles on their faces.

"How much did you have to drink, Jason?" Merissa is not happy.

"One beer. You know he's a lightweight." Jackson drunkenly laughs.

I look at Jackson just to see if he's going to look me in the eyes, but he doesn't. David congratulates Jason and gives him a hug. Jason and David have become great friends over the past year. I hate to say it, but in a way, he's taken Jackson's place as someone who's present in our lives on a daily basis, and Jackson hates that.

"How are you doing, Jackson? It's been a while." David reaches out to shake Jackson's hand, but he sees an unsettling face in the near distance that freezes him completely.

"Who invited Allie?" He asks.

I also notice the loud, desperate mean girl who tried to hook up with Jackson more times than I can count. She's on the phone and it looks like she's looking for someone specific. Jackson's phone rings and that same caller ID from last night appears, The Devil. He rolls his eyes and denies the call. I don't know who The Devil is but this bitch Allie is making her way over to us.

"I did NOT invite her, Jason. Why the hell is she here?" Merissa looks to Jason, but Jason looks clueless.

"Hey little townies! You missed me?" Allie walks up to Jackson and wraps her arms around his waist and slides her other hand inside of his tuxedo jacket. Jackson tries to step away from her, but she steps closer.

Jason, Merissa, and David look at me in concern while Jackson holds his head down in shame.

"What the hell is going on?" Merissa asks again this time alarming a few of the guests.

"I'm Jackson's plus one. Actually, I'm his plus two." Allie boasts and looks directly at me then rubs her belly.

I feel David's protective nature kicking in and he slides his hand down my waist to grab a hold of my hand. My body stands still and stiff but I feel my soul dropping to my knees.

Jackson looks at me, regretfully. "I'm sorry, Parker. It's not what you think. I didn't want you to find out like this. Can we please talk in private?"

"Jason, get your friend out of here, now." Merissa turns her back to Allie and Jackson and pulls me in for a hug. Jackson steps towards me but Jason and David stop him from coming any closer.

"This is what you had to tell me, Jackson? Why do you continue to hurt me?" I wish I could speak without my voice breaking. I wish I could make myself stop crying. I wish I could tap into the powerful Parker that just walked down the aisle without a cane, but instead my strength is gone and I feel as weak as I was a year ago.

"I'm sorry, Ris. I shouldn't be doing this on your wedding day." I try to wipe my eyes, but my tears are flowing like a waterfall.

"It's okay, babe. This isn't your fault." Merissa consoles me and Allie walks nearer to us.

"Jax, why is she crying? This is good news. She should be happy for us. I'm giving you what she can't."

Allie has no shame. My life is a game to her and I'm a joke to Jackson. I look to Avery and Izzy who are making their way over here.

"You don't wanna mess with a Waylen sister. Let's go." Avery and Izzy grab Allie and escort her out the back courtyard and off the Pierce Estate.

Merissa and David are still consoling me while Jason is still in disbelief.

"We're gonna talk about this one time, Jackson. Then, you're gonna walk out of Parker's life and never bother her again."

Jackson's jaw tightens, but he nods to Merissa's demand.

"So, you two idiots planned this? You wanted to bombard Parker, for what? Why would you do this to her? Why would you invite that broad to our wedding? I told Jason that he needed cut you off a long time ago. I told him you're a selfish bastard who only cares about yourself but he was adamant that you're doing better. You were even apologetic. You're his brother, but brothers don't do this. Friends don't this. If you ever loved Parker, you wouldn't have done this to her!"

Merissa's crying for me, and I feel embarrassed for her. I nudge her shoulder and step forward to be face to face with Jackson.

"Do you have anything to say? Is it true? Did you get Allie pregnant?" He can't even look me in the face. Tears fill his eyes and I turn his cheek so he's forced to see me.

"Did you get her pregnant, Jackson? Are you having a baby with her only a year after the baby we had together died?" I try my hardest to keep a straight face but as soon as I say baby, my defenses break down. "Please Jackson. Be a man and tell me the truth. Tell me what you wanted to tell me last night when you made love to me. Tell me what you had to say when you kissed me right here where our baby used to be. Say it, Jackson!"

"Yes." He breaks down in tears and whispers in my ear. "I'm so sorry. I never meant to hurt you."

"But you always do." I respond and step back into safe territory next to Merissa, David, and Jason.

I woke up this morning feeling optimistic about a friendship or maybe even a future with Jackson again, but I'm thankful for harsh truths and painful realities. I'll walk away from Jackson with a healed body and a mind and heart that are still a work in progress which is still a million times better than being disillusioned by the fantasy of Jackson Sands.

"Goodbye, Jackson."

Chapter 14

Goodbye Jackson - Jackson

My name is Jackson, and I'm an alcoholic.
"I honestly can't tell you when it all began, but I remember the first time I felt like it was the answer to my problems. I was fourteen. I remember my mom and dad had been crying for days waiting for the results of her latest scans. They thought the cancer came back, but it was equally worse. It was an infection that kept her sick for a couple of weeks. I'd been so stressed and worried to the point I'd get migraines. I just needed something to calm me down, make me relax, make me feel nothing. I was always feeling something and for once I just wanted to feel nothing. I would secretly have a few sips of whiskey and beer every now and then when my parents would have their friends over, but on this particular day, I went in the garage and stole one of my dad's bottles of vodka that he kept hidden for special occasions. I drank half of it. It was gross, but I downed it so fast because I've seen enough tv and older adults to know that if I drink enough, I'd feel better, and I did. I stopped crying for a couple of hours. I stopped worrying and I felt safe in my sleep because being awake and in constant fear of the unknown was physically exhausting, mentally dreadful, and emotionally agonizing. It's hard to describe, but I felt warm and comforted, and the older I got, the more painful life became which made me constantly crave that warm, comfortable feeling at the bottom of a bottle.

"I'm here today, but I probably shouldn't be. Somebody's been watching over me because I haven't, but it's been three years since I had my last drink. I know I have a long road ahead of me, but I'm thankful to this group, my sponsor, my dad, my best friends Merissa and Jason, and my mentor Wayne Waylen. Without your support, I would've been dead on my living room floor instead of accepting my three year sobriety chip. I love you all and thank you for believing in me."

My support group, family, and friends erupt in a loud round of applause at my three year sobriety ceremony. This day means so much to me because it reminds me that I'm stronger than my addiction and I'm on the right track to recovering the life I threw away. I'm ready to make amends with the people I've hurt, most importantly, I'm ready to face the person I caused the most devastation to. I doubt Parker wants to hear what I have to say and she has every right to turn me away, but I have to try to make amends.

"Congratulations, Jackson! We're so proud of you! Isn't that right, Jax Jr.?" Merissa stands next to my four year old son as he jumps up to give me a high-five.

I pick him up and spin him around, and though he doesn't often express his emotions, he gives me a hug and it's the best feeling in the world.

"It's been a wild ride, son." My dad pats me on the back. Our relationship had been on the outs since my mom passed away but we reconnected three years ago and we both realized we needed help beyond a simple conversation or outing to a game. We needed therapy, and once we dealt with our grief, my dad got his son back and I got my dad back. I needed him so badly over the years but now that we're here, we're going to do everything we can to ensure we never lose each other again, for our sakes and Jax Jr.'s.

"When are you coming to town for the ribbon cutting?" Jason asks.

"Jax has a piano session and Allie won't be able to pick him up so it'll be late. I'll fly in around 9 p.m."

"Of course, Allie's busy." Merissa folds her arms and rolls her eyes at the mention of Allie's usual absence in Jax's life.

"Cut her some slack, Ris. She's a busy woman. She's taken over her dad's company so she's always traveling, and she's still trying to figure out how to build a better relationship with Jax."

I've tried to help my dad, Merissa, and Jason understand Allie's lack of daily involvement in our son's life, but I've come to understand that everyone needs time to cope with the reality that life doesn't always happen the way you plan and our son's recent diagnosis of Asperger's syndrome is a lot for her to handle. She's had a difficult upbringing and she's easily triggered by our son's outbursts and communication style.

"But that's okay isn't it, big man? We're gonna have lots of fun before daddy has to go away for a few days." Jax Jr. doesn't respond but I know he enjoys spending time with me just as much as I enjoy spending time with him.

After dinner with my family and friends, I give Jax his bath, we watch wrestling, and I put him to bed. This is my life now. It's the peace and stillness I never knew I needed and never thought I deserved, especially since the day I started to hit rock bottom, the day of Merissa and Jason's wedding.

5 years ago

Jason and Merissa are the blueprint for young, everlasting love in Beverly Mills. My best friend's wedding is two months away, and I almost didn't receive an invite. In order for me to be Jason's best man, I have to abide by three rules the entire wedding weekend:

1. Stay away from Parker
2. No plus ones
3. No drinking

I can do that easily. Contrary to what people say, I don't drink that much, and I don't bring women around my friends or family. After the accident, I kept away like Parker and Wayne warned me to, but I couldn't stay away for too long. So, while I technically haven't seen Parker in a year. I still try to find ways to connect with her and to let her know how sorry I am for ruining our relationship and throwing away our future. After a few months of silence, I text. I call. I even leave messages for her at the hospital, but Parker wants nothing to do with me.

I don't hear from her until six months later. She must've found out I paid off her student loans and hospital bills. I know she's angry, but I'm so excited to see her name pop up on my phone screen.

"Parker?" I answer.

"Leave me alone, Jackson. You think you can just buy me off with your money?"

"What? No! You got hurt because of me. You don't deserve any of what's happened to you. I just wanted to at least take one or two burdens away." I explain to her, but she doesn't want to hear me.

"Oh, Jackson, you have my undying gratitude for paying my hospital bills and school loans. How should I ever repay you? Do you want me to get on my knees with my broken leg? Do you want me to screw you like the dozens of women you flaunt around at parties? What the hell do you want from me, Jackson? I have nothing left to give to you. I'm in rehab right now. Maybe you should find a certain type of rehab of your own."

As much as it hurts to hear Parker tell me to stay away from her, it feels so good to hear her voice. I wish she could feel how much I hate myself for being the reason our family is broken. I wish she could see how miserable I really am for being the reason we can never start a family ever again.

After that call, I decided to move on and focus on my new career in the NFL. Winning in football is easy, so much easier than winning in life. I dominate on the field and almost won a championship my rookie year, but with fame and notoriety comes temptation and the constant need to do whatever it takes to stay on top.

The first time I slept with a woman other than Parker, I'll be honest, I was drunk. It was just sex. It meant nothing and so did the sex with every other woman that followed. I was invited to all the hot Miami clubs and yacht parties, and I transformed from the innocent country boy to the biggest playboy in sports in the matter of a year, but my reckless behavior caught up with me the night after the ESPY awards two months ago.

My teammates planned a party at my Miami beach house per usual and I was drinking per usual. I may have even taken a few Vicodin for my shoulder pain which explains why I don't remember much from that night. At any rate, my teammates and I are drinking and have loads of beautiful women hanging around us.

I'm usually very careful about how I deal with the women I have sex with. I use condoms. I don't kiss. I've only gone down on one woman, and I don't get attached. I've got too much to lose and I've already made a year's worth of mistakes that I'm still trying to make up for.

The party is loud and mind numbing and I need to take a break so I walk to my room with my drink in hand, but I hear clicking heels behind me. I don't let women sleep in my bedroom so I turn around to stop the eager groupie before she can go any further and I immediately recognize who she is.

"Surprise, stranger!" I can spot that loud shrieky voice from a mile away and when I turn around, I see Allie Oxford, an old college classmate who's been obsessed with me since freshman year. She was never an ugly girl, but she looks different, more superficial than back in college and she's wearing pounds of make-up and horse teeth veneers.

"What are you doing here, Allie? Why are you in my house?" I lean against my wall and try to regain full awareness of the situation, but I'm too far gone to do so.

"The same reason these other people are in your house – to have a good time, duh." She responds in a giddy, valley girl manner.

"Well, I'm tired and I'm going to bed so enjoy the party." I turn back around to head to my room but Allie grabs my hand to catch up with me.

My back faces the wall and I'm dazedly staring at her blurry face. "Jackson, I'll be happy to keep you company. I'm sure it must be lonely not having someone to keep you warm at night." She rubs her fingers down my chest then puts her hands down my pants.

"So, you are as big as everyone says." She smiles and continues to tug.

"Stop, Allie. I told you. I'm tired. I don't feel like this right now."

I frequently drink a lot and often enough to know when I'm about to pass out for the night and I don't want to do it on my hallway floor. I push her to the side to go to my room and lock the door so I can feel nothing and enjoy a long, interrupted night of blackout rest, but she's persistent and follows me to my room anyway.

"I want you, Jackson. I've always wanted you, and I can feel that you want me too." She whines.

"If you tug on a dick long enough, it'll want anyone, now move."

I move her to the side and I lay on my bed, but again, she follows me. I can't even recall how much time has passed but Allie's naked and she's pulling my pants down. The next thing I remember is her going down on me. I moan involuntarily but that's the last thing I remember. I have no idea what happened after that. I don't know if we had sex, but I do know if the roles were reversed, it'd be called rape.

The next morning, I wake up with a pounding headache and a half naked woman next to me petting my chest. It's Allie, yet again.

"What are you doing in my bed?" I jump up and try to get as far away from her as possible.

"We were sleeping, Jackson. That's what you do after you have a long night of wild, passionate sex." She smiles and stretches out wide on my bed.

"We didn't have sex. Last thing I remember, I was telling you to leave."

"Oh Jackson, stop playing dumb. We definitely had sex. Your sheet stains prove it."

"I was fucked up, Allie. You knew that and you still tried to have sex with me?" I'm pissed off and on the verge of hyperventilating. "What is wrong with you? You're sick. You took advantage of me when I was drunk!"

Unfazed, Allie gets out of my bed, walks up to me, and kisses me on the lips, "Jackson, it sounds like you're trying to make it sound like I – hmm…sexually assaulted you? Now what would everyone think once they find out a big, strong football star like yourself cried rape by a tiny, helpless beauty heiress that could have any man that she wants? Get real, Jackson. I didn't do anything you didn't want. You were definitely hard for me and you moaned as loud as a virgin. I bet Parker could never make you hit notes that loud."

"Get the hell out of my house, you psycho!" I scream and point towards the door, but she doesn't move.

"Calm down Jackson, I was just joking! Lighten up. We really did make passionate love last night and you enjoyed it as much as I did. I know you did. I know you wanted me since school. You were just too distracted by your hillbilly girlfriend to realize it."

"Don't ever mention her name again. You wish you were half the woman she is."

Allie grits her teeth, puts her clothes back on and hits me below the belt, "Well, if the rumors are true, *she's* half the woman I am especially if I end up being the one who has your baby. Last night did get pretty intense."

She winks at me and marches out the door and hopefully out of my life for forever. I can't believe I was so stupid and reckless, yet again. I keep making bad decisions that have even worse consequences. On top of that, my shoulder is throbbing and it's too soon for me to get another script without raising any red flags. I need to drink something hard to numb this pain and help me forget about what I did last night or what happened to me last night rather.

Day before wedding

That night and the morning after haunted me for days. I used to be in control of my life, but over the course of three years, since my mom died, everything has unraveled. Now, I'm here and back to the present, a day before my best friend's wedding, staring at a text from an unknown number that says, *Hey, it's Allie. I'm pregnant.*

I can't believe what I'm reading and I literally can't believe anything she says.

Allie: Your read receipts are on. Respond to me Jackson!

Jackson: What do you want me to say? I don't even remember sleeping with you

Allie: Well, I do and now I'm pregnant!

Jackson: How many other people were you sleeping with Allie? It was only once and I know I couldn't have been the only guy you randomly had a one night stand with

Allie: Well, guess what Jackson? You are and you're the only guy I've had unprotected sex with in months 💚

Jackson: Tell me the honest truth. Did you plan this? Did you plan to get pregnant? You know I wouldn't have touched you with a 10 ft pole

Allie: Careful Jackson, I hold all the cards right now and if you don't want a big announcement on ENews then you better fall in line and accept that you're gonna be a daddy.

Jackson: So, you're keeping it?

Allie: Of course, I am. We're a family now and maybe you can get over your ex and realize that we'd be a power couple.

Jackson: You're crazy. I'm out of town. We'll talk later.

Allie: I know you're in Beverly Mills for the Pierce wedding. They're high society like my family. I want to come.

Jackson: You're not coming anywhere near me or my friends.

Allie: Or your precious Parker?

Jackson: I'm not kidding. Do not come here. It won't go well. We'll talk when I get back. Just give me time to think.

Allie: Hmm…Ok, I'll try.

This is a disaster. I just need to get through this weekend without interference from Allie and deal with this situation another time. It's been a year since I've seen my friends, and I'm calling them friends lightly. Ever since the accident, I pushed everyone away and I haven't been back to Georgia since. I figured it's for the best, and if this secret comes out, I don't think I could ever return.

Yet tonight, I've tried my best to avoid Parker but I find myself looking at her out the corner of my eye, and I couldn't control myself when we were alone on the bus together. My body burns with passion when I look into her eyes but my heart also breaks when I see her limp through the pain she's had to suffer on my behalf. I've cowardly tried to escape the trauma that she's forced to endure. I'm a monster for torturing her with my presence, but it's been torture not having her in my life.

Wedding Day

Last night, I stupidly made my way back into Parker's bed and she may say she can handle what we did, but I know I made my way back into her heart as well. A year a part isn't long enough to erase a lifetime of love and all I want to do is carry her burdens like she's carried mine since the day we met.

I don't want this day to be over because I know she'll never speak to me again if she finds out about Allie. I don't want to twist the dagger that's already in her heart. How much pain can someone take until they break entirely? I can't chance this any longer. My phone's been ringing constantly, and Parker's getting suspicious.

The Devil: I'm coming to the wedding.

Jackson: You aren't invited. I'll call the police.

The Devil: Lol. Yeah right Jackson! And cause a ruckus?

Jackson: Please don't do this, Allie. You're gonna make a fool out of yourself.

The Devil: Bye Jax! See you soon.

I don't have time for this. I felt alive again last night but now I'm flat lining. I should just anticipate the shit storm that's about to happen and proceed to breaking rule #3 and drink my ass off.

"Goodbye, Jackson."

Allie was just escorted out, and Parker just gave me what feels like is her last goodbye. She's had enough, and I pushed her to the point of no return. All of the wedding guests are looking at me in shame, even my dad, who I haven't spoken to in three months.

So, I have no choice, but to escort myself out, too. I have nothing left and no one left to clean up my mess this time. I'll leave with Allie and embark on this journey I never would've chosen for myself nor would I ever wish on anyone else.

I stand in front of Allie's car and she curls her arm around mine. "I knew you'd come to your senses."

Leaving this reception together marks the end of a life I wish I would've made the best of. I'm leaving my dad, my friends, my home, and most importantly Parker, and I know it's for the best because she doesn't deserve the hand that I've dealt her.

A few weeks later, I'm at Allie's ultrasound appointment where the doctor is also performing a prenatal DNA test. I told Allie I won't contribute anything to her or this baby's life until I have proof it's actually mine. This is our first time together since the wedding and I'm not one to hope for the best, but I've been praying for the results to be in my favor for weeks.

I always imagined moments like this except the woman laying down with the jelly on her belly was Parker not Allie.

"Would you like to hear the baby's heartbeat?" The doctor asks.

Still removed from the situation and a little too buzzed to care, Allie answers for me. "Yes, we'd love to hear!"

She's so excited about this baby and while I want to be a father, I don't want it to be like this and definitely not with this person. I can't bring myself to play happy with her so I'll just stand back and watch this unreal situation from afar.

However, when I hear it and see it, something changes inside of me. This small little sweet pea on the screen is real. It's so real that I see it wiggling. I hear its strong heart beating and I'm overwhelmed with an emotion that I've only ever imagined, an emotion I can't even explain, a different type of love. I hadn't even noticed that I'm not standing against the wall anymore. I'm next to Allie, by her side, squeezing her hand tight. I'm going to be a father and I want to be good for him. I desperately need to.

A week later, I find out the results were as Allie said they'd be and I've accepted what it looks like my future will be. I want to give my child a good life like the one I had except without the sadness, the sicknesses, and the pain.

"Are you ready to meet my parents?"

"As ready as I'll ever be."

Allie grabs my hand and squeezes it tight. I agreed to meet her family and she's pretty much given me the run down. She comes from old money. Her parents plan to retire in a few years and she stands to inherit the family's billion-dollar fashion empire. Her parents are very conservative, judgmental, and stuck-up. They're everything that I'm not, and today they're meeting the man that 'knocked' up their daughter. Of course, that's the story Allie is telling them, but we know the truth. Anyway, I'm just here to fulfill my duties and do whatever she says so she doesn't keep me away from my baby.

I release a huge breath of nervousness and we walk into the Oxford family mansion. Her parents are standing in the middle of their grand foyer. They don't walk to us; we walk to them. So weird.

"Mom, it's so good to see you." She hugs her mom and I notice the Regina George mother-daughter vibe they have going on. Again, weird.

"Allie, my precious girl! You're so gorgeous and beautifully thin to be so far along. I can't believe I'm going to be a grandma already! And you happened to shag a football star?"

Mrs. Oxford turns to me and hugs me enthusiastically. She's so happy that I actually can't help but smile. I know what a person looks like when they mix pills and booze and she's definitely on a plane right now.

Mr. Oxford, on the other hand, is not pleased. "Come Jackson, let's sit down and have a drink."

Now, we're talking! We sit down in the Oxford's living room where he pours me a glass of scotch and he cuts to the chase.

"So, when are you marrying my daughter?"

I nearly choke on my drink and laugh.

"Uh, sir. Allie and I aren't together. We're not getting married."

"Don't be silly, Jackson. We're definitely together and we're definitely getting married, daddy."

Allie smiles at her dad like a little puppy waiting to get a treat then she looks at me sideways and tries to get me to play along. No thanks.

"We're not getting married. I have no interest in your daughter and I'm not gonna lie to you and say I am." I look Mr. Oxford directly in the eyes.

Mrs. Oxford is outraged and nearly walks out the room. "Mr. Sands, we invited you into our home. Have some respect for our daughter!"

"Pipe down, Martha. I knew our nitwit of a daughter wasn't dating this kid." He shakes his head, turns to Allie and glares at her with a look of disgust. "That useless thing in between your legs couldn't get him to stick around, huh? You can't do anything right."

Whoa, I wasn't expecting that response. Mr. Oxford swallows all of his drink in one gulp.

"Oh, Stephen. It's okay, maybe he'll grow to love her. Isn't that right, Jackson? People grow in love all the time, and I'm sure Allie will do everything in her power to make sure you're happy. Our grandbaby deserves to be raised in a two parent home." Mrs. Oxford tries to build a case for a marriage of convenience.

Allie runs to her father whose seething in anger and gets on her knees and places her hand on his upper thigh like she's begging for mercy. This father-daughter dynamic doesn't feel right. What the hell is going on?

"I'm sorry, daddy. I didn't mean to embarrass you. Mom's right, though. I can fix this. I can be the respectable woman I was raised to be."

"You know the conditions you have to meet to take over Oxford Beauty - married with an heir to the fortune. Who's gonna marry you, now? You're a pregnant slut who can never find a decent man. All your friends are married and you've been chasing after this boy for years. You're pathetic."

"I'm sorry, daddy. I can make this right, I promise."

"What'll make this right is for you to get rid of this abomination. You're not gonna embarrass me by trolleying around like a whore. I see enough of your antics online and the last thing I'm gonna do is let you ruin everything I've built."

Mrs. Oxford gently lays her hand on Mr. Oxford's arm, but he violently jerks it away and nearly raises his hand in the form of a back hand slap. She flinches like it's second nature and she looks at me as to remind him that I'm present. It's taking everything in me not to beat him to a pulp.

This encounter is so bizarre that I'm speechless. I thought I was just meeting the grandparents of my soon to be kid, but so far, I've been told to get married, Allie kneeled to her dad like a servant, Mrs. Oxford is high as a kite, and Mr. Oxford is a monster. This is some twisted shit. What have I gotten myself into?

Allie lowers her head and stands up to pull me aside to chat. "Jackson, I'm sorry about everything. I'm sorry about the way I went about getting pregnant. I'm sorry about what happened between you and Parker. I'm sorry I messed up your life. I'm gonna be sorry for the rest of my life, but if you do me this one favor, I promise to never bother you again ever."

"Uh, if this one favor is marrying you then that isn't a favor, Allie. It's marriage! I'm sorry that you have a shit family, but I want no parts of this scheme. You've already conned me into fatherhood. I'm not marrying you, too!"

"What've you got to lose, Jackson? You have no friends. You have no family. The girl you love will never love you again. You're lonely and so am I. We can learn to make one another happy. I don't need your money and you don't need mine. You could even have sex with other women. I don't care! I just really need this. Do it for our baby's future. We can raise this baby together and give our son or daughter a home, a much safer and happier one than what I had. Please, Jackson."

I know this is a terrible idea, but she does have a point. Everyone I love is already gone out my life so I don't have anything to lose. I just don't think I can justify seeing Allie's face every day knowing what she did to put us into this situation, but I also don't want her to have to rely on her father for any help.

"If I agree to do this, then you have to agree not to leave our kid unattended with your parents. No overnights, no baby-sitting. None of that, and your dad cannot be around our kid unless I'm present."

"I wouldn't dare, Jackson. You have no idea what type of sick man my father is and I'll die before I ever leave him alone with our baby especially if it's a girl."

I see fear, hatred, and pain in Allie's eyes and as much as I hate her, I still feel sorry for her.

"Okay, I'll do it. I'll marry you." I can't believe I'm agreeing to this, but I'll do anything for this child starting with raising it in a happy, stable, and loving home.

When we get back to the hotel, I call my dad to tell him what I'm sure much of what he already knows given the drama that occurred at the wedding, but I'm even more nervous because I don't know how he's going to react when I tell him I'm getting married.

"Hey, son." He doesn't sound too excited to speak with me.

"Hey, Dad. It's been a while," My tone is somber and I feel like a little boy who just wants his dad's approval. "I miss you."

"Oh, that's a surprise since I haven't heard from you in months." He responds sarcastically.

"There's been a lot going on."

"Well, humor me then, I need a good laugh."

"Well, you're going to be a grandfather."

"Yes, I know."

"You don't sound very happy."

"You don't either, Jackson. So why should I be?"

"I'd think every parent would be happy for their adult child, who's doing pretty well in life, by the way, to have a kid."

My dad still sounds unimpressed. In fact, he even laughs. "I don't know what you want me to say, son. Congrats on getting a random woman pregnant? This isn't the life I wanted for you and if you call what you're doing pretty well in life then I'm sorry that your mom and I didn't raise you better."

"Wow, I was stupid to think you'd be happy for me. You haven't been happy since mom died. I lost both of my parents that night."

My dad doesn't respond, but I hear his heavy breathing over the phone.

"I'm sorry, Dad."

"No, you're right, Son. We haven't been very good to one another over the years, have we? I'm sorry about that. Your mom always took care of us and now we're a mess."

We both laugh as we think about the glue that held our family together. While the moment is still, I decide to make a confession.

"Dad?"

"Yes, Jackson?" He warmly answers.

I'm hesitant to share, but I muster the courage and inform him, "I'm gonna marry Allie."

He's silent for a moment then says, "Why?"

I didn't quite think about the why, but I answer, "Because it's the right thing to do."

Absent of emotion, he blankly asks, "Says who?"

"Um, me, I guess."

My dad sighs. "You don't have a great track record for making good decisions lately, Jackson. I don't think this is a good idea. Just because you got this girl pregnant, doesn't mean you have to marry her."

"But I can give my kid the type of home you and Mom gave me." I explain.

"No, you can't." He declares. "Your mom and I loved and respected one another. If you don't have that, then your kid's gonna be just as miserable as you. Don't do it, Son."

"I don't know, Dad. I have to try to make it work. I've screwed up so many people's lives. I don't want to do the same for my kid."

"Well, maybe the best way to do better is to get better. Maybe, that's the key to giving my grandkid the life he deserves."

I stare at the many empty bottles of rum and vodka in front of me and wonder if he's referring to my drinking, my depression, or my anxiety – or maybe all three.

"Hmm, maybe I will. I'd like to get better, if I can."

My dad replies, "Can is always possible. I'm gonna get some rest. I had a huge project today and your old man needs sleep. I'm glad you called, Son."

"Me too, Dad."

As soon as I hang up the phone, I hear a knock on my door.

"Hey, it's me, Allie."

I just finished having a somewhat positive conversation with my dad and here she comes to interrupt my rare moment of peace. I swing the door open and I see Allie dressed in a short satin robe.

"What do you want, now?" I leave the door open and sit as far away from her as possible.

"So, I was thinking about a marketing strategy for the engagement. While we're here in Atlanta, I'm thinking we can tag ourselves at various boutiques, restaurants, and maybe stop in Cartier so paparazzi can get a few photos of us shopping for rings. We're gonna be trending for months. Then next week, we'll announce the pregnancy on whatever talk show pays us the most money. What do you think?"

"Why would you want everyone to be in our business? They'll figure out this whole thing is a sham in no time."

"Not true, Jackson. It's called controlling the narrative. We'll show everyone what we want them to see and they'll know what they know based on what we tell them. Just sit back and let me do my thing, okay?"

I shrug my shoulders and let Allie devise her plan to further ruin my life and eliminate my chances of ever getting back into my friends and family's good graces.

By the time she finishes making phone calls and sending texts, my calendar is booked up with tv, radio, and podcast interviews for the next three weeks.

"This is insane. I start training again in a few weeks, Allie. I'm not going to have time for all of these fake shenanigans."

"Well, that's a good thing. If you're too busy to spend time with me, maybe you'll grow to miss me." She's really banking on this growing in love idea.

"Doubt it. Can you leave now? We have an early morning flight back to Miami."

She pouts and even tries to dangle her breasts in my face, but I see the empty drink bottles on the table and all I can think about is the night she screwed me over and found a way to trap me. I know she's not blameless because I did have sex with her, but at the same time I didn't. I didn't want to, and I hate her for it. I hate that the mother of my child is someone who's manipulative, evil, selfish, twisted, and broken just like me. The mother of my child should've been Parker, but I guess we all get who we deserve in the end, and in my case, it's with someone who's as undeserving as me.

Six months ago, if you asked me how life was going, I'd say terrible, but I'm halfway through football season and we're still undefeated and this arrangement with Allie is really working out. I play along with this engagement ruse and she's kept her promise of having limited contact with her dad. I think we're as happy as we can be, given the circumstances.

"I'm fucking miserable, Jackson!" Allie throws my Rookie of the Year award across the room and almost hits me in the head.

"Allie, what's going on? You almost hit me!" I try to escape Allie's wrath but she's throwing anything she can find my way.

"I've been living in your house for months and you haven't touched me yet! You bring women home after partying all night long and make a fool out of me by letting them sleep over and walk past me like I mean nothing to you!"

"You said I could sleep with other women so what's the problem?"

"The problem is that you don't want to sleep with me! Why, Jackson?"

"We've been through this already, Allie. I don't want to sleep with you. It wasn't a part of the arrangement. You need to calm down. It isn't healthy for the baby."

"Screw you, Jackson. I'm leaving. I can't let you do this to me any longer. I need more."

"What do you mean, more? C'mon, Allie." I grab her wrist to try to get her to stay but she turns around slaps me in the face.

"What the hell? You hit me! What is wrong with you? Can we just talk?"

"What is there to talk about Jackson? You wanna talk about your drinking? You wanna talk about your pills? I'll be glad to tell the whole world about that. I'll let them know about that little hurt shoulder of yours, too!"

"Allie, you better not or I swear –"

"Or what, Jackson? You're gonna go cry to Parker, huh? You think I haven't read the drunk texts you send to her professing your undying love like a stupid little pussy whipped bitch? You think I don't know about the car you bought her last week? You little backstabbing prick! I hate you!" Allie throws a glass bowl and hits my throwing shoulder so hard my body loses its balance.

I feel the pain pulsate from the top of my shoulder down to my hand. "My shoulder! What the hell did you just do, Allie?"

She quickly snaps out of her rage and runs toward me to try to lift my hanging limb. "I'm so sorry, Jackson! Let me see."

I yell, "Get away from me! Go call the team doctor."

"No way. You can't let anyone know we were arguing. It'll ruin our reputations. Let me see," Allie looks closely at my shoulder and moves my arm back and forth. "Oh, it's just dislocated. I can pop it back into place." She nonchalantly states.

In agonizing pain, I pull away, "You're gonna make it worse. This is my throwing arm."

I start to panic and scream. I'm in so much pain, and I'm at the mercy of a psycho.

"I can do this, Jackson. My mom's popped mine back into place before plenty of times and I can't tell you how many times I made a sling for my mom's arm. Let me help you. It's the least I can do." She talks about her childhood abuse like it's normal.

I lean over the kitchen island counter, bite on a washcloth, and close my eyes in anticipation for Allie to fix the damage she just caused. She grabs my wrist then pulls my arm forward and straight out in front of me. I feel it snap back into place but I'm still in just as much pain as before. Allie runs to one of the bedrooms and comes back out with a pillowcase. She folds and cuts it into a triangle then places my arm inside it like a cradle.

"Where are your pills?" She indifferently asks. "I know you have stashes everywhere. Shoutout to your Dr. Dealer, by the way. It'll help ease your pain for tonight, but you need to come up with a story to explain this to the doc tomorrow."

I take my medicine and try to figure out what just happened. "Allie, I don't care how angry you feel about me doing what we agreed to do. You have no right to hit me, and now you probably ruined my entire football season!"

"I know. I'm sorry, Jackson. I never wanted any of this to happen. This isn't the type of environment I want for our baby. Tonight is exactly like what I used to see when I was a little girl. I just got so angry and tired of feeling hated and unwanted and add these stupid pregnancy hormones to the mix, I'm just a monster."

Allie's crying hysterically and as much I don't want to lie, I do it to help her calm down.

"You're not a monster, Allie."

Shocked by my words, she softly responds, "Really, you don't think I am? You're not saying that just because you're drunk, are you?"

Drunk or not, of course, I think Allie's a monster. She's a horrible person!

Yet, I lie again, "No, I don't think you're a monster at all. You're just tired and pregnant and stressed."

Allie wraps her arms around me and it's the first time we touched since the night I blacked out on her, and as she starts to let go, I feel a faint kick.

"Oh my god, did he just move?" My eyes are bright with excitement and joyful emotions finally begin to arise.

"He did! Jax Jr. just kicked!"

I place my hand on her bulging belly and he kicks again. Our fight becomes a distant memory and we share a moment that makes us forget who we are and how we got here.

She looks me in the eyes and with my hands still on her belly, she closes the space between us and kisses me, and I don't stop her. While we're caught up in the moment, Allie turns around, hikes up her dress, and leans over the kitchen island for me to enter her from behind.

"Get inside me, Jackson. Treat me like a dirty whore." The sound of her voice nearly makes me sick, but I have so much pent-up rage right now that I'd release it into anyone at this point.

"Shut up and bend over, Allie." I pound into her like a heartless savage and the more dissociative I am, the more it drives her wild. I disgust myself, yet she's turned on.

"Harder, you bastard!" She screams out loud. I do as she says and within seconds, her body shutters from a long-awaited orgasm by me and as much as I don't want to with her, my body betrays my heart and mind and releases as well.

When we finish, we gather ourselves, and Allie tries to have small chit chat as if what we just did is going to be a regular thing.

"I told you we can find ways to make each other happy." She smiles.

"I only did that so you can leave me alone, Allie. That was –"

"Intense." She answers.

"Toxic." I rebut. "You're the worst thing that ever happened to me."

Allie's smile quickly fades and she goes back to the twisted person I know her to be.

"I am to you what you are to Parker." She laughs.

She grabs an old-fashioned glass from the kitchen cupboard, pours a drink of scotch up to the brim, hands me another Xanax and Vicodin, and pats my hurt shoulder.

"Get some rest, future husband."

I go to sleep high, repulsed, and defeated. I'm ashamed of the man I've become. Yet, I accept my fate because after everything I've done to Parker, Allie is who I deserve.

The Miami Thunder were undefeated this season until Allie dislocated my shoulder. I've missed three games which resulted to three losses. I consulted with three doctors who claimed I should take the remainder of the season off to correct my previously and now further damaged shoulder. However, I finally found a doctor who determined it was okay for me to get back out on the field and right in time for the playoffs. I threw my way to victory and next weekend is the moment I've been waiting for, the opportunity to play on the biggest stage in sports – the Superbowl.

Home life is still unstable. We fight and we fuck then I go to my side of the house and Allie goes to hers. We have to figure out a better way to communicate because the baby will be here in a few weeks and the arguing, violent tantrums, and tension is unhealthy for all of us.

"My dad wants tickets to the game, Jackson."

"Tell him to buy them. He can afford it."

"He wants VIP seating. Make it happen, please."

"Too late. It's not happening. Papa, punch you in the face can find his own way."

Allie pushes me as hard as she can and curses me before walking away. "You're such an asshole, Jackson. I hope you break your arm and lose."

I'm used to being put down and told off now, but at least Allie's temper will likely be tamed for the next few weeks while my dad moves in with us to help out when the baby comes.

Later in the evening, while enjoying a beer and reviewing game tape, I hear a loud cry from the bathroom.

"Jackson! I think my water just broke!"

I frantically rush over to help her. Our hospital bag's been packed for months but the baby isn't expected to arrive for a few more weeks so we're completely unprepared for this moment.

"Jackson, we need to get to the hospital, now!"

I grab our belongings and hurry Allie to the car. We arrive to the hospital in record time and our obstetrician and her team are prepped and ready to go. I send a text to my dad and Allie's mom to let them know what's going on.

Baby Jax Group Chat

Jackson: Get ready. Baby's coming early.

Martha: Oh gosh! I'm booking the next flight out right now.

Frank: Ok. Remember to stay calm. Be there for Allie. I'll be there in a few hours.

Martha: I can't wait to see Baby Jax! Jackson, have you changed your mind about Stephen at all? He really wants to see his grandson.

Jackson: I haven't changed my mind, AT ALL. See you two soon.

After a shot of epidural and three hours of labor, my son enters the world. I could've never done what Allie just did. From carrying him to pushing him out, I can't help but admire her strength and watching her hold and kiss our baby is one of the most beautiful sights I've ever seen.

Yet, am I wrong for still wishing she were Parker? Am I sick for imagining her in this bed holding our baby? I prevented a moment like this from ever becoming a reality for us, and now I have to settle for a carbon copy, dark twisted version of happily ever after with a woman that hates me and makes me hate myself even more, but now that Jax Jr. is here, maybe we'll both change for the better. Maybe I *can* grow in love with Allie, for our son's sake.

"Jackson, do you want to hold your son?" I'm so nervous. For months, I've been googling fatherhood and reading parenting articles, but I completely forgot to look up how to hold a baby.

I respond with a hesitant nod. She passes Jax to me and I cradle him in my arms. He's so small and delicate. He's innocent and untainted by the sins of my past. This is my redemption, my chance to right my wrongs and start life over on a blank slate. I love you son and I promise I won't hurt you like I've hurt everyone else in my life. You'll be the one person I won't let down.

A week has passed and life couldn't be any better. My dad and Allie's mom have been a huge help. I forgot how good it felt to feel a part of a family and Jax has brought us all closer to one another. My dad and I haven't spent this much time together since before my mom passed, and Allie and her mom have been inseparable with Mr. Oxford temporarily out the picture.

Everything's fallen into place and I feel confident about the big game today. Spending time with Jax Jr. and my dad gave me an adrenaline rush which initially made it easier for me to go cold turkey off the alcohol and pills. It also helped that my dad's thrown away every bottle and beer can in my house, but now I'm restless and itching for a drink to take the edge off. There's so much pressure on me to win this game and I chose the wrong time to be sober.

Before I head into the locker room to prepare for tonight's game, I check my phone to see if I received any messages from my dad or Allie, but to my surprise, it's a text from Parker.

Hi, it's been a while. Jason, Merissa, and I are rooting for you. We love you, Jackson!

Parker still loves me. That's the only motivation I need to play my best today. Her support and love alone will help me fight through these damned withdrawals. I have to push through my throbbing shoulder pain, sweaty palms, nausea, shakes, and anxiety for the next 60 minutes. I can do this.

"Jackson, they're knocking your ass down out there. You gotta throw that ball sooner or you're gonna be down for the count. Let's go guys, protect our quarterback! One touchdown is all we need. Let's bring it home!" Coach Hart motivates the team to close the game with the win.

It's third & goal with twenty-three seconds left of game play. My men are covered and I'm out of options. The defense is closing in on me so I quickly cut to the right to shake them off and I run eight yards into the end zone until I'm completely clobbered by three defenders. There's a pile of multiple 200 plus pound men on top me. When it's cleared, all I hear is the ref blow his whistle and I see him signal a touchdown. My teammates go crazy and lift me up off the ground. The crowd erupts in chaos. I can't believe I did it. I won the Superbowl!

This moment feels so surreal. My mind is blown and my body's numb. I don't even notice my limp arm until the trainers and team doctors rush to me during an interview to temporarily place it in an emergency sling.

"Jackson Sands, you played like a legend in the making today so much so you re-injured your shoulder but you're still unfazed. What a way to lead your team! What was your mindset throughout today's game?" The sports anchor asks.

"I was just thinking about making the next play for my teammates. We worked hard all season for this moment and it was a collective effort. We have the best coach in the league, the best staff, the best offense, and the best defense. Miami Thunder, let's go!"

This victory high is on another level. I'm so excited in this moment and I want to make sure the world knows why.

"Anything else you'd like to say before I leave you to celebrate?" She asks.

"Absolutely, I just want to say I wouldn't be here if it weren't for my mom, God rest her soul, my dad, my newborn son Jax Jr. my best friends Jason and Merissa, and Parker. I love you!"

This win is all for Parker. Whenever I win in life, it's all because of her.

After the on-field celebration, the team's popping bottles of champagne to commemorate our victory. I know I shouldn't drink. I know I promised not to, but this is a momentous occasion so one drink won't hurt. It's just one drink.

Days later, I awake to find my dad and Allie standing over me in my bedroom. My dad looks disappointed and Allie looks annoyed while holding Jax Jr. over her shoulders burping him.

"I told you he was okay, Mr. Sands. Jackson does this more often than you know. By the way Jackson, nice speech." Allie walks out the room and slams the door.

"Son, we haven't seen you since you left last week. Your teammate said you arrived home days ago, but he just dropped you off this morning. You've been passed out for hours and Allie said this is normal. What happened to not drinking anymore?"

"Dad, please not now. I'm exhausted and I feel like I've been ran over by a truck." If I were in my right mind, I'd never shoo my dad away, but hangovers make savages out of anyone.

With an elevated voice, my dad angrily demands, "Jackson Sands! Get your ass up and treat me with some damn respect!"

Instantly alert, I open my eyes and sit at attention. My dad has never raised his voice at me before. "You're a father, now. You can't keep drinking and partying like you don't have any responsibilities. You should've been home taking care of your son, but instead you've been doing the exact opposite. You're behaving like a child and those days are over."

I lean my head back on the headboard and let out an exhausting sigh. "Yes, sir. I apologize."

"Don't apologize to me. Apologize to your fiancé and your son and I hope saying sorry doesn't become a habit. I'm packing my bags and going back home and I told Allie to do the same if you continue on this self-destructive path."

Before my dad leaves the room, he sorrowfully turns back to me and says, "You and your mom are still the two most amazing people in my life. When you're done running away and decide to come home, I'll be there with open arms. Goodbye, Jackson."

I'm a twenty-five year old young man, but my body feels like a fifty year old crash dummy. I've been taking hard hits to the body since high school. It's my third year in the NFL and I don't know how much more damage to my shoulder I can take. I underwent three surgeries this past summer for my fractured clavicle, rotator cuff tear, and dislocated shoulder. I overworked myself during rehab so I can get back on the field before the season begins, and I've had to take twice as many scripts to mask my pain this time around. Yet, here I am. I'm on the verge of becoming a two-time back-to-back NFL champion.

Allie's been on this kumbaya kick ever since her mom left her dad and moved in with us to help with Jax Jr., and they've been going to therapy which is like the 'in' thing to do now. I come home when I can, but it isn't easy being around them because I didn't choose this life for myself. The life I want is the one David has. He and Parker have 'made it official' and she looks happy. I could never give her that.

But hey, the blogs, social media, and tv all say that Jackson Sands has it all and I guess that's all that matters. That's what my life has come down to – fakery and fuckery.

I just wish I had people around who knew me. I wish I had people around me that could see that I'm lonely and I need help because I'm not strong enough to get better on my own. I'm not strong enough to confront the pain that's kept me shackled for nearly all my life. I need my mom. I need my dad. I need Jason. I need Merissa. I need Parker. I need Parker more than I need to breathe and I don't know how much longer I can survive living like this. I'm past the brink of depression. I've been sitting on a bus stop of hurt and despair for years waiting for someone to see me, waiting for someone to hear this voice inside of me scream out like I screamed the night my mom passed away and Parker held me in her arms and wrapped me in her comforting embrace. I need to know if I'm still redeemable. I need someone to show me that there's more to life that what I see. There has to be more than loneliness, tragedy, and despair.

While I'm sitting in the corner of my room with my knees to my chest, rubbing my bruised shoulder and rocking back and forth drinking a beer and lost in my dark thoughts, Allie quietly enters with a bag in her hand and our son in his carrier.

"Jackson, I'm leaving and I'm taking our son with me."

I say nothing. It's for the best.

"Jackson, did you hear me?" Allie puts the carrier and bag on the ground, walks closer to me and kneels down.

"I'm sorry that I contributed to your pain. I'm sorry for everything. I don't want Jax to be without his father, but you're sick, Jackson. It's like you have a switch that you turn on in front of cameras and on the field but as soon as you come home, you shut yourself up in a room and drink 'til you pass out. I thought I could handle it – the drinking, the pills, the women, the partying, the hate, but I can't. I grew up with it but I can't let our trauma affect our son. I'm moving back to Atlanta. Goodbye, Jackson."

I don't even watch her leave the room. I just cry in a corner and imagine Parker holding me and rocking me to sleep like she did the night my mom died.

A week after winning my second Superbowl ring, I receive a long text with a drafted statement from Allie's PR team in response to a photo circulating of me and another woman in a compromising position. She and the Thunder media team also arranged a series of interviews with major media outlets as an attempt to fix the poor reputation I built for myself. My party boy lifestyle is now affecting the organization so appearances aren't optional, and I have to clean up my act or else face the consequences.

I pop a few Xannies and wash them down with a dash of Jack Daniels and ace almost every interview on the Jackson Sands Redemption tour except this one.

This reporter is an idiot.

"Thank you so much for sitting down with me, Jackson. How does it feel to be the youngest quarterback to win back-to-back NFL championships?"

"I still can't believe it. It's humbling, that's for sure, but I wouldn't be here without a great organization and a strong support system."

"Speaking of support system, your mom must be so proud! Her son's a superstar and he's also considered one of the most eligible bachelors in the nation. Things must've been tough since the love of your life recently broke up with you, but have any of the special ladies we've seen you out with had the chance to meet your mom?"

I say nothing.

"Is the notorious Action Jackson shy?" She asks.

"No, I'm just dumbfounded at how dumb you are."

"Excuse me?" The reporter looks to her producers confused as to how to proceed.

"I only loved two women in my entire life. My mom, who's dead by the way, and Parker Waylen. She's love of my life not Allie Oxford."

"I'm sorry, Jackson. I had no idea about your mother. My apologies."

"You can find that information on Wikipedia. I thought I was here to talk about football not my love life. Are you a sports reporter or a gossip columnist?"

"I beg your pardon, Jackson Sands? I am a well-respected journalist. You're clearly as unhinged as they say you are."

"Okay, lady. Whatever you say. This is a waste of my time. Go elsewhere and gossip about my trash engagement."

"Well, whoever Parker Waylen is had the right idea to leave you, Jackson Sands!" She yells.

I get out of my chair, throw my mic down, and exit the live tv interview. My agent's gonna kill me.

I've been shut up in my home for days drinking, crying, sleeping, and drinking, crying, and sleeping some more. Every tabloid and gossip account on social media are calling me a drugged out alcoholic trainwreck, and they're exactly right. I can't even refute it. Not to mention, I embarrassed Parker. I really wanted to impress her. I wanted her to see I was changing for the better, but I'm a con. I know she'll never speak to me again, and I don't blame her for it.

I've officially hit rock bottom, and there's nowhere for me to go from here. I'm weak, and I've relied on everyone else to give me strength throughout my entire life and when it was time to pull myself up by the bootstraps, I failed. I'm ashamed of the man I've become. I've been doing the same thing over and over for years and experiencing the same pain over and over again for years. I've lasted long enough. I've suffered long enough. My mom would know what to do, but she's gone. Parker would know what to do to help me, but she's gone, too. God, I'm such a fucking burden. I always have been and I always will be. How can I make it all stop? I want to stop hating myself. I want to stop feeling worthless, but I only know how to make myself feel numb which is exactly what I need to do right now.

That's exactly what I'll do. I'll hope for both the best and the worst. I hope to die. I hope to spare everyone the misery of being associated with me. I hope to see my mom again. I just want to see my mom again. I hope that everyone understands why this is the right thing to do. I hope everyone understands that I can't take the pain of living anymore. They say weeping may only endure for the night, but joy never came for me. Pain is temporary for some, but it's become my life and now it's time to permanently end it all.

After I ingest a cocktail of benzos and opioids, and get ready to truly feel nothing, I receive a text from Parker.

I saw your interview. You are so much better than what I watched. You're the son of Debra and Frank Sands. You're strong, perseverant, loving, and kind. You've overcome too much in life for you to get to this point. I've forgiven you for what happened, but what I can't forgive is the hatred you're harboring against yourself. You are not worthless. You are not a failure. You just need help, Jackson and there's nothing wrong with getting the help you need to live a healthy, happy life. Jackson, I know you're lonely and depressed. I know you're hurting. You've been hurting since the day we met and you've been suffering since the night your mom died. We may not ever be together again, but I'll always be your friend and I'll always love you, no matter what, Jackson Sands. I love you IN SPITE OF what you've done. I love you IN SPITE OF who you THINK you are. And I love you IN SPITE OF what you think you deserve. You're stuck in your sorrow right now, but it won't always be like this because despite everything, you are still wonderfully, beautifully, and fearfully made. I know you'll do the right thing and get the help you need, but until then Goodbye Jackson.

I pick up the phone and dial Jason's number. I haven't spoken to him in two years. I don't know if he'll answer, but I need help. I don't know how long I can stay conscious to call out for help, but I don't want to die. I want to get better, but my thoughts have taken over and there's a tug-a-war between the strength Parker just gave me to hold on a little while longer and the darkness that's been trying to suffocate me since I was a kid. I DON'T WANT TO DIE. Not now. Not yet.

"Jackson?" Jason answers his phone and I try to mute my cries so he can hear me clearly, but I'm too overwhelmed with sadness and desperation.

"Jason. I need help. I can't – I can't do this anymore. I'm sorry, I didn't know who to call. I have no one left."

He frantically, "Where are you, Jackson?"

Barely coherent, I mumble, "My house in Miami."

Jason says, "We'll get the jet ready and be there in two hours. It's time to come home."

Hours later, I wake up in a hospital room. I see my dad, Wayne Waylen, Jason, and Merissa with excited and relieved expressions on their faces.

Parker's text gave me strength, and Jason, Merissa, my dad, and Wayne just saved my life. After struggling for over ten years with addiction, depression, and despair, my journey to recovery finally begins.

CHAPTER 15

JACKSON 2.0 - JACKSON

Sobriety Year 1

It's been a year since I had a drink of alcohol or taken any type of opioids or benzos, and I'm grateful beyond belief that I've made it this far thanks to words that have comforted me since I was a little boy, *Because despite everything, we are still wonderfully, beautifully, and fearfully made.* It gave me the strength to make that phone call and finally cry out for help.

The day I tried to end my life, Merissa and Jason called my agent and publicist to discreetly rush me to the nearest hospital where the doctors pumped my stomach and by the time I awoke, most of the people I pushed away for years were by my side supporting me – my dad, Jason, Merissa, and Wayne Waylen.

After I was discharged from the hospital, I met with my coach, the team president, the doctors, and my agent, and we came to the conclusion that I shouldn't renew my contract. My publicist spun the real reason why I decided to take time off and I made an official announcement to the media a week later.

"Thank you all for coming today. We're here because I have an announcement that impacts my future and the future of the Thunder Organization. As you all are aware, my arm's taken quite a beating since my senior year of college. Like many other players in the league, I've played through injuries and even managed to win two championships, but all at the expense of my physical health. My shoulder is damaged beyond immediate repair and I've decided to take time off to focus on the proper pain management and rehabilitation needed for me to live a healthy life, now and after I retire from football. My sole focus will be my health during my time of leave. Thank you for respecting my privacy and all questions may be directed to my team."

I make a beeline to my truck and my driver takes me directly to the tarmac so I can board Jason family's private jet where he, Merissa, Wayne, and my dad wait for me.

"Are you ready to do this?" Jason asks.

With sigh of determination, I respond, "I finally am."

I used to envision rehab as this gloomy, caged prison meant to scare people away from doing drugs and alcohol, but it's the exact opposite. From the moment I checked in, I felt welcomed by the staff and counselors, and while my recovery's been difficult, my treatment has been as twice as beneficial.

"Mr. Sands, are you ready for your six month evaluation?" Dr. Asher asks.

Trying to mask my nervousness with a hint of confidence, I respond, "Yes, ma'am."

Dr. Asher, another staff worker, and I sit in her office to discuss my progress.

"Mr. Sands," She says. "When you first got here, I have to be honest with you. You were a wreck."

We all laugh because I'd be a fool to disagree. I checked in with an optimistic attitude, but by day two, my withdrawals start kicking in and I felt like the walls were closing in on me. I wanted to claw through my stomach to make the pain stop and I was shivering like a Southerner in New York on New Year's Eve. The longest I'd gone without drinking or taking pills in the last four years was four, maybe five days max.

"I remember. I was a mess. I thought I was dying." I admit, shaking my head at the memory, surprised at how far I've come.

Dr. Asher smiles. "But you didn't, did you? You realized you can survive without the pills and alcohol. You realized you can be content with just yourself." She encourages.

"I can. It does feel different. You may think I sound dumb, but I haven't slept this well in years and when I wake up, I actually feel energized." I embarrassingly confess.

Yet, Dr. Asher's sincere tone reassures me, "I don't think you sound dumb at all. I don't think you're dumb either, Jackson. In fact, you sound like many recovering addicts who forgot what life was like before their addiction overshadowed it."

"Well, I like it, but it's only been six months. What if I can't stay sober? It's easy in here. I have you and our sessions, but out there it's just me, and when I'm alone, I make terrible decisions." I voice my fears as think about the weight of my future pressing down on me.

But Dr. Asher motivates me and lift a bit of the heaviness from my heart. "From what I see, one of the best decisions you ever made was coming here which is the first step to creating a new life for yourself and that is something you should be proud of."

With a sigh a resignation, I reply, "I guess, you're right."

With a light-hearted smile, Dr. Asher concludes, "And I guess you aren't as wretched as you think you are."

A smirk forms on my face as I think about the possibility that I may not be the monster I've always thought I was. For years, I judged myself for being reckless. I chastised myself for being sad. I criticized every action I made. I beat myself up so bad that I felt worthless. No matter how much money I made, no matter how well I played on the field, no matter how much Parker would tell me how amazing I was, no matter how much my mother encouraged me, I still felt like I didn't deserve to be happy or be loved. Nevertheless, my self-perception has changed over the past six months.

I don't think I can be good, I know I am good and I deserve to live a happy life.

The room gets quiet and Dr. Asher hates silence. So, she prompts, "What are you thinking, Jackson? Speak up. I can't hear your thoughts."

Responding with honesty, I share, "I'm thinking about what happens in the real world, when I'm no longer confined to this bubble."

Dr. Asher leans forward and emphasizes her point, "You make a commitment to yourself to stay sober. For years, you failed because you promised to change for the sake of everyone but yourself. You said you'd get better for your mom. You said you'd get better for Parker. You said you'd get better for your son. But you never made a commitment to get better for yourself. It's time to do that, and I believe you're ready. You know how to cope, and you have a strong support system. Channel that strength inside of you, but most importantly use our network. Go to your meetings – once, twice, and three times a day if you have to. Don't let your guard down and be mindful of your thoughts when you feel sad, angry, stressed or anxious. It sounds difficult and tedious, but I promise over time, being this aware becomes a part of who you are. And if you mess up, it's okay. The beautiful thing about being human is that every day is new chance to start over. Does that make sense?"

"It does. It absolutely does." I answer, feeling a surge of hope.

She probes further in a quest for commitment, "So, tell me Jackson, what are you going to do when you get back out in the real world?"

I sit back in my chair and rub my hands on my thighs and think about my new beginning. "Well, first things first, I'm going to a meeting. Then, I'm going to go home to work on my short-term and long-term goals. I have a lot of work to do."

Dr. Asher smiles, then affirms, "And I believe you're going to succeed, Jackson. We believe in you."

I exit the Sober Minds Drug and Alcohol Rehab Center of Atlanta with a renewed sense of self. I'm ready to be the man my mom always said I would grow to be. I'm ready to trust myself. I'm ready to encourage myself. I'm ready to communicate better. I'm ready to accept love and happiness. I'm ready to be Jackson 2.0.

After I visit a nearby support group, I feel energized and ready to take on the world, but when I enter my condo that I only purchased for the sole purpose of hosting wild alcohol and drug infused parties, I find myself thinking about who I was six months ago and what I need to do right here and now to prevent myself from falling back into bad habits. I unfold my paper to remind myself that there's a better way to live.

My drinking triggers	My coping strategies
HALT: Hungry, Angry, Lonely, Tired	Support group, meeting, sponsor
Anxiety and depression	Therapy, hobby: cooking
Loss and tragedy	Counseling, meetings
Bad memories	Good memories
Shoulder pain	Rest, self-care
Party scene	Family, friends
Sadness	Positivity
Stress	Exercise

My short-term goals	My long-term goals
Buy a house and make it a home	Live sober. Stay sober.
Make up for lost time with Jax Jr.	Thrive in real estate
Enroll in real estate course	Make amends • Merissa • Jason

	• Dad
	• **Parker**
12 months of sobriety	Give back to Beverly Mills
	• Help friends achieve their goals
	• Drug and alcohol rehab facility
	• Hospital expansion

While I'm planning my schedule for the next few days, I receive a knock on my door. I look through my peephole to see who it is, but my line of sight is covered by balloons. I take a deep breath then open the door to see my friends, who I'm sure are ready to celebrate my return.

"Jackson!" Merissa's loud voice travels through the door and she rushes over to give me a hug. "Six months sober, who would've thought?"

I look at her closely and I even have to take a step back, her frame is still small, but her stomach is hard to ignore. "Is there something I need to know?" I look back and forth between Jason and Merissa.

I see the smile breaking through Jason's poker face and I give them a celebratory hug.

"I really thought my dress made me look conspicuous! Please don't tell anyone, Jackson. Only you, Parker, and a few family members know. We'll make an announcement once we're in the safe zone." Merissa rubs her belly and drifts off into her own wave of sadness as she thinks about her last pregnancy and the miscarriage that followed.

I was too consumed with myself back then to support my friends, but I'm here now and they're stuck with me. "I understand, Ris. Come and sit down. You should relax, no standing."

"Oh goodness, so you're gonna be one of those types? I'm still an adult Jackson. I can take care of myself."

"Here we go, again. There's no point in trying, Jackson." Jason shakes his head. "I've been trying to get her to relax for weeks. She's a stubborn one."

"Oh hush, you two. By the way Jackson, you have a special visitor that should be here any minute." Merissa informs me.

Right on cue, I hear a knock on my door. "It's open!" I yell from the living room and see my door open slowly to reveal my dad holding my son. It's been well over six months since I've seen Jax Jr. and he's gotten so big. I give them a hug then the moment turns into an emotional Sands family reunion.

"I missed you, Dad." Tears flow from my eyes as we hold our embrace. It feels like I haven't seen them in forever so much so that I'm afraid to let go.

"Daddy?" My son calls me dad for the first time. Well, maybe he has before, but this is the only time that matters because it's the first time I'm in my right mind.

My dad passes Jax Jr. to me and I'm shocked by how much he's grown. He looks at me like I'm a stranger, but calls me daddy again. I missed nearly two years of his life, and I'll be damned if I ever miss another day ever again.

Sobriety Year 2

I know hitting rock bottom was what I needed in order for me to get my life together, but I really wish I would've known how good it felt to live sober much sooner than later.

My dad and I expanded the family business. I purchased Sands Construction and it's now a subsidiary of Sands Family Enterprises. I've been able to leverage my NFL contacts to quickly build my client portfolio and I'm now one of the youngest, most successful commercial real estate developers in the nation, but my proudest career achievements are giving back to the community. My real estate developments have all contributed to the health and well-being of individuals who struggle with mental health, alcohol and drug addiction, physical injuries, and cancer-related illnesses – all of which have greatly impacted me throughout my life.

I couldn't have done it without the support of my friends, family and my sponsor. I'm finally at a point of stability in my life, and I don't want to be one of those people that toot my own horn, but I've become a pretty good dad, too. Allie's still crazy, but she's a decent mom. Once her dad stepped down from the company, she became, in her words, 'the boss bitch.' She doubled their profits and she's finally the respected cut-throat businesswoman she never thought she could be. Take that, Mr. Oxford.

Recently, we've come to an agreement that her work responsibilities, travel schedule, and the amount of time and special care needed to nurture Jax is too much for her to handle right now so Jax lives with me on the weekdays.

We also noticed his unique social interaction skills and lack of expressiveness a few months ago, but it didn't cause us concern until recently when his daycare, couldn't calm him down or figure out why he was upset. He broke out into a rage, but it wasn't because he was angry, it was because no one could understand what he wanted or how he felt. I mean, he's still only a toddler and while other kids his age may be more communicative, Jax Jr. is still a brilliant work in progress. His school called him a problem. The doctors call it Asperger's Syndrome, but I call him a prodigy. We enrolled him in a childcare center for the gifted and I've seen a tremendous amount of growth already.

I'm going to take advantage of these years for as long as I can because I know they go by fast and pretty soon I'll be a grandfather like my dad who can't get enough of Jax Jr. I'm pretty sure he likes him more than me. Jax, my dad, Mr. Waylen, and I have even started going on monthly fishing trips like we used to do when I was a little kid.

Jax is perfect, and he even has a special place in Jason and Merissa's hearts. After Merissa suffered another miscarriage, Jax and I stayed with them for a few days to serve as a source of comfort during their time of grief.

It was the least I could after they've supported me through every tragedy in my life, and now Merissa's suffering yet again.

Today is the day of her sister Iyanna's funeral. She died last week of a drug overdose. Since we were kids, I watched Iyanna's drug addiction tear their family apart over and over only for them to still remain intact and hopeful that one day she could overcome her struggles. There were always glimmers of hope during her months of sobriety, but it only takes one mistake, one slip up, to fall back into darkness, and it happened to Iyanna more often than not, and if I'm not mindful and let my guard down then it could also happen to me.

I haven't been back home in Beverly Mills since the wedding, and so much has changed, especially the people. I've been anticipating this moment for an entire week, but I've been waiting for this opportunity for years – to be reunited with Parker again. I don't know the next time I'll be able to see her so now is my chance to make amends to the person who deserves it the most.

Parker has always supported me through thick and thin, but I was too emotionally closed off to accept her love. I've let go of all hope of us getting back together, but if she'll allow me to make amends and take ownership of all the pain and heartache I caused her then I'll be forever grateful to her for the rest of my life.

Parker and David walk into the funeral home hand in hand. She looks more mature and refined than the years prior, and she's more beautiful than ever. I try to stalk her social media accounts here and there, but she recently blocked me after we exchanged a few likes on each other's photos. From the little information I could squeeze out of Jason and Merissa, she's nearly done with her residency at Emory Hospital and she wants to open up her own practice soon. She's so incredible, and I may give off Allie stalker level vibes, but sometimes I schedule business meetings near her hospital with hopes of running into her. I mean, we live in the same city, but we live in completely different worlds. I've wanted to see her for so long. I just want to know if she's happy. I want to know if he's given her the unconditional love that I couldn't give her and today I'm gonna find out.

After the funeral, I see David walk to the driver's side of the car I bought her a few years back, but Parker looks back at me and to my surprise, lags behind. Maybe she wants to speak to me as much as I want to speak to her.

Breaking the silence, I venture, "Hi, Parker."

I didn't think I'd ever say those words again, and while my smile is wide, hers is tight.

She responds with a cold edge, "Jackson."

She still hates me, but that's expected.

"It's good to see you. You look wonderful given the circumstances we're here of course." Without even thinking, I reach my hand towards her face and touch a lock of her hair. "I love the haircut. It matches your personality."

"Thanks, Jackson," Her voice slightly softens, and she tries not to smile, but I know she still feels something for me. "But how would you know my personality? We haven't crossed paths in years."

With sincerity, I continue, "No matter how long we're separated from one another. No matter how far apart we are. I'll know you, always just like you'll –"

She interjects, "Love you, always?"

We smile at one another for what seems like forever until Parker glances back and remembers that David is in the car and he's staring at us through the window.

Parker hurries, "I should get going. Maybe we'll see each other around."

I half-jokingly suggest, "If we stop hanging out with Jason and Merissa on separate days then we can."

She shakes her head and adjusts her tone, "You know it's not that simple. *We* aren't that simple, to just be friends."

I'm frustrated because she's right, even right now as we stand, I just want to kiss her.

With determination and hope, I plead, "Maybe we can try or you can give me the chance for me to prove to you that I'm a man of my word. Everything I do is intentional now." I step closer to her and brush my hand against her cheek. "Everything, Parker." Our panting hot breaths raise goosebumps on our arms and our hearts beat in sync. Our lips are inches away from one another, but the hard slam of a car door interrupts this destined moment.

She pushes my arm away and frantically steps back. "Sorry, Jackson. I almost made a huge mistake. We can't be around each other." She turns around and walks to her car. I plaster a fake smile and wave my hand in the air to greet David from afar. He looks pissed and embarrassed, and I could only hope he finally realizes that Parker may be in love with him now but not always.

Sobriety Year 3 – *Present Day*

I'm coming home. Atlanta's treated me well, but it's time for me to give back to Beverly Mills.

Sands Construction already made a huge impact with the Beverly Mills Beautification Project which has contributed to the influx of new residents over the years. We recently renovated historic Beverly Mills. We restored the town's government complex, and this weekend we'll break ground on the new hospital wing. This is just the beginning.

And did I mention that Parker moved back home? And that she's single? And that I am, too? I don't mean to sound like an opportunist, but if the opportunity presents itself, then why not?

"The city of Beverly Mills is once again proud to partner with Sands Family Enterprises to contribute to the beautification of this booming city. The construction of our hospital's new Cancer Research Facility marks the beginning of our investment into the health and wellness of families and patients across the nation. We'll employ the most revolutionary oncologists and equip them with innovative, leading-edge technology to help combat cancer and prolong lives. This is a wonderful day and I am proud to be the mayor of Beverly Mills and it feels even better to stand here next to my best friend and Beverly Mills native, Jackson Sands. This is only the beginning everyone!"

Business owners, reporters, and residents applaud Jason, the youngest and most popular mayor Beverly Mills has ever elected into office. He sure knows how to put on a show. I'm not a fan of the spotlight anymore. I prefer magazine or podcast interviews so when we cut the ribbon and the crowd disburses, my anxiety dissipates and I feel relaxed.

After the ribbon cutting ceremony, Jason and I head to dinner to meet up with Merissa and Parker. I'm so nervous right now. We're all just hanging out as 'friends' but Jason and Merissa are known for their schemes and this outing could easily be considered a double date. Not to mention, Merissa is more giddy than usual.

Unable to contain her excitement, she remarks, "Isn't this restaurant nice?"

Merissa points out the dim lighting, the fancy seating, and the romantic atmosphere - this is definitely a double date. Parker enters through the doors and stops the moment she sees me. Her smile quickly fades into a grimace, and she marches up to the table and scowls at Jason and Merissa.

Parker explodes in feigned indignation, "What is this? Why do y'all insist on putting us together? All our frickin' lives you smush us together into these uncomfortable situations. How dare you betray my trust, Merissa!"

Parker looks so cute when she's fake angry. She's trying to keep a straight face but she's also looking at me out the corner of her eye.

She turns to me in scrutiny and asks, "Are you in on this, Jackson?"

I innocently lift my hands and shake my head, "Nope, had no idea, but I'm not complaining." I sit back in my chair, button my suit jacket and give Parker a little smirk.

Parker whines and plops down in the chair next to me, "Ugh, y'all are so annoying. Let's get this over with."

Merissa amusingly rolls her eyes and gets to the heart of the matter. "Now, that you're done being a little diva, we brought you both here to get something off our chests and out in the open."

Concern shows on both of our faces as the conversation turns serious.

I anxiously ask, "Is everything okay? What's the problem?"

Jason and Merissa grab one another's hands and Merissa continues to speak, "We're really annoyed with the two of you."

Baffled, I defend myself, "What? What'd I do? I don't even live here." Last time I checked, I haven't pissed my friends off in years."

Merissa cuts me off and urges, "Oh, Jackson. Shut up and listen. We're not splitting days between you two anymore. For years, we've had to rearrange our schedules to spend time with you separately throughout the week and it's exhausting. I'm going to work from home a lot more and limit my activity. Jason and I are going to try for a baby again for what may be the last time. After so many miscarriages, I'm not sure we can take any more heartache and we want our best friends around, the both of you."

Jason adds, "We need your support."

Parker and I look at one another and I'm sure she agrees that it's time for us to step up. Merissa and Jason have been there for us for every argument, every tragedy, and for me and all of my screw-ups. This is not just important to them; it's important to all of us.

Parker speaks up, "I'm so glad you guys are gonna try again. We'll be there every step of the way."

Eager to show my support, I join in, "Parker's right. Whatever y'all need, we'll support you. I'll make sure Jason leaves the house when he annoys you."

And Parker, always the planner, adds, "And I'll make sure Merissa doesn't work past 4 p.m. We're pumping the brakes on her workaholic tendencies. I'm setting up the group chat right now."

Okay, maybe this was a bad idea. Merissa and Jason did it again. This is the most Parker and I have communicated in years. Our elbows are even rubbing together and it feels so natural to be this close to her. We stay at the restaurant long after we've eaten. The conversation is flowing, and in this moment, I realize that I made the right decision to come back home to Beverly Mills, but most importantly I made the right decision to come back home to Parker.

Jason laughs and kisses Merissa on the cheek, "All right, I'm gonna get my wonderful wife home so we can get to work."

Parker reacts in playful disgust, "Ew, you two are so gross. It's so cute."

After they leave, Parker suggests we take a walk so who I am to deny her right to exercise?

"You've really done a great job with revitalizing the city. It's the perfect blend of old and new, ya know?" She looks around to see the lively, diverse groups of people walking the streets. From young and old to singles and families, Beverly Mills is the place to be." She compliments.

With modest pride, I reply, "It's the least I could do. Beverly Mills and the people who live here saved my life too many times to count."

She curiously probes, "If that's so, then why in the world has it taken you so long to come back home, Jackson? Your dad and random employees have been roaming around the city and you've been nowhere to be found."

I explain, "Why would I visit? Jason and Ris were in Atlanta up until a year ago and my dad travels back and forth because he's in this weird 'I don't like to be by myself' phase. But if I may be honest, I think he should start dating, put himself out there."

Parker then cautiously asks, "Are you dating anyone, Jackson?"

I push my excitement at the though of her showing interest in my dating aside and answer, "No, not right now. I tried to here and there, but my schedule's too busy."

She chuckles, "You'll always be too busy, Jackson. So, do you just intend on being single forever?"

I hint at my true feelings, "No, I'm just waiting for a second chance from one person in particular."

Parker smiles. My attempt at flirting is working.

She suddenly suggests a change of scenery. "Let me show you my office. It's right over here."

I tease, "Ah yes, the world-renowned Beverly Mills Pediatrics and Childhood Psychology. I've been waiting to receive an invite."

She laughs, "Oh whatever, Jackson, no one has banned you from coming here. Your company did most of the work anyway, and I'm sure my parents – actually, I know my parents sent you an invitation to our grand opening."

I nod. "They did, but that was before I knew you and David broke up. I didn't want to cause any more issues between the two of you."

Parker acknowledges our wrongdoing. "We both did our fair share of damage. Hell, you sneezing would've caused an issue between us, but that's the past, right?"

I agree, looking forward, "Absolutely."

We walk into Parker's office where I admire her academic achievement plaques on her walls, but I stop when I notice a more poignant achievement and it's an array of wall photos that chronicle her path to learning to walking again.

She reflects, "Amazing, huh, how the human body heals? I love these photos. They remind me of how strong I am. I thought I was broken."

Moved by her resilience and she's overcome, I express my admiration, "Bruised, not broken. Despite everything, nothing could break you. You're the strongest person I know – so wonderfully, beautifully, and fearfully made."

We interlace our fingers with one another and enjoy a moment of silence until I turn to Parker and finally ask, "May I kiss you?"

With a soft voice and longing heart, she answers, "You may."

It's been years since I've been fortunate enough to touch her lips and I want to take my time and savor this moment, but my greediness and neediness won't allow me to move in slow motion. I want to give her my all. I want to be sensual, tender, sexual, aggressive, rough, and passionate all at once, and to my surprise, she lets me have my way.

I deepen my kiss and my hands travel down Parker's breast then to her waist. Her moans are driving me crazy. I'm a man unhinged and I need to stop myself before we cross a line that she'll regret. She starts to unbuckle my belt but I finally gain enough awareness to stop her.

"Jackson, what's wrong?" We're both panting hard and struggling to catch our breaths.

"This, what if you regret this? If we cross this line, I don't want to go back. I want to move forward with you, Parker. Tell me we can move forward."

"We can try, Jackson." Parker barely finishes her sentence before she unzips my pants, but before she could grab ahold of me, I lay her back on the desk, eagerly pull her panties to the side, and bury my face in her sweet, warm, wetness.

"Jackson, don't stop."

She doesn't know this but I won't stop. I can't stop. Not now. Not ever. I lift her off the desk and push her back against the wall. She wraps her legs around my waist and I thrust deep inside of her. It's been a while since I had sex this good so I don't know how long I'll last. I push her to the edge with my circling thumb and after a few more thrusts I feel an explosion of wetness all around me. She yells out in pleasure and I'm so glad I can finally release as well.

"That was the best sex I've ever had." I admit, still breathless and sweaty.

"You came so fast. Reminds me of prom night." She laughs.

"I don't see how I even lasted that long, a few more seconds and I would've been in tears. No one's ever made feel like how you make me feel, Parker."

She gives me a peck on the lips, throws me my shirt, smiles and says, "We should get going."

We clean ourselves up and put our clothes back on. As amazing as our sex was a few minutes ago, I feel Parker distancing herself already.

"So…do you want to grab dinner tomorrow before I leave town?"

I see the regret on her face. "Jackson, I don't really think –"

"Parker, really right now? I asked if you'd regret this."

"Jackson, this is a lot. We have a lot of history, but we can't just pick up where things left off. Every time we hook up, you screw things up. I can't go through that again. I'm too old to keep making the same mistake. Unstable relationships aren't cute to me anymore."

"Please, Parker. I love you. I've never stopped loving you and I know you never stopped loving me. Always, remember?"

She takes a deep breath, taps her forehead against mine and we cross our pinky fingers.

"Always, Jackson."

I feel so alive in this moment. We give each other one last kiss goodbye, and agree to meet for dinner tomorrow night. However, she ghosts me for the next three months, instead.

Chapter 16

Then there was David - Parker

Two years ago, Jackson did it again. Every time I think he can't hurt me anymore, he finds a way to completely gut me open. We slept together the night before Merissa and Jason's wedding then Allie tells me they're expecting a baby the very next day. Oh, but get this, just a few months later, he's engaged!

I'm sure they have lots of sex, and I'm sure they'll have a happy, healthy marriage with lots of babies. He probably loves her more than he ever loved me. I bet he respects her more than he ever respected me, too, but onwards and upwards as they say.

I don't need Jackson, anyway. My leg has fully recovered and I'm able to walk again without a limp or cane, and I'm twenty-five which is practically thirty so I don't have time to harp on what coulda, shoulda, woulda been anymore. I'm a resident physician at Emory Hospital and I'm optimistic about my future in pediatric medicine.

I never realized how much I loved kids until David set me up with a part-time job working in the hospital's children center during my last semester of med school. I don't know if it's a craving because I can't physically birth one, but I'd love to be a mom someday. For years, I was depressed because I thought that choice was taken away. I was deprived from experiencing an essential piece of motherhood – pregnancy. However, as years passed, my heart mended, and I understand that there are many ways to be a mother, and I look forward to nurturing my own children one day – maybe even with David. I mean – Jackson settled down so why shouldn't I move on…and settle.

"Parker's daydreaming again!" Avery yells out loud to get my attention. We're enjoying a Girls Night In at David's apartment while he's away at a conference. I practically live here until my new apartment unit is ready for me to move in.

"Avery, do you have to scream in my ear?"

"Yes, she does. We've been trying to get your attention for three minutes. You know how hard it's been to pull you away from David for the past few months? We finally have you all to ourselves and you're still thinking about him!" Izzy complains.

"I'm actually not solely thinking about David. I'm thinking about what I want for myself in the next five years."

"Make sure it's good sex because you're definitely not getting that right now."

"Avery! I told you that in confidence."

"Don't worry. I already know. She told me in confidence!" Izzy reveals.

Merissa yells from the bathroom "Then, Izzy told me in confidence!"

"So, are y'all just having secret conversations about my sex life behind my back?"

"Sometimes." Merissa shrugs and holds a pregnancy test in the air. "Still negative, ladies." She collapses on the couch next to me and exhales a sigh of frustration. "We've been trying to get pregnant for a year now, and even before that, we were only relying on the pull-out method for protection. So, why haven't I gotten pregnant, yet? Maybe there's something wrong me."

I rub Merissa's back and run my fingers through her hair, "Oh Ris, there's nothing wrong with you, but maybe the both of you should see a fertility specialist. They may offer some recommendations to help you conceive. I'll go with you, if you like?"

"Would you really, Parker? Thank you!" Merissa sits up and squeezes me so tight I can barely breathe. "I've been hesitant to bring it up to Jason because it'd be so awkward for the doctor to tell me my poon poon doesn't work in front of my husband. But wait – are you tagging along for moral support or for your own personal reasons?"

"A little bit of both?" I admit to the girls without hopefully taking the attention away from Merissa. For weeks, I've been contemplating what happiness looks like for me. I once thought it'd be impossible to have it all, but as I continue to work through my grief and make up for lost time, the more determined I am to be whoever the hell I want to be and do whatever the hell I want to do – have a successful career, find a loving partner, and start a family. I want it all and I will have it all someday.

Merissa's gives me another enthusiastic hug. "Oh, Parker! This is so exciting! I'm so glad you changed your mind about freezing your eggs."

"Congrats to both of you ladies on chasing your dreams and not taking no for an answer when life serves you lemons! Now, moving on to the next topic of discussion. Let's talk about David." Avery turns the tv off and my conniving sisters and best friend stare at me like they're about to stage some type of intervention.

"Uh, what is there to talk about?"

Avery takes another swig of her wine, Merissa rubs my back to brace myself for the conversation to come, and Izzy gently rests her hand on my knee and says, "You've had a rough couple of years, sis, but we've seen you emerge stronger, more independent, feistier, and more beautiful than ever before. You reclaimed your life back after being let down by Jackson so many times."

Avery interrupts, "And we're rooting for you which is why want to make sure you don't backtrack by entertaining thoughts of a life with Jackson."

"We were just talking about moving forward in life – career and babies. Why would I go back to Jackson? I have no interest in him whatsoever, not after everything he's put me through."

"I'm sorry, but I call b.s., Parker!" Avery interjects. "If Jackson suddenly became the man you always claimed he'd be, walked up to you right now, and asked you to choose him or David, then you'd choose Jackson."

"I don't live in a world of hypotheticals." I respond.

"That response is exactly how I know you're not over him. He's a brooding jerk, Parker. You dodged a bullet and everyone can see that but you."

Merissa takes over. "Jackson's been fighting demons his entire life, Parker. I haven't spoken to him since the wedding, yet I still love him like a brother, but I love you more, and there's no telling when Jackson's going to overcome his issues. Are you seriously going to wait around for him to change?"

"I love Jackson. I always will. Y'all can't make me feel any different, but I promise you I'm not chasing after him anymore. I'm committed to David and David only."

Avery asks, "Then why aren't you even putting in half the effort that he's put into your relationship? Just two months ago, you complained about how boring your sex life is. You even compared you and David's sex life with you and Jackson's. And last week you went completely silent during our double date when the topic of marriage came up, but now you're talking about having a baby? Who do you want a baby with – David or Jackson? Your mind is everywhere! It's like you won't allow yourself to be happy and stable with anyone but Jackson, but newsflash hun, happy and stable doesn't exist in Jackson's world. You need to accept who he is and what you two will never be. Move on, Parker."

My girls are reiterating what I already know. For so many years, I believed there was no one else in this world who could love me like Jackson loves me, but to be honest, David loves me better, yet I still can't bring myself to love another as purely as I've loved Jackson. I committed myself to him before I even knew what love was. He'll always have a piece of me which is why I can't give my all to David, and it seems, for now, he's okay with me giving just enough.

"David's great. He's absolutely wonderful. He's handsome and kind and patient, and unlike Jackson, he communicates and doesn't shut me out. It's a breath of fresh air. *But,* when Jackson touches me, I get goosebumps. The hairs on my arms stand and my body temperature spikes. Every kiss is passionate and every interaction whether we're happy, sad, or angry is just intense. It's an intensity that David just doesn't give me. Being with Jackson gave me a constant high, and I'd be lying if I said I don't miss that feeling. It's an –"

"Addiction," Merissa says. "Everything about you and Jackson is obsessive and addictive and destructive and toxic. It didn't used to be but the last few years were and he isn't getting any better, Parker. Every few months, you backtrack and reminisce on the good while overlooking the bad of your relationship. Don't waste David's time if you're still in love with the idea of Jackson Sands. Jackson's had a head start on learning how to please you. Tell David what you like. You can't expect for him to read your mind, and if he doesn't bring the intensity that you crave then maybe you should bring it and set the tone for your relationship. Most importantly, you need to remember, the emotional high you're so drawn to with Jackson also contributed to all the turmoil you've experienced throughout your relationship – petty arguments, neglect, the drinking, the insecurity, the co-dependance, the unhappiness, the *accident.* There was no balance, Parker. You and Jackson are drama and chaos. That's not a healthy relationship. It was a disaster waiting to happen, and it did."

"Okay, y'all can leave!" I yell out in frustration. "So much for a fun Girls Night In. Our schedules are all so busy nowadays and we barely get to see each other, yet you want to start an argument out of nowhere over my love life. I am happy! I'm happy! I love David! I love David! He's perfect for me. We take care of each other, and it works. I love him. I love him. I freakin' love him!" I repeat it so much that my heart may finally be convinced.

My breathing is heavy, and I'm exhausted from telling lies to myself. "I love David and I love Jackson. I love Jackson so much." I can't hold my resolve for much longer, and I break down in defeat.

"I can't let him go. He's everywhere. He's on tv. He's on every social media feed. He's on billboards. He's in ads! He's constantly on my mind. His face is still etched on every shattered piece of my unhealed heart. I love him, always and I can't make it stop. Every thought I have whether good, bad, irritated, or happy is about Jackson. He's the father of the child I'll never have and the man of my dreams that'll never love me like I deserve. Yet, here I am, still in love with him while David offers the entire world at my feet. How can I let go of him when we're an extension of each other? Even despite waking up in a hospital bed bandaged, broken, and literally emptied out, I still hold on to the idea of rewriting our story together and one day creating our own happy ending. There's no way three bad years should overwrite a lifetime of love and history. The good does outweigh the bad, and hate is temporary but our love is in spite of. Y'all think I'm stupid and I probably am. I have to be to still be in love with a man who's now in love with another woman, but that should be me. I should be his fiancé. I'm the mother of his child!"

My friends stare at me. I'm sure they're stunned by my outburst. I've tried to keep my cool for months but Jackson still has my heart. Avery allows me to melt in her arms.

"It's okay, Parker. We just want you to move on and be happy. I won't pretend to understand how you feel, but we're here for you. Take all the time you need to heal."

The next few days are rough. I avoid David as much as I can, but it's hard to do so when we work at the same hospital. My responses are short and my kisses are dry. I'm still trying to digest the admission of my unbreakable love for Jackson. I know a future with him is impossible. I know he's moved on and has a family of his own now. I need to accept reality and I need to force myself to accept simple and easy. So many people wish they had simple and easy and that's what David is. It won't be easy for me to accept, but I'll try it. I have to try. Jackson isn't an option for me anymore and I need to open myself up to new possibilities of love without heartache.

"What's got you in such deep thought over there?" David sneaks up behind me and nibbles on my ear. I've temporarily tucked away all thoughts of Jackson to prove to myself, my girls, and David that he's the only one who has my undivided attention.

"Hi, handsome. How was your day?"

"Nope, don't change the subject. You were tearing up over here. Penny for your thoughts?" David's so old fashion it's borderline cheesy, but he's stable, honest, and brings me peace. Everyone deserves peace.

"Okay, promise not to freak out?"

"I promise, for the most part."

"I was thinking about our future together. You've been working so hard and I know you want to open up a practice of your own here in Atlanta, but I was wondering if you ever considered home."

David pulls me close and caresses my cheek, "Do you want to move back home to Beverly Mills?" He places a sweet, tender kiss on my lips and lifts me up on my kitchen counter.

"It's actually always been a part of my life plan. Merissa and Jason are going to move back soon, and when I finish my residency, I'd like to open up my practice there, but I want to make sure we're on the same page. I don't want to do long distance."

"I agree. I'll try to go where you want me to go, Parker. My life is with you and wherever you are is home to me." He kisses me again, but this time more passionately. Then, he lays his head on my chest and listens to my heartbeat.

"Dr. Gallinari, what are you doing?"

"I'm just enjoying the moment. I love this sound, this pace, your presence is everything to me. I love you, Parker Waylen."

My heart is conflicted. I do love David and I want to be in love with him, but I don't know if I am because the only comparison I have is my love for Jackson which is an unhealthy representation of being in love so I don't know if my feelings for David equate to being in love.

Yet, I run my fingers through his hair and lay my head on top of his and respond, "I love you too, David."

The moment's interrupted when my cell phone pings. "Who is it and why are they interrupting our lovey dovey time?"

David checks my phone, but I worry when he doesn't say anything. "Babe, who is it?"

"It's a message from Jackson." He reveals.

The mood is totally ruined, and David steps back to observe my next move. I read the text and throw my phone on the couch.

"He wants me to watch some interview that he's gonna do tonight. He says he wants to prove to me that he's changed. I don't want to entertain his antics. Let's just enjoy our evening together, I can think of so many *other* things we could be doing besides talking about Jackson."

"Parker, if you want to watch the interview then feel free to do so. I won't feel any type of way. I trust you, and I know what we have is solid." David confidently remarks.

If he only knew how much I doubted us just a few weeks ago. He would definitely feel some type of way.

"Are you sure?" I ask. "You wouldn't feel uncomfortable?"

My relationship with David is what some may call a slow burn. I waited a year until I finally agreed to be his girlfriend. Even saying 'agreed to be his girlfriend' sounds so dispassionate and unnatural, I'd never have to agree to be Jackson's anything, we were just always meant to be. With

David, it's different, he doesn't do anything wrong, it's just sometimes 'us' doesn't quite feel right, but only in the moments when Jackson is mentioned.

"Parker, should I feel uncomfortable? I'm only living in his shadow every day. You drive the car he purchased for you after he broke your heart. He paid your tuition bills. Everyone asks you how he's doing when we go back home. He randomly texts you whenever he feels like it, and you may say you're over him Parker, but if you were really over him, then you would've at least blocked him by now. It's like you're anticipating his return, so should I be worried?"

"No, David, I swear," I grab his hand and give him a reassuring squeeze. "I know it can't be easy being around my friends and family when they retell old stories or ask questions about Jackson, but please know that you make me happy and I want this, okay? I don't tell you thank you enough for being such a patient and understanding boyfriend. I don't know how you put up with me and my baggage."

"It's not baggage, but it is a heavy load to carry." David caresses my cheek with his hand and moves my hair out my face. "Sometimes I feel like you miss the chaos of your old life. The dramatic tales of Parker and Jackson." David's usually a master at disguising his frustrations, but he doesn't bother hiding how he feels tonight.

"Well, just think about how far I've come. Jackson used to consume all of my thoughts."

"And your heart." David interjects.

"But not anymore. I'm choosing to give my heart to you."

"I'll take what you can give me. I don't want you to feel like I'm pushing you to open yourself up to me. I don't know if our relationship will ever measure up to what you and Jackson had, but I promise to try my hardest to put a smile on your face every day."

"That's sweet, but it's also a tall promise. How do intend on keeping it?"

David picks me up and carries me to his bedroom. He gently lays me down on his bed like a delicate flower, but I wish he'd throw me on his bed, instead. I wish he expressed a greater sense of urgency for me. I want him to want me so bad that he rips my clothes off and has his way with me, but he slowly pulls down my underwear.

"David, stop teasing me. It drives me crazy in a bad way." I whine.

David presses his lips to my clit and sucks agonizingly slow. I try to maneuver his head to gain better positioning and even buckle my hips to hint to him that what he's doing isn't working. My complaints to my girls are valid. We've been together for months and for as much as David succeeds in fulfilling my emotional and mental needs, he still lacks in pleasing me sexually. I thought it was a small price to pay for happiness, but I don't think I can take the dissatisfaction anymore.

I grip his hair with my fingers and motion his body to move upward to end this sad session of oral sex. I nudge David's legs apart to help him align himself with my entrance, and when he enters inside me, I feel good, but not great. I feel pleased, but not spent. I want him to make me want more, and right now, this isn't even enough. David hates it when I mention Jackson's name, but he's all I know. Sex with Jackson is so passionate, but sex with David is like a task, and I think I've settled for this because, a part of me fears, that if I'm honest with David about how he doesn't please me the way I like, he'll learn how, and he's a perfectionist so I know he'd eat me out so good I'd play re-runs in my mind for days, and that scares me. Am I really ready to stop fantasizing about Jackson and let David be great?

I'm running out of so many legitimate reasons to not be in love with this man, and I'm fighting against the fact that Jackson Sands may really be a person of my past. I can't keep comparing David to Jackson and I know the best way to build intimacy is to learn one another's likes and dislikes. If I want this to work, then I have to speak up. I should tell him what I want which is to touch me like Jackson touches me and fuck me like his life depends on it.

"Okay, okay, that's enough. David, stop." I buck in defiance against him. Startled and alarmed, David pulls himself out of me.

"Is something wrong? Are you okay?" He checks my body for bruises and breaks, but oh how I wish he would break me off good!

"I'm fine, David. I want to please you."

"You do please me, Parker."

"And I want you to please me," I hold up my hand to prevent him from responding. "Which is why I think I should tell you what I like. I never told you how I like it, how I need it. Is that okay?"

David looks at me with his endearing eyes and his lips curve upwards into a smile. "That's all I want to do, Parker. Tell me what to do and I'll make you feel like no one's ever made you feel in your entire life."

That statement alone just turned me on. I push David's head back down for his first lesson. He blows his hot breath on me and I feel familiar tingles move up and down my spine.

"Flick your tongue up and down in a quick paced rhythm." I command and he does as he's told. "Now, ease your finger inside me."

Again, he does as he's told and I can barely think straight at this point. His tongue is amazing like an organ in a symphony! Why didn't I do this before? Why have I deprived myself?

"Does that feel good, Parker?" He asks in a low, raspy tone.

"Yes David, don't stop."

David's tongue and finger both alternate between pleasing me. He finds a melodic rhythm that comforts my body.

I begin to feel overwhelmed and I yell so loud that I feel a sting in the back of my throat. My orgasm feels like it's been waiting to be released for months but David still won't let up. He continues until another orgasm breezes through my body like a calm storm. I feel relaxed, relieved, exhilarated, spent, and beyond satisfied.

When David comes up, he lays next to me with a big kool-aid smile.

"You've been holding out on me, David."

"You've been holding me back by not being honest with me, Parker."

Still sweaty and slightly embarrassed by my multiple orgasmic performance, I bury my head into David's chest, but he lifts my chin with his finger and forces me to look him in the eyes.

"I'm sorry. I'm no virgin, of course, but I'm not experienced in this area so to speak. This is all still new to me, being with someone else, but I promise, I'll be vocal for now on."

He pulls my face even closer and brushes his lips against mine.

"That's all I ask." David proceeds to suck my neck, and I release a soft moan.

"Do you like this?" He asks. I incoherently respond yes while I get lost in his soft kisses and lay flat underneath his body.

He grazes his fingers up and down my inner thigh and I feel my temperature rise all over again. "How do you want it, Parker? We can do this all night long."

My eyes go wide and before I can even respond, David's lips crash against mine. We kiss until our lips are swollen and bruised. David stands near the edge of the bed while I lay flat and wonder what he's going to do next. He pulls me nearer by the legs and wraps them around his neck and plunges into me so hard it feels like he's hitting a bone. I've never felt this much pain and pleasure in my life – not even with Jackson.

"David!" I yell in ecstasy, and within seconds, he pushes me to the brink.

"Not yet, Parker." He struggles to speak.

I plead to release, but he picks me up while still inside of me and sits on the bed so I now straddle him with my legs tightly wrapped around his hips. He takes my breath away with a kiss and looks deep into my eyes.

"I love you, Parker." He whispers.

"I love you, David."

We both let go together for the first time, and for the first time since we've been together, I *only* thought of him and him *only*.

Days have passed since my first night of mind-blowing sex with David, and let's just say every night afterwards topped the night before. Our sexual chemistry was the only missing piece to our relationship, but now, that's resolved and I'm ready to continue working towards a happy future with David.

I can't wait to tell Avery and Izzy all the juicy details during our coffee shop chat.

"Ladies, we have so much to catch up on." I'm so excited to dive in, but Avery is anxious to discuss some news of her own.

"Uh yeah, like how we can't believe Jackson made an ass of himself on national television!"

"Parker, your picture is everywhere! You're totally trending right now. Check this out! #whoisparkerwaylen #jacksonsfirstlove #savehimhesahotmess #parkerthehomewrecker"

Izzy shows me the posts and threads where strangers, groupies, fans, and Allie's minions are circulating photos of me and Jackson from elementary, middle, high school and college.

"What the hell?! This is crazy! Can you report these profiles? People are sharing my personal information. It's an invasion of my privacy!"

"Did you not watch the interview?" Avery asks.

"I did. We did, David and I. It just further affirmed the fact that Jackson is still on the hot mess express and I'm finally living a content, stress-free life without him."

And this is the truth. Seeing Jackson on that tv screen broke my heart. I wanted to immediately reach out to him. I saw the hurt and pain he was in. I felt it, and I know he's lonely. I know he's alone, but I can't be there to save him anymore, and for the sake of my relationship with David, I don't want to.

"Wow, Parker. I'm shocked." Izzy sits back and folds her arms and looks at me in disappointment.

Confused, I ask, "Why are you looking at me like that? One minute you're telling me to move on then the next you want me run to him? Make up *your* minds!"

Avery clarifies, "We don't want you to go back to being Jackson's lap dog, but you were still his best friend. You know him better than anyone. Ray Charles can see that he's down and out right now. You know how I feel about Jackson. He's no good for you, but he's family and we love him. You love him and I know you care about his well-being. Remember, it was you that helped him get back in therapy. It was you that was there when his mom died. It was you that kept him out the dark place, but I think he's trapped there now, Parker."

My sisters are right. I've been so caught up in my happiness that I disregarded Jackson's helplessness. I told him I'll always be there for him no matter what and he needs me now.

I respond, "I'll call him."

"Good idea. What are you gonna say?" Izzy asks.

"I have no idea," I shrug. "On second thought, I don't think I should call. I wouldn't know what to say on the spot. It might get ugly or he may not even answer."

Avery reaches over the table to place her hand on top of mine. "Send a text. Let him know everything will be okay. What would the old Parker tell Jackson when his mother was sick? What would the old Parker say to Jackson when he's putting himself down? What would the old Parker say to him when he's a drunk mess? What would the old Parker who was madly in love with Jackson say? Be his anchor one last time. I'm worried his life depends on it."

I send Jackson a text to encourage him to keep fighting. He probably won't read it. It probably won't help, but the least I could do is to remind him of how loved he really is.

I saw your interview. You are so much better than what I watched. You're the son of Debra and Frank Sands. You're strong, perseverant, loving, and kind. You've overcome too much in life for you to get to this point. I've forgiven you for what happened, but what I can't forgive is the hatred you're harboring against yourself. You are not worthless. You are not a failure. You just need help, Jackson and there's nothing wrong with getting the help you need to live a healthy, happy life. Jackson, I know you're lonely and depressed. I know you're hurting. You've been hurting since the day we met and you've been suffering since the night your mom died. We may not ever be together again, but I'll always be your friend and I'll always love you, no matter what, Jackson Sands. I love you IN SPITE OF what you've done. I love you IN SPITE OF who you THINK you are. And I love you IN SPITE OF what you think you deserve. You're stuck in your sorrow right now, but it won't always be like this because despite everything, you are still wonderfully, beautifully, and fearfully made. I know you'll do the right thing and get the help you need, but until then Goodbye Jackson.

The past two months have been stressful. I've worked so hard to create an identity outside of being Jackson's girlfriend, but now the entire world sees me as not only his girlfriend but a whore, and Allie is milking every bit of publicity she can get, garnering sympathy from millions of strangers who have a blind, misguided hatred for me.

I get vile, disrespectful DMs on social media and patients try to inconspicuously snap photos of me at the hospital, and I'm sure my colleagues probably gossip about me and my new fake, scandalous personal life. It's embarrassing and hurtful, and I haven't heard back from Jackson since his little stunt. I don't know what he's going through right now, but it's nothing compared to the undeserved hate I'm receiving nearly every day.

I can't believe he blew up my life yet again, and to make matters worse, David's been targeted, too. He receives so many messages like *You should dump her. She's trash. You and Allie should get revenge. Why are you still with a cheater?* He shouldn't have to deal with this type of harassment.

"Another no caller id text?" He sets a box of my belongings on the dresser as we move into my new apartment.

"Unfortunately, yes. I'm just ignoring all unsaved numbers."

"You should get your number changed. Every weirdo, psycho, and pervert have your number now. It's dangerous. Some stalker could find a way to hack or track your phone and do God knows what. The thought of you getting hurt drives me crazy."

"I'm a big girl, David. I'm not afraid of some bullies. Besides, I've had that phone number since high school. I can't change it!"

"Well, we need to do something. Maybe talk to an attorney about taking legal action against the blogs and Allie – definitely Allie."

"That girl's so rich. She's gonna bury me in court fees alone. I don't stand a chance against her. The calls and messages will die down eventually, but I'm really sorry. I hope you haven't gotten too much flack at work because of this."

"At first a little, but it was mostly from the women." David smiles at me to gauge my reaction and yes, I'm jealous.

"Oh really? What'd they have to say? And you better not have gotten hit on by the same women who were smiling in my face at the holiday party."

"Ooh, jealous Parker is really turning me on right now."

"Oh no you don't, David. Seriously, are women really throwing themselves at you?"

"No more than the usual. Listen, we can't control Jackson's behavior. We had no idea he was going to do something like that."

David may not have known Jackson was going to bomb that interview, but I did. I had a feeling that Jackson would be drunk and go to extreme lengths to 'prove his love' for me then completely make a fool out of himself. We may not communicate, but he just keeps making these grand gestures to show how much he loves me and how apologetic he is, yet the only thing I've ever wanted him to do was to get help.

I never asked him to pay my hospital bills. I never asked him to pay off my school loans. I never asked him to buy me a car. And I never asked him to periodically put money in my bank account which he just did last week – a secret I think I'm going to keep from David. For once in my life, I'm pouring into myself after years of giving my all to him.

David changes the conversations, "On a brighter note, you have an entirely new apartment that needs to be christened. I can't get the thought of you naked and screaming my name while I make love to you on the counter, the bathroom, the balcony, your office, *this dresser*."

"David, you are so nasty!" I flirtatiously laugh and get hot and bothered by his forwardness.

David lifts me up on my dresser and spreads my legs, but our sexy time is disrupted when I accidentally knock over a packaged cardboard box filled with mementos.

"Just ignore it." I tell him as I pull him near for a kiss, but he looks down at the messy mixture of photos, old clothing, and index cards and he's too distracted to continue. David bends down to read and sift through my belongings.

"What is all this?" He asks, but he already knows.

It's Jackson. It's our memories. It's our love story. It's our childhood. It's our adolescence. It's our college memories and everything in between. It's my life.

"It's mostly trash." I lie. "I need to look through everything and see what I can throw away." I try to play it cool, but sometimes, when it comes to Jackson, I'm a terrible liar.

"Trash, huh? So, you don't mind if I throw away his shirt?" David grabs Jackson's old college jersey and shorts and stands next to the trash can.

"Definitely get rid of that! But just so you know, you owe me some of your lounge around sweats now." I joke attempting to hide my reluctance.

He observes my façade, "Okay, what else can we get rid of? What about this picture?"

"Are you kidding me? This is a pic from one of our monthly fishing trips. I think I was nine in this photo and my dad forgot to pack the bug repellent that weekend. We got bit up so bad. You can see the bitemarks on us in this photo. And Mr. Frank, Jackson's dad, had the bright idea to rub mud on our arms to detract the mosquitos. That was a terrible idea! Our moms gave us oatmeal baths when we got home and they cussed out our poor dads. That weekend was so much fun." I laugh so hard while thinking about the fun we had back in the day and I notice that David is trying to connect, but he can't because this is a memory for me and Jackson to bond over, not Parker and David.

"Okay, what about this one? This is literally a photo of you laying your head on Jackson's shoulder." He describes with a hint of jealousy.

"I don't know, David. I remember this day. Mrs. Debbie, Jackson's mom, got really sick from chemo. Jackson didn't eat or sleep for days. We honestly didn't think she'd make it that time around, but she did. Me, Jason, Merissa, and our parents were in and out the hospital for a week in support of the Sands. This picture isn't about me and Jackson. It reminds me of the bond our families share. It reminds me to never give up on the people we love. Always be there for them whether it's Jackson, Merissa, or you. I'll always hold out hope for the best outcome in every situation, no matter how bad it looks."

I give David a kiss of confidence and he holds me in his lap as we look through various vacation, birthday, prom, graduation, and college photos. It's impossible to throw any of them away because although they contain Jackson, they're also major memories and milestones in my life.

"We have so many years to create memories together David, and as much as I wish Jackson wasn't a major part of my life up until now, that's just not the case, but I do look forward to our future together and the photographs that we'll take to document our love story."

"We live in a digital world now. Our life is on social media not in photo albums. These photos feel more special than a post online. These feel like something you'd past down to your kids and grandkids. I want to create a legacy with you, Parker, but you and Jackson began building that years ago, and sometimes I feel like I'm just a pit stop on your journey to rebuilding that legacy with him, again." He confesses.

I assure him, "But I'm here with you, David. I want marriage and a family, too. That's the legacy we can build. There's nothing stronger than that."

His eyes widen in full surprise and hope. "And you want that with me? Parker, can you honestly say that you want to marry me? You're not just saying that to make me the happiest man on earth?"

"I'm saying I want all of that with the man I love. I'm committed to you and I'm ready to start our future together, if that's what you want. I know it'll be difficult given I can't get pregnant, but…maybe we can explore other options? If you want? I know it isn't ideal, but we could still have a child together. It just may not be easy or traditional. I know you deserve to share the pregnancy experience with the person you love, but I hope what I can give is enough for you. I hope it can make you happy."

A tear of uncertainty falls from my eye. We haven't had the baby discussion yet. It's a fear and a deep-seated insecurity of mine. I avoided being in a relationship again for so long for this exact reason. David's always been sensitive, loving, and supportive during my recovery and especially when I told him about the hysterectomy, but did he think we'd be in a relationship back then? Probably not. Did he envision his life being married to a wife who couldn't get pregnant? Probably not. Did he imagine bypassing the whole pregnancy and childbirth experience with the love of his life? Probably not. Yet, I chose to take a risk at love again because of the person he is and I hope I'm not wrong. I hope he wants what I want and I hope he wants it with me.

David wipes my tear with his thumb, grabs a hold of my hand and kisses my knuckles. It's a kiss of comfort, confidence, and optimism for the future.

"I can't imagine my life with anyone else, Parker. You're perfect. Thank you for choosing me."

He sprinkles kisses all over my body and removes my doubt with passionate love making which conjures a feeling I've never felt before. Tears run down my face in the midst of our heated moment of passion and for the first time in forever, the love I've always given away is finally reciprocated back to me. David is giving me the love I gave to Jackson and I never want to let this go. I want him to love me, always like I've always loved Jackson, and now I'm certain that I'm in love with them both.

Chapter 17

A Bond that Can't be Broken - Parker

Death is a part of life, but no one can convince me that it's still natural. Suffering, struggle, and loss are inhumane experiences accompanied with the human condition, and today we're here to mourn the loss of someone who has struggled too long and suffered even longer. For Merissa, disappointment ends where tragedy begins, as of late. Three weeks ago, she and Jason found out she miscarried, again. Two weeks later, Iyanna was found in a nearby town, dead from a lethal mix of cocaine and methamphetamine.

I know life isn't fair but it also shouldn't be cruel. Although Merissa's family stopped trying to force Iyanna to go to rehabs and psychiatric hospitals, they still held out hope that one day, she'd have a desire to want to stop using, but the day never came. And today, we're back in Beverly Mills to say goodbye to her tormented soul.

"Words can't express how losing a loved one feels. It's like having a part of you taken away, and lately I feel like I keep getting robbed. So many people we love get taken away from us undeservingly, and we're left to deal with the pain. At times, my pain feels greater than my strength, but when I get to that point where I feel like I've lost too much, I close my eyes and think about the gratifying moments I've been blessed to capture as lifelong memories. I'll always love Iyanna, and the memories we made will help sustain me through dark times. Many people don't remember who she used to be before her addiction, but I do. Many people may see her as weak, but she was the strongest of us, and even the strongest hurt. And when they hurt, they hurt the most and unfortunately, she discovered the worst ways to deal with her pain. I'm not a philosopher or a pastor or have divine understanding, but I choose to believe she isn't in pain anymore. I choose to believe she's in a better place than the mental hell she'd been caged in all her life. We'll miss her so much and I promise to dedicate my life to helping young people who struggle with mental health and drug addiction like she did. Thank you all for coming to honor my sister."

After other family members also speak their piece, Merissa and her family somberly leave the funeral home. Throughout the years, I'd overhear Mrs. Hernandez say 'one of these days, her next hit may be her last' and though many parents of addicts have this thought at the top of their minds far too often, no one actually expects to bury their own child.

Merissa's grief is unmatched and as her best friend, I should be there to support her during this time, but I can't be there in the capacity that she's always been there for me. I can't because today is Jackson's day and tomorrow is mine. This year, I've had to share my two best friends with Jackson which has been awkward, uncomfortable and a strain on my relationship.

I know that some bonds are unbreakable, but Jackson has been given chance after chance, even after he committed numerous unforgivable acts against me. Yet, I've been forced to accept him back in my life, and though it's indirectly, it hurts equally the same. David's hurting too. Jackson's presence is affecting his confidence in our relationship. It's affecting his ability to trust me, but most importantly, I feel like he's losing hope in the future that we planned together. We've been so happy for nearly two years, but I feel like I'm losing him because of my inability to keep Jackson out of our lives.

I really didn't think anything of it, until I was 'caught' so to speak. Some months ago, when Merissa and Jason began spending time with

Jackson again, I accidentally liked a photo of them together. From there, Jackson liked a few of my photos and I kept liking his in return. I thought it was innocent, and I had no idea David could see the photos I like on social media. Those stupid privacy settings! When he noticed my activity, he decided to look through my search history, which I admit, after liking a few photos of Jackson accepting philanthropic awards, I became curious and went down a deep, dark rabbit hole. I googled him, and I found out he's doing so well. Instead of being on TMZ, he was featured in Business Digest as the #1 entrepreneur on the rise. He's so different from the Jackson I watched have a meltdown on national tv. He's so different and I was so intrigued. For a moment, I wondered if that was the Jackson, Debbie and I always believed he'd grow to be.

Since then, David questions my thoughts and desires and even second guesses himself, but today is a test of my will. I avoided eye contact with Jackson during the funeral, but I can't keep avoiding him and at some point, we have to make a truce so we can end joint custody over our best friends.

Reflecting on the emotional ceremony, I share, "Merissa did well to keep her resolve during her speech. I feel so sorry for her. She deserves a break from all the heartache. I just wish I could be there for her more."

David puts his arm around my shoulder as we walk to my car. "You're there for her as much as you can be, Parker. The circumstances suck, but your support isn't unnoticed and Merissa knows you'd be there for her every second of the day if you could."

Frustrated, I express my concerns more forcefully, "It's not enough, David! I need to talk to Jackson. It's not fair that he gets to be there for them when I'm the one that's never left their side. He needs to be reasonable and go away. It's only right for us to support them today. Why would they want an addict around, anyway!"

David cautions, "Parker, I really don't think that's a good idea especially given our recent issues."

Undeterred by his concerns, "My best friends are hurting and Jackson doesn't deserve to be the person that comforts them."

He protests, "Are you really going to walk away from me to speak to your ex? Parker!"

I am and I do. Before David can say anything else, I turn around and walk towards Jackson to give him a piece of my mind. I sense David's frustration and jealousy and I hear his huffing and puffing, but I don't care. I'll be damned if Jackson's friendship with Merissa and Jason takes precedence over mine.

When I reach Jackson, his glare is so serious and enticing that I nearly forget the reason why I walked over in the first place. I haven't been face to face with him for years and based on how heavy I'm breathing and hot I'm feeling, he could probably have his way with me, if half the town weren't surrounding us. He looks so demure, so classy, so wealthy, so healthy, and so handsome. He looks like the man version of the boy I fell in love with and I need to stop staring and come back to my senses before I forget who he really is and the pain he's caused me.

"Hi, Parker." Jackson greets me with two short words that I ashamedly have been longing to hear.

Since he's arrived back on the scene, my curiosity has piqued so much that it's been driving me crazy. I want to ask him so many questions like where have you been? What have you been doing with yourself? What happened between you and your psycho ex? Where's your son? Why are you here? Why don't you just leave and never come back? Do you miss me?

But instead, I respond as coldly as I can. "Jackson."

He flashes his flirtatiously cocky smile that's always broken down my walls and continues to speak as if the fire burning between us doesn't exist.

"It's good to see you. You look wonderful, given the circumstances we're here, of course." He boldly takes a lock of my hair and moves it away from my face.

My body shivers at his touch and I, without even realizing, close my eyes and imagine his hands touching every part of my body.

He charmingly continues, "I love the haircut. It matches your personality."

I question his familiarity, despite the warmth I feel, "Thanks, Jackson, but how would you know my personality? We haven't crossed paths in years."

Then, he continues to prove that we'll always be familiar with one another when he says, "No matter how long we're separated from one another. No matter how far apart we are. I'll know you, always just like you'll –"

I cut him off to finish what our minds and hearts already know with hope and fear, "Love you, always?"

Nothing else we say even matters at this point, and before we know it, we're so close to one another I can see the small hairs on his upper lip. His eyes are hungry for me but his mouth is even hungrier. We're in a trance and I take one step closer so our bodies can finally reunite for a taste of one another, one small taste, but suddenly my senses begin to heighten as I notice the stares and hear the whispers. And when I turn around, I see, my love, David, fuming and hurt.

I take a step back then fretfully and regretfully leave to return to the life I decided was better to live – a life without Jackson and a life with someone who makes loving him light and easy.

After the funeral, David and I head to his parents' house for their monthly Gallinari Family Lunch, but before we spend time with his family, I want to clear the air and address that embarrassing and unacceptable interaction that just occurred.

Although David's extremely tight-lipped right now, I can tell there's a lot on his mind and a lot that he wants to say.

"Hey," I place my hand on his forearm and proceed with caution as he tightly grips the steering wheel. "I'm sorry."

His response is unexpected. He laughs and says, "Sorry for what, Parker? What exactly do you think you did?"

"Well, I shouldn't have…lingered?" I state, hoping I used the right word.

He amusingly retorts, "So, you're not sorry. You don't even know what you did wrong."

I remorsefully confess, "I do! I just want to make sure I apologize for the right reasons. I know the entire situation was wrong, David. I am sorry. I disrespected you and our relationship."

David raises his tone in astonishment, "You shouldn't have even went to him, Parker. We just left the funeral of your best friend's sister. Yet, you could only think about Jackson! This is crazy!"

"I said I'm sorry. My intentions were good, I swear. It's just – I can't explain how flustered I get when I try to confront him." I try to explain as my words tumble out in a rush.

David rolls his eyes, shakes his head, and chuckles. "You still don't get it."

Desperate for clarity, I press, "Get what, David? I obviously don't so stop beating around the bush and tell me how you feel."

He bears his emotions, "Sometimes, I feel like you've been playing me for almost two years. I give and give and give to you, but it isn't enough and I'm tired, Parker. I need more from you or else I want nothing at all. One minute you're madly in love with me, the next minute your damn near locking lips with Jackson in front of all of Beverly Mills like I'm some lame fool! I can't take this any longer. I love you, but the way we love just isn't the same. You've proven it to me time after time again and I overlooked it, but not anymore."

"What're you saying, David? Are you breaking up with me? You better not be breaking up with me. I said I was sorry! I'm really sorry. I don't know what's gotten into me lately. I can admit, I've been beside myself and making foolish decisions, but I love you." I plead.

David looks like he wants to forgive me, but he maintains his will. I know I screwed up. I'd be devastated if he gave another woman googly eyes in front of everyone. I'd be devastated if he wanted anyone other than me. David's my present and my future. I need to make this right and I know just exactly how. It may not be the best solution or the healthiest or the most mature, but I know it'll ease the tension between us before we have to spend time with his family.

I look at David with apologetic eyes and he already knows I'm up to no good.

"Parker, not now. I'm not falling for your charm this time, not until you admit that this isn't working. I'm not gonna let you embarrass me again!" He firmly declares.

Blah, blah, blah, yaddy, yaddy, yaddy. To shut him up, I slide my hand up his thigh, and I inch up a little higher to massage him.

His voice changes from stern and angry to breathy and powerless. "Parker, please stop."

His eyes are on the road as he tries to adjusts his body to reject my advances, but I lean over to whisper in his ear.

"David, I'm so sorry. I love you." I lick his ear and undo his belt.

"Parker, we're almost at my mom's house."

"Then, drive slower." I seductively whisper.

When I pull it out, I eagerly take all of him into my mouth.

He demands, "Touch yourself while you choke, Parker."

My eyes widen from shock and excitement.

I know I shouldn't but if this is how he talks to me when he's angry, I think I should piss him off more often. I bring David so close to the edge that he almost swerves off the road.

"Screw this." He takes a sharp turn onto a dirt road filled with trees.

I lift my head to see what's going on and it looks like we're in the middle of nowhere.

"David, what are you doing?"

"I'm doing you." He slides the seat back and pulls me on top of him.

I'm paranoid and freaking out, and I look around for cars and bystanders. "Someone might see us."

"Maybe, that's what I want. Maybe, I want Jackson to see us. Maybe I want him to know you're mine."

I lift up my dress and David roughly pulls me down on top of him. In the finale of our angry, lustful experience, he wraps his strong hand around my throat until the rush, the excitement, and the chaos possess bodies. When we come back to earth from the sinfully blissed hell we just dragged one another down to, we breathe heavily and avoid eye contact. I sit back in my seat and we hold hands as we pull up to David's parents' house to portray ourselves as being happily in love.

Before David knocks on the front door, he gives me a kiss on the cheek then whispers in my ear, "Lately, you've brought out the worst in me. I hate that. I hate who you're turning me into and I *don't* forgive you."

My heart drops, but before I can respond, our instincts kick in and we smile wide for the Gallinari sisters who greet us at the door.

"Parker!" David's younger sister pulls me in the house and they all give me a big group hug.

"Well, hello sisters. It's great to see you, too."

It's been a few months since I've spent time with his parents and sisters, but they've always welcomed me with open arms and I love the idea of being an official member of their big loving family one day. As David speaks, there's a softness in his eyes that I haven't seen in months. I know it isn't sincere, but maybe time with his family is something we both need to remind us why we chose one another. We love one another and some bonds can't be broken – mine and his or maybe, I'll realize that it isn't our bond that can't be broken, but mine and Jackson's instead.

After catching up with David's sisters, I venture off into the kitchen to offer assistance to Mrs. Gallinari.

"Hi, Mrs. Beth!" She's busy pulling muffins out the oven but as soon as she hears my voice, she turns around and embraces me like the loving mom she is.

"Parker, you look radiant even in black on such an unfortunate day. How's Merissa?"

"She's doing okay. She's been through a lot these past few months so she and Jason are going to go on an extended vacation to grieve, relax, and reset."

"That's good to hear. They're such good people. I'm so glad my son has such a lovely friend group. Where is he, by the way?"

"He's still trying to make his way in here. He got past one sister. He has three more to go."

We both laugh and Mrs. Beth sets down the plates of food and walks over to me. She looks me up and down with a steady smile.

"Parker, you make my son so happy."

"Thank you, Mrs. Beth. He honestly makes me the happiest woman in the world."

"Hmm." She maintains her steady smile.

"You make David happy now, but you won't for much longer. You can only fake it for so long, Parker and as much as I like you, I love my son more. I'd love to have a daughter-in-law. I'd love to be a grandmother, but I can't have those things if my son's obsessed with a girl who's obsessed with another man."

Mrs. Gallinari picks up her phone to show me a photo of me and Jackson that someone must've snapped after the funeral. I'm ashamed and embarrassed, but Mrs. Gallinari doesn't care. She sets down her phone and picks up a knife to continue preparing lunch.

"Like any mother, I'll do anything for my children and I don't care how adorable you are, how funny you are, how smart you are, or how great your sex may be, if you continue to play with my son's heart, I'll do whatever I need to do to protect him from you. Now, I'd appreciate it if you stop torturing him. He's a good man and he deserves to find someone who loves him just as much as you love that Sands boy. If you can't love him like that then leave him alone."

Humbled, afraid and humiliated, I nod at Mrs. Gallinari's demand, but once again, the energy shifts when David walks in.

He wraps his arms around my waist then hurries over to his mom to kiss her on the cheek. "My two favorite women."

"Hi, baby. How's Mama's favorite son doing?"

"I'm doing well, Ma. What are you two talking about?"

She doesn't even give me a chance to answer, "Oh you know us, just having girl chat about you. Isn't that right, Parker?"

"Absolutely. Your mom was telling me a few stories from your awkward teenage years, of course."

"Alright, I'm leaving, right now!"

"Oh, don't be silly, David. Come help Parker and I set the table. It's time to eat!"

During lunch, I remain quiet and paranoid wondering if David's dad and sisters also received the same picture. I understand his mom's anger and suspicion of me, but I just wish we had the chance to resolve this issue before we became the hot gossip of Beverly Mills.

David notices my silence as well and leans in to check on me.

"Are you okay?"

"Yeah, I'm fine. I'm just feeling a little unwell."

David's youngest sister overhears me. "Parker, you're sick? Do you need any medicine?"

"Oh no, I'm fine, just a bit under the weather – a tummy ache is all."

She gasps and innocently oversteps. "A tummy ache? Could you perhaps be pregnant?" She asks in excitement.

Only David and his parents are aware of my accident. His sisters were too young at the time to be looped into the town gossip back then and now a dark cloud looms over the table.

I'll do anything to change the subject. I'll say anything and that's exactly what I do.

"No, not pregnant. However, we have discussed children." I look to David to give him the go ahead to announce the happy news we've been wanting to tell our parents for months, before we hit the rough patch, of course. I caught David off guard and I see he's annoyed and hesitant to speak.

"Well Son, the suspense is killing your dad and I. What *news* do you have?" Mrs. Gallinari glances at me as a reminder of our conversation in the kitchen.

"Mom, dad, you're all aware of a previous situation that affected Parker's ability to conceive."

His sisters profusely apologize but I assure them it's okay and I squeeze David's hand to continue.

"Six months ago, Parker froze her eggs. We've been together for almost two years, and Parker will be done with residency soon so we intend on getting married and starting a family."

Mrs. Gallinari nearly chokes on her food. "Wow! You two seem to have it all figured out, huh?"

"Not at all, mom, but I do know that we love each other."

"And while I'm not pregnant, I know David's the man I want to marry and have a child with."

He lifts my hand and kisses my knuckles. For a moment, I feel the gentle comfort of the man I fell in love with a year ago. I should've never betrayed his trust which planted seeds of insecurity that's now blocked us from seeing the path ahead of us.

"I look forward to the proposal and wedding, Son. I know your mom's excited. She's been wondering when she'll have a grandchild to spoil." Mr. Gallinari joins his daughters in congratulating us on taking a major step forward together.

From now on, my focus is on David. Building a future with the man of my dreams is at the top of my priority list. David's a good man, a man who loves me, a man who cherishes me, a man who puts me first, a man who has put up with me placing him second, and a man whose mother has now given me an ultimatum – love him always or leave him forever.

When David and I get back to Atlanta, he's too emotionally drained to address our issues, but I'm not. I want to be with him and he's invested too much into our relationship for it to be thrown away. We didn't speak in the car, and David's grabbing a pillow and a blanket to sleep on his couch so the last thing I want to do is let this argument fester any longer than it needs to. I grab his hand and pull him back to the bed.

"If anyone should be leaving. It's me. Should I go back to my place?"

"No, Parker. Please stay. It's late out and I know you don't like to drive in the dark."

He's so thoughtful. Sometimes I forget how well David knows me. I've avoided driving at night ever since the car accident.

"Sleeping in the bed without you is just as frightening. Please, lay with me, David."

We get under the covers and lie next to one another. I place my hand on his chest and allow the warmth of his body to envelop me.

"Do you want to talk?"

"Not now, Parker. I'm so tired. It's been a long day, a long week, a long couple of months. Let's just rest." He resigns.

"But I can't. I'm in love with you, and I'm sorry for making you feel insecure. I'm sorry for making you feel like you aren't good enough. I'm sorry for embarrassing you at the funeral. I'm sorry for revealing our pregnancy plans to your parents. And I'm sorry for acting in any way that would give you the impression that I prefer Jackson over you. I'm yours David and you're mine."

He kisses my knuckles then pulls me in closer to kiss my lips.

"Thank you, Parker. I needed to hear that."

"We're endgame, David."

"There's no ending to us, Parker. This is forever."

Finally, after months of torture, David's forgiven me and we can move on and plan our lives together. I'm one step closer to everything I want and deserve – career, love, marriage, and family.

We're officially at the two year mark! Our anniversary is today and we're going to David's family lake house for the weekend to celebrate. David's been hush hush for weeks about his plans but he did say it will be a "night to remember." Merissa and my sisters are convinced that David's going to propose to me, but I'm not so sure. Yes, we've been happy for the past few weeks, and David's been hinting that he has something he wants to tell me, but I still don't know – the more real the possibility of marriage is, the more nervous I get. For the last two years, I've focused on my desire to get married, but I haven't actually considered what being married to David would look like. What would that mean for my future?

"Are you excited about this weekend?" David asks as he drives us to Lake Lanier.

"Excited is an understatement! We need this mini-getaway so bad. We've both been working so hard at the hospital. I'll be glad when my residency's over so we can move back to Beverly Mills. Now that Jason and Merissa moved back, it makes all the more sense for us to do the same. You can open your first clinic and I can join Merissa's practice."

David looks over at me and I notice he isn't as enthusiastic as I am.

"Is something wrong?"

He's hesitant to answer, but proceeds anyway. "Yes and no. You know how I've been telling you about a potential business opportunity?"

"Yes, what about it? You've been so secretive."

"Well, I was going to wait to tell you until the details were finalized but I might as well spill it. A few of us from the PT Center are going to open a practice. We built our reputations as some of the best DPTs in the area. We reviewed the numbers. We found a location and an investor to fund it all."

"Wait, wait, wait. Just slow down for a minute. You're going to open your own practice? Dr. David Gallinari, I'm so proud of you, baby!" I bask in David's good news and lean over the console to give him a kiss.

"The timing of this works out perfectly! You'll have your clinic in Beverly Mills and Merissa and I will –"

"Well, about that, the only stipulation our investor made is for us to open the first location in Atlanta, and I won't be able to move back home for at least a few years until we hit our revenue goal to open a second location."

David looks back and forth between me and the road ahead and waits for my reaction. Merissa, Jason, Jackson, and I have always discussed moving back to Beverly Mills after school and two of the four of us are already fulfilling that promise.

"Well, who is this investor? Why don't you negotiate? Beverly Mills is the hottest city to move to right now. Surely, he can see the value in this."

"It's Be Strong Investment Group. We've only communicated through his executive assistant and attorney, so I don't know much about the head honcho, but they're legit and they have an excellent reputation across the healthcare industry."

"That company sounds vaguely familiar." I try to think back to where I heard that name from but nothing comes to mind.

"I'll send you their website information when we get settled in." David notices my shaky hands and places his on top mine to calm me down.

"Hey, say something. Your excitement went away and now you look down."

"I'm happy, babe. I promise. I'm just thinking about how we could make this work. We're a little too old, but at the same time too young, and altogether too busy to make a long-distance relationship work. I can see us starting off right with daily phone calls and video chats, but as we get busier and more successful things will change. We'll eventually resort to sporadic texts and weekly phone calls that end up getting rescheduled. Then, we'll eventually lose our spark, and I know that's not what neither one of us wants."

"That won't happen, Parker. We'll find ways to keep our relationship fresh. We've come too far to let distance tear us apart."

"You're right. I guess we'll be okay." I flash David a smile and look out the window for the remainder of the ride.

For David, it's a gratifying silence filled with optimism and hope, but for me, I feel nothing but dread and worry. I want the best for David, but staying in Atlanta isn't what's best for me, and if we can't find a better compromise then I may never get the happy ending I deserve.

My worries temporarily fade away when we finally arrive to the lake house. When David said he was taking me to his family's cabin I pictured a small, comfy two bedroom near the woods, but this is a country oasis! David's family is so down-to-earth and he's so humbled that I always forget that their wealthy, but this architectural masterpiece is a very good reminder.

He opens the door and in front of us are a group of people readying their stations.

"Parker, welcome to my second home growing up. This is William, he's our house manager. If you need anything, he'll be here to assist us this weekend. This is Chef Heidi. She's the best culinary artist in the North Georgia and she'll cook whatever you have a craving for. Last but not least, this is Angie and Mike, our masseuses for the day."

"Wow, hi, everyone." I wave shyly to the crew. Mr. Williams takes our belongings to the main bedroom while the rest of the staff continue to work.

"David, your home is so beautiful. It has everything we need! We don't even have to leave the cabin this weekend."

"And we won't. We have a pool, the lake, a sauna, a nature trail, and a 24-hour wait staff. I want you to relax. I sense the discomfort you have from my news earlier. I want this weekend to be special and provide both of us with the clarity we need."

"Clarity is definitely at the top of mind right now. You treat me so well, David."

We take a moment to embrace one another then head to the wellness room for our massages. We take off all our clothes, lay on the tables, and kick off our weekend of relaxation.

"This is just a short drive from our apartments. Imagine us doing this every weekend, if we stay here. Beverly Mills can always wait."

"It sounds tempting, David, but I've been waiting to return home since I left for college. How long do I have to keep waiting?"

"Not long, Parker. I promise."

"I honestly get the feeling you don't want to move back. When I think back to our conversations, I've always been the one to mention moving, and you'd just co-sign or not say anything at all. And you know what? The more I think about it, I've also notice you've been driving out the perimeter lately to look at houses. So, be honest with me, David. Do you even want to move back to Beverly Mills?"

It's much easier for me to have this conversation while we're laying on the table unable to look one another in the eyes.

He sighs. "Home has different meanings for us, Parker. I want to lay down roots up here. I've built meaningful relationships with clients and I've built an excellent reputation, but most importantly, here is where you and I fell in love not in Beverly Mills. If I move back home, I'll have to start over and I'll always be reminded of your relationship with Jackson. That town is perfect for you and him, but not me and you. Would you really ask me to do that?"

"I just asked and now I have my answer."

This conversation doesn't make me feel any better, but David does have a point. Beverly Mills is where Jackson and I fell in love. It's where we made plans to return home and build a life together. It's not fair to try to make David fulfill the dreams that we shared, but I also can't put my career and personal aspirations on hold for him.

"Would it make you feel better if I try to renegotiate the contract? Maybe I can include a guaranteed second location clause for Beverly Mills. We could potentially move one to three years from now. The investor is dead set on Atlanta and they want me to be the main point of contact for all business logistics."

These investors are so pushy, and I don't want David to get involved with any company that's going to pull all the strings. I need to research this Be Strong Investment Group.

Something just doesn't feel right and as I think about the *Be Strong* name for a little while longer, it finally dawns on me. Be Strong, Hold On was the name of Jackson's non-profit back in college. That sneaky, manipulative little runt. He's the investor, and he's trying to break us up. I can't believe he'd interfere with my life like this!

"Parker, you're mumbling over there to yourself. Is everything okay?"

"Yes, David. Everything's fine. This massage feels so good. It's hard to keep quiet."

There's no way I can let David know about my suspicions until I speak to Jackson. A part of me wants to believe Jackson wouldn't be so cruel, but I'm wise enough to know that he'd do anything to get his way, no matter who gets hurt, and I can't let him hurt David. I can't let him succeed at ruining what we have.

When our massages end, David heads outside to swim a few laps in the pool and I hurry upstairs to shower and get to the bottom of Jackson's evil plan.

I call Jackson's phone but he doesn't answer so I send him a text.

Jackson, call me now. It's urgent. We need to talk.

Less than a minute later, he video calls me and I don't hesitate to answer – naked under my robe and all.

Jackson, looking as handsome as ever, amusingly greets me, "Parker, what a pleasant surprise to see you and all your glory."

I clear my throat and close my robe to cover my breasts. I didn't even have time to mentally prepare myself for this conversation so I'll just play it straight.

With a firm voice, I press, "Jackson, are you the man behind Be Strong Investment Group? Don't lie to me."

Jackson unapologetically, and even proudly admits, "I have no reason to lie to you. Yes, that's one of my companies."

He has no shame!

"Jackson," I yell. "Why the hell are you funding David's business? You think you're slick but you're not! I know what you're doing. You're trying to come in between me and David."

With his twisted logic, he retorts, "I'm not, Parker. David's the one who came in between us. How can you not see that?"

In disbelief, I exclaim, "You sound like a crazy person!"

A softness creeps into his voice as he responds, "I sound like a man who's in love with you, Parker."

I plead for clarity and understanding, "You've always had screwed up ways of expressing your love, Jackson. David's a good man and you're using him like a puppet. You're messing with his career. How could you do this to him? To me?"

He desperately explains, "Parker, I swear I didn't plan this. He and his colleagues reached out to my company. They were looking for funding, and my assistant just happened to bring me the file."

I skeptically question, "So, this is all just a coincidence, huh?"

He hesitates like he has more to reveal. "Well, some of it."

That damn Jakson!

"Tell me everything, now!" I demand. "I don't know if I can forgive you for this."

Jackson earnestly explains, "Okay, I'll tell you everything. After our interaction at the funeral, I knew you still cared about me and I also knew that it was getting close to the time for us to move back home to where we fell in love in Beverly Mills. Our best friends have already made the move and I just want us all to be happy." He reveals his deep-seated intentions. "So, I'm funding Jason's bid for mayor and I purchased and already began renovating the office for Merissa's practice with hopes of you joining soon. I know you want to move back, and you have less than a month left in your residency so I'm just trying to help push the needle for all of us to achieve our goals and be together again."

I'm so torn. He makes such bad decisions with the upmost audacity.

"Jackson, you can't treat everyone like pawns. You can't make these decisions for us. You can't control people!"

He insists, "I promise you, Parker. It's not like that at all. I owe Jason and Merissa. I owe you and I'll give away all my money if it means I could give back at least half of what you all have given me. I wish I could tell you everything, but not like this. Just know, I'm not trying to manipulate anyone. I'm just trying to show up and be present in the lives of the people who have always looked out for me. You included."

Still skeptical, I counter, "Save it, Jackson. How is making my boyfriend stay in Atlanta for the next couple of years looking out for me? You know that's a deal breaker for me."

He quickly responds with resolute ignorance, "I don't know what you're talking about."

I sharply fuss, "Stop playing games. The only way you'll fund David's clinic is if it's located in Atlanta. How is that not interfering with my relationship?"

He sincerely asserts, "Parker, I promise on everything I love – you and my son that that's a lie. The contract specifically stated Beverly Mills but David made my team specify it to say anywhere in Georgia. I was hoping he'd choose Beverly Mills because I know that's what you want. It was all a part of my plan for you to move back home. I'd never do that to you, Parker. You have to believe me."

But I assert my unwavering trust in David, "Well, I don't, Jackson! David has never lied to me. He wouldn't do that to me."

"I'll prove it. I'll have my assistant email you the contract. I just wanted to do some good in your life after doing so much bad and I thought helping David would show you that I can put aside my feelings for you and make amends or maybe even build a friendship. This was me extending an olive branch. I knew you'd eventually figure it out, but I guess it was bad idea." Jackson regretfully concedes.

I agree, "This was a terrible idea, Jackson. You have no idea how many obstacles David and I had to overcome because of our past relationship *and* recent behavior. Just send me the contract because I need to know the truth and if you really want me to be happy, then you'll pull out of this project. This isn't right, and if David finds out, it'd be the end of my relationship and the end of any chance of you and I ever being friends again."

"I'm sorry, Parker. I'll fix this. I promise." Jackson pledges.

"I don't want your promises. I just want you to let me be happy. I have that with David."

He scoffs like the striking, immature but bold man he is. "We can be even happier, Parker. You're choosing to be happy with him, but what we have is so much deeper. You can't ignore how you feel about me and you can't forget how I make you feel. I love you enough to keep reminding you that we belong together."

My heart's beating so fast and I can't tell if it's because I'm angry at him or because I agree with him, but either way, I need to focus on David and find a way to break the disappointing news to him.

"I have to go, Jackson."

"Parker, wait! Don't hang up, yet." He pleads.

"What do you want?" I impatiently ask.

With a slight smirk, he says, "Just to get one more look at you. I don't get to see you often, so pissed or happy, I'll take what I can get. You look beautiful."

He stares at me through the screen and I return the same level of fondness, but I hear footsteps up the stairs so I abruptly hang up the phone.

I called Jackson to confront him for inserting himself into our lives again, but now I'm angry with David. If Jackson's telling the truth, then that means David's never had any intention of moving back to Beverly Mills. He didn't even give me the courtesy of discussing other possible cities, and now I wonder if I can even trust him to tell me the truth.

"There's that troubled look again!" David playfully teases. "I take you away to a southern paradise only for you to show the worry lines on your face every hour we've been here."

"I know. I worry way too much." I reply, attempting to hide the truth.

David sprinkles me with kisses and motions to the bathroom.

"I'll be happy to distract you even if it's just for a few minutes." He unwraps his towel to reveal nothing underneath.

Now pleasantly distracted, I smile. "Dr. Gallinari, are you trying to seduce me?"

"Is it working?" He flirts.

I ease him towards me and respond, "Maybe you should come closer and find out."

David leans in to hover over me and although my mind is still cluttered with thoughts of his possible betrayal, I push them aside so I can enjoy a moment of intimacy.

Our naked bodies are now pressed against one another and we're rolling on the bed tussling for dominance. However, I left my recent calls screen open and the back of my arm accidentally presses against the last call in my log while making out with David.

Our moans are too loud to hear the outgoing ringer, but a deep voice is loud and clear when he answers.

"You miss me already, huh?" Jackson could've said anything, and of all the most indecent moments, he chose this one to flirt.

"Is that Jackson?" David pulls the phone from underneath my body and raises it to our faces so we see Jackson on the other side of the screen and he sees us naked and exposed.

"What the hell is going on?" David reacts furiously.

"David, it's not what you think. I can explain. Jackson was just –"

David cuts me off and hangs up the phone in Jackson's face. "Clearly waiting for you to call him back."

I desperately try to explain, "That's not it at all. There's nothing going on. I called Jackson to discuss something important with him that involves you and me. I wasn't going behind your back! I'm trying to fix something that Jackson did."

Yet, David ignores me and walks out the room. "I'm going to take a shower in the other room. I'll see you downstairs at 6 o'clock for dinner. You have a whole hour to talk to your precious Jackson."

David's so angry and while I understand why, I'm not actually in the wrong this time. I'll clear up everything during dinner, and I'll also address the email Jackson just forwarded to me that confirms that David's lying to me and Jackson is telling the truth.

Once we have this conversation, I just know the rest of our weekend will be perfect. We can work through anything. This isn't the end. Forever can't be over this soon.

David's dinner instructions were clear – wear a short and tight dress that hugs every curve, and now I can barely breathe. When I step out the door to go downstairs in my dusty rose dress, I notice there are beautifully lit candles throughout the house and the floor is covered in hundreds of rose petals all the way down to the last step. I stand at the top of the balcony and look down to see David smiling up at me. I wish I could say he's a sight to see, but I can see the weariness and discontent behind his smile.

"You look stunning." He says as he meets me at the bottom of the steps to escort me to the backyard patio for dinner.

"I feel like royalty." I admit in awe of the elaborate setup.

"You are royalty, Parker." David places a sweet kiss on my knuckles and pulls out my chair for me to sit, a gesture so tender it almost makes me forget the tension between us.

Blushing, I manage a shy, "Thank you."

When we're seated, I take the initiative to explain the Jackson incident from earlier.

"I just want to apologize. That situation with Jackson isn't a situation at all. I contacted him because I recognized the name of the investors funding your clinic."

Confused, David asks, "Okay, and what does that have to do with Jackson?"

I hesitantly drop the bomb, "It's his company."

Initially, David looks both stunned and appalled, but after a moment of silence, he takes a sip of wine and says in disbelief, "So, my girlfriend's ex-boyfriend is funding my business? Is this some kind of sick joke? Why is he doing this?"

"I'm so sorry, David. He was adamant that he didn't know at first, but when he found out, he just wanted to help from the goodness of his heart." I explain with hopes of soothing his frustration.

Yet, he counters, "How is any of this from the goodness of his heart? He wants to control me because he doesn't have control over you anymore."

I defensively remark, "That's not fair. He never controlled me, and I told him to pull out."

David's voice rises with each word, "How can he even do that now, Parker? How can *you* just kill the deal? I have business partners. It's not just about what I want. I feel like I'm backed into a corner. This is my life, my livelihood! What good person would do something like this?"

"I know. I'm sorry. I can fix this." I assert and offer a solution. "We just need to tell Jackson what we want out of this deal and he'll agree to it. I promise you, he will. He wants to fix this."

"Why are you still defending him, Parker? Look what his obsession with you has done to me?" He laments. "He forced me into a business deal. I've put up with the social media flirting, the calls, the texts, the inappropriate looks, but now, you and Jackson are messing with my career, my passion."

Feeling unfairly blamed, I protest, "Why are you lumping me into this? I didn't do this, David! This was all Jackson."

He exclaims, "It's always gonna be Jackson, Parker! He will always be in our lives!"

David lowers his voice and The tension between us momentarily pauses as Chef Heidi and her team serve the first of our three-course meal.

"We're going to start you off with a refreshing red citrus salad with berries, pears and pomegranate drizzled with honey. Enjoy."

David and I proceed to eat our salad in tense peace until his phone rings. He looks at it then puts his phone back in his pocket.

I ask, "Who was that?"

"My mom." He blankly responds.

Wrought with sadness, I still try to lighten to mood. "I miss her. She doesn't call me anymore. I don't think she likes me very much."

As his anger boils over, David sharply replies, "At this point, what reason does she have to like you, Parker?"

Hurt by his harshness, I snap back, "Really, David? That's rude and uncalled for. I don't care how angry you are, don't disrespect me."

"I've been disrespected by you for two years." He accuses. "I kept telling myself you're healing, you're focusing on school, you're finishing your residency, you're this and that. You're everything but committed to me."

I earnestly plead, "I'm fully committed to you. I've never cheated on you. I don't know how many times I have to say it to convince you."

He clearly states, "Action. I want you to act like you love me and not someone else."

Now, my irritation seeps through. "Ugh, here we go again. You're infatuated with Jackson and you're letting him get in your head."

His voice escalates, "Are you serious right now? Listen to yourself! You and Jackson have crossed too many lines to count. I know you kept those boxes of memories. Half of the clothes in your drawer belong to him. Even your car is a constant reminder of him. And let's not mention the secret you've been keeping about him paying your bills!"

"He does not pay my bills!" I fiercely counter.

He bitterly scoffs, "Cut the crap, Parker. He just deposited $3,500 in your account a few weeks ago and he's been doing it since we've been together. Your emails come to my phone, remember? You think I'm stupid, and maybe I am for thinking you could love me as much as you love him, but don't humiliate me even me more than I already am."

David's right. I can't believe I didn't recognize how strong Jackson's presence still is in my life, and I never acknowledged it because if I do, I'm afraid that I'll have to remove every inch of him from me, and that isn't something I think I'll ever be willing to do.

Chef Heidi announces the next course and attempts to pierce the heavy air with a lighter tone, "Our next dish is a honey glazed filet mignon with steamed asparagus and garlic mashed potatoes. Enjoy."

When she exits, I attempt to mend the rift between us. "I've sent mixed signals to you throughout our relationship. I know that, but I'm past that. I know who I want, David."

"You want Jackson. You always have and I know you always will." He responds with resignation as if he's accepted the painful truth.

I try to convince both David and myself, "I don't want Jackson. I want you."

With his voice weary from the emotional toll of our relationship he counters, "You can't want me, but be in love with someone else."

My eyes flutter and my voice cracks under the strain of my conflicted emotions, "Why can't I love you both? I'm in love with you and I want to be with you."

"I can't share your heart with Jackson, anymore. Our relationship started off great. We built a genuine friendship that blossomed into something beautiful, but you couldn't let go. I feel like you eventually tried to mirror our relationship to reflect the relationship you and Jackson once had – tense with too many emotionally draining days and petty arguments followed by passionate make-up sex. I can't sustain that. I can't be your Jackson anymore, Parker." The finality in his tone signals the end of his tolerance.

With a shred of hope left, I reiterate the promise I made the both of us. "I don't want you to be. I love you, David Gallinari. I want to marry you and start a family in Beverly Mills."

At the end of his with and at the beginning of his new resolve, David confesses, "I'm never moving to back home, Parker!"

"Is that why you lied to me about the contract? I know you could've moved to Beverly Mills. You should've told me. You've never lied to me until now." I confront him in rare disappointment.

He admits, "I haven't done a lot of things until I joined you in your toxic bubble. I barely recognize myself lately."

Feeling betrayed by his omission, I retort, "That's no excuse for lying to me."

A sad chuckle escapes him, "I'm sorry that I'm not perfect. I lied to you to avoid another conversation about moving. Our entire relationship has been about what you want, and never about me. I haven't made a decision for myself in two years," He tries to control his anger then lets out a soft laugh. "You know what's funny? I make one mistake and you're torn, but Jackson's made twenty years of mistakes, yet you still love him more than me."

The tension lingers as Chef Heidi serves the final course. "This desert is simple with a lovely surprise on the inside. Enjoy."

David tries to intervene but it's too late. "Oh crap! No, no, no, no, don't lift the top!"

The plate contains an opened velvet ring box with a cupcake inside and a beautiful diamond ring on top. David looks at me with tears in his eyes, and I'm left speechless. The beauty of this moment is overshadowed by the raw honesty and painful admissions of this evening.

He heartbreakingly reveals, "I planned this weeks ago. I didn't think tonight would go down like this."

"It's beautiful," I breathe out, the awe in my voice mingled with a hint of sorrow over the dream that seems more like an illusion now. "Have you changed your mind? Do you still want to marry me?"

With a voice laced with emotion, David hesitantly asks, "Truth for truth?"

I nod yes.

His confession cuts deep with both love and pain, "I knew I wanted to marry you that day I saw you walk down the aisle without your cane. I never stopped wanting to marry you, but I don't think you ever wanted to marry me. I just think you wanted to get married, and since Jackson wasn't available, you chose me and ever since he's been back in our lives, you've unraveled and sabotaged our relationship every chance you could get. Your turn. Could you ever love me more than you love Jackson?"

"No," I honestly respond. "But I still love you. I won't leave you. I'll support you. We can make this work."

"No, we can't, Parker." He declares with sad resolve, which marks the end of our shared illusions.

My heart plummets as my dreams of having it all disappears. I stare at a future I just threw away. This is the end. Tears fall down our faces, and I grab his hand from across the table.

"So, what do we do now?" I ask, struggling to accept our fate.

David gently says, "We go to bed and enjoy our last night together and tomorrow we go our separate ways."

David and I make love to one another while bathing in each other's tears. What we share is different from anything Jackson and I ever had. David took care of me when I was too weak to move, too broken to stand, and in too much pain to enjoy the pleasures of being loved in spite of my circumstances. He's shown me what a healthy, loving, supportive relationship is. He raised my standards and now there's no going back, and I'm forever thankful for him.

Before we drift off to sleep, I tell my last truth for truth. "I don't want this to be the end."

He sighs, "Me neither, Parker, but I deserve to experience what you and Jackson have – a bond that can't be broken."

Chapter 18

One Step Closer - Parker

Jackson and I have been dating for six months and I couldn't be happier, but I fear our fairy tale may be ending soon. The hospital expansion is coming to a close, and we have some difficult questions to answer regarding our future.

Our schedules conflict with one another, but we've managed to find a decent balance. Jackson splits his time between Atlanta and Beverly Mills. Tuesday through Friday, he's with his son and runs the business from his home base, but Saturday through Monday he's here with me in Beverly Mills. I know it isn't the most ideal situation which is why we really need to discuss what the next step is for us as a couple. I don't want a part-time relationship. I want to wake up next to the same person every day for the rest of my life, and I don't want to continue down this path if Jackson isn't willing to be that man for me.

We need to have this conversation soon because we're making strides in the right direction, and he's clearly serious about making our relationship work this time around. I mean, he has to be serious about us because today I'm going to meet the most important person in his life, Jackson Jr.

I've thought about this moment since Jason and Merissa's wedding day. I wondered if I'd ever meet his son. I study every photo Frank posts of him online. I researched ways to connect with kids with Asperger's all week long. I bought three different gifts and I finally settled on Roman Reigns and Sammy Guevara wrestling action figures that I really hope he likes. I wonder if he'll like me and if he could grow to love me like a step mother. I've been worried so much that I've had numerous panic attacks.

"Are you ready to meet Jax Jr.?" Jackson asks.

"No. What if he hates me? He's gonna see his dad with some strange woman, and I doubt he's going to like that."

"It's impossible to hate you. Besides, he's my mini-me so I'm positive he'll love you."

"If you say so, Jackson. Where's your nanny? The suspense is killing me!"

"She'll be here any minute."

A black truck pulls up from around the corner and a young girl exits the vehicle with a tall and stocky toddler. Jax Jr. looks just like Jackson and Frank except much cuter, and the closer they get to us, the more nervous I get.

"Hi, Mr. Sands. I have a hefty package to deliver to you."

"Package? I'm a five year old boy name Jackson." Jax Jr. clarifies who he is to his nanny.

"Oh, that's right! There you are, Jax. I'm gonna miss you buddy."

"I'm only gone for a weekend, Miss Katie. Please make sure my turtles get fed and don't forget to delete my dad's football games if there isn't enough space to record wrestling."

Jax and his nanny give one another a hug and she and the driver depart to go back to Atlanta. Jackson lifts him up and they embrace one another.

"I missed you, Son."

I've never seen this side of Jackson. I imagined what type of father he'd be. It's all I ever dreamed about before my accident. I wanted to be his wife and the only mother of his kids. I wanted to have as many kids as my body would carry and now, it won't carry any, but seeing Jackson with his own makes me feel reassured. I hope I fit in and I hope I'm here to stay.

"Jax, I want you to meet someone very special to me. Her name is Parker. Parker, this is the coolest five year old ever and I mean ever."

Jax smiles at Jackson's silly enthusiasm and introduces himself.

"Hello, Parker. It's nice to meet you." He extends his hand out for me to shake.

He's so stiff and proper. I feel like I'm meeting an adult instead of a little kid.

I bend over and shake his hand. "It's nice to meet you, too, Jax. Your dad told me that you love to wrestle."

"I do. I beat him up a lot, and one day he had to wear makeup to work to cover up his black eye."

"That's right. I sure did. I don't see how women do it. I was smudging foundation on all of my paperwork. It was a mess."

"Well, maybe you can take a break from beating up daddy and play fight with these awesome wrestlers that I happened to believe are really popular, but hard to get."

"Dad, look! These are collectible items! Miss Katie looked everywhere online for these, but couldn't find them. Thank you, Miss Parker."

Jackson winks at me and I take a huge sigh of relief. Jackson, Jax, and I walk the park's trail and get to know one another more.

"Miss Parker?"

"Yes, Jax?"

"I saw you before in daddy's bedroom."

I stop walking and glare at Jackson, but he shakes his head like he has no idea what Jax is talking about. This kid is onto something. He's my eyes and ears into Jackson's life outside of Beverly Mills so I need to be strategic and pump as much information out of him as I can.

"Jax, please tell me more about when and where you saw me in daddy's bedroom."

I raise my brow and smirk at Jackson, but he rubs his hand on the back of his neck shyly and lowers his head in embarrassment.

"It's your picture on daddy's nightstand. It's you, daddy, grandpa, and grandma."

"It's a photo from our junior year when my parents surprised us with a homecoming visit."

"I remember that! What a good weekend. A beautiful memory."

"He has more photos and drawings of you too. There's one in my playroom. It looks like scribble."

"It's not scribble, Jax. He's referring to the MASH game we used to play. I think we were in 6th grade and it said we'd be married in a mansion with two kids. I uh – I always kept it as a reminder of what I always wanted my life to be like with you."

"Aww Jackson. You're so sentimental, it's sickening."

"Says the woman who hoards every photo of me and piece of clothing I've ever owned."

We roam the park, laugh, and play with Jax for another hour then eat lunch in downtown Beverly Mills. When we arrive back to my house, I lay Jax down for his nap and go back to the living room to cuddle with Jackson on the couch.

"That little boy is a ball of energy, and he's so adorable. I never met someone who could talk about wrestling for hours and he's so smart, it's scary! He knew stats and everything. I didn't even know wrestlers had stats!"

"He wasn't always this talkative, though. A year or so ago, he probably would've just stared at you and made you feel extremely uncomfortable. It honestly scared me, but once he was evaluated, everything changed. I was able to learn how to adjust to his behavior patterns and I really started to understand him more when I started going to behavioral therapy with him.

I know he has a long way to go, but he even made a few friends this year who also have similar personality types as him. Their conversations are very interesting and very never ending!"

"I love listening to you talk about him. You're an amazing father."

"Thanks, I still feel guilty sometimes about not being there for him when he was a baby. I was such a mess back then, but I'm thankful for our village. His mom, grandma, my dad, your dad, Merissa, and Jason."

"And now me?" I look at Jackson with hope that he sees me as a permanent fixture in his son's life.

"Yes, you." He caresses my face and kisses my forehead.

"So, I've been wanting to ask this question for years, but why Allie? Why'd you choose her?"

I can sense this is a sore subject for Jackson. His body is tense and he struggles to form an answer.

"I never chose her. Most of my short-lived NFL career is a haze. I was drunk every day and high off pain killers and anti-depressants and Allie took advantage of my state of mind one night. To this day, I still don't know what happened."

"She assaulted you?"

"I won't say that. As much as I have matured into a better man, I still don't think I'm ready to accept what may be the truth. So anyway, after the wedding, I felt like I lost all my friends and family for good so I agreed to be Allie's…companion so to speak. It was the fake relationship from hell. My anxiety was always on ten and I was extremely depressed. We were diabolical. I was messed up and so was she and her family."

"So, how did it end?

"Well, although she was unbearable back then, my destructive behavior was worse so she did us both a favor and left, and she took Jax with her. I was devastated but it was the right choice."

"Would you ever be with her again so your family could be complete? You know, the two-parent home thing?"

"It doesn't matter how many parents are in the home, if you can't get along then it's unhealthy. I don't want Allie. I never did and I never will. What you and I have right now works. I want you, and I know you'll be an amazing mom one day to Jax and our other children."

"I love you, Jackson."

"I love you too, Parker. This is just the beginning."

"Hmm, speaking of beginnings, are you going to move out here or not, Jackson?"

"Well, that was a smooth transition." He laughs.

"I'm serious. Three days aren't enough for me. I didn't sign up to have one of those weird celebrity relationships that you're used to where you barely see one another. I want a real-world relationship."

"It's not that simple. My business is in Atlanta. Jax's school is there, and I don't want to pull him out after all the progress he's made."

"I understand that, Jackson, and I'd never want Jax to feel uncomfortable or be taken away from familiar surroundings, but there's another top-rated school less than thirty minutes away in Greer that specializes in working with gifted kids like him. And we both know that you can work anywhere in the world. I'm not asking you to uproot your life. I'm asking you to build one with me."

"It's a lot to think about, Parker. Let's just table it for now."

"No, Jackson. Let's talk about it, right now."

"Sorry, no can do. My phone is ringing."

Jackson steps into the kitchen to answer his phone and all I can hear on the other end is high-pitched screaming.

"Calm down, Allie. No, absolutely not. I've asked you and your assistant to review the paperwork for months! You initially said you were okay with it so what's the problem, now? The enrollment deadline was approaching and I had to make a decision. It's a great school!"

I can't figure out what their argument is about, but I do hear her say my name.

"Oh, come on! You're being petty. She has nothing to do with it. Yeah, whatever you say. I'll see you soon."

He sits back down on the couch, except this time, he looks frustrated and stressed.

"What happened? Allie didn't sound very happy."

"Co-parenting woes. It's nothing for you to worry about. I promise, we never have these types of issues, but she *is* going to be in town next weekend and I have a request."

"Spit it out, Jackson."

"Can you clear your schedule to meet with her? I'll be there with you, of course, but I think we should sit down and squash this college-aged beef y'all have going on."

"She's the one with the problem, Jackson. I still don't know why she ever hated me. I did absolutely nothing to her."

"Well, next Saturday you can find out."

"I can't. Merissa's baby shower is Saturday afternoon, remember? And I'm hosting it!"

"Dammit, I forgot about that and it's one of those coed couples' showers so I think Jason wants me there."

"Exactly and no plus ones this time! Allie better think twice before crashing this party. She does not want to deal with pregnant Merissa's wrath."

"Okay, what about dinner, Saturday night?"

"Jackson, you're killing me! I'm gonna be too tired to meet with her. Merissa's being a complete mom-zilla. She's been on my case about the décor, the games, and the unnecessarily fancy menu she and Mrs. Pierce planned."

"It's really important to me. I really want you to meet with her. Just trust me, this is all a part of a larger plan."

"Okay, fine! I don't know what you're planning, but I don't like this, Jackson. I feel like I'm being pushed into some type of sister wife situation."

Jackson laughs but I'm dead serious. The thought of being around Allie makes me feel uneasy. She stalked my man when we dated, finally got him then had a baby, and later sent her minions after me online. Now that we're back together, she probably hates me even more.

"Thank you, Parker!"

"Yeah, yeah, Jackson. She just better not call me a hillbilly or bumpkin. I am *not* the same sweet country girl from college."

"Ooh, feisty Parker is really turning me on right now."

We share a brief moment of flirtatious banter and playful touching until we hear a pint-sized voice echo from the bedroom.

"Dad?" Jax Jr. is awake and we hear the fear and confusion in his voice so Jackson runs over to tend to him.

"It's okay. I'm right here, Son."

"Where am I?" Jax asks in a tearful cry.

I walk up to him and drop to my knees to caress his back until he calms down. To my surprise, Jax lets me pick him up and carry him to the couch to sit between me and Jackson.

"I've never been here before. It's very small."

There's still a hint of fear in his voice, but Jackson allows me to take lead. I work with children every day, but this is different. I feel like this is a moment to show Jackson how well I could take care of his son, but most importantly, this is my chance to build a connection with, hopefully, my future stepson. When I was younger, I never envisioned that my family would look like this, but now, I desperately pray that it does.

"Yes, it's small especially compared to your home. Do you like it, anyway?"

"I do, but I'm sleepy and hungry, again. Can we eat so I can go back to sleep?"

"Absolutely. Someone told me that you love to eat pizza and I happen to have a delicious pepperoni pizza on my counter. You want a slice?"

Jax's eyes open wide and his frown quickly fades away.

"Yes, please! Dad, may I have some pizza?"

"C'mon. We'll all sit at the table and eat."

We load our plates up with greasy pizza and regrettably have an eating contest. Jax is definitely just like his dad. By the time they finish their second slice, I'm still eating my first.

After dinner, I manage to win the silly face contest and Jax wins charades. This day was packed with non-stop child's play and I wouldn't mind doing this for the rest of my life. This feels so right and so unforced, but it's all just a dream right now because this can never be real if Jackson doesn't move to Beverly Mills.

"Alright, Jax, it's getting late. Let's head home to grandpa's house."

"Do we have to go? Can we stay with Miss Parker?"

"I'm glad you had fun, but not tonight. We didn't pack a bag of clothes and," Jackson playfully sniffs his son's armpits. "You're kinda smelly."

"I am not! I smell like my granny's special spray – mint and fresh linens. Don't I, Miss Parker?" Jax steps closer to me and I take a big whiff of his shirt.

"You sure do! Umn, I love this smell. When I was kid, I used to rub your dad's clothes on my skin so I could smell just like this."

"Did you, really?" Jackson asks.

"I may have done it a few times." I shrug and maintain a poker face. I did it quite often.

Jackson laughs and continues to gather their belongings.

"What's on your schedule for tomorrow? Any fun plans for you and Jax?"

"Well, the weather is nice so it's only right to enjoy a day at the beach, and then we're taking a really hot doctor out to dinner when she gets off work." Jackson steals a kiss when Jax Jr. isn't looking.

"Ooh, well I definitely look forward to going out with not one but two handsome men! What should I wear?"

"I can't say what I really want you to wear while little ears are around so jeans and a t-shirt are fine, but afterwards…" Jackson winks.

"I get it Jackson. I'll look my best in my birthday suit." We try to keep things as PG as possible around Jax Jr. so Jackson kisses my forehead then I stoop down to shake Jax's hand but, instead, he embraces me with a hug.

"Thank you for being my dad's girlfriend, Miss Parker."

Still clasped in his embrace, I look at Jackson but his expression is unreadable. He looks shocked yet calm and content.

"Alright, buddy. I'm glad you had fun today with my *girlfriend*?"

I just realized we haven't actually made our relationship 'official' yet. Of course, we're together, but we haven't said it out loud. I didn't think we needed to especially after that hot kiss at my parents' anniversary party. We were in the blogs for nearly two weeks and my lame social media profile went from 1,100 followers to 12,000 in two days! You'd think our public displays of affection would be enough to solidify our status, but not for Jackson Sands. He needs to hear me say this.

"Yes, Jackson. I am your girlfriend."

His face lights up like a little kid on Christmas. He loses his reserve, picks me up, and fiercely kisses me. I know he's been waiting for the moment to call me his girlfriend again, but little does he know is that I'm hopelessly anticipating the moment I call him my husband.

"Sorry, I got a little excited. I gave up on the thought of being yours again years ago until recently and sometimes I feel like this is all too good to be true – where we are right now, together, and in love again. It feels like a dream."

I subtly lean into Jackson and wrap his arms around my waist and place my hand on his heart.

"This is all real, Jackson."

Jax yanks on his dad's pant leg to hint that he's ready to go. Jackson, Jax and I embrace one another one last time before they leave. I collapse on my bed to find comfort in our 'official' declaration of boyfriend and girlfriend. Yes, I sound immature and maybe even pathetic, but how I look and sound still don't compare to how I feel about Jackson. What we're building isn't what we've had in the past. This type of love feels better. It doesn't feel new, it feels fixed. And I finally feel like I'm getting closer and closer to everything I ever wanted and everything I deserve.

Chapter 19

Always Meant to Be - Parker

How many baby showers does the typical mom-to-be have? For Merissa, it's five! We threw a work shower. Jason's office threw a shower. Mrs. Pierce and Mrs. Hernandez threw a 'glam-ma' baby shower, and they had a virtual baby shower for those who can't attend today's shower. This baby has more clothes than me, Merissa, and my sisters combined!

I enlisted Avery and Izzy to help me decorate the Pierce estate, but Jason's mom is so picky about her expensive art and statues so we're settling for a minimalistic design which is everything Merissa hates.

"What in the basic manilla envelope is this?"

Merissa wobbles in the main living room angrier than usual and on a war path. She snatches decorations off the wall and yells at the top of her lungs.

"I specifically said I wanted to feel like I'm at a Georgia football game! This is boring and I hate earthtone colors."

"Merissa! You're not supposed to be here. Besides, the party doesn't start for a couple more hours. We can fix this. Just calm down, okay?"

"How can I calm down when my decorations are sad and the outside food tables look a mess! Where are the centerpieces? Where's the food? I need food. I'm starving!"

My sisters and I are afraid and our assurances are making Merissa panic even more. She breaks down in tears right in front of us and Mrs. Pierce and her staff come rushing in to her aide.

"Oh, Merissa, honey. Those third trimester hormones are getting to you, aren't they? C'mon, I'll take you upstairs and run you a nice, warm bath to help you relax. Your friends are going to make sure they give you the best baby shower you could ever dream of."

Mrs. Pierce leads Merissa upstairs and turns her head around to wink at us. I'm going to assume that gives us the go ahead to tacky up her elegant home and backyard for a Georgia Bulldogs themed baby shower.

"How in the world are we supposed to uglify this house in less than 5 hours? How do you make red and black look sophisticated?" Avery asks. "We aren't professionals. Merissa wants 5-star elegance and we're more like the Party City type of girls."

"We can call in reinforcements?" Izzy suggests.

"Already on it."

I call Jackson and explain the situation then ask if he and the guys can come over to help out. Less than thirty minutes later, Jackson, Jason, Deacon, and Gabe arrive, but their hands are empty and their wearing linens shorts and flip flops as if they're getting ready to go to a yacht party on the beach.

I frantically run to Jackson to give him a hug and Deacon walks up to Avery and plants a kiss right on her lips.

"Aww, they're back on again!" Izzy calls out the obvious elephant in the room and Avery's instantly annoyed and ready to deflect.

"I'm gonna stop you right there. Deacon and I are just friends. End of story. I'll be happy to discuss this with you another day. Our focus right now should be Merissa and the beautiful baby shower that we're struggling to put together."

"Fine by me, Aves. I just know love when I see it." Izzy gushes.

"And I know when someone needs to be loved on, if you know what I mean." Avery looks back and forth between Izzy and Gabe until Izzy gives in.

"Okay, okay. You win! I'll leave you and your love story alone for now." Izzy laughs.

I direct my attention to Jackson who looks confident, calm, and outrageously handsome. He's smiling while my sisters and I are in a state of panic.

"Let's go to breakfast." He says with a care free attitude.

"Breakfast? How can you think about food when Merissa's having scary pregnancy meltdowns and we still have to pull off a decoration miracle. And why are you dressed like this? We have work to do!"

"I have everything handled. I commissioned a team to come over and decorate the house – inside and out. The caterers, baker and candy artists are all on track to arrive at 2 p.m. And I even have a team of stylists booked so all of you can meet Merissa's strict hair and makeup policy. In the meantime, we need to eat and based on how Merissa sounded on the phone with Jason a few minutes ago, she's very hangry right now. So?"

"Fine! I trust you have everything taken care of Jackson, but if this goes sideways then the blame is on you."

"Deal. Now, let's go."

We all head out and go to The Nook for breakfast.

"This is just like old times, isn't it?" Gabe says.

Deacon agrees. "Yeah, except we're older, settling down, and even having babies."

Merissa taps her fork on a cup to get everyone's attention.

"I want to thank y'all for being so patient with me. I've been really irritable and snappy lately and it's just a lot. Baby Pierce is kicking my butt right now. I'm really sorry."

Jason rubs her belly and kisses her cheek.

"It's okay, baby. Jace Jr. is just a chip off the old block. You know us Pierce men like to drive you crazy, and you're handling us like a champ. You're the strongest mama I know."

"I agree with my brother-in-law over there. Ris, you're a rockstar. I couldn't imagine walking around with that heavy load. My back would've broken a long time ago."

"Aw, Gabe. You never give compliments. Thank you, little brother."

"Well, good morning to my favorite group of Beverly Millers." Miss Marcie, our favorite waitress greets us with a warm smile, coffees, and biscuits.

"Miss Marcie, how are you this morning?" I ask.

"I'm doing much better now that y'all are here. Jackson, your dad just left a few minutes ago."

"I'm sure he did. If I'm not mistaken, he comes here every morning for a coffee, pancakes, and to see his favorite waitress."

Jackson sits back in his chair and winks at Miss Marcie. She blushes and tucks her hair behind her ear.

"Jackson, does your dad have something going on with Marcie?" I whisper in his ear.

"I think so. He's been cutting his hair more and hanging out a little later than usual. I even caught him ironing his shirts last week, and Frank Sands does not iron clothes."

"Well, how do you feel about your dad dating again?"

"Honestly, I'm relieved. It's been almost ten years since mom passed away and one thing I've learned since then is that life gets lonely especially when you've been with someone for so long and they're suddenly gone from your life. My dad deserves to find happiness and love again."

We sneak in a quick kiss while everyone at the table is distracted, but one person in particular taps Jackson's shoulder from behind.

"Ahem." The scratchy voiced woman clears her throat and Jackson immediately recognizes it.

"What a coincidence that I'd see all of you at once in this small little po' dump town."

It's Allie Oxford in the flesh. Everyone turns to look at the woman who knows exactly what to do and say to make you tick and Jackson's demeanor has changed completely, that is until we see a pint-sized Jackson Sands holding her hand.

"Hey, mom. Dad, Parker, Aunt Merissa and Uncle Jason are all here."

Allie rolls her eyes, but still ushers Jax Jr. to us so he can give hugs to Jackson, Merissa, Jason and I. His cuteness makes everyone smile.

"Hey buddy! I had no idea you were gonna be here this morning."

"Mom was hungry, but she didn't want the hotel food. She said it was beneath her so we came here, but then she said this was even worse."

"Alrighty, little man, you're talking too much." Allie looks annoyed and grabs Jax's wrist to pull him closer to her side.

"Jax," Jackson looks at Allie sternly. "You aren't talking too much, isn't that right, Allie?"

She adjusts her tone and corrects herself.

"No, you aren't at all. Actually, you want to sit next to Merissa and Jason? You can talk as much as you want."

"Is that okay, Aunt Merissa? May I sit next to you?"

"Absolutely! Come on over."

Jax runs over to sit next to Merissa and Jason and Jackson pulls an extra chair up to our table for Allie to sit.

"Is it okay if we add two extra people to the table?" He asks everyone, but specifically looks at me.

Avery sneers at Allie and answers for the entire table.

"Your adorable son is always welcomed Jackson, but I can't say the same for psycho Barbie over here."

"Well, it doesn't seem like y'all have a choice so I'll just sit right here next to my ex-fiancé."

Allie flashes a teasing smile and puts her arm around Jackson's shoulder. Her attempt to gut my confidence and self-worth I gained over the last eight years fails, and Jackson removes her arm from around his shoulder.

"Allie, everyone knows our engagement was fake. Everyone knows I never liked you. And everyone knows I'm in love with Parker. There's no need to embarrass yourself any further. We aren't you're little social media followers."

"And I have twice as many followers as you so if you don't want that secret getting out or better yet if you don't want the world to know how much of a witch you are, I recommend for you to sit down and lay off my big sister." Izzy threatens.

"Whoa! Izzy, where'd that come from?" I ask.

"We love you, Parker and we aren't gonna let this desperate girl tear you down."

"Aww, thanks Izzy, but she can't, no matter how hard she tries."

Clearly outnumbered and embarrassed, Allie lets down her defenses and speaks.

"I'm not here to fight so I apologize for comin' in hot. I haven't gotten the chance to officially introduce myself. I'm Allison Oxford and I'm sorry for being a bitch."

"Jax is right there. He can hear you." Jackson chides.

"Right, sorry. I keep forgetting he retains everything. Well, anyway, thank you for letting me eat with y'all. I don't have too many friends so I look forward to seeing how these cheesy little friend meetup things work."

This woman is so annoying but at least her mouth is shut for now.

"It's so nice to get out that house for a few minutes! I know I've been driving your mom crazy with all of my mood swings and I know I apologized already but I really am sorry you guys. I appreciate everything you've done for me. Y'all are my family."

"Stop apologizing, Ris! You and Jason are the glue that holds us all together. You're the reason Jackson and I are together again. Hell, you helped us get together in high school. And we love how supportive you've always been to each other. I just hope we can get to where y'all are someday."

"Oh, you definitely will! Jackson would be a fool to fumble that ball again." Merissa laughs.

"I don't know, babe. Parker's actually got a prize on her hands. Jackson is handsome, rich, successful, and kind. He's a great friend. He's persistent and he's sober. I mean, he's a catch." Jason states his case.

"I'm touched, Jason." Jackson playfully places his hands on his heart.

"Well, why don't you go marry him? You never talk about me like that, Jason!"

"Don't worry Jason. I feel the same way about you and Jackson." Deacon says.

"For sure." Gabe chimes in.

All the guys fist bump one another from across the tables.

"This bromance is way too much!" Avery laughs.

Allie giggles at the interaction.

"It's actually kinda cute, but I do agree with Jason. Jackson's a catch."

"Are you seriously trying to flirt with Jackson in front of my face?"

"I don't mean it in that way," Allie clarifies. "What I mean is I had the unfortunate experience of knowing the ugly, dark Jackson and I may have even contributed to his downfall. So, who he is today versus he who used to be is completely different. You're the best dad in the world, Jackson."

"Thanks Allie."

Allie then looks at me.

"And thank you, Parker."

"What did I do?"

"When Jackson first told me he was going to lead this hospital project in Beverly Mills and others to follow, I figured it was a front for chasing after you again, and I thought he'd neglect our son or even worse – relapse, but that hasn't been the case. Instead, he's introduced you to our son and as much as I hate to admit, Jax Jr. is completely obsessed with you just like his dad, and surprisingly enough, I don't mind. Anyone who treats my son like their own is okay in my book."

"Thanks, Allie. I really appreciate that."

"You're welcome, but don't expect any more niceties from me."

"Oh, I'm no fool. I know you're still a snake."

"Touché, Parker." She smiles back at me.

"This is by far, the most random breakfast ever." Izzy laughs.

"Do y'all mind if two more random people join?"

A distant voice chimes in from behind us, and like Jackson easily recognizes Allie's voice, I immediately recognize David's. He hasn't visited Beverly Mills since my parents' anniversary party, at least that I know of.

"David?"

"Hey Parker. How's everyone doing?" He and Pia both wave to the table and we can't help but notice her cute little baby bump.

"Oh my god, congratulations." I may be overdoing it a bit, but I jump up to hug both of them, and unlike the fake pleasantries from months back, Pia greets me with a genuine hug and smile.

With everyone seated at the table, some people meet for the first time and others catch up on old times, and when I get up to go to the restroom, so does David. I stop him when he exits the men's room by placing my hand on his forearm. I haven't touched him in so long, and I even feel a warm tingly buzz through my body. It's the chemistry of our past, but it feels different now because I have my Jackson and he has his Pia.

"I really am happy for you, David."

"Thanks, Parker." He stares at me like a nervous schoolboy for a moment then looks me directly in the eyes. "May I speak candidly?"

"Of course."

"About two years ago, I was sure it'd be you and me forever."

"I thought the same, David."

"Did you, really? All cards on the table."

I think about his question and finally admit what I've always known to be the truth.

"I wanted it to be you so badly. I loved you so much, but I was always deep in love with Jackson. I'm sorry, David. I felt guilty about it for so long. I hope you don't think I wasted your time. Your friendship and our relationship changed my life."

"It changed mine, too. It hurt knowing how much you still loved Jackson after everything he put you through, but it helped me appreciate Pia more than I could've ever imagined, especially after she left me."

"What? She left you? What happened?"

"Well, the anniversary party happened. I distanced myself from her, and I started to imagine a life with you again. She left me so fast and I was miserable! I threw away happiness for a pipedream and I took for granted the peace she brought to my life. I felt so incomplete without her. I knew I had to get her back and prove to her that she was the only one for me."

"That's sweet, David. I can tell she makes you happy and I know she loves you. She made that known at the party. You deserve each other."

"Thanks Parker. I'm rooting for you and Jackson. He turned out to be a great guy after all."

"He always was."

David and I hug and sit back down next to our significant others. Jackson looks at me strange.

"Is there anyone in particular that I should be concerned about?" He raises his brow.

"Ooh, are you jealous, Jackson?"

"Well, I mean, Dr. David does look like one of those soap opera actors. Maybe he swept you off your feet again or something." He shrugs.

"You're the only man who can sweep me off my feet."

I kiss Jackson on the cheek and everyone at the table enjoys their meal. This is the oddest group of people, but I feel close to every single person even Allie who happened to play nice with my sisters and friends. Life always comes to a full circle, and I'm starting to feel like mine is almost complete. I'm only missing one important piece and that's Jackson's commitment to moving back to Beverly Mills.

Before we leave for Merissa's baby shower, Allie asks to speak to me. Jackson insists on joining, but both Allie and I agree that we're mature enough now to have an adult conversation without any name calling or hair pulling.

"So, you and Jackson again, huh?" She says sarcastically.

I stand firm and speak confidently.

"Yes, us again, but this time, there's no going back and forth and no one's going to come in between us."

"Well, that's good to hear because I'd hate to see Jax Jr. heartbroken if y'all break up. He's a special boy and he doesn't like change so just promise to be constant in his life. It's bad enough that my work keeps me away from him so much. He'll need another mother figure and you may not think I know you well, but I do, and I know you'll be loving, protective, patient, and nurturing to Jax just like you've always been to Jackson."

Allie's heartfelt honesty isn't a side of her that I'm used to. She's being vulnerable and speaking as a mother who has accepted that her son will have a stepmother one day and I appreciate her openness and acceptance of me.

"You have no idea how much I appreciate your kind words. I adore your son and I'll only ever protect and love him. I imagined this conversation going a lot differently than this!"

"Me too, but just like Jackson's grown, so have I. So have we all. It's so nice to see that you aren't wearing a sweatshirt, shorts and Ugg boots for once." She laughs.

I roll my eyes. "I knew your kindness was too good to be true. Can I ask you a question?"

"Sure."

"Why'd you hate me for so long? I never did anything to you."

"It had nothing to do with you, at first. I come from a very screwed up home and I was taught to use my body, money, and manipulation to get whatever I wanted, but back then, I couldn't get Jackson. He was the college superstar who was in love with his childhood sweetheart. It made my blood boil, and from the outside looking in, your relationship was perfect. I wanted to be you, and I hated you for that, but when I finally got him, I realized how much of a trainwreck he was, and I hated you for making me want what I thought was a loving relationship. You were at the center of everything. I lost count of how many times he called me your name. By the end of our arrangement, I was nearly at my wit's end! I blamed you for my choices and when Jackson decided to get sober, I was ecstatic! He rebranded himself and everyone started praising him for being such an amazing businessman and philanthropist. He was everything a girl could dream of in a man, and I wanted to be with that Jackson, but he shot me down and said his heart belonged to you. So, I hated you again."

"Well, do you still hate me?"

"No, I'm clearly outnumbered by him and Jax Jr. so I have no choice but to accept my reality. I accept you in my life and since there are no cameras around to record this conversation, I apologize for any wrongdoing I've ever done to you."

She extends her hand, but I give her a hug, instead.

"Thank you, Allie. You really have changed."

"I have. Now, stop touching me, and we can cancel our dinner date for tonight. I really want to get back to the city. Being around you and your friends really makes me feel all chummy on the inside."

"Us hillbillies are growin' on you, huh?"

"I'm ashamed to admit, but yes. So goodbye!"

After Allie leaves, Jackson can hardly wait to hear what happened.

"So…"

"So what, Jackson?"

"C'mon, Parker. What'd y'all talk about?"

"You, obviously. Just know we're on much better terms than before. She's not on my shit list anymore, and I'm not on hers."

"Oh, thank God! She doesn't have any bearing on our relationship or future, but I just want her to understand that you're here to stay and she needs to get over whatever gripes she has with you."

"Well, that talk worked."

"Now, let's go celebrate our best friends."

I sometimes forget how much power, money, and influence Jackson has because to me, he'll always be my best friend and the man I've given my all to since 3rd grade. However, today I see how demanding and meticulous he is as a businessman and it's as equally as sexy as him being my hometown country boy.

The Pierce Estate looks like something out of a magazine. At the last minute, the event decorators collaborated with Izzy's floral team to create a beautiful rose flower wall. The backyard looks like a red and black gothic romance novel and the dinner table is adorned with black vase centerpieces with red floral arrangements on top. He even purchased my beautiful red dress and hired a full beauty team to help us get ready for the shower. This had to have costed a fortune, but it means nothing to Jackson. He's still the same man he's always been. He'll go above and beyond for the people he loves, and today, he saved the day.

All of our friends and family are here and the previously frantic Merissa is now calm and in her element as the sweet, classy best friend and beloved Mayor's wife we know her to be. After we eat and Merissa opens her gifts, she makes an announcement for all the guests to hear.

"We want to thank all of you for coming out today. Jason and I can't even begin to describe the joy and love we have in our hearts right now and if it weren't for our parents and our best friends, we would've given up hope and stopped trying years ago which brings us to this moment. Since we were kids, there were two people who always took care of us. We've been there for each other for all of our highs, but most importantly, we've been there for each other through every tragedy we've faced. Jackson and Parker, we have a gift for the two of you."

Merissa's callout catches us off guard, but we come to the front to accept their gift, anyway. Jason reveals a beautiful sculpture of two angels and a baby.

"We've always shared our lives with one another and we would love to share our child as well. Will you be Jace Jr.'s godparents?"

The guests smile and say their awes. Jackson hugs Jason and tears flow down my eyes as I hug Merissa.

She whispers in my ear, "You've always had so much love to give and I'd be honored if you'd pour your love into my baby's life like you've poured into ours."

"Of course, I will. I love you, Merissa."

It's a beautiful way to end an eventful day. My guilt over breaking David's heart is gone. The tension between Allie and I is relieved. I'm officially a godmother. Life couldn't get any better than this.

After the guests leave the party, our friends and family all stick around to hang out in the backyard. I opt to stay inside to assist with the party clean up, but my mom and dad call out to me in a panic from the gazebo.

"What's going on? Is everyone okay?"

"We're fine," She laughs. "We just decided to yell like banshees to get you to stop cleaning and come out here to relax. Jason and Merissa want to play a game."

"A game? The party's over! What are y'all up to?"

"Nothing. We're just reminiscing about our mischievous days. How about a game of Truth or Dare, for old times' sake?" Jason asks.

"Really, right now? This is hardly the time to play Truth or Dare. The last time we played that game with our parents around, we got put on punishment for weeks! I think not."

"Aw, c'mon, Parker. We're grown now! You wouldn't dare say no to a pregnant woman, would you?" Merissa pouts her lips and begs me to play.

"Okay, okay! But I'm not playing long. These heels are killing me and Jackson, Jax, and I need to get going soon."

Speaking of Jackson, I haven't seen him in nearly an hour. He must've got pulled away for a business call, but it's unlike him to be m.i.a. for so long.

"Has anyone seen Jackson?" I look at Frank who's standing next to Jax Jr. and my parents.

Everyone has a goofy dumbfounded look on their face like they're aware of something that I'm not.

Jason re-commands my attention. "Truth or Dare, Parker?"

"Ugh, truth."

"Is it true that you want to marry Jackson?"

"What kind of question is that? Of course, I want to marry Jackson. You could've asked me anything and you came up with the obvious. I'm going back inside."

"Simmer down, sis," Merissa says. "Jackson, truth or dare?"

"Truth." He says.

I feel a tap on my shoulder and I turn around to see Jackson on bended knee wearing a sharp black suit and holding a velvet box that reveals a flawless, perfectly cut diamond ring. I'm in shock. I knew this day would come soon, but I didn't know when or how it'd happen. Jackson is the only man I ever wanted to spend the rest of my life with, and this is the moment I thought, at many times, would never happen. This is the moment I dreamed about. This is the moment I hoped for. This is the moment I prayed for.

"Is it true that you want to marry Parker?"

"Yes," His hands are shaking and I hear the nerves in his voice. "Parker, they say perfection is impossible but I see it in you. You are the most beautiful, loving, devoted, and forgiving person I ever met in my entire life. You saw me through my hurt and you healed my pain. You make me a better man. You make the best man. The love you give me is Godly and if you give me the chance, I promise to love you every day the same way you've loved me my entire life – whole-heartedly, endlessly, and always. I know our love story didn't always go the way we planned, but I think this is how it was always meant to be, and I want us to continue writing our love story together as one, here in Beverly Mills. Parker Eliza Waylen, will you marry me?"

"Yes, Jackson. Yes, I'll marry you!"

Relieved as if he's surprised I said yes, Jackson slides the ring on my finger, lifts me up and twirls me around. Our friends and family cheer for us and I show off the beautiful diamond on my finger.

"I love you, Jackson Sands."

"I love you, future wife."

Chapter 20

Love You, Always - Parker

Four months ago, Jackson casted away all my fears regarding our future. He's been planning our lives together since he stepped foot back in Beverly Mills a year ago. I've been nagging him about moving back home for good, but little did I know, he had already purchased two homes within the first few weeks he arrived – our dream home on the beach and one in-town near work and family.

I finally feel like I have a family of my own. Jax Jr. enrolled in a nearby school two months ago, and we've all been living together full-time. At first, it was a difficult adjustment. I never lived with a kid before and he certainly never lived with anyone else but his mom and dad, but now we're a happy family.

Everything feels surreal, and I still can't believe that I'll be Mrs. Sands in less than 24 hours.

Jackson stretches out wide in *our* king-sized bed and rolls on top of me. "We finally have the bed all to ourselves! I hadn't slept that good in God knows how long. There's no little person kicking us and I finally don't have to fight for your attention."

"I can't help that Jax is more interesting and a better cuddler than you! It was super sweet for Marcie to help your dad watch him this weekend. We needed some alone time."

"Yeah, Marcie's great. Dad's head over heels for her, too. She reminds me a lot of you and my mom — straight-forward and uncomfortably bold, but still nurturing and sweet. We must have some type of fetish or something." He side eyes me.

"Jackson, are you saying I'm an acquired taste?" I playfully hit his chest.

"I'm saying, every woman that's ever been important in my life has been unique. I think that's a better way putting it."

"Attaway to dig yourself out a hole."

"Hey, question? Are you sure you don't want to skip your bachelorette party and spend your last night as a sexy single with me? I promise I'll make it worth your while." Jackson asks.

"Now, why would I miss the chance for young hot strippers to put their junk all up in my face?"

"Parker, I swear if anyone makes a move on you it'll be the last performance of their life."

"What happens in the beach house stays in the beach house, Jackson. You'll never know."

"Yeah, right. How wild can you, Avery, Izzy, and Merissa actually get? This will be Merissa's first time away from the baby. Avery's been knee deep in cases and Izzy and Gabe are doing their bucket list challenge. Everyone's stressed out and busy and no one really has time for a party."

"Jackson, I cannot believe you're trying to convince me to skip my own Bachelorette party!"

"It's just a suggestion! I can give you three very important reasons why you should stay home with me."

"There's nothing you can say to make me bail."

"Is that a challenge?"

"Definitely. Tell me why I should stay in the bed with you all morning."

"How about I show you instead?"

Jackson pulls me in for a sensual kiss and slides his right hand into my panties.

"Ask me for reason #1?" He whispers in my ear and uses his thumb to apply pressure to my sensitive nerves.

I playfully squirm and try to wiggle away, but Jackson is strong and I want every bit of him on and inside of me.

"Say it." He presses harder.

"Give me reason #1."

I helplessly relent and he slides two fingers inside me.

"Jackson!"

"Do you want me to stop?"

I shake my head no and he tactically moves in and out of me while stimulating my nerves with his thumb. He lifts my shirt over my head and moves his left hand to my breast flicking it back and forth while kneading and nipping my other breast with his mouth.

"Jackson, it's too much!" I manage to cry out in the midst of heavy panting and moaning.

Jackson doesn't respond. He only ravages my body even more until I feel a strong unexpected orgasm hit me so hard my arms and legs go stiff and my mind goes blank. Jackson looks at me with a boyish smile and I cover my flushed face.

He then slides down to line his mouth up with my throbbing center.

He kisses it gently and says, "Parker, you made a mess."

"No, Jackson. I can't take anymore!" I push his head away.

"Ask me for reason #2."

"No." I shake my head.

He runs his fingers down my thighs then lightly tickles my skin with his tongue. He's torturing me and my legs are shaking uncontrollably.

"Ask me, Parker."

"Please, show me reason #2!"

Excited from my submission, Jackson flicks, licks me, and rigorously sucks until I feel my body weakens. This orgasm takes all of my energy and nearly sends me to sleep. When he finally comes up for air, he gives me a sweet kiss on the lips.

"Don't go to sleep on me, yet. I still have one more reason."

"I'm so tired, Jackson. I don't think I can handle anymore."

"You're the strongest woman I know, Parker. You can handle anything. No matter how big, can't you?"

"Yes, Jackson. I'm ready now for reason #3."

Jackson quickly adjusts my position to sit me on my knees with my butt tooted up, and my hands pressed against the headboard. He gets behind me and rubs his hardness against my drenched entrance then plunges inside of me. We both revel in the pleasure of how good we feel.

"I want to wake up and do this every morning. Do you want that?" He whispers in my ear. "I can't wait to marry you, Parker. Tell me you're mine forever. Tell me this is mine forever."

"It'll always be yours. I'm yours for the rest of our lives, Jackson."

Eruptions spring from both of us so powerfully that it saturates my insides and drenches his now limp, emptied length. We collapse on the bed and fall back to sleep in one another's arms. His three reasons worked.

After a much needed nap, we prepare to separate for the day. The next time I'll see him is when we say 'I do.'

"I don't want to be away from you tonight. I miss you already." Jackson confesses while holding me in his arms.

"I don't want to either. This is our first time away from one another in four months. This life we're building it feels so peaceful, so stable, so deserving."

"Finally." He kisses my cheek and turns my body to face his. "I have something for you."

"Jackson, stop spoiling me! You've given me everything I could ever dream of. What could you possible give me now?"

Jackson pulls two cards from his nightstand and places them in my hand.

"Appointment cards. I'd been trying for weeks, but the earliest fertility and surrogacy appointments I could book were after the honeymoon. I hope that's okay. I hope I didn't overstep. I just wanted you to know that I want the same thing you want. I've wanted it for years. You're an amazing mom to Jax, but I know you want a baby with me and I desperately want one with you. Your mom told me you froze your eggs years ago when you were dating David. We never talked about this. I know you had plans to start a family with him, but I know in my heart that we were meant to have a family together. Is this something you still want? If not, it's fine, I'll –"

With tears of happiness flowing down my face, I kiss Jackson to shut him up and show him how much I appreciate his mindfulness.

"It's all I ever wanted Jackson – you and a family. Thank you for this. I love you so much, Jackson Sands."

"I just can't wait to hold a mini-Parker in my arms." He laughs shyly.

"Jax will be the best big brother and you'd be the cutest, protective girl dad."

"I'm actually getting nervous thinking about it."

"Well, let's table this topic for now and focus on our wild night with our friends to commemorate our last night as single adults!"

"Well, you have fun. I'll be sober, of course, and apparently Jason rented out that new cigar lounge for us to hang out at. It sounds boring. Our Bachelor party's group chat is called A Gentlemen's Affair."

"Jason's now the most boring person on earth ever since he became a dad! At least Merissa's letting her hair down. Check out our group chat name."

I show Jackson our Bachelorette party's group chat and he immediately loses it.

"Parker Picked a Dick!"

"Yup! My phone will be on silent so no cock blocking!"

"This is ridiculous. I'm going to AA."

"Is the party seriously driving you *that* crazy?"

"I wouldn't give you the satisfaction, Parker," Jackson smiles. "But no. Actually, I was thinking about what we discussed the other night. You know, about becoming a sponsor."

"Jackson, are you really gonna do it?"

"You convinced me, yes. You believe in me and your faith helps me believe in myself."

Jackson works extremely hard in and outside our home. He has a hyper-stressful career and it's easy to relapse when under pressure all the time. It takes a toll on him when deals fall through because he's responsible for hundreds of his employees' livelihoods and he hates letting people down. The old Jackson would drink his problems away, but my Jackson doesn't. When he's hyper-stressed or recognizes when he's having an anxiety attack, we, as in me, his therapist, friends, and family, help anchor him back to a safe, peaceful state of mind. He's been sober for four going on five years. He and Merissa are building Beverly Mills' first Drug and Alcohol Rehab Center and recently, a recovering alcoholic from his AA group asked him to be his sponsor. Jackson is past the point of redemption, he's simply remarkable.

"I'm so proud of you, Jackson."

After we eat a late breakfast, we pack an overnight bag and go our separate ways to spend time with our wedding party.

Since Jackson purposefully tried to steal me away for the day, I missed my previously scheduled bachelorette breakfast with my mom and my girls, but Merissa used her connections to have a catered lunch instead.

She decorated Jackson's – I mean *my* beach house to resemble a spa. Our day of pampering begins, and the first item on the list are our our mani and pedi appointments!

"Who bails on their own bachelorette activities?" Avery asks.

"Parker, because she was too busy having lots of pre-marital sex!" Merissa jokes.

"Hey! Mom's right here." I remind Merissa and my sisters.

"Uh, mom's been having a lot of sex for a whole lot longer than all of you." My mom reveals entirely too much to the group.

"Ew." Avery gags.

"I'm just saying girls. It gets even better when you're older."

"Mom!" Izzy yells.

"Oh, stop being prudes. I know you girls have been having sex since you were teenagers – with the exception of you Izzy, but I know you've been getting busy lately, too. Don't think I haven't noticed."

"I'm impressed, mom. You're like the female 007. How do you know these things?"

"I was young too, duh."

"Okay, so given your experience with love and marriage, what advice do you have for Parker?" Merissa asks my mom.

"Hmm, my advice is simple. Have fun. Don't be one of those super serious boring married couples who don't joke around or flirt. I can't tell you how many times laughter and affection helped your dad and I overcome hard times."

"I don't think we have a problem in that department. I think I'm pretty funny."

"Says who?"

My sisters and mom laugh at Avery's response.

"Y'all don't think I'm funny?"

"Not like, comedian funny more like it's funny to watch you blow up at Jackson. You're definitely the most dramatic one of us, that's for sure." Izzy explains.

"So, I'm funny when I'm the butt of the joke, got it."

Izzy rolls her eyes. "The dramatics are comin'. It's about to get funny."

"Wow! Y'all are the worst!"

"Says the girl who used to have nervous breakdowns when she couldn't find her pencil." Merissa laughs.

"Ooh or the girl who calls ten times in a span of thirty minutes, and when you finally answer what does Parker say?" Avery asks.

"Hey, whatcha doin?" Izzy laughs.

"I'm not that bad!"

My mom pats the top of my hand. "You are, baby. You really are, but that's why we love you, of course."

"Avery, can I ask you a question?"

"Of course, big sis."

"Do you still hate Jackson? Do you think he's changed? Your opinion means so much to me."

"Parker, I never hated him. I just," Avery sighs. "I hated what you went through to get your happy ending. I wish it didn't have to be so traumatic for you. I never believe anyone deserved to go through hell just to get a piece of heaven, but I realize I was wrong. Everyone's love story is different and now that I know everything you two have been through together and apart, I know y'all are meant to together. No one makes you happier and I'm happy for you, Parker. Jackson loves you so much and we all know how much you love Jackson Sands!"

I can't hide my blushed cheeks as I think about how much I love Jackson, but Avery's right. I've lost so much in order to build a life with him, but I wouldn't do anything differently because if I did, we would probably still be together in a toxic relationship marred with anger, chaos, and dysfunction. I'm not twenty years old anymore, and I only have space for happiness, love, support, and respect. I wouldn't have any of that if it weren't for my past which is why I don't regret any of it.

"I do love me some Jackson Sands!" I admit.

"And I love him for you, Parker, and I finally have a grandson!" My mom says delightfully. "And I have a feeling I have so many more grandchildren on the way."

"What the heck, ma! What's gotten into you?"

"Nothing's gotten into me, but apparently penises have gotten into my daughters! Everyone's *booed* up now."

"Oh, my goodness, speaking of penises. We have a surprise for you later on tonight, Parker. So, let's get wasted and enjoy the rest of your spa day. We're gonna need all the rest we can get."

A few hours later after we've eaten and had a few margaritas, Merissa and Avery pull out a bag of colorful wigs and skimpy frilly mini dresses for us to wear.

"Whoa! I look like a sexy anime character meets go go girl." I do a little a twirl in the mirror and take a selfie to send to Jackson, but Merissa snatches my phone out of my hand.

"Don't you dare send that to Jackson. He's gonna lose his mind knowing you look this hot in public."

"Hold on, we're going out in public looking like this? You're the mayor's wife! I'm a doctor! Avery's a respected lawyer. And Izzy's innocent!"

"I'm not that innocent!" She yells.

"My point is, there's no way we're leaving out the house looking this scandalous."

"Don't worry. I got us covered," Avery hands everyone a trench coat. "Now if this isn't inconspicuous then I don't know what is!"

"Oh, here's the final touch." Merissa places a sash around me that says *Parker Picked a Dick!*

This is so embarrassing! We aren't in college anymore. This is not about to go according to plan.

"Let's go ladies. It's time to get fucked up!" Merissa yells.

As soon as the driver picks us up, Izzy starts to send emails. Avery says she needs to take a quick power nap, and Merissa whips out her breasts to pump and dump. And Jackson thought his crew was lame…

"I cannot believe y'all." I complain.

Merissa releases a sigh of relief, "Whew! This feels so good right now. My boobs were throbbing!"

Avery lays her head on my shoulder, "I haven't slept in weeks. This case is driving me insane."

"I have to make sure the floral arrangements are perfect for tomorrow!" Izzy panics.

"But don't worry Parker, once we get out, we'll be back in party mode, I promise!"

I can't help but laugh at my best friend and sisters' attempt to be young, wild, and free again. I check in with Jackson to see if he's having as much 'fun' as I am.

Parker: Hello, my love. What are y'all up to?

Jackson: I'm so glad you texted. I'm trying not to bother you during your wild night out, but I'd have more fun hanging out with our parents than our friends right now. Jason just told us his top 3 favorite diaper brands. Deacon's sulking over Avery and I think Gabe is sleep.

Parker: We're in the same boat. Are we officially the cool couple out the bunch?

Jackson: I used to have my doubts, but yes. We definitely are.

Parker: I want to see you!

Jackson: Find an excuse to go home in an hour?

Parker: Deal.

Now I know why Jason and Merissa were so keen on spending the night together before the wedding. I feel so anxious. I just want to hurry up and fast forward to life as Jackson's wife.

When we arrive downtown, I notice the mischievous looks on my girls' faces. We're at the cigar lounge where Jason's hosting Jackson's Bachelor party.

"You didn't actually think we were gonna be wet blankets all night, did you?"

"Y'all scared me for a minute! What are we doing here?"

"Tonight, your name isn't Parker. It's Pink Fantasy and you have a special someone who's in need of a lap dance." Merissa explains.

The girls and I enter the lounge and Jason directs me to the private VIP room where Jackson sits in a chair wearing blindfolds.

"Jackson, are you ready for an out of this world experience with Pink Fantasy?" Jason asks from afar.

"With who? Jason, what the hell are you thinking? Parker's gonna kill all of us! You know she's batshit crazy!"

Everyone laughs including myself. I throw my trench coat down on the floor and try my hardest to disguise my voice.

"Hi, big daddy. Someone told me you're getting married tomorrow."

Jackson takes a deep breath and scoots his chair back every time he hears my heels take a step forward.

"It's okay, big daddy. I don't bite. You can touch." I tease him.

"No thanks. You may not bite, but my fiancé fights. I'm practically a married man. Jason!" He screams.

I've never seen Jackson so squeamish. This is so hilarious. Time to up the ante.

"I need some music, boys!" I yell out to our friends.

The sensually slow and intoxicating music begins and I move closer to Jackson whose still blindfolded and afraid. I lean in close and nibble his ear, but I mess up because he takes a long whiff of my scent and smiles.

"You smell so familiar. What's your name again?"

"They call me Pink Fantasy, but you can call me anything you want."

I take his hand and run it along my fishnet stockings.

"Hmm," Jackson smiles. "Can I call you my fiancé's name?"

What the hell? What is Jackson up to?

"Wouldn't she be mad if you were calling other women her name?"

"She's not here to find out now, is she?"

Jackson reaches his hand out to feel me, but I slap it away, and grind on his lap.

"You can only touch when I say you can touch, big daddy."

"Pink Fantasy, you're gonna make me take you home."

"What would your fiancé think about that?"

"If you want, I'll ask her to join us."

I gasp in shock and anger.

"I hate cheaters."

"I'd never cheat on Parker or Pink Fantasy. I know how my fiancé smells. I know every curve on her body," Jackson slides his hands down my hips. "I know how Parker sounds when she speaks," He pulls me closer and whispers in my ear. "I know how she sounds when she moans."

He lights a fuse in my body and a moan escapes my lips.

"I know my Parker and right now, I've never been so turned on in my life."

I sit down on top of him and I lift up his blindfold.

"You're the sexiest fantasy I've ever had."

We make love passionately and in public.

"I can't believe we just pulled a Jason and Merissa – sex in public! And big daddy? Where'd that come from? I really tried not to laugh." Jackson teases.

"It was the only thing I could think of at short notice! We had a cheesy porn moment so it fit the occasion. And speaking of our best friends, we gotta get back out there."

"Put your coat back on. This work of art is for my eyes only, you hear me, Pink Fantasy?"

Jackson pats my butt and we enter the main lounge to rejoin our friends.

"Hmm, it sounded like some fantasies were being fulfilled back there, huh?" Jason looks to Jackson.

"Why do we have such perverted friends?" He laughs.

"It's officially a tradition amongst us. Jason and I had a wild night of sex the night before our wedding. Now, you and Parker. Hopefully soon, Avery and Deacon and perhaps even my bull-headed brother and Izzy. Alright, are y'all ready?" Merissa asks. "The real party begins now. It's karaoke time!"

Jason and Merissa open the doors to usher in old friends, former teammates, Beverly Mills' residents, and colleagues we've known from throughout the years.

For hours, we sing cheesy songs, laugh, dance like there's no tomorrow, exchange memorable stories, and I even see the girls sneak in the VIP lounge for a few quickies with their significant others. I know every day won't be smiles and laughs but I'll take any day – good or bad, as long as I'm surrounded by these amazing people.

As we near the end of the night, the Beverly Mills crew all sit around to chat.

"So, we all know the story of your infamous pinky promise, but after tomorrow, what's gonna be the next one?" Deacon asks.

"Hmm, good question." Jackson answers. "Our promise isn't ending. Parker and I will continue to love one another day every day for the rest of our lives just like we always have." He turns to smile at me.

"Well, I propose we all make a group promise." Avery raises her mocktail. "Let's promise to never stop supporting one another. No matter where we live and no matter how far we grow apart, if we need each other, then we show up."

"That's easy! Y'all are hands down the most important people to me," Izzy says then smiles at Gabe. "I promise to be your #1 supporters."

We all make an official vow to show up in each other's lives like we always have time after time again.

The party goes on, but my girls and I need to leave to go back to the beach house. We're tired, anxious, and ready for the big day, but before we head off, Jackson pulls me to the side.

"Are you sure you want to do this tomorrow? I'm only giving you one chance to change your mind?"

"Are you kidding me, Jackson? If I could, I'd marry you right here and right now. I've waited too long for this. Can you believe it's finally happening?"

Jackson embraces me and says, "I've imagined this. I've wished for this and I've prayed for this. Yet, I still can't believe it's actually happening. I still can't believe my dreams are finally coming true. I love you, always, Parker."

My parents' home is the most beautiful wedding venue in Beverly Mills. The botanical wonderland is complete and just like my parents said, I'm the first person to get married here. The sage green, champagne and light terracotta color scheme blends perfectly with the natural greenery. Everything looks so beautiful…except me. I've been ugly crying all freaking morning. This is the makeup artists third time fixing my face, and she's getting fed up. Everyone's getting fed up with me.

Avery rubs my shoulders and tries to accomplish what Izzy just failed to do.

"Parker, you have to chill out. You're never gonna walk out of here if you don't stop crying."

"I can't help it. I can't believe I'm getting married. What if Jackson changes his mind? What if our marriage doesn't work out? I was googling late last night and it said 50% of marriages end up in divorce. What if we're a part of that 50%? What if he just wakes up one day and decides he's over it. You said it yourself. I'm dramatic. I'm a lot to handle. What if he gets tired of handling me?"

"Okay, we need reinforcements. Mom! Parker's getting cold feet!"

Our mom comes rushing in to save me from taking off on a horse like the runaway bride.

"Parker, stop talking right now. Just breathe. Deep breaths." She advises.

My mom's calmness stills me. For a moment, I stop crying. I stop talking, and I just breathe.

"Parker," Mom says. "You look exquisite. Jackson's going to take one look at you and bawl his eyes out. Today, you're marrying the love of your life, and y'all will have great days, good days, bad days, and maybe even worst, but as long as you stay committed to one another, everything will be okay. Do you hear me?"

I sigh, "Yes, ma'am."

"Everyone's waiting on you so pull it together. Debbie and I used to imagine what this day would look like, and there were times when I thought it'd just be a dream, but the day is here and there's no way in hell, I'm gonna let you regret not walking down that aisle. Stand up tall and be the beautiful, confident, and deserving Waylen woman we raised you to be. Now, let's freshen up our makeup and get out there and celebrate this momentous occasion."

After I dry my eyes and refresh my face, my matron of honor and my bridesmaids, walk down the aisle.

I hear Jax Jr. announce, "The bride is coming! The bride is coming!"

Everyone stands to await my arrival and my dad waits for me by the back doors. I adjust the cathedral train of my lace dress and lock arms with my dad. When we turn the corner, we see everyone. Tears flow down cheeks and mouths gasp with oohs and awes, but my only focus is Jackson.

He looks at me and starts to sob. My dad speaks to me as we walk down the aisle together.

"You're almost there, Parker. You got this."

I try to sniffle and hold back my tears, but the moment is too emotional. It's too unbelievable, and it's been a long time coming.

"We're here, Parker. You're so beautiful and amazing. I couldn't have prayed for a more wonderful daughter."

My dad gives me away to Jackson and we face one another and stare as if it's love at first sight. He wipes my tears and I wipe his.

Pastor Owens begins the ceremony.

"We're gathered here today to witness the holy matrimony of two people we love and hold dear to our hearts. Jackson Sands and Parker Waylen are childhood sweethearts with an unbreakable bond and today, they've decided to begin the next chapter of their lives together. They've written their own vows to express their eternal love for one another. Jackson, you may proceed."

Jackson's hands are shaking but he still manages to pull an old, ragged letter from his suit jacket.

"I haven't been this nervous in years so please excuse me if I stumble. I've been trying to write my vows for a few weeks now, but I struggled to translate my feelings onto paper, until my dad happened to give me this letter a few days ago," Jackson pauses and I caress his arm for support.

"It's a letter from my mom. She told my dad to make sure I open it on my wedding day. So, forgive me, if I say something crazy because y'all know how she was."

Tears fill every guests' eyes as Jackson reads a ten year old letter from his mom.

"My one and only Jackson. If you're reading this, then I'm no longer here, and if my prayers were answered then Parker is standing in front of you looking like the beautiful, graceful goddess she is. I know life hasn't treated you fair, but God sends angels for everyone and Parker is yours."

Jackson pauses again to clear his eyes.

"She is the sun to your moon. She adds reason to your chaos. And she's your guide when you're lost. I don't know how many months or years it will take you to heal from being an anxiety-stricken kid who saw too much and lived too little, but through it all, I know Parker has always been there for you and will continue to be there for you. So, when you get better, please promise me that you'll protect her. Promise me that you'll love her.

Promise me that you'll give her the world because you are hers. I may not have lived a long, adventurous life, but it was worth it knowing you and Parker would come back to one another someday. The way she loves you is the way I love your father. It's the way Jolene loves Wayne. And it's why I'm thankful that I get to have her as a daughter. It's why I look forward, even after death, to her being the mother of my grandchildren. She is your soulmate and I hope you both know that I passed peacefully knowing that you have each other. Through the good times and the bad, I know that your love will withstand. I know it's been hard and I know it's been painful, but look at you two now. This is beautiful. This is love. This is forever. This is always. And this is the life that you deserve. I love you Jackson and Parker and I thank God for answering my one last prayer."

Jackson tucks the letter back into his suit jacket and tries his best to regain his composure, but he can't.

"I love you, Parker Waylen and I'll fulfill that pinky promise we made to one another in third grade. I'll never leave you and I'll love you, always."

Tears flow from my eyes as I now struggle to speak.

"Well, I don't think I can top that so I won't even try, but I will say that loving you, Jackson Sands, has been worth every laugh, every teardrop, every fight, every heartbreak, and every kiss in the world. When I told you that I'll love you, always, I didn't mean forever. I meant in spite of. In spite of everything we've been through, I have always loved you and my love for you is still growing every day. Our worlds have been shattered so many times, yet here we are with mended hearts and more whole than ever before. I'm so glad that we never gave up on one another because this is the happiest I've ever been in my entire life. Dreams can't compare to the life we share together. You've given me love, confidence, trust, security, laughter, hope, a son that I love so much, and a wonderful future to look forward to. I'm in awe of who you've grown to be and I look forward to growing even more, together. While other people may want a love story, I just want you, Jackson Sands. I've always only ever wanted you. Thank you for loving me and I promise to love you, always, in spite of anything."

Jackson and I exchange rings and we wait to hear those final words.

"Jackson, you may now kiss your wife."

Our kiss is filled with smiles and tears. It's an intimate moment between us. It's a moment we discussed in high school, throughout college, and years in between. It's a moment I once stopped believing would happen, but now, it's a moment that I'll never forget.

From the outside looking in, many people could never understand why I always believed in Jackson Sands. They could never understand why I always remained hopeful in the man I knew he'd become, and I never even bothered to explain because he was meant for me and I was meant for him – and no one else ever mattered. When I felt broken, I still knew it was him. When I thought all was lost, it was still him, and when I felt love didn't love me anymore, Jackson re-emerged – different, better, healed, and whole. Through it all, we never broke our promise, and our bond always remained.

So, without further ado, I'd like to finally utter the words I've been waiting to hear my entire life.

"I am *the* one and only Mrs. Jackson Sands."

EPILOGUE

I guess you can say we didn't waste any time after our romantic 14 day honeymoon in the Maldives.

We're pregnant! Well, kind of.

After three tries, the artificial insemination finally worked, and I'm so thankful to our surrogate, Melena. She's had to put up with my late-night check-ins, Jackson's meal plan recommendations, our emergency doctor appointments every time she had a cramp, my unplanned shopping trips, Jackson's anxiety attacks, and our overbearing tendencies. You know – typical Parker and Jackson behavior.

But today's the big day! Melena went into labor early this morning, and our family's pouring in to await her arrival.

Avery rushes through the hospital doors. "Where's my niece? I caught the earliest flight available to get here."

"She isn't here, yet. I'm gonna go back in to check on Melena and make sure everything's okay. Mom temporarily kicked us out the room because she said we were stressing her out. Thank you so much for coming at such short notice, Avery."

It's been months since I've seen my sister. She and Deacon's breakup caused a rift in our friend group and things haven't quite been the same since.

"You know I'll always be here for you, Parker. I've missed you so much. Where's Izzy?"

"She's going back and forth between this wing and Gabe's."

"What? I thought he was getting better, and what about the baby? She's high risk!"

"There's so much to catch up on. We'll have to discuss later."

"I understand. Go check on Melena."

My parents are in the room while Deacon and Frank are calming Jackson's nerves.

Deacon walks over to Avery and tries to speak.

"Not now, Deacon. This isn't the time or place."

"I just wanted to speak to you. Just give me five minutes."

"Stay away from me, go find your precious Alyssa!" Avery yells at the top of her lungs, bumps Deacon's shoulder, and walks away.

"Is the baby here yet?" Izzy's checking in on us again and waddling over to me with her pregnant belly.

"Baby girl, please sit down." I beg Izzy.

"I can't, Parker. There are way too many important life events happening at once."

"Well, sit down so you don't go into labor and add another one to the mix."

"How's Gabe doing?"

Izzy's expression falters as she shakes her head. "We'll talk about it later. Jason and Merissa are with him but they said they'll be over here shortly."

My parents come rushing out the delivery room and call me and Jackson over.

"It's time," My mom says. "Remember, stay calm and be there to support her just like you practiced."

We nod our heads, take a deep breath, and hold onto Melena's hands as she pushes.

My goodness, the strength of this woman. "Good job, Melena. You're doing great!"

"We see her head! Just one more push!" The doctor says.

She pushes as hard as she can and nearly breaks our hands in the process, but it pays off. Our baby comes out with loud, powerful lungs and the nurses quickly grab her to weigh her in and wash her up.

The room is filled with emotion. Melena's exhausted and closes her eyes to rest while Jackson and I are filled with joy.

"Would you like to hold your baby?" The nurse asks.

I'm still in disbelief and cry, "My baby," The last time I was in a hospital room, my tears were filled with pain and grief, but the tears flowing down my face right now are tears of joy, gratitude, and pure love. "Please!" I respond.

I sit down in the rocking chair and I hold my daughter for the first time. She's perfect. She's absolutely perfect.

"Oh Jackson, she has your eyes."

Still in tears, he kisses our baby girl and says, "She's so beautiful just like you."

"Hi baby. We're your mommy and daddy. We love you so much."

Before we move to a private room, we thank Melena for everything and make sure she's tended to as needed. Without her, I wouldn't have this perfect little mixture of both me and Jackson.

After we have a few minutes alone with our newborn, we hear a knock on the door.

"May we come in, now?" My mom's voice rings through the walls.

"Come on in!" I excitedly yell.

Frank, his wife Marcie, my parents, and Jax Jr. make their way in.

"We'd like to introduce you all to Payton Debbie Sands."

Marcie comforts the emotional Franks Sands. "What a beautiful name, Son." Frank says.

"She's so small," Jax Jr. touches her tiny feet. "Be careful with her, Dad. Your hands are big and you're clumsy sometimes. My little sister is special."

We smile at Jax Jr.'s protective nature and allow the nurses to come in to care for Payton while our siblings and best friends join us as well. I look around the room and admire my beautiful family. I think back over the years when I thought all of this – my marriage, my family, and my life, could only be a dream. I turn to Jackson and see peace, happiness, and fulfillment on his face. I grab his hand and speak softly in his ear.

"This is everything we ever wanted. This is the life we deserve."

He kisses my forehead and says to our daughter, "You are wonderfully, beautifully, and fearfully made."

Thank you for reading the Love in Beverly Mills Series
Book 1: Love You, Always - Parker and Jackson
Book 2: Love You, Finally - Avery and Deacon
Book 3: Love You, Til the End - Izzy and Gabriel

Printed in Poland
by Amazon Fulfillment
Poland Sp. z o.o., Wrocław